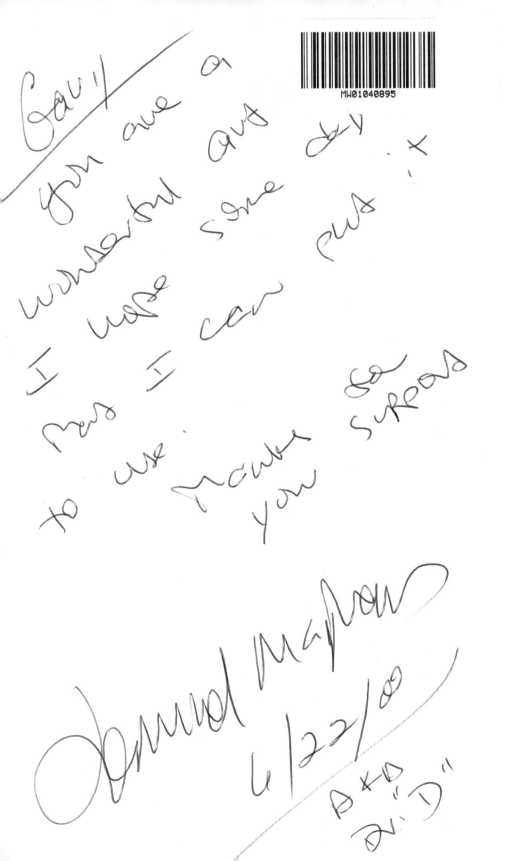

Gary

you are a
wonderful and
I hope some day
mad I can put .×
to use . maybe so
you surround

Donald McBow
6/22/00
D ×D
D "D"

PIANA

PIANA

Lemuel Mayhem

Published in the United States
by Mayhem Tale Enterprises

ISBN 1-888519-01-0

Library of Congress Catalog Card Number: 99-69080

Printed by Jostens Graphics,
Winston-Salem, North Carolina

Cover design by Clinton Bryant

Inquiries should be addressed to:

Mayhem Tale Enterprises
P. O. Box 690935
Charlotte, NC 28227-7016 USA

Dedicated to

Hazel, Carmen and Front Ro, my family and my foundation. They serve to inspire me on a daily basis.

The women in my life Mom Dawkins, sisters, Faye, Linda and Johnnie and Willie, my girl Friday.

Constance Holloway who changed words and untwisted sentences and made good prose better prose.

Debbie McKinney who made a manuscript look like a book.

Dr. Bobby Gibbs for his work on the photography.

Monica Link and Ramon Perry for acting as models.

Lynette Barnes-McGill for providing initial research.

Dr. Couch whom at North Carolina College during the 1964 - 1966 period inspired me to like History.

Clinton Bryant the young artist who gave night and day effort toward designing the cover.

Clara Jones Music Studio for expert tutelage in playing the piano.

Much thanks to Theautry Green for his unrelenting effort to bring this novel before the eyes of the public.

PROLOGUE

He'll be ridin' on a smoke cloud,
ridin' on a smoke cloud

Emanuel sat at the piano. His sprightly fingers effortlessly danced across the keys as his mother's soulful voice enlivened the otherwise mournful lyrics. He would have heard her voice even if she'd sang quietly, even if she were miles away, instead of just beyond the open window beside him. It was a triumphant blend of the musical talents of two oppressed people—mother and son shackled by slavery. There had been other victories, but none so important as this. For the first time, he seized the opportunity to play as his mother sang.

Ridin' on a smoke cloud

But it would be his last effort at making beautiful sounds on this magnificent instrument. The first and the last times he would play as his mother sang.

Piana

I wan' cho' ta ride dat smoke cloud ta heaben, ma son

Her deep voice pierced his soul, arousing the multitude of passions repressed over the past eighteen years of his life. But he could express his emotions now without inhibition or punishment. The veil was lifted, soon to be vanquished to the hereafter. Minutes later, he would be dead. The seething, crackling fire had already engulfed the periphery of the room. A single flame left his eyes burnt shut, his face puffy, his lips swollen. *Sing to me, Mother, sing to me your death song,* he pleaded in his thoughts. He was not inclined to believe that she'd missed his supernal message. Her beautiful voice was her reply.

> *I'll meet cho' dere someday.*
> *Ride dat smoke cloud ta heaben, ma son,*
> *'cause dat is de only way.*

Neither was he inclined to escape his predicament. What for? He was scarred and blind. Moreover, he was a slave like the rest of his kind—adorned with the color black and the title Negro. What for? Winnie, his wife for nearly a lifetime but so few months, was dead, too—a victim of the same scorching fire that would orchestrate his end.

When yo' smoke cloud land in heaben, ma son

What for? He had had freedom, but it was no more useful than his color, the telltale sign of enslavement.

Gib yo' 'spect ta de grace ob God

What for? He was now blind and disfigured. Who would care

10

for him? Who would tolerate his newly acquired handicap? The system that he knew and was, although involuntarily, a part of didn't tolerate such infirmity. He had but one choice. He knew it. His mother knew; she told him so in her passionate, melodic outburst that seemed to quiet the unforgiving flames that edged ever closer.

And when He hab time ta lend yo' an ear

He had to crowd a short lifetime of practice and teaching into these last few moments. His unerring fingers crossed the keyboard synchronously with his mother's voice—teasing every note and caressing each sound. Crash! Crash! Part of the ceiling fell to the floor, just missing the piano. His play became more urgent but no less accurate, as did his mother's voice.

Tell Him dat life down here is so hard

Bell sang even louder as great yellow flames besieged the house like an army about to subdue its enemy. Her impassioned pleas were for her only son, not to save his life—what life? Like her, he had been a slave—but to give him contentment and guidance so he could find his place—a place where he could play his music right alongside Gabriel as he blew his horn.

I wan' cho' to ride dat smoke to heaben, ma son,
I'm gonna meet yo' dare someday

Hers was an impassioned plea—a plea to God almighty to take her son—just as he had taken his own son from the tomb. There was no other glimmer of hope—certainly, not on this earth, not in this life. The Lord giveth and the Lord taketh away. She heard his musical farewell and responded in kind just as if they had practiced together a thousand times.

Yes! She would meet him there someday, but not now—if she could help it, not too soon. She had a grandson now. Someone had to love him and protect him, and show him the way.

> *I wan' cho' ta ride dat smoke cloud ta heaben, ma son,*
> *'cause dat is de only way.*

His agile, nimble fingers began to slow—accuracy and precision gave way to indistinct, troubled sounds. Bell couldn't bear to watch. She closed her eyes as her sweet, melodious tones melted into muffled cries. Their enchanted spiritual chain was broken and the earth-shaking noise from the crumbling, burning house signaled the end.

She thought: *No mo, Lawd! Please, no mo!*

BOOK ONE

CHAPTER ONE

"Good-bye, Auntie Mame," Kathryn cried hoarsely. Long before the ship had left the dock, she'd started shouting her good-byes.

As the vessel carried her farther away, Kathryn had to strain to see her aunt's frantic motions, her hands signaling what could no longer be heard . . . I love you . . . I'll miss you . . . Have a safe trip . . . Come back soon. Far too soon, she was unable to see even that. A sudden loneliness crept over Kathryn as she looked out over the vast ocean. Her long ocean journey to America had begun.

For a while, Kathryn stood clinging to the side rail, crying in earnest, until a booming voice, thick with Irish brogue, jolted her out of her misery.

"Are ye all right, Lass?" Kathryn whirled around. The voice belonged to a burly man whose ruddy face was framed by an unkempt, fiery red beard. It was the captain.

"Yes, I'm fine, Sir," Kathryn replied as she dried her tears.

"Ere ye a native Englishwoman, Lass?" asked the captain, who towered over her. "And if ye are, y'r aye pretty one at that."

"No, no, Sir. But I've lived there at least one-half of my life."

"Will you be returning to England anytime soon, Lass?"

"I hope so. I surely do."

"Well, don't ye be worried about a thing. The journey will be over before ye know it. And now I'll be begging your pardon, Lass," he said. Then the captain retreated and a big, muscular black man—no doubt a slave serving as a cabin boy—quickly fell into step behind him. Just then, Kathryn realized he had been there throughout their entire conversation, motionless and silent. His grim appearance unnerved her, and she was seized by fear. I must get away, Kathryn thought frantically, and began to walk in the opposite direction in hopes of finding her cabin.

She took five steps, lost her balance, and tumbled to the deck as seasickness quickly began to envelope her. Everything was moving, swirling like a whirlwind inside her head. Kathryn tried to stand but collapsed again. She vomited but was too sick to feel shame. Finally, she lay motionless, eyes closed, afraid to stir. Then she felt someone tugging at her shoulders. When she opened her eyes and saw the black man lifting her, Kathryn vomited again. She was nearly relieved to hear the captain's voice.

"Aye, Lass, you've got a wee bit of the seasickness an' ole Dan'l 'ere will take ye to me cabin—an' don't ye worry none; 'e's gentle as a furry kitten." Terrified, Kathryn opened her mouth to protest. Don't let this man touch me, she so desperately wanted to say, but exhaustion gripped her, pulling her into the blessed sanctuary of unconscious and her past.

Jessica Chiles looked toward the ceiling. It took all the strength she could gather just to open her eyes. Slowly, the ceiling was fading away. Only a miracle would allow her to realize her twenty-ninth birthday, just one week away—August 3, 1819.

Six months earlier, Jessica Chiles had been a ravishingly beautiful woman—vibrant, strong, full of life and energy, so much so that she felt constrained by plantation life. Her discontent was the source of much guilt; after all, she was married to Sir Edward Chiles, owner of one of the wealthiest plantations in Charleston, Echo Holler. They had hundreds of slaves; she had but to awaken each day and summon one of the many house servants. Like most women of her class, there were few challenges or achievements--just conformity to the restrictions of the social order of the day, *le petite delicacies*, the appropriate pastime of privileged ladies. Dead or alive, she would not allow her daughter, Kathryn, to be victimized by such an order.

Kathryn was nine years old and in every way the reincarnation of her mother. She had fiery red hair that glowed as it caressed her beautiful face and soft skin. It was common for Sir Edward to receive the compliment from his friends—Kathryn is going to be as beautiful, if not more, than her beautiful mother.

Jessica saw this beauty in her daughter, but there had to be more—unseen, untested, unnourished creative ability. Oh, how she had yearned to find it within herself during her lifetime. Her chance was about to be stolen from her but not from Kathryn. She made Sir Edward promise that, upon her death, Kathryn would be sent to England to be cared for and tutored by Madame Edwina Bartholomew, a longtime friend of the family and musical scholar.

"Wake up, Lassie! Wake up, Lassie, or ye will be sleepin' away the whole voyage."

"Where am I? How long have I been here?" Kathryn mumbled as she struggled out of her slumber.

"Two hours, Lassie," said the captain. "But a girl as pretty as ye is welcome to me quarters as long as she wants."

"Your quarters!" she exclaimed. She spotted the big black man behind her and her attention was immediately divided.

"That's right, Lassie, this be ma cabin. With ye bein' alone an' so sick, Ole Dan'l an' me didn't want to leave ya alone an' not know how ye are."

"Oh, I see." Deftly, Kathryn brushed her hands across the front of her dress, just to be sure all was intact. She felt uncomfortable. "I'd best be going. Thank you for your kindness, Captain."

"As ye wish, Lass. Ole Dan'l 'ere will show ye to ye cabin."

"No! No! Please! That won't be necessary. I can find it, I assure you. You've done enough and I don't want to take up any more of your valuable time," replied Kathryn nervously. The thought of being accompanied by the black man frightened her; he always seemed to be looking at her out of the corner of his eyes.

Despite the captain's urgings, she managed to leave his cabin unescorted.

Day after day, as the voyage progressed, Kathryn spent hours reminiscing. Her favorite spot was up on the deck where she could stare at the vast ocean and submerge herself in the past.

Kathryn arrived in England on October 22, 1819. Initially, she was very surprised to find out that Madame Edwina Bartholomew was much older than her mother. Although not the spectacle of beauty that her mother was, she had a charismatic charm that mellowed Kathryn almost immediately. Furthermore, her stately, well-mannered decorum enlightened Kathryn as to why her mother wanted her sent there. Auntie Mame, as those much younger than she were instructed to call her, was a delightful person to whom Kathryn would gladly have given the title of mother. No later than the day after her arrival, Auntie Mame began to direct Kathryn's education of English life and culture.

The mornings were filled with history lessons. From the earliest time, it seemed that the English were always fighting about something. There was the invasion by Julius Caesar and the Romans at some unimaginable time B.C. Her scorn for the Romans grew adamantly as she surveyed Hadrian's Wall. Such a useless countryside barrier—built for a war that never happened. How foolish, Kathryn thought. As she listened to Auntie Mame's scholarly excerpts on the history of the English, she romanticized the Norman invasion as something beautiful and perhaps necessary. It was during this time that there were great warrior knights and big castles. It was easy for her to imagine herself a fully grown princess living in a great castle with a handsome knight suitor.

The afternoon quickly became Kathryn's favorite time of the day. This was the time that was dedicated to learning to play the piano, and she loved every second. Auntie Mame's love for music and Kathryn's desire to learn brought them even closer together, no different than mother and daughter. Kathryn was gifted with extraordinary musical talent. Before long, she was being nurtured on the classical pieces of many of the great composers.

Mozart. They spent whole afternoons exploring the many great works of this composer. She studied both of Mozart's minor key concertos. She practiced the G-Minor concertos with such an impassioned plea and fervor that seemingly she was calling out to Mozart himself to come forth and offer critique. She gave sincere effort toward mastering all fifteen of his piano concertos. When she first saw the opera *Don Giovanni* performed, her efforts were all the more rewarded. Thereafter, she made it a point to see every Mozart opera made available to her—*The Impresario, The Marriage of Figaro, The Magic Flute,* etc.

Haydn. Kathryn had many triumphant experiences at the piano playing Haydn's music. She especially loved *The Emperor's Hymn.*

She remembered that Auntie Mame always developed goose bumps when talking of Haydn. She had seen some of his London performances from which came twelve symphonies. Auntie Mame, for sure, was in love with the man, Kathryn thought.

Handel. One of the most challenging tasks laid before Kathryn was to transform Handel's *Messiah* into the language of the piano. Auntie Mame would only accept perfection and perhaps her approach to teaching music was unique, partly because she would not accept restrictions. A piece of music made for one instrument was made for all instruments, she would say.

Beethoven. Kathryn relished the idea that just as Auntie Mame had been in love with Haydn, she, too, was in love with a musical poet named Beethoven. She only knew the man through his music. His death a year before her departure from England was her most devastating experience while there. She had lost her chance to ever know the man in person, so she delved evermore deeply into his musical work. Perhaps, she thought, there were hidden messages that would help her know and understand this man.

A gentle sea breeze washed over Kathryn, reminding her of her present journey. She was still on the deck. Just a few feet away, a galley mate tossed some spoiled meat over the side of the ship. She lifted herself on tiptoe so she could peer over the side rail. She saw sharks gnawing savagely at the meat. As she watched in fascination, the strains of Beethoven's *Symphony No. 3* filled her head. The sharks' frenzied feeding paralleled the sudden unleashing of pent-up energy, much like the symphony's first movement, the *Allegro Con Brio,* followed by a slower return to peaceful serenity—*Marcia Funebre.*

When the feed was over, the sharks swam away much as though nothing had happened.

"Aye, Lass, wouldn't lean too far forward. Them sharks looks mighty 'ungry," the captain said.

Kathryn turned to face him. "Captain, I didn't know you were behind me." She knew without looking that the black man was also there.

"Be careful, Lass. An awkward wave and ye'll be tumbled o'er the side."

"Thank you, Captain. I'll try to be more careful." The captain started to move on, then stopped. "Lass," he said, "will ye give me the pleasure of 'aving dinner with me in my cabin this evening?"

Kathryn didn't see how she could refuse; the captain had been so nice. "Yes, Captain, I would like that very much." He thanked her, then left with his servant in tow. Kathryn hoped that the black man would not be present.

Left alone again with only the noise from the Atlantic waters to break the silence, she rekindled her thoughts of the past. Together, she and Auntie Mame had coursed the triumphs of musical history. They studied the harmonic sounds of Bach in fugue, concerto, and symphonic form; the symphonic tones of Mozart; and the rapturous genius of Beethoven. Without a doubt, to her, Beethoven was the greatest. His music both stunned and stimulated her. Auntie Mame's exact words had been, "His genius will not be equaled in my lifetime, nor surpassed in yours." Kathryn would have gladly dismembered a limb if it would have meant extending his life.

"I trust, Lass, that ye 'ave enjoyed ye time aboard me old packet, the Saint Dervis."

"Yes, Captain. The journey has been delightful so far, at least, after I got over my seasickness." As Kathryn spoke, she eyed the small feast being set before her. Her mouth watered as she surveyed the stewed chicken, macaroni, hot rolls, pickles, soup, boiled cod with potatoes, turnips, and roast turkey. This was certainly not the meal she'd once heard the crew sing about as they worked:

> Oh the cook, he's mixing up his bread!
> Yo-o-o-ho, heave the man down!
> And when you eat it, yo'll be dead!
> Yo-o-o-o-ho, heave the man down!

Kathryn smiled. "Some of the songs the men sing are so funny. The words are so cheerful and lively, I could listen to them and watch the ocean all day," she said.

"Aye, Lass, a livelier crew never set sail on the water and I'll wager me packet rats against the best of 'em."

"Oh, I see," Kathryn said. A hush fell over the room. Though she had tried to pretend otherwise, Kathryn was as uncomfortable now in the cabin as she had been that first day.

"Dan'l!" the captain screamed. "Bring me my best brand of whiskey." Suggestively the captain inquired, "Will ye be partaking of a drink, Lass?"

Kathryn didn't quite know what to say; no one had ever asked her to drink before. "No, no thank you, Sir."

The captain ate heartily and drank throughout the meal. With each drink he took, Kathryn grew more uneasy, "Dan'l," the captain bellowed, "more whiskey!" The obedient servant retreated to the galley to fetch the liquor. But just as he approached with the beverage, the ship lurched, heaving the black man right into the midst of the table and food before he rolled onto Kathryn's lap.

"Idiot, buffoon! You nigger swine!" the captain bellowed.

"I'll teach you to mess up . . . " He pummeled the black man with his fists. "You bastard!" he bellowed.

"No! No! Captain!" Kathryn shrieked. "He couldn't help the fall! Stop beating him!" She pulled and tugged at the captain, but he continued the beating, oblivious to her efforts to stop him.

Minutes went by before the captain achieved some measure of sobriety and realized what he was doing. "Sorry, Lass. Didn't mean to show off like that." But as the black man attempted to get to his feet, the captain kicked him. "Now git out, nigga. I should've known that swine could nay be trusted to attend an evening for a beautiful lass. Now git out!"

Kathryn watched the servant rise from the floor, his face streaked with sweat and blood. He left the room, silent as always. Instantly, the captain reached for Kathryn and attempted to embrace her. She pushed him away, more angry than fearful.

"I'd best be going now, Captain," she said icily. Her tone seemed to startle him; for a moment, he stood motionless. It was all the time she needed to escape from the room.

Once in her quarters, Kathryn locked the door. Her heart raced; her hands shook. Now she was frightened. The knock at the door, though no surprise, completely unnerved her. "Sorry about what happened, Lass," said the familiar voice. "That stupid nigger . . . "

Kathryn took a deep breath. "It's all right, Captain," she replied slowly and deliberately, trying to conceal her newfound terror of this man. "But now I would like to get some sleep." Her heart sank as she watched the captain's fingers slip through the door and deftly open the inside latch and enter the room. "Now Lass, ye old captain has apologized. Let's be friends." He closed the door behind him. He had a vicious, stalking look in his eyes.

As he walked toward her, Kathryn's only recourse was slow

retreat to the nearest wall. "Y'r a pretty little thing, Lass." She cringed with fear as her muffled screams amplified the moment.

"Ever been with a man before? I bet you . . . " As he lurched toward her, he was stopped instantly in his tracks. A big, muscular arm with a viselike grip curled around his neck. The captain's face was turning red-purple as the black man tightened his choke hold.

Horrified, Kathryn watched in silence as the captain desperately struggled to free himself. Then she stared in disbelief at the black man's mouth as he struggled to speak: His tongue had been split right down the middle. Never releasing his grip, the black man dragged the now-unconscious captain from the cabin.

Again, Kathryn closed the door, this time barricading it with every item in the room that she could move. Exhausted, she lay on her cot for hours in the darkness.

As she slept, the ship edged closer to port side. Charleston had already been sighted in the distance. But the crew was frantic; the captain and the black man had vanished. Kathryn was blissfully unaware of it all; she'd willed herself back to England, to the precious last moments she'd spent with Auntie Mame.

"Kathryn, I have a gift for you," said Auntie Mame. "It's a going-away present."

"Thank you, Auntie. You shouldn't have. I'll be returning just as soon as I can."

"I doubt that," her aunt said. "Some handsome beau in Charleston is going to change your mind about that. Now go on, open your present."

"It's beautiful!" Kathryn cried. "It's the most beautiful diary that I've ever seen."

"Over the years, we have had many joyous occasions, just

sitting and talking," Auntie Mame said. "Now when you think of me or need to speak to me, pen your thoughts into this diary and address it to me. Then I will know your thoughts. I'll feel your emotions."

When she finally awakened, Kathryn recorded in her diary the horrifying events of that night in her cabin. The rest of the voyage was uneventful. The first entry into her diary was dedicated to the maimed black man, whom she had so feared.

Earlier, she stood watching the water churn under the stern of the ship. She created a poem:

> *Dark secrets, perilous waters*
> *All a part of yon blue and deep*
> *Relentless in grip on all afloat*
> *Pregnant with life*
> *Solemn auditor of death and destiny's end*
> *No blemish, no scar*
> *Scavenger to all and for all before*
> *Gone! Gone are the captain and the black man*
> *to be heard from no more.*

CHAPTER TWO

The South was beside itself. A native son, Andrew Jackson, was a candidate for the presidency of the United States. He'd chosen John C. Calhoun, a local boy from South Carolina, as his running mate. Kathryn, who arrived in Charleston on August 16, 1828, had never envisioned her homeland in such a euphoric state.

Still, her return hardly went unnoticed among Charleston's aristocracy. And it seemed that almost none of her old friends had forgotten her. Kathryn wished she could say the same.

What Kathryn had remembered was the beauty of Echo Holler, her family's plantation. It was peaceful here, she thought, just the kind of serenity she needed after her near-assault at the hands of the white captain and the equally traumatizing rescue by his black slave. No doubt because of what had transpired, she was now acutely aware of the many slaves attending the plantation.

There were men, women, and children of every age, every shape, and size, every shade of brown. But each one lacked the same thing: an identity. Not so for the big black man on the ship, whose face was now permanently etched in her mind.

She decided not to tell her father about her tumultuous sea journey. He would surely be repulsed and would not allow her to set foot on a ship again. That must not happen. She simply had to get back to England, Madame Bartholomew, and her music.

She had to. She would tell her father of her plans later.

"Kathryn, my dear," Sir Edward said as he walked onto the porch where she was standing. After kissing her lovingly on the cheek, he gazed admiringly at his only child. "I trust your return home has been as exciting for you as it has been for me."

"Yes, Father, it has been so much fun. There were times in England when I didn't think I would see this most beautiful place again. I appreciate your arranging for me to come home."

"This is your home. This is where you belong, and one day when I die, this will all be yours. You need to start giving strong consideration to the young man of your choice who will help you run it."

Kathryn didn't have the heart to tell her father of her intentions. For now, she decided, it was best that she play along. "You mean marriage?" she asked.

"Well, yes. Is that wrong of me?"

"No! No! I suppose not. It's just that I have never given it any serious thought."

"Well, perhaps you should. I won't live forever, you know! Furthermore, a young lady with such astounding beauty as yours will be suited by every eligible bachelor far and near."

"Yes, Father. Tell me more," Kathryn said with a laugh as she grabbed her father's arm and led him off the porch into the garden.

"You must look with a cautious eye amongst the makeshifts and scalawags who would have you purely for your purse. The man of your choice must be of the highest social standing and possess enough wealth, at least, to equal yours. He must come from Charleston's highest social order, noble in his efforts, Southern in his heart, and most importantly, a gentleman. Fortunately, in Charleston, there are many to choose from. You have been away a long time. Most of your old friends, you have forgotten. I thought a lawn party here at Echo Holler would be an excellent way to renew old acquaintances and meet new ones. Well, what do you think?"

She had no intention of living in America, let alone marrying here, she thought. Even so, she couldn't bear to hurt her father's feelings, so she decided to humor him. "How exciting! And when will this party be?" she asked brightly.

"Sunday week, perhaps. I'll alert the servants to begin preparations and ready the invitations," said Sir Edward. From his jacket pocket, he pulled out his pipe for a smoke.

Kathryn quickly wrapped her arms around her father's neck, startling him. "That's sweet of you, Father," she said, her voice filled with infectious delight.

Sir Edward was moved.

"It'll be the best party that we have had at Echo Holler in years," he told his beguiling daughter.

August was one of the hottest months of the year in Charleston. All the animals, large and small, furry or feathered, were paralyzed by the scorching heat—all except the mosquitoes and gnats, who seemed energized. Most of Charleston's elite had taken up residence at their summer homes, content to leave the affairs of the plantations to an overseer and the slaves while they took advantage of the city life. But, those who left returned for Kathryn's homecoming party. Already, word of her presence and stunning beauty had swept the community. No doubt, it seemed that every eligible beau within riding distance of

Charleston had come to Echo Holler on this hot Sunday afternoon.

Elegant carriages, with their drivers nearby, dotted the magnolia-lined lanes. Nothing was left unadorned—the drivers wore their Sunday best, carriages gleamed, and horses were groomed until their manes shone like sparkling glass. The belles and beaus promenaded about the gardens seeking relief under shade trees or from their glasses of mint julep or cool water. The servants weaved through the crowd, refilling glasses with ice-cooled drinks. They, too, were decked out in their best service attire.

In the midst of all this gaiety, Kathryn made her entrance. She stepped onto the wide veranda on her father's arm. Almost instantly, the crowd started moving in their direction. Guests inside the house filed out. Those strolling in the garden and lanes came forward for a closer look.

The crowd surveyed her. Kathryn wore a blue dress, modestly cut in front and in the back, exposing her soft, flawless skin, and a neck piece accented by a blue sapphire broach. Her long red hair, unadorned, cascaded well below her shoulders. Awestruck young ladies eyed her with envy; would-be suitors prepared to woo her.

Sir Edward and Kathryn then made their way onto the grounds, where he began introducing her to the guests. Countless young men approached her; almost all asked whether she remembered them.

Truthfully, she didn't, but this was no time for blunt honesty.

Then, two men approached—one was older, the other a much younger man, perhaps twenty or twenty-two years of age. She immediately noticed how handsome the youngest man was. Soon, they were face to face. The tone of her father's voice told Kathryn that this meeting would be different from the rest.

"William and young William, how good of you to come," he said.

"Edward, you know that I wouldn't miss this event for the world. And this must be Kathryn." He paused for a moment before continuing. "My dear, you are as beautiful as the rumors have made you."

"Kathryn," her father said, "you remember William Littlejohn Sr., and William Littlejohn Jr.?"

"Yes!" Kathryn exclaimed. "From Lakeview, next to us. We used to play together. At least, I tried to play with you," she told the younger man as she flashed an impish smile.

"That's right," the younger man quickly responded. "How are you, Kathryn?" Their eyes met and—for a brief moment— locked. "I was the little boy who never wanted to play with you because you were a girl, and as I remember, a pretty good tomboy at that."

"Yes! Yes! How nice to see you again, William. You've changed," she said approvingly.

"For the better, I hope. And so have you."

Sir Edward interrupted. "Kathryn, I guess this party might be perceived to be a celebration for the return of both you and young William. He just recently completed law school studies at Yale University."

"Well, Mr. Littlejohn, you must be very happy and proud to have your son home," said Kathryn.

"Just as pleased as I'm sure Sir Edward must be about your return, my dear." He kissed her gallantly on her cheek, then turned to Sir Edward and said, "Edward, let's leave these two young folks alone so that they can get to know each other better."

They stood silently for a moment before their eyes met again. Kathryn thought William was the most handsome man she had ever seen, quite different from the way she remembered him as a boy. He must be almost six feet tall, Kathryn thought, as she gazed into deep blue eyes and imagined caressing his waves of pecan-brown hair. It was true that, many years ago, when the families had visited each other, he never liked to play with her.

No matter how much his parents had insisted that he be courteous, he would always manage to scamper away to the hills where he'd shout at the top of his lungs, trying to produce an echo.

"Do you somehow get the feeling that this was all planned, our meeting, I mean?" Kathryn asked. "This party, our returning home at the same time."

"I most certainly do and I couldn't be more pleased. I hope you feel the same."

"Well, yes, I suppose I do."

And they spent the rest of the party together, the obvious envy of all.

Kathryn and William spent every spare moment together thereafter. The following week the couple and their fathers were invited to the home of Joel Poinsett for breakfast. Kathryn recollected that this early morning gathering was one of the key social events of Charleston. Invitation only. Most of Charleston's elite, as well as important visitors to the city, would be in attendance.

Kathryn was quick to take to her host, Mr. Poinsett. He was of short stature but affable and an accomplished storyteller who made his many adventures abroad sound so interesting. But Kathryn and William were oblivious to Poinsett's mesmerizing ways with the other guests, so intently were they focused on each other.

After breakfast was served, they ate quickly then set out for a stroll in the gardens. There, amid the privacy of one of the gardens, William gently pulled Kathryn to him. Their lips met, then parted. Kathryn reached for him quickly, pulling his lips down to hers again. Over and over they kissed, their passion mounting. Only the jerky, chiming movement of the humming-birds disturbed the silence. Then William spoke.

"Will you marry me?" he asked breathlessly.

"Yes! Yes!" Kathryn said without hesitation. "I will. I love you so much!"

Theirs had been a whirlwind romance which captivated all who knew about them. Here was the perfect couple: the gorgeous daughter and handsome son of two wealthy Charleston planters.

Not to be made light of was the fact that their two plantations, Echo Holler and Lakeview, were located side by side. Now two months later, Kathryn and William would be wed at Saint Michael's Cathedral, standing side by side—much like their families' plantations.

That Saturday afternoon at Saint Michael's, the church bells rang in the marital hour. The wedding began promptly at 4 p.m. before an overflow crowd. After the attendants made their way down the aisle, the organists began to play the wedding march. A hush fell upon the crowd as Sir Edward appeared at the rear of the cathedral with his beautiful daughter on his arm. Her white, floor-length gown was made of imported fine silk and trimmed with European lace. A veil concealed her face, causing all to wonder, as she passed them on her way down the aisle, whether she could possibly be even more beautiful on this day. She joined hands with William at the pulpit as their fathers stepped aside.

In her excitement, Kathryn heard few of the pastor's words. But the ones she was able to focus on were, to her, truly magical.

"Lady Kathryn Chiles, do you, being of sound mind, body, and thought, take into the bonds of holy matrimony William Littlejohn Jr.?"

"I do."

"Do you, William Littlejohn Jr., being of sound mind, body, and thought, take into the bonds of holy matrimony Lady Kathryn Chiles?"

"I do."

"Then let the angels of connubial bliss announce across this sacred land for now and the hereafter that you are now man and wife."

William lifted her veil. They gazed at each other lovingly and kissed, tenderly at first, then with such passion that they drew applause.

The reception was held at William's Charleston town house.

Kathryn and William immediately raced up the stairs to the second floor, a little anxious to get away from the crowd. As they passed the door of the study they could hear angry voices. They paused to listen. "David! You could at least do this family the honor of being present at your own brother's wedding."

"Father, I'm home . . . "

"Yes, and already you've begun to see how far you can go toward depleting my liquor supply. Must you have a drink in your hand every moment of the day?"

"Well, it isn't totally necessary, Father, but it is a means of soothing one's pains."

"What pains? You've never worked a day in your life. You've used your stipend for nothing of measurable accomplishment, but to squander on the next harlot or bottle. You've . . . "

William opened the door to the study as David completed his father's statement. "You've done nothing since your mother died except demean your own and this family's existence." Voraciously he gulped his drink until his glass was empty. "Is that what you were going to say, Father?" Then he turned to his brother. With a flourish, he extended his hand. "William, my father's favorite. Congratulations are in order, I hear. This must be the lovely Kathryn of whom I've heard so much."

"Kathryn," William said brusquely, "this is my younger brother, David. As you can see he drinks too much, and even at his best he is a loudmouth and a troublemaker."

David turned all of his attention to Kathryn, ignoring William's remarks. "My dear Kathryn, if looks are a proper measure, then you most certainly are deserving of all the good commentary that prevails regarding you." He curtsied and kissed the back of her hand. "Now I shall take leave to my own quarters and give the room a chance to defuse. My dear lady, it was so nice meeting you." Then he left, liquor glass and bottle in hand, as William and his father watched in stony silence.

Kathryn didn't know what to say. She remembered little about David when they were children, except that he preferred the company of his mother or one of the slave children. William had made little or no mention of his brother during their courtship, but what was said suggested that there was no love lost. Kathryn recalled that she and William had once talked about the future of the plantations and about what would happen if his or her father died. "Your father is lucky," she recalled saying, "he has two fine sons who will inherit his wealth and lands."

William had exploded. "No! He has two sons who will share his monetary wealth, but only one son who will inherit the land, and that's me. My brother is a squandering fool whose only goal in life is to receive his monthly stipend. I'll gladly continue his support should something happen to Father, if he will only stay away from here." William's animosity toward his brother shocked her. Too bad, she thought. Such a handsome young man, every bit as handsome as William. Too bad he is not yet twenty and has such a penchant for the bottle.

David Littlejohn lay in his bed awaiting the return of his usual state of sobriety. He was certain that his act had been convincing; he had given his usual drunken performance. Now, thoughts of his brother's wife occupied him. She was the most beautiful and charismatic person that he had met in a long time. And even though their relationship had long been sour, David hoped that William and Kathryn would have a good life and that she would find him deserving of her charm and beauty.

He turned his thoughts to more pressing matters. He had to book passage to Philadelphia as soon as possible. There was to be another secret meeting where he would have to deliver certain financial reports.

How much money should he request from his father this time? David knew that, as always, his father would part with it so he could rid himself of this son. He would use it to fund his efforts, on which many lives depended. And it was imperative that he maintain the utmost secrecy.

As he prepared for bed, David eyed the nearly full bottle of liquor that he had taken from his father's study. Lifting it off the nightstand, he poured the bottle's addictive contents out the window.

CHAPTER THREE

Just before daybreak, Kathryn roused herself from a deep, peaceful sleep. She turned over to face her husband, still sleeping and cozily nestled under the covers. Kathryn smiled as seductive memories of the night before came rushing back, a night filled with tender caresses, lingering kisses, ardent lovemaking.

As a lover, William had been the ideal—considerate and patient, a skilled teacher who reveled in guiding her to ecstasy.

Later that day, they would leave on their honeymoon—a tour of Europe that would last three beautiful months and end at Auntie Mame's. So elated at the thought of seeing her aunt again, Kathryn was now too excited to go back to sleep. She slipped into a robe and walked to the window to glimpse the beautiful moonlit night. What a grand and glorious time for a honeymoon, she thought. A soft poem came to her mind:

> *Heaven's lit, a glow of love*
> *Purity, whiteness shown clearly like*
> *the wings of a dove*
> *Fly away, fly away, o' valiant wings,*

symbol of affection
Let your permanence be encased
by the ephemeral air around you to
secure your presence forever
Heaven's lit! Dove afloat
Your guardian star beckons
With the soft shine of light
Fly away! Fly away!
Carry the message of love
to all who await thy presence
throughout the night.

After a lengthy trip, they arrived in France a weary couple. But their exhaustion was short-lived; France's aura of romance quickly rejuvenated them.

Kathryn and William supped at the finest dinner theaters and partook of other entertaining fare before departing France on a course through the Swiss Alps that ended on the Italian peninsula. They boarded a boat from Naples to the Island of Messina. On the way, they marveled at the bright red flames coming from the Stromboli volcano. Kathryn savored the beauty of the blue carpeted sea and the mountainous volcano. How beautiful it would be, she thought, to set this scene to music. Later, they visited picturesque Rome with its ancient ruins and hot dusty trails. Aware that they were standing on the same ground that great generals and kings had trampled upon, William and Kathryn were truly in awe. They traveled back to the Italian mainland and set their itinerary for the return to Switzerland, through Germany, and into Vienna. Then they backtracked to Paris before going to visit Auntie Mame in England.

As the boat docked in England, Kathryn was filled with nostalgia. Her formative years had been spent here under the watchful eye of someone whom she grew to love. She could hardly wait for their driver to take them on this short carriage ride into the cool, foggy night. William was exhausted; he only wanted this stretch of the trip to end so he could rest. He slept during the entire carriage ride. Not Kathryn. In her excitement, she almost forgot to awaken William as the carriage pulled up to No. 8 Caraston. Upon arrival, she was at the front door, knocking vigorously. William followed. Auntie Mame met them at the door.

She embraced Kathryn tenderly and greeted William.

"I am so glad that you sent me a letter letting me know of your arrival," Auntie Mame said once they were all inside.

"However, I've already booked passage for both of you on the next ship back to Charleston. You see, I have terrible news. William, your father died after you left. Apparently, he took ill with fever and never recuperated. It was all so sudden."

William was speechless for a moment. He sat in the nearest chair with his head buried in his hands.

"My father is dead! I can't believe it. He was as fit as anybody when we left."

"Well, according to Sir Edward, your immediate return is imperative." She reached for Kathryn, who stood teary-eyed at William's side. "Dear, dear Kathryn, I have missed you. I so looked forward to seeing you and getting to know this handsome husband of yours. However, you must prepare to leave by early morn'." She turned to William. "It seems that your younger brother is all that there is to see to the affairs of Lakeview until you return and Sir Edward didn't sound too confident that he was capable. I do hope that I'm not offending you."

"No, no. You've been most kind and indulging. Thank you for making all the arrangements for our hasty return home."

"Well, Sir Edward indicated that the land situation back there is sort of perilous, something about a tariff and secession."

The next morning, Kathryn and William were up and about early to depart for Charleston. Auntie Mame had already prepared a filling breakfast of hot tea, eggs, and muffins that energized William and Kathryn for their hasty departure.

"I bid you God's speed, my children. Hurry, don't miss your ship. You will be returning on the *Mava Fase* and I know the captain to be a dependable man."

William was the first to exit after bidding a solemn good-bye. He waited for Kathryn outside the carriage as she and Auntie Mame fervently embraced.

"I shall miss you even more, my child, now that I have had this brief glimpse of you after so many months. Here, take this wedding present. It will seal our friendship forever. There is a letter inside for you to read when you are safe aboard ship. Good-bye, my child."

"I love you, Auntie Mame. Thank you for being so nice and thoughtful." They hugged again, then parted. "I'll miss you and I'll write soon."

"Please do."

Later that night aboard ship, as William lay asleep, Kathryn pulled at the ribbon that sealed the gift from Auntie Mame. As she opened the package, she could see that the collection of musical pieces inside were all her favorites—Handel, Mozart, Beethoven. There was also a letter. She lit a candle. Excitedly, she began to read:

January 27, 1829

Dear Kathryn,

    Most lovely and only child that I have known as my own, I know and feel that you will never be able to return to me—at least not permanently.

You see, dear child, I am somewhat familiar with the ways of Charleston and I knew at once upon your departure that your beauty and charm would send out signals to every eligible and ineligible man to behold and conquer. Surely, William is deserving and he will see in you the extraordinary person that I have come to know and love. I trust that you will be happy.

I have but one regret and that is that the world shall never come to know of your extraordinary talent for music and the piano. You are subdued by an un-yielding era that promotes a credo that a woman's place is in the home. Such a tragedy! After all, what is the substance in us that restricts talent and creativity as part of our birthright?

Remember that the sweetest berry can sour and life has its tribulations for us all. I've always found comfort sharing thoughts with a friend. Remember, you can always reach me in spirit through the diary I gave you. Here are copies of the musical pieces that we shared throughout the years. Who knows? Perhaps you will find a willing student who will benefit from your instruction.

Love Always,
Auntie Mame

Kathryn marveled at how much this voyage differed from her first trip to America. This time, she had William and felt secure in his presence. But it was hard to not think of that other journey or the evil captain or what would have happened if the chivalrous black man hadn't intervened. She owed that slave her life, yet she could never tell anyone of his heroics—or her gratitude. She was forced to bury both deep in her soul.

CHAPTER FOUR

As soon as he reached Charleston, William went to his father's graveside, high up on a hill overlooking the sprawling plantation. He was now lord of the manor, but at that moment—next to his father's final resting place—he felt more like a child. Atop the hill, William was able to survey the vast lands of Lakeview and Echo Holler. When Sir Edward dies, he thought, Kathryn will be the sole heir to his plantation, and the Littlejohn holdings would automatically double. It was the perfect time to produce heirs to the family fortune. But first, he had to rid himself of David. To William, that wasn't much of an obstacle; he knew his brother's price.

At Lakeview, David descended the stairs, outfitted for departure. Kathryn stopped him. "David, are you leaving?"

"Yes, dear Kathryn, I'm afraid that I've worn out my welcome."

"Nonsense, I've hardly spoken to you."

"Part of this plantation is yours," she said, then stopped as she remembered William's vehemence about who would run it. "Isn't it?"

"Perhaps there is some truth to what you say, but I don't think that my brother would agree with you," said David. "Well, I must be off, dear lady. It would be, shall we say, untimely to have a scene now. Please forward a message to my brother and tell him that he knows the amount of my stipend as well as the address to which it should be sent. Now, I must bid you farewell," said David.

Sadly, Kathryn watched David as he stepped into a waiting carriage. Even death couldn't unite her husband and his wayward brother, she thought. Would she ever find out what had divided them? Jonathan, the butler, approached as she stood in the foyer.

She took note of Jonathan's gray hair and toothless mouth and remembered that he had been around for years. Perhaps he could provide the answer to her question.

"Jonathan, come here, please. I want to ask you something," said Kathryn as she directed him to the sofa in the parlor.

Jonathan looked panic-stricken. A slave-servant never sat with master or mistress. Kathryn patted the seat beside her. "Sit down! It's all right. Sit down!"

"Yes'm."

"I want you to tell me about David and William. Why do they hate each other so?"

Jonathan didn't hesitate.

"You see, Missy Kathryn, it happened a long time ago," Jonathan began.

"Go on, go on," Kathryn said anxiously.

"David was about ten or twelve years old. Ya know out here on these plantations, dey so big an' all, the massah's young'uns plays wit' slave young'uns an' I guess sometime thems young'uns forgets that there is a difference. An' that's what happened to li'l David, or Massah David."

"Keep going, what happened?"

"Well, you see, li'l David had this li'l slave friend. His name was Jermie. These two boys did everythin' together. They fished together, they climbed trees together, they ran together, and they hunted together. Then they begin ta wrestle and sometime fight together, as boys will do. Well, Missy, one day they was out in the yard foolin' around. The slave boy was 'bout the same age as Massah David. They was wrestlin' in full view of ole Massah Littlejohn, who began to take notice. No matter what Massah David tried, he couldn't outwrestle that li'l slave boy.

"Time and time again that slave boy threw Massah David to the ground. Well, by now Massah Littlejohn was madder than a striped snake. He called David a girl and a sissy who would never be able to control his slaves an' he sent William over to beat up the slave boy. An', bein' a full foot taller'n li'l Jermie, it was easy for him to do. Pert near beat the life out o' that li'l boy, and lef' him on the yard to bake in the sun. Well, ole Massah Littlejohn applauded Massah William for bein' brave an' manly and they both left the li'l slave boy to die. Well, Mrs. Littlejohn was livin' then. She an' Massah David carried li'l Jermie to his cabin where, after a day or so, it looked like he would live.

"Then, one mornin', David woke up to go find his friend. When he entered the yard he saw a wagonful o' slaves jus' pullin' away from the front. There was Jermie, sittin' in amongst 'em. They caught each other's eye, but there was nothin' li'l David could do.

From that day to now, he never had much o' nothin' to do with his brother or ol' Massah Littlejohn. Just his mother. When she died, he asked to be sent away to school. You see, Missy Kathryn, to Massah William an' ol' Massah Littlejohn, they just sent away an' sol' a li'l slave boy; but to Massah David, they sent away an' sol' the only friend he done had in the worl'."

At that moment, William entered the foyer. "Kathryn, where are you?"

Jonathan nearly tumbled to the floor as he tried to get to his feet. "I'm in here, William," Kathryn answered calmly, "in the parlor with Jonathan."

By the time William entered, Jonathan was already at attention. William eyed Kathryn and kissed her on the cheek.

"Kathryn, are you all right?" he asked.

"Yes, I'm fine, thank you. Perhaps I should ask the same of you. You saw your father's grave?"

"Yes, I did, and now I must have a word with David. Where is he?" asked William sternly.

"He's gone. He left a message that he was sorry he had to leave without seeing you, but he thought it best and that, when you found the time, to send his stipend to the usual address."

"Of course," William said. He looked a little relieved when he added, "Stipend, huh? Worthless no-good. Well, perhaps I shall skip supper—maybe a glass of warm milk. I'm really tired and worn out from the trip and everything else."

"Fine, I will have Gertie bring along a glass of milk," said Kathryn, and they parted with a kiss.

The next day, Kathryn urged William to accompany her to Echo Holler. The greeting was cordial but subdued as her father met them in the parlor, his customary pipe in hand. "Sweet Kathryn," he said lovingly as they embraced.

"Father, it's good to see you. How have you been?"

"Fine as can be expected. And William, I'm sorry about your father. It happened so suddenly." His eyes were filled with concern.

"Yes, yes I know," was William's reply. "I appreciate your thoughtfulness."

"Kathryn," said Sir Edward, "would you mind awfully much if I took William away from you for a moment? I do need to speak with him in my study."

"As you wish, Father," Kathryn said before heading out to the veranda.

"Come along, William, this way." He led William to his study where they settled into plush leather chairs.

"I don't want to bemoan your father's death too much, but it was awfully untimely. All the planters sort of looked up to him for leadership during this nullification thing, and before we were barely organized, he was gone." He paused for a moment and placed the pipe between his teeth. "William, I don't need to tell you how perilous times are for the South in general, and Charleston in particular. Every proud Southern gentleman that's worth his salt must fervently rally together if we are to nullify the conspiracy to frustrate our way of life with this abominable, ill-begotten taxation on our imports-even to the point of secession if necessary."

"I couldn't agree more, Sir Edward."

"I knew I could count on you, my boy. The Littlejohn name means something in this neck of the woods and in the absence of your father, others are going to look to you for advice and to see what your stand will be on this most critical issue."

"Well, you can count on me, Sir. My father always used to say to me, in private of course, that there is only one thing more important than the Union and that is the Southern way of life. Perhaps, when Jackson is well into office, being the Southerner that he is, we can finally rid us of this damned tariff once and for all."

"Perhaps, but the local planters association wants other assurances, just in case."

"What do you mean?"

"William, let me come straight to the point. This association to which your father belonged is prepared to send an emissary to open up independent lines of communications with our European markets just in case secession becomes our only alternative. Once you have been introduced to the group in your father's stead, I would like for that person to be you."

"But Sir Edward, I don't see how I can. Who would run Lakeview, and more importantly, what about Kathryn? We've just married and we haven't had a chance to spend much time together."

"Well, there's no one who knows better than I how big a sacrifice this would be for you. Nevertheless, you are the perfect candidate—young, well-trained in law, and with strong Southern interests. Yet, you are little-known outside Charleston and your departure to Europe would be less likely to cause a stir amongst our Northern friends. Not to mention the fact that the man who keeps our European markets open will wear a big feather in his hat amongst Southern politicians. We are going to need young, strong, aggressive leaders to see us through this tariff problem and no matter what, you, like the rest of us, are caught right in the middle." He paused for a second then added, "It could put you at the helm of the Southern leadership if secession is our only alternative."

"I'll have to think about it, Sir Edward, and naturally I'll have to speak with Kathryn. I don't mind telling you that the idea appears to carry a critical amount of intrigue."

"There's no rush for an answer, but think about it and we will talk again," Sir Edward replied.

That night as he and Kathryn readied for bed, William decided not to mention Sir Edward's offer yet. Instead, he focused on his growing excitement as he watched Kathryn disrobe and slip into bed beside him. They began to explore each others' bodies, but William found the approach orderly and possessing of a routine that was foreign to him. No reckless abandon or animal passion. But no matter; his other liaisons would fulfill that need, he thought.

Once again, William thought of the child he and Kathryn still did not have. His father had begun to mold him into a Charleston aristocrat at an early age, and he was ready to do the same for his son. Maybe there would be many sons, maybe just one.

The number wasn't important. What mattered was that no child of his would be like his brother David. He would see to that.

CHAPTER FIVE

The year was 1831. Andrew Jackson was about to complete his first term as president of the United States. He had left no doubt that he was a strong supporter of the Union, even if it meant severing ties with the South; moreover, he had denounced any support for secession as an act of treason. To make matters worse, emotional sentiment against slavery began to swell in the North. Some called it unconstitutional. When William first saw this "Yankee gibberish" in some paper called *The Liberator*, he could hardly believe the words spread out before him were those of a white man. " . . . I shall strenuously contend for the immediate enfranchisement of our slave population. I am aware that many object to the severity of my language, but is there not cause for severity? I will be as harsh as truth, and as uncompromising as justice. On this subject, I do not wish to write or speak or think with moderation. No! No! Tell a man whose house is on fire to give a moderate alarm. Tell him to moderately rescue his wife from the hands of the ravisher; tell the mother to gradually extricate her babe from the fire into which it has fallen; but urge me not to moderation in a cause like the present. I am in earnest

—I will not equivocate—I will not excuse—I will not retreat a single inch—and I will be heard . . . ”

These words incensed William to such a degree that he knew he had to enter the fight. Now, the country was just one year away from another presidential election and if current events were any indication of whether the tariff would be sustained, Southerners were about to be had. The not-unfamiliar refrain of revolt, secession, and nullification began to surface.

Many Charleston aristocrats and poor farmers alike decided to attend a statewide Nullification Convention which was to be held in Charleston in July.

William Littlejohn was among the conventioneers and was appointed to a special committee, after being nominated by Sir Edward, to investigate how to keep the bargaining tables open with the European markets should secession become a reality. It was unanimously decided that he was to be a member of a committee traveling to England for this purpose. William knew the situation was urgent and felt it was his duty to go; now he had to tell Kathryn. How would she take it? Her own father saw the urgency.

The committee members were not allowed to take their wives. He hoped she would understand.

Conversation at the Littlejohn dinner table had become such a rare event that its initiation by William always meant bad news. To hear her husband speak of political affairs was even more cause for Kathryn to worry, but she listened. “We discussed having our own separate states under a separate flag at the convention again, and there are those of us who feel that we should put some plans into action,” William said.

“You mean secession from the United States?” asked Kathryn.

“Perhaps. It may be our only alternative.”

Kathryn braced herself. “And my father,” she asked cautiously, "what does he have to say about all this?"

"Of course he agrees with the idea of secession, which brings up another point. I've been nominated to a special group who will travel to England soon. Sir Edward asked me to be a part of that committee. I am afraid we were asked not to take our wives for fear of danger should the Unionists try to repel our efforts."

"Well, what about you? I'm afraid for you. Is there any real danger?"

"Oh, of course not." He got up from the dinner table to kneel at her side.

"I'm going to be fine. But I know I've spent so much time away from you in the past several months, and now this. I love you and I want you to understand that only something as serious as this situation could pull me away for so long. Please say that you understand."

She lovingly stroked his face and gazed into his eyes. "I do. I know that you must go. I'll miss you so much, especially when I'm out on the plantation. However, Jonathan and Gertie will do very well taking care of me."

"We should be gone no longer than six months and I promise never again."

Tears flooded Kathryn's eyes as William continued to talk.

She touched his lips softly with her fingers to silence his promises; they both knew there were some he might be unable to keep.

On the day of his departure, Kathryn, along with Jonathan, watched from dockside as the huge wooden craft with tall poles and graying sails moved farther and farther from port. Kathryn's nose detected the fishy smells mingling with the humid breeze that drifted off the blue-green water, the expanse of which was almost unimaginable. She focused on the distance, out there where the sky and water intersected, until she felt the world was closing in on her. She grew dizzy.

"Are you all right, Missy Kathryn?"

"Yes, Jonathan, I'm fine. Let's go."

During the ride home, Kathryn cried silently. She felt as alone and just as imprisoned as the harnessed horse that pulled her carriage. She had not told William her secret: pregnant, again. This baby had to live. She had felt pregnant on one other occasion, but early on, she had had massive bleeding with clots and intense pain. She had decided to not tell William until she was sure she wouldn't lose this baby. By the time William returns, she thought, I will be well into the pregnancy. Please, God, don't let anything happen to this baby, she prayed.

William wanted Kathryn to stay in the Charleston town house for the duration of his trip, but this proved much to her dissatisfaction and she remained only long enough to hear her doctor's words: "Yes, you are pregnant." She had Jonathan gather her belongings into the carriage and they set out for Lakeview.

She had grown accustomed again to plantation life, and when the dreaded loneliness ensued she would play the piano, walk in the lush garden, sit alongside the lake, or have someone saddle a choice mare and ride for hours between the two plantations. Her father's health was failing now and she didn't want to be far away in case of an emergency. But with the baby, she would have to choose only the most delicate of pastimes. She felt the spiritual presence of life within her and longed for the day when she would feel the swift kicks in her womb. Often she massaged her abdomen softly with her hands, just as she would hug and cuddle the child gently when it was born. She felt more complete as a woman than ever before.

On this particular morning, Kathryn awakened at her usual

time just after sunup. She looked toward the window for the telltale rays of the sun preparing to usher in a brilliant day.

There were none. She got out of bed and walked to the window. The sky was gray and overcast. A gentle but steady breeze whipped the curtains around like a kite on a windy spring day. Kathryn did not feel at her best this morning. She thought breakfast might help, so she washed her face and hands at the water bowl. Not bothering to take off her bedclothes, she went downstairs. By the time she reached the breakfast room, she was wracked by severe cramps. Her back against the wall, she slowly slid down and curled into a fetal position on the floor. Misery and pain engulfed her. "No, you can't take my baby!" she screamed. "No! No! I won't let you!"

By now Jonathan and Gertie were at her side. "Missy Kathryn, Missy Kathryn, whud wrong wid cho? Lawd, dis chil' is burnin' up wid de feva. She wetter dan one o' dem ole hosses of Massah Littlejohn's after dey win a race," Gertie cried.

"Let's carry her to bed," said Jonathan as he bent over to pick her up.

"No! No!" shouted Kathryn. "You must hurry and fetch the doctor. Go now, Jonathan, and hurry! Go now!"

"Yes! Yes, Missy, I'm gone."

"Gertie, Gertie," she talked in gulps. "You go get Ole Nanna and hurry. I'll be all right here until you return."

Gertie was so overweight that her running pace was no better than a fast walk. But she tried to hurry. As she reached the front porch, she saw a lone horseman dismount. "Missy Kathryn, Missy Kathryn, she done took terrible sick wid de feva. She in der on de breakfast room flo'. Hurry, I's got ta go fetch Ole Nanna," she said to the rider.

David ran to Kathryn's side. She was sweating profusely, ashen, and weak. He grabbed a towel from the kitchen and began to pat her moist forehead. He tore at her gown and began to sponge her whole body, then noticed the pool of dark blood between her legs. Despite her pain, Kathryn was aware of David's presence, in which she took comfort.

With herbs and medication in hand, Ole Nanna took off from her nearby cabin after hearing the news from Gertie. She was at Kathryn's side in no time. "I needs me some warm water. I needs me some towels and I needs a lot of 'em," Ole Nanna barked. David obeyed her commands; he knew Ole Nanna had delivered every child, black or white, that had been born on the plantation, including him and his brother. Nobody argued when she took control.

Ole Nanna's examining ritual never varied. First, she bent over the mountainous stomach to look at it from all angles. Then she felt the stomach, ever so softly, with her roughened but skillful hands. Usually, before she began to work, she would remove a neck piece from her neck and place it over the navel. If it fell off, she would replace it. This time, she did not take off the neck piece. Rather, she took a handful of herbs and placed them in one of the moistened towels given to her by David.

She placed this around Kathryn's groin in diaper fashion. When she finished, she gathered her sack to leave. On her way out, she stared at David before silently shaking her head.

David attended to Kathryn's every need. Under his watchful eye, Kathryn slept most of the day, which allowed David to gaze at her beauty. Silently, he acknowledged his attraction to her—and his guilt.

It was late that evening before Jonathan returned with the doctor, who also had a healthy respect for Ole Nanna's abilities. When he saw the diaper and herbs that she had left in place, he knew what to expect. He removed the diaper; miraculously, the bleeding had been kept to a minimum. He was in with Kathryn only a short while, departing after leaving a vial of medicine with David to ease her pain. It was all he could do.

A week passed before Kathryn was steady on her feet. Throughout her convalescence she had warned David to not tell her father what had happened since it could have an adverse effect on his health.

One week later, she insisted that David let her out of the house so they could ride to Echo Holler. She refused a carriage.

The ride was slow and not without some discomfort. She rode sidesaddle, but still she looked elegant in her blue riding outfit. She and David stared at each other before Kathryn broke the silence. "I haven't seen you take a drink for the whole time that you cared for me," she said with a gentle smile.

"I guess it was because I was so busy. I didn't feel that I needed it," he responded.

"David I must thank you for taking the time with me. I know you must have more important things to do and I don't think I would have made it without you."

"Nonsense, you're quite some lady and you would have made it because that's the kind of stuff you're made of. If you were my . . . " he cut the sentence short.

"If I were your what?" Kathryn asked.

"Oh, nothing. What will you tell William about the baby?"

"Nothing. He didn't know that I was going to have a child. So I won't tell him anything. You see, that was not my first loss. As a matter of fact, that was my second. It seems that the privilege of motherhood will escape me forever."

"Oh, don't say that. You must keep trying."

"I don't know. I'm not so sure that I want a child for the right reasons. Just selfish reasons. With William being gone so much, it would be company for me, or maybe if there were a child,

William would stay home more. I'm not so sure that it would be fair to a child."

David leaned over and pulled both horses to a halt. He looked at her admiringly and this time, he didn't try to shift his gaze. For the first time, he admitted to himself that he was falling in love with her. He wouldn't say it, for he knew she was too much of a lady to solicit infidelity, but he conveyed it with his eyes; they beamed the message unyieldingly to her.

"If you were my wife," he began again, "there would be no need for you to try to entice me to remain at home. My daily efforts would be to please you and love you. I could spend a lifetime with you just savoring the tender moments that we would spend together."

Kathryn was speechless. David's words and the realization that her feelings toward him were changing in a dangerous way distressed her. She resolved to brush them off as simple passions stirred in a time of stress. But her hand instinctively moved to gently stroke his face. "David, my dear, sweet David," she said. "I . . . ".

She stopped as he clasped her hand and brushed it across his other cheek. "You don't have to say anything," he told her. "I know this must have come as a surprise, but I think I've felt this way since I first saw you."

"David, it's the most lovely thing I've heard in a long time. But I would never do anything to help widen the gap between you and William. I simply couldn't."

"I know and understand," he said as he released her hand.

They both rapped their horses to begin the ride back to the plantation.

When they reached Echo Holler, Kathryn hurried to her father's side. She found him in his usual spot in a rocking chair near the window. Kathryn could see the toll his illness had taken.

His face was heavily wrinkled, skin dry, hair thin and lifeless. It took all of her father's energy to muster a smile, but he acknowledged her presence by pulling one corner of his mouth to the side. The other side of his mouth and face was paralyzed from a stroke that was slowly draining the life from him.

"Father," Kathryn said, kneeling at his side. "David is with me; you remember David, David Littlejohn." Sir Edward grasped David's hand weakly and gave it a shake.

"How are you, Sir Edward?" asked David. Kathryn's father was silent as he struggled to look up at the visitor who was speaking to him. Kathryn turned to the servants to inquire of his health.

"How has my father been doing?"

Old Claude, the elderly black man who seemed every bit as decrepit as Kathryn's father, spoke up. "He be doin' all right. He's a little weak, but we goin' to take care of 'im, just like he done us all dese years."

For Kathryn, the ride back to Lakeview was a much more solemn trip.

"I've never seem him look so bad. I guess I just wasn't prepared for that," she said about her father.

"What happened to him?" David asked. "The last time I saw him he was as strong as an ox."

"He had a stroke recently and he's been going downhill ever since. I'm really surprised that he has lived this long. You know, he really needs someone to help run the plantation. I just simply don't know how."

"Well what about the overseer?"

"Oh! He's been with father for years and I trust him just as much as Old Claude. But still, he's not in the family." Suddenly she pulled her horse to a halt and looked at David. "You know that when my father dies he has left all of this to me, which means it will be a part of Lakeview. You should really give some thought to coming home and looking after Echo Holler and Lakeview. I'm sure William would agree. What with his political aspirations, he should be glad to have someone in the family available!"

"Just hold on a second. Who says that I want to run a plantation, yours or anybody else's?"

Kathryn disliked the tone of David's voice. He had been so wonderful over the past two weeks—not the shiftless, drunken, irresponsible person whom she'd met on her wedding day. But now, his voice signaled the return of his former self. "Well, why not? You are the only other surviving member of the Littlejohn clan who could. Plus, it would give you a chance to earn the stipend you receive."

David took offense to her statement, but he decided not to show it. "Well, why not? My brother makes the money and I spend it and enjoy it for the both of us."

"You know, when you speak like that, you sound like a different person. Not the same person whom I have grown to like over the past two weeks. How quickly things change!"

"Yes, don't they, though." David quickly assumed his former role as wayward brother. It was the only way he could survive being around Kathryn, loving her, yet not being able to hold or caress her as his own. He rapped his horse hard and it galloped away as fast as it could. All the time, he felt like snatching Kathryn from her horse and taking her with him. He was falling deeply in love with her. Never before had he admitted such a thing to himself. To make matters worse, the lady was not his to have: she belonged to his brother. He decided to leave immediately. After all, he would have to hurry if he was to make the next meeting on time.

On the day that William was expected to return, Kathryn dispatched a carriage driven by Jonathan to Charleston. He returned the next day with Master William. Kathryn and William greeted each other with great affection. As they embraced, Kathryn noticed the two other passengers in a wagon. One was a large, muscular black man who appeared incapable of a smile. He looked to be about twenty years old. The other was a young Negress of about the same age who looked nothing like the field hands that Kathryn knew. Her skin was soft and smooth, devoid of wrinkles brought on by an unrelenting sun. Her body was straight, not bent from years of performing heavy tasks normally meant for men. Her hair was jet black, lively, and sprang out from her head like so many needles from a porcupine's back. She possessed a womanly figure that men of both races were sure to notice.

"Who are they?" Kathryn asked, motioning toward the passengers.

"That big black's name is Buck. The girl is called Teresa. I'm gonna use her as a chambermaid. Buck's a field hand. I got a real good bargain on these two while I was in Charleston."

"Do we need more hands?" asked Kathryn.

"Well, we can always use another hand around the place. Come on, let's go in. I'm tired and hungry," William said, caressing Kathryn as he led her inside.

The overseer took Buck to the slave yards; Jonathan directed Teresa into the house to the cellar, where she would sleep. She studied the cold, damp room. Wine bottles protruded from little shelf-like pockets along the wall. A small, dirty window barely let in light. The bed was the only inviting item there; it was covered in clean sheets and appeared large enough for two people.

That evening, Kathryn and William sat on the porch for a long while. He had spoken so much about his trip and—for the most part—the voyage was uneventful and to some degree successful. The committee was now hopeful that the foreign markets would be sympathetic toward Southern secession, since Northern dominance would mean more taxes on exports to America.

Kathryn reported to William that her father was still in poor health and that the doctor had been summoned on several occasions. She did not speak of the pregnancy or the loss of their baby. The miscarriage had amplified her insecurities about being a woman. She knew how badly William wanted children and she felt she had failed him. And she had already warned Gertie and Jonathan to not speak of what had happened. She was glad that William was away long enough for her to heal, for he was certain to make love to her tonight, as he always did when he'd been away.

After a short silence, William asked her to retire with him to bed. Darkness came earlier now, and they left the porch to enter the house. Upstairs in their room, William kissed her gently and softly on her lips and face. He caressed the nape of her neck as he tickled her ear with his tongue. His hands moved to her breasts, massaging each until the nipples pointed rigidly.

Kathryn responded to his gentle urging with soft kisses and moans. Though she submitted to William completely, her love-making had no urgency; her excitement was minimal and she faked orgasm.

When it was over, for reasons unknown to her, she thought of David. She was fearful. What was happening to her?

William lay still on the moistened sheets, still too excited to fall asleep. Although infidelity, not abstinence, was his lifestyle when away from home, his nature was still alive and wanting. He decided to rest for a while and arouse Kathryn again. He turned to face her, but she had already turned her back to him. Maybe it's just as well, he thought. He always thought himself a good lover and he tried to be gentle with Kathryn, but, of late, he had begun to doubt his virility. Four years of marriage and no children, no son. Maybe something was wrong with him, he thought.

Maybe his juices did not carry the substance of life. He had to know. He had to find out.

He'd first seen Teresa with a slave dealer as he left the ship in Charleston Harbor. She had a certain sex appeal that aroused him physically as no other black girl had done before. He decided he had to have her as his chambermaid, and bargained with the owner to make the purchase. He felt a little guilty, but he found solace in the fact that rendezvous with slave women were common among planters. Anticipating his first encounter with Teresa, William grew erect as he lay in bed next to Kathryn. He nearly paid the girl a visit that night but restrained himself for that perfect moment.

William had ordered Buck to bed down with a young wench that everybody called Bell, short for Sociobell, so named because she had been quick to smile when she was young. By age fifteen, life as a field slave had taken its toll. Her hands were tough and her nails ragged. The smile had disappeared into a tight, grim face.

Yet, there was something about her that attracted Buck. For the first time, he wanted to love a woman as his own. He soon found out that under that hard shell of a woman, there was a softness that wanted to give love and be loved. But like himself, she felt there was no room for trust or caring in the life of a slave, that is, unless you were not fearful of the hurt that was inevitable.

One day, Buck and Bell were at Lakeside fishing, a privilege that made Sunday a special, long-awaited day. They were sitting close, side by side, and spontaneously, Bell began to sing. Her voice was forceful, soft, and beautiful. Buck looked in amazement at Bell. The smoothness of her voice, the ecstatic moans and groans that she used to embellish her music surprised him. They had been together for weeks and never before had she sung a note.

"Yo' neba told me dat yo' could sang. I've neba heard nothing so good."

Tears welled on Bell's lower eyelids as she continued:

> *I sings to yo' 'cause yo' makes me happy,*
> *I sings to you' 'cause yo' makes me sad,*
> *I sings to yo' 'cause yo' makes up fo'*
> *all dat I lost*
> *and some dat I neba had.*

> *Dis life ain't nothin' to me, fo' I*
> *met yo', yo' see*
> *my body ain't mine tho'*
> *it now seems my life has some meanin'*
> *a new dream and my parts now*
> *makes up one whole.*

> *I sings to yo' 'cause yo' makes me happy,*
> *I sings to yo' 'cause yo' makes me sad,*
> *I sings to yo' 'cause yo' makes up fo'*
> *all dat I lost*
> *and some dat I neba had.*

> *Ma fears fo' life wuz dulled by so much*
> *toil and strife*

It difficult to know if I breathed
I open ma eyes, what now, much to ma surprise
I can hear, I can feel, I can see . . .

Buck realized that this frail, not too pretty young girl in a rapidly aging body had aroused in him emotions he never knew he had. They both looked out across the lake as they drew closer together, trying to envision what was in store for their uncertain futures, both afraid. Afraid to say I love you.

It did not take long for Teresa to learn what her duties were as chambermaid. She administered solely to the needs of Master Littlejohn when he was in his study. She brought his food or wine when requested, she served his guests. Almost always, these were male friends to whom she would bring tobacco or drink as they conversed mostly about the politics of the day. Sometimes one of the visitors would make mention of her— something like, "Does she make a good bed, William?" Sometimes a visitor who had too much to drink would take liberties and pinch her bottom. She had to act as if nothing had happened. She hated it when that happened. She had seen enough back bedrooms and slept on enough clean sheets to know that the comfort was not for her. She knew what she was there for and had learned to expect as well as pretend to enjoy it, but she didn't like being pawed at by every male visitor in the house.

The study was all but forbidden to Mistress Kathryn and any female visitors. Little wonder, thought Teresa, since it was here that Massah Littlejohn and his friends talked about their concubines perhaps as much as their politics. The scenario was usually the same and the bedroom was situated conveniently nearby. Such was the case with Massah Littlejohn.

The first time she heard footsteps descending the stairs to her bedroom was about a week after she got to Lakeview. It was late in the night and Teresa knew everybody else in the house had to be asleep. She knew what was about to happen and was a bit anxious to see what her new lover would be like. When Massah Littlejohn entered her room he didn't say anything, but walked toward the bedside and lit a candle. Teresa's already nude body silhouetted sharply against the white sheets. William undressed slowly, never taking his eyes off the bed where she lay. After he was completely nude, he opened a bottle of wine that he had brought from the cellar. He sat beside her on the bed, drinking his wine in large gulps. After finishing each glass, he massaged her beautiful naked body. It wasn't long before they were both relaxed and enraptured by each other's nudity. They rubbed, they caressed, they kissed. This came as no surprise to Teresa, for she learned long ago that within the shelter of these back rooms, white men became very loving of their courtesan slave women. What did surprise Teresa was what happened next. Massah Littlejohn drew a fistful of cotton from his jacket and lay back on the bed. He demonstrated what he wanted done. She was to massage his whole body with the soft cotton until it tingled with excitement. Then they would make passionate love. Only the moist smothering kisses muffled Teresa's screams of pleasure. She wanted to please him and apparently she did, for there were frequent repetitions of that night to follow. After the first encounter, Teresa thought, that white man sho' did like to use cotton in a funny sort of way.

Kathryn was happier with William over the past six months than she had been in a long time. One reason was that he had been home consistently for that period without having to spend nights away—something that had not occurred for a long time. But the year was 1832, an election year. This had more than historic meaning for Kathryn. Again, she would be left alone. Sir Edward was one of Charleston's local delegates to the first Democratic Convention in Baltimore. But because of his failing health, he could not attend. He asked William to attend in his place, and her husband accepted without hesitation. The Southern position and, especially, the tariff were key issues. Kathryn would have to stay home and attend to her father as well as manage the estates.

William's departure was delayed by a slave. It was Buck. After six months on the plantation, he had tried to escape. It was a priority for him to be caught and returned to the plantation before William left for the convention. He had to be taught a lesson.

"Get the hounds and give them Buck's scent, then let them loose," said William to Big Sam, the black overseer. All the local planters who could be alerted quickly set out with William, Big Sam, and the hounds to find Buck, and they did. He was brought back to the plantation, tied in harnesses, and given fifty lashes, his bleeding back left exposed to the sun. When she was allowed, Bell pulled Buck into their cabin and she and Ole Nanna administered to his wounds. Buck was beaten so badly that he could not muster enough energy to talk. Bell cried and pleaded with him.

As she nursed Buck's wounds, Bell was filled with self doubt.

The both of them had entered forbidden territory-man and woman slaves emotionally attached and in love. Slaves were supposed to produce babies for their masters just like cows produced calves and hogs produced pigs.

Her errors were in duplicate, she was in love and she had not produced any babies. Such a relationship would be frowned upon by the master.

Within a matter of days, Buck was made to return to the fields. But now both feet were shackled and he was made to crawl between cotton rows. He knew that one day, somehow, he had to get away. There were rumors in the quarters about slaves who successfully escaped to the North; almost every week there was a new story. This excited Buck. The only way he and Bell could be together was for him to get away and come back to get her. For sure, the massah would make his demands known again. A big strong slave like Buck was not only good for the fields but also for stud. But he no longer wanted to spread his pleasure around. He only wanted one woman now, and that was Bell.

David almost didn't hear the words spoken to him by his companion. His mind was somewhere else—deep in the South— in Charleston, South Carolina. He thought of Kathryn every free moment. Never before had he a reason to want to return home since his mother died. His father and brother long ago had formed a union that made him feel like an outsider.

"What! What did you say? I'm sorry, my mind was somewhere else," said David.

"I said it's important that we extend our railway activities deeper into the South, and we need conductors that we can trust to get the job done. Men like yourself who are from the South and know the South well. Our activities as far as Virginia, North Carolina, and Maryland have been very successful but not farther south."

"Yes, I agree." David knew what his companion was hinting at and before Kathryn, he would have rebutted with a strong no! I shall return to the South for permanent residence under no circumstances. But now he could be near Kathryn. "But if this person was to be successful as a conductor, his return to the South would have to be inconspicuous, and I'm not so sure that my reputation for roaming and philandering would not cause concern if I were to settle in some responsible position; furthermore, what would that position be?"

"On the contrary, I should think that your reputation would help you go unnoticed that much more. Didn't you mention sometime back that your sister-in-law's father was in failing health and there was no one to run the plantation? Well, it would be nice if you could somehow secure the position, don't you think?"

"Well, I don't know, I honestly don't think my brother would hear of it."

"Think about it, David. We could use you down there. Maybe something will work out."

Kathryn lay cold, wet compresses across her father's head.

The searing summer heat added even more to his discomfort. Then there were the godawful mosquitoes that made the nights almost unbearable. Sir Edward had refused to go to the city. "I have spent my life on this plantation and I refuse to die somewhere else," he said emphatically. Kathryn had not argued strongly, for she knew she could not change his mind. As often as she could, she would spend the day and night at Echo Holler. More and more, she felt the sting of loneliness. She had nostalgic reflections of the time she and David spent together during her illness and their long ride together to see her father during her convalescence. Less and less did her thoughts include William.

Not only had she become accustomed to his long absences, she had accepted them as a way of life.

She missed David and wished he were with her.

CHAPTER SIX

In 1832, Andrew Jackson was reelected to his second term as President of the United States. South Carolinians and Southerners alike enjoyed a brief revival of their interests and, again, felt they had a president who not only understood their grievances but would resolve them as well. Almost three weeks after the election, William Littlejohn attended a convention in Columbia, South Carolina. Afterward, he hosted a Christmas party at Lakeview to tell everyone of the news from the convention. Guests indulged in good food and drink while musicians performed soft, sweet music. As always, the women and men soon divided into two groups: The ladies congregated in the parlor to engage in chitchat; the gentlemen inevitably wandered off to William's study to talk politics—a subject that, for the most part, was for their ears only.

Teresa circulated among the guests, refreshing each man's drink, as William began his report. "Gentlemen, as you may well have expected, the convention unanimously voted the tariff of 1828 and 1832 null and void." The men broke out in thunderous clapping and wild cheers. Joy was clearly evident on their faces.

"Furthermore," William continued triumphantly, "the convention ruled it to be unlawful and against the best interest of the South for agents of the Union to collect the duties." More boisterous applause erupted, and the men's raucous mood seemed impossible to subdue. William's next sentence changed all that.

"Gentlemen, the convention further asserted its strength and dedication to our cause by admonishing the United States government that secession would be our only recourse, should further efforts be geared toward collection of the tariff." This time, the applause was barely audible and not one smile could be found on the faces of the now-solemn guests. William raised his glass. "Gentlemen, may I propose a toast: preservation of the Union, only without taxation."

Every man held his glass high. Then the click of glass filled the room, followed by silence as each man drank his wine.

The stoic faces of his male guests told William that they all knew exactly how grave the situation was.

Satisfied that he had conveyed the proper message, William decided to elevate his guests' mood. "Gentlemen, enough about politics. We are in the Christmas season and about to enter a new year under Andrew Jackson. Let's go out and join our wives and sing our Christmas carols loud enough to let all Yankees know that Southerners know how to enjoy the spirit of Christmas."

As if on cue, Teresa moved to the rear of the library to open the huge double doors. The men spoke in hushed tones as they filed out past her. William was the last to leave the room. When he reached the doors, he paused at Teresa's side and pinched her bottom. A quick smile crossed her lips and she offered no resistance.

To William, Teresa looked as if she had put on some weight,

especially around the middle. This caused him a bit of concern, but he made no inquiry as he exited the room.

President Andrew Jackson's reply to the South Carolina proclamation was as bold and stern as the precipitating document.

"The Constitution is still the object of our reverence, the bond of our Union, our defense in danger, the source of our prosperity in peace . . . Fellow citizens of my native state, let me not only admonish you, as the First Magistrate of our common country, not to incur the penalties of its laws, but use the influence that a father would over his children whom he saw rushing to a certain ruin."

The rank and file of the nullifiers shared William's shock and dismay over Jackson's strong statement. They felt he had betrayed his South Carolina constituency. All stood in applause when the legislature passed the nullification ordinance. All believed civil war was inevitable, which is why they fully supported Gov. James Hamilton's requests for 3,000 volunteers and another 10,000 for a state guard. The threat of war was real to all but the blind and uncaring.

Big Sam saddled two horses and gathered the dogs before rushing to the big house to fetch his master. He had to hurry so that nigger Buck wouldn't get too far away. He reined in both horses at the front of the mansion, hastily dismounted, and reached the front door in two strides. He pounded on it until Jonathan appeared. "I gots ta see Massah Littlejohn. I gots ta see him quick."

"Well, he's in the study, this way."

Big Sam didn't wait for Jonathan to show him the way; he knew where to go. "Massah Littlejohn," he said at the entrance to the study, "dat big Buck done run away again!" announced Big Sam.

"He's what?"

"He done run away again."

William was infuriated to the point of speechlessness but not for long. "Get my horse and send one of the boys to alert the other planters that Buck has escaped," he told Big Sam. "I'll be outside shortly."

William and Big Sam spent most of the day looking for Buck but returned to Lakeview empty-handed. The next step would be to organize a search party, consisting of all the available local planters, and to head out again. In the morning, his group of men and dogs would begin the hunt, ending only when they found Buck.

Then, William would show him and all the slaves on his plantation who was boss. There would be no more running away and no rebellious types likely to incite unrest or revolt against me. "I am the master, and I'll not have a nigger causing any trouble here on this plantation."

When Kathryn inquired about the unsuccessful search, William told her that a larger search party would be organized and set out the next day.

"You look exhausted," Kathryn said.

"I am."

"Why don't you go up to bed. I'll have Gertie bring supper up to you."

"That's a good idea," replied William as he walked wearily toward the stairs.

"What will you do to him when you find him this time?" Kathryn asked quietly.

William began his ascent. "I will fix it so that he will never run away again!" he uttered grimly. He said nothing else to her; such indelicacies were not to be discussed with ladies.

William slept fitfully that night. Buck's actions triggered in him an unease that mirrored the concerns of the entire South. Every slave owner secretly feared the certain consequence of having a servant run away: the spread of rebellion and free thought among those left behind.

Still restless, William shifted his thoughts to the Twenty-Second Congress and its debate of the tariff issue. He found solace in knowing that John C. Calhoun represented South Carolina and the entire region. Calhoun, unlike Andrew Jackson, had not yielded to Unionist propaganda and pressure. In fact, he had resigned as vice president of the United States to devote his full attention to the tariff fight and guarding the interests of the South. And not a moment too soon, William thought. The rift between the nullifiers and the Unionists had grown. The Union had its Force Bill, which granted it the right to collect the tariffs, but the South had a tariff compromise that, in time, would reduce the tariff to a minimal ad valorem tax. Still, William thought as he drifted to sleep, these were only temporary measures.

A few hours later, William roused himself from bed, dressed quietly so as not to disturb Kathryn, and headed downstairs to the kitchen. Gertie had already begun breakfast, and soon had it in place before him. William thought Gertie looked troubled, and reasoned that it was because of Buck. She had been his "nanny" and attended to him as a mother would. William usually cared little about what slaves thought, but Gertie was different.

"What's the matter with you, Gertie?" he inquired. "You've got that I-want-to-tell-you-something look on your face."

"Yassah, ain't cho' noticed Teresa's belly is gittin' bigger 'n' bigger?"

"She's going to have a baby? Dammit!" he shouted as he pounded the table with his fist. "What else is going to happen?"

He took a moment to think. "Gertie, I want you to rouse Teresa and have her pack her things and be ready to leave in the morning."

"Yassah, Massah Littlejohn."

Jonathan appeared.

"Jonathan, I want you to take Teresa along to Mr. Myers in Charleston. You may leave early in the morning, even if I have not returned. Should Mrs. Littlejohn ask, just tell her that I was made a very good offer for Teresa's services. Bring me my pad and pen."

"Yassah," Jonathan said as he left the room.

When Jonathan returned, William pushed his breakfast aside and quickly scribbled a note to Mr. Myers.

> *Dear Sir:*
>
> *I write this letter to inform you of my wishes. I have sent my girl, Teresa, in the company of my house boy, Jonathan. As you can see, she is a likable wench who is not hard on the eyes at all.*
>
> *She is impregnated and I would like for you to sell her for the highest price with a gentle reminder that the buyer will be getting two for the price of one.*
>
> *When you have finished with his services, please direct my house boy, Jonathan, home with your response.*
>
> *The best of health to you,*
> *William Littlejohn II*

"Jonathan, tomorrow morning, carry this letter of introduction along with you to Mr. Myers," William said as he folded the note.

As quickly as she could, Gertie headed from the kitchen to

Teresa's room in the cellar. Tomorrow morning, she would help Teresa get packed and ready to go before the mistress came downstairs. That way, there would be fewer questions, less suspicion. But today would be her last one on the plantation and there was work to be done. She entered the cellar. "Git up, gal, git up!" she yelled at the sleeping figure in the bed.

Teresa stirred. "What's the matter?" she mumbled.

"Yo' git yo' butt up, gal! Yo' is goin' wid Jonathan in de mornin'." Already, Gertie was gathering clothes and stuffing them in a bag next to the bed as she talked.

"Why I have to go?"

"Jes git yo' butt a movin'. When dat belly gits ta swellin', dats when yo' gots ta leabes here. An' yoin's is. Na' git up. Dar's work ta be done befo' mornin'."

"Will I come back?" Teresa inquired halfheartedly. Somehow she knew the answer to that question.

"Gal, don't be crazy. Yo' ain't neva comin' back here. Yo' job here is finished."

Teresa rose. As she began to gather her things, reality sunk in even deeper. Worse, she was now afraid. She had grown to like clean sheets and a warm place of her own in which to sleep. Now, she must leave; her destiny was—once again—uncertain.

Buck realized that his best route to freedom was through the swamp and marshlands of outlying Charleston. He traveled without rest throughout the day and as much of the evening as he could before the darkness ensued. Still, he knew he had traveled only a short distance; with each step, the water and mud pulled him back a little. It seemed even nature was on the white man's side, Buck thought. He felt like giving up, but his heart knew but one direction and that was away from the whip and the lash; from the endless toil in the relentless hot sun; from the sharp, deep hunger pangs that gnawed at him each night; from the woman whom he was allowed to impregnate but not to love. He had to take this journey. It was the only way for him to arrange an escape for Bell.

Buck fell asleep in the chilly marsh, covered with mud and weakened by hunger. But his mind did not rest; it replayed every detail of his last altercation with the massah.

"Buck, you got that little wench of yours' belly big?" the massah had asked.

"No, sah, massah. We's been tryin' but ain't nothin' happnin' yet."

"Well, now, you listen to me. Just because you married this gal, Sociobell, doesn't mean that you have to stop seeing these other gals. I want you to sleep with some of those other ninnies and get me some young'uns here by next spring. Tonight, you sleep with Sarah. Something is wrong with that gal you married. Fifteen years old and still no young'uns, something's wrong."

Buck hadn't liked what he'd heard. He had found a woman that he loved and wanted to be with for the rest of his life. Maybe there was something wrong with her, but she was his.

"No, Suh, Massah," he said defiantly. "I gots my woman and dats who I wanna be wid."

"Nigger, you'll be with whomever I say."

"No, Suh, boss, I got ma woman," Buck said steadfastly.

All activity around them ceased. The other slaves in the yard knew there would be trouble; no slave was allowed to talk back to his master. William knew he would have to hold fast lest he lose the respect of his slaves. So he took out a horse whip and began to swing at Buck's body. Buck was beaten until he fell to the ground. Too weak to rebel, he was tied to a whipping post and beaten again.

As he lay there in the marsh, Buck conjured up a different outcome. He pictured himself grabbing the whip and slinging his master to the ground. Then, he saw himself reach for a nearby bush ax. As he stood over his master, he slowly raised the weapon higher and higher above his head, and then . . .

Yelp, yelp, yelp, yelp. A pack of barking hounds jolted him back to reality.

The dogs arrived as he attempted to rise. They cornered him as if he were a prized rabbit and sank their teeth into his flesh, shredding what was left of his tattered clothes. He burrowed himself into the muck as the animals tore into him. Defeated, he accepted death as his only salvation.

"Yo, hounds," he heard his master call out in the distance.

"Git back there, dogs; git back there!" The dogs retreated instantly. "Leave some of him alive. Gonna show them other niggers what happens to uppity slaves. Gonna show them this one last time."

Buck lay crumbled, his body bloodied from head to toe, clothes—what was left of them—in shreds. The slightest movement caused him almost unbearable pain. But for one brief moment, he smiled. He had scored a minor victory. He had acknowledged his love for Bell and defended his rights. A man who had no control over his manliness, he reasoned, had no manliness.

The next morning, Teresa arose early at Jonathan's wake-up call. For a moment, she sat on the side of her bed while tears rolled down her face. She had tried so hard to please her massah, thinking and hoping that attending to his needs would ensure her a permanent home.

Later, as she and Jonathan pulled away from the plantation in a wagon, she wept openly. Where would she end up now? Who would be her new massah? Would she end up a field slave like the ones she could see in the distance, already up before the full break of day? Then there was the baby, her baby, Massah Littlejohn's baby. Would she be allowed to keep it and care for it or would it, too, be sold into horrible slavery as soon as it was of age? Teresa gazed upon Lakeview's private lake. So many times she had dreamed she would stroll along its shore in the arms of her massah as he whispered sweet, soft words in her ear.

It was only a dream, she knew, but it had helped her survive.

This time when she looked toward the lake, she saw a line of men across the way. She recognized Massah Littlejohn and some of the men she had served in his chambers. And there was also a lone, bedraggled black man among them. Sometimes he walked, sometimes he fell to the ground and was dragged along. She barely recognized him as the man who had come to Lakeview with her. She was sickened by the sight. Better to dream, she thought, as she reentered her fantasy world. There, she saw Massah Littlejohn blowing a soft kiss her way, and she knew he would be joining her and the baby some day.

CHAPTER SEVEN

The early morning dew drenched Bell's bare feet as she frantically raced up the path to the big house. She'd made that trip almost every day of her life; never had it seemed to take so long—until this particular morning. Looks like I'll never get there, she thought. Maybe she'd better call out to her mistress.

"Missy Kathryn, Missy Kathryn," she panted. It was no use; she was far too tired to raise her voice to a shout.

Two carefree yard hounds yelped at her feet, oblivious to her angst. "Missy Kathryn, Missy Kathryn," she cried feebly, then, "Git away dog, git away dog!" She kicked angrily at her unwanted companions, to no avail.

It no longer mattered. She was there now, stumbling toward the back porch, staggering up the stairs. Only then did the hounds stop; they knew not to enter the house. Bell burst into the kitchen. Completely unaware of her surroundings, she saw nothing until she reached the stairs. She paused to catch her breath. "Missy Kathryn, Missy Kathryn!" Her cries went unanswered.

At the top of the stairs, she was confronted by a row of closed doors. Which one led to Miss Kathryn's room? She began her search, opening doors to unoccupied rooms. "Missy Kathryn!" she shouted hoarsely. "Missy Kathryn!" She rushed into another room.

Finally, a bed with someone in it! She could see Miss Kathryn's fiery red hair scattered about the pillow. She rushed to the sleeping woman's bedside, shaking her vigorously. Kathryn protested sleepily. Bell had no choice but to jerk away the covers and resume her shaking. "Wake up, Missy Kathryn, wake up!"

"What's wrong, Sociobell? What's wrong with you this morning?" Kathryn's words were barely audible as she struggled to rise.

"Missy Kathryn, yo' wake up!" Tears poured down Bell's face.

Kathryn swung her legs over the bed and stood. She grasped the frantic slave girl's shoulders in an effort to calm her.

"Tell me what's wrong, Bell. Tell me!"

"Dey don' caught dat nigger man o' mine. Dey gon' kill 'im, Missy Kathryn. Dey gon' hang him 'til he dead!"

Kathryn began searching for her robe. "Massah Littlejohn gonna hang 'im," Bell whimpered. "I knows he is."

Kathryn knew, too. She was keenly aware of how much anger, hate, and fear had built up in her husband for the renegade slave.

Kathryn ran toward the window. In the distance she could see the mob of white men unleashing their assault on Buck, savagely beating and stomping their hapless victim. Not far away was a tree from which a noose had already been hung. Kathryn bolted from the room with Bell on her heels. Both charged down the seemingly endless flight of stairs, through the foyer, and onto the veranda. They dashed across the yard, closing the gap between them and the men in the distance. "William," Kathryn screamed.

"William . . ." Suddenly, she stopped in midcry. Not Bell. The distraught servant continued to run at breakneck speed, hurtling toward the body of the man now suspended against the sky. She saw his feeble last kicks of life, and still she ran. She saw the spasms jerk his body, but even this did not deter her. At last she reached her beloved Buck. She started to speak, to tell him that everything would be all right, but only at that moment did she grasp what had happened. Buck was gone; in his place was a grim, lifeless form whose head—still trapped in the noose—had flopped to one side. So had his tongue, which dangled from his mouth. Bell stepped closer to search the eyes that stared blankly ahead. She raised her hand, sweeping it down over the eyes to close them.

Bell balled her hands into fists and clasped them together.

She shut her eyes and allowed the ugly rage to surface. "God, why did yo' let dim kill 'im?" she cried out. "He all dat I got." She crumpled to her knees, raised her arms heavenward, then froze.

Somehow she regained her composure and arranged herself in a squatting position. She began to survey the men who now surrounded her. All, including Massah William, seemed to wear the same sinister smile.

Finally, someone reached up and unceremoniously cut the rope. Buck's body fell to the ground in front of her. She sat motionless, staring straight ahead, until she felt a familiar touch. It was Ole Nanna, tugging at her shoulders, forcing her to rise and walk away.

Kathryn had watched the deadly drama unfold. Now teary-eyed, she walked back to the house. She knew she should be grieving for the dead man, but her thoughts were of William. Already, she felt a distance between them.

William Littlejohn was triumphant; he had captured and hung the only slave who had dared challenge him. One by one, he thanked the men who had aided him. They gathered their things and headed toward home, leaving Buck's body for the field slaves to retrieve. William set out on foot toward the mansion. He knew full well what he'd find: a house and a wife both cloaked in silence.

He was right. Kathryn did not utter a word the entire day. Silently, they retired to bed, where Kathryn positioned herself as far as she possibly could from William. She'll come around, he thought. After all, this was only her first hanging.

To all who knew him, William seemed indifferent to the day's event. As night descended, and he was left alone with his thoughts, he found it harder to escape the turmoil that raged inside. Now he desperately struggled to justify his actions. He told himself that it was the divine providence of all white men to dominate the black barbarians, to maim—and even kill—if need be. He recalled his father's stories about slave rebellions and plantations being burned to the ground as masters and mistresses slept inside. "My boy," his father had told him, "you've got to control the slave like you control any other animal. Show him who is boss, either with a lash or a rope around his neck. This, he understands and this he will obey."

Then the words of a friend from South Hampton, Virginia, who had survived the wrath of Nat Turner, bolstered him. "I beseech you to be most careful and observant in your dealings with the slave populace," his friend had once written, "for even the most docile seem to have the ability to turn ravenously mean, a killer of white men, a molester of white women, and a batterer of white children. During my days, I know only anguish and apprehension for this wretched beast that some of our less learned whites would refer to as our fellow man. At night, I know only constant fear, and would not dare repose without a gun close at hand; for it would seem that somehow, darkness nurtures the wretchedness that causes these most unusual animal-like creatures to brutalize us whites who were kind at heart when we introduced them to civilization."

So vivid were William's thoughts of insurrection that he soon struggled against the troubling images in his sleep.

"William! William! Wake up!" Kathryn was sitting up in bed, shaking William as hard as she could. "Wake up! Wake up! You are having a nightmare!"

William awakened, sat up in bed, and stared at her in silence. He was grateful for the darkness for he knew it concealed the fear he was no longer able to suppress. Kathryn lay down again. In a matter of minutes, she was asleep. But not William. He couldn't sleep; he didn't even try.

One month later, as the early rays of light pierced the darkened sky, Ole Nanna awakened and looked out her window. Another brilliant, sunny day was about to dawn. She turned her head in the other direction, toward Bell's sleeping figure.

Before long, Bell stirred, then raised up on her pallet. Her eyes were swollen and red; she didn't appear to have rested much.

"Bell, yo' all right dis mornin'?" asked Nanna.

"I s'pose," she mumbled before falling silent again.

Nanna rose and began her chores. Finally, Bell spoke again.

"I ain't seen no blood."

Nanna kept on going. Intent on preparing the tiny cabin for the slave children she was about to attend to, Nanna hadn't heard Bell's words. "Hurry, chile, yo' got to git to dem fiel's," she told her.

"Dey ain't been no blood f'om me," was Bell's reply.

This time, Nanna stopped.

"How long?"

"Since befo' Buck don run away, befo' he wuz killed," she said.

"Lay down on de flo'," Nanna instructed her. Hurriedly, she loosened Bell's garments so her stomach and private area were exposed. She pressed in on the lower part of Bell's abdomen, just above the bladder. Then she examined the lips of Bell's vagina, her experienced fingers searching for familiar signs. "Yo' gon' hab a baby. Gon' be a boy chile," Nanna said confidently.

When Buck was alive, Bell used to pray that she would become with child. Now he was gone. Maybe he would be alive today if I'd had a baby sooner, she thought sadly. Tears cascaded down her cheeks. She felt so hopeless. She didn't want a baby, not now, not without her Buck. But it was too late. Maybe, she thought, maybe I can kill it when it's born. Immediately, she dismissed the idea, knowing she could never go through with it.

All right, she told herself. I'll have this baby, but it will be the last. No more, she vowed, no more.

Still, she cried. "Don't want dis baby. Don't want dis baby to lib like dis. Guess I hab ta hab it."

"Yes, chile." Nanna told her. "Yo' hab a big boy jus' lak Buck wuz."

"Be killed like Buck wuz, too, s'pose," Bell replied bitterly.

"No! No! Ma chile, yo' can't think lak dat. De Lawd works in His ways. Ain't gonna be dis way always. It ain't. Yo' bring dat chile right on in dis worl' an' raise him jus' lak he wuz a king. De Lawd wuz once a slave, too."

"De Lawd wuz a slave?" Bell queried.

"Sho wuz. Just lak yo' 'n' me," Nanna replied.

"Bell's tears began anew. "Nanna, don't want no mo' young'uns ab'ta dis un'. No mo'. Kin yo' fix it?" she pleaded. "I knows yo' kin. Seen yo' do it."

Bell was now hysterical. Before she knew it, Nanna had drawn back her right hand and slapped her hard across the face.

Instantly, she grabbed her, cradling her in her massive arms

83

like a baby. "Ab'ta dissun'," she whispered in Bell's ear, "dey won't be no mo', 'cause Ole Nanna gon' fix it."

Nestled securely in Nanna's bosom, Bell finally began to settle down. Only one other thing troubled her. "If dey is a Lawd," she asked aloud, "den why niggers got to go through all a dis? Dey ain't no Lawd up dere. Dey ain't no Lawd fo' us."

BOOK TWO

CHAPTER EIGHT

With Christmas just weeks away, Charleston braced for a winter predicted to be one of its coldest. There was even talk of a white Christmas, a prospect the white folks found delightful. Not so for the slaves, who dreaded spending even one frigid day or night in their drafty old cabins. Even the thought of leaving those cabins was cause for dismay. This meant they'd have to traipse around in tattered shoes that provided no protection against the elements, and share their worn-out coats—the grown folks, not the children. Coats and shoes were luxuries the little ones didn't get until they were much older.

Bell was nearing the end of her last month of pregnancy, and Ole Nanna was making an extra special effort to care for her. She would not allow Bell to do any heavy lifting, and performed many of her chores. Ole Nanna was convinced that Bell was going to have a Christmas baby and all the slaves knew it. The spirit of the season was alive and well among them. If there was an extra blanket, a spare piece of clothing, or an extra morsel of food, it would be discreetly left at the door of Bell's cabin. A Christmas baby was perceived as a gift from God and a blessing for all. A child born on that day had to be special, and the holiday would be even more joyous. A girl-child would be received with certain disappointment, but a boy-child would be praised and revered as a sign—a message from the Lord!

True to Ole Nanna's prediction, Bell's baby arrived in the wee hours of the morning on December 25, 1833.

"Waaa, waaa, waaa, waaa, waa." The newborn's terse cries filled the small, one-room shack.

After what seemed like an eternity in labor, Bell could finally rest. Quiet and alert, she raised up on her elbows so she could see herself. Sweat seemed to run from every pore of her body. Her lower torso was still awash in the warm liquids of childbirth, which Ole Nanna gently wiped away with freshly laundered bedding.

Bell looked down at the wiggling, wailing infant by her side. She listened intently to its cries, trying to determine its sex. Loud and strong, she thought, so it must be a boy.

Anxiously, she pulled at the blankets to fully expose the child's groin. A moist, sausage-shaped organ squirted urine into the blankets. It was a boy! Throughout her pregnancy, she had asked God for a male child; it was her belief that a boy could better withstand the hardships of slavery.

Bell almost forgot the pain in her lower abdomen as she cradled and caressed this new creature. Was everything all right, she wondered, as she studied her son. Gently, she felt his moist, curly hair. She wanted to see his eyes, but he kept them tightly closed as he continued to cry. She touched his broad nose and watched his nostrils flare. His chest swelled like bellows and emptied vigorously as each new cry began. Every now and then there would be long pauses between the end of one cry and the beginning of another. The child's face would turn bluish-red; each time, Bell thought he'd surely stop breathing. Then, an even louder scream would follow and Bell would relax. She found the baby's erratic breathing, not his crying, to be truly unsettling.

Bell grasped one of his hands as it fervently reached into the air, fingers spread apart to grasp anything within reach.

"One, two, three, four, five," she counted aloud, taxing her limited mathematical abilities. All there, she thought. She repeated this exercise as she examined the other hand and both feet. The baby struggled aggressively in her arms. This made Bell feel proud. "Strong boy, jus' like yo' pa wuz," she told him.

"Hush up, naw, boy, yo' mammy gotcha naw. Hush up, naw! Gonna feed ya naw, 'cause if'n I don't yo' gonna wake up evabody dats sleepin' 'n' some folks dat dead. Hush up, naw!" Bell said softly. She tugged at the old shirt she was wearing, lifting it to expose her breast, and guided her son toward her engorged nipple. He quickly began to suckle. Bell could feel a part of her flow into the child. She snuggled him closer as she rolled slightly onto her right side.

Fatigue began to overwhelm her. Suddenly she felt a pounding, cramp-like pain high up between her legs and a hot liquid trickling from her groin. Slowly, Ole Nanna raised one of Bell's legs and stuffed a piece of cloth between her thighs that also pressed against the groin. She leaned over on Bell's hip and thighs, applying firm pressure. Meticulously, the old woman continued to work, offering no explanation for what she had done or was about to do. For years, she had been the midwife for the plantation; she offered explanations to no one.

The child had drifted off to sleep. Even though the lower half of her body seemed to pound with pain, Bell also began to doze. Every now and then she'd awaken with a start, immediately checking to see if her sleeping baby was all right. What a beautiful, delicate creation, she thought during one of those moments. Then all kinds of doubts tugged at her. A tear collected in the corner of her eye as she remembered her plight and that of her child. Maybe I should try to escape, Bell thought. She looked around the room to see if Ole Nanna was asleep. Sure enough, she was curled up on a pallet in the corner. Childbirth was no longer an unusual event for her; she found it easy to sleep soundly once it was all over.

Bell hoped Nanna had not forgotten her promise: There would be no more.

No more children.

CHAPTER NINE

For William, the birth of Bell's child was no more cause for celebration than that of any other slave's, though he did give orders to add an extra chicken to the holiday food supplement. It seemed so strange, William thought, a slave gal can bring a healthy boy child into the world, but my wife, after six years of marriage . . . none. Perhaps this was the real reason they had decided to stay away from the Christmas parties. More than anything else, it was a painful reminder of how special Christmas day was—for those with children.

On Christmas morn, William presented to Kathryn a copy of *The Canterbury Tales* and a collection of music, some of the choice works by her favorite, Beethoven. She gave him a pipe and house jacket that Auntie Mame had sent all the way from England.

Life was back to normal at the plantation. Kathryn had managed to push the horrible memory of Buck's lynching to the back of her mind, though she certainly hadn't forgotten it. And now that the issue of nullification had been put on hold, William was spending more time at home and things were better between he and Kathryn. More and more, Kathryn thought about bearing children, and what having a son would mean to William. She believed she had come up with an idea that offered some hope. Kathryn knew she could count on William being in an upbeat mood because of the holidays, so she decided that this was the perfect opportunity to broach the subject of children. That night, she snuggled closely against William's chest as they lay in bed. Her heart began to pound as she started to recite the speech she had rehearsed a hundred times. "William, I've heard of a doctor who is giving a lecture series at the University of South Carolina," she said. "He is a specialist in obstetrics and diseases of women and children. I thought perhaps I might have him examine me to see why I haven't yet become with child."

William was already convinced that Kathryn was the reason he did not have a son; after all, Teresa had confirmed his virility.

"Who is this doctor?" he asked suspiciously.

"His name is Dr. Gunning C. Bedford, and, like I said, he is a specialist trained in diseases of women."

In William's mind, the issue of family and self-pride had to be considered. What if word got out to his friends? Besides, he just didn't like the idea of some stranger examining his wife.

"I don't think that this is a good idea," he replied tersely.

"Why not?"

"I just don't. There are some things that should just be left alone."

"But I want to have a baby. I want to have your child so badly."

"I know. And it will happen in time. I'm sure it will. Just wait and see."

Kathryn wasn't so sure, which was why she wanted to get Dr. Bedford's opinion. But she knew it was best to not press the issue with William.

She also knew she was going to see Dr. Bedford.

William and Kathryn spent the last week of the year in Charleston, and Kathryn secretly made arrangements to see Dr. Bedford at the university.

She found his examination room dark and uninviting, but the doctor quickly put her at ease. Nevertheless, she left his office distraught and disappointed. After asking only a few questions—and without performing a physical examination—the doctor told Kathryn that he wouldn't be able to help her. How could he make such a decision without examining her, she wondered. Kathryn was no prude and had been more than willing to submit to an examination—even though such activity was frowned upon for women. Bitterly, she concluded that the medical profession was not the enlightened society it pretended to be.

She told William nothing of her experience.

For some reason, William's drinking episodes—which were generally few and far between—grew alarmingly more frequent. He always overindulged as the new year approached, but this time was different, and Kathryn was worried.

On New Year's Eve, William and Kathryn were among the many Charleston notables attending festivities at the Planter's Hotel.

The soft minuets and waltzes playing in the background could barely be heard over the roar of hundreds of guests—many of them drunk, like William.

"You've had too much to drink," Kathryn told him. "I think we had better go."

"I'm just having some fun. What the hell, it's New Year's Eve. Relax a little," William said before stumbling across the room toward some friends.

Kathryn stayed but only to watch over her husband. Alone and miserable, she spent the evening thinking of David.

Hours later, when they finally arrived home, Kathryn all but carried William to the bedroom. He babbled on and became crude and rough in his approach as he tugged at Kathryn's clothes.

Kathryn managed to push him onto the bed. Now she was rid of him; he was too inebriated to cause her any trouble. "Teresa . . . cotton," he mumbled. The words made no sense to Kathryn, but it didn't matter. William was already fast asleep. Kathryn knew he would not awaken before noon the next day.

Still, she decided to sleep in the bedroom next door.

Teresa's new home was on a plantation in Natchez, Mississippi. Her duty was to serve as nanny for her mistress' two-year-old child, Robert, and a newborn named Bertram. She was allowed to keep her own child as long as she first attended to the needs of her mistress' children.

Winnie, short for Wilhelmina, was now three months old. Teresa decided on this name since it reminded her of her child's father. When the two boys were asleep, Teresa spent every spare moment with her own child, whom she adored. She was still inclined to fantasize and often pictured herself as William's wife and the grand mistress of a great plantation.

When she wasn't wrapped up in a world of make-believe, Teresa talked to her daughter in a careful and deliberate manner, the same way white folks did.

"Your father is a white man and he owns a big plantation—so big that you can't see all of it, even from the highest ground.

I'll bet that he misses us and he wishes that he was here with us, so he could take care of us for the rest of our lives—but he can't. But we understand, don't we? It's those other mean white folk that will not let him be with us because he's white. But we know, just as soon as he can, he is gonna look for us and when he finds us he will take us to the North where we can live like decent folks." To hear her talk, it was nearly impossible to tell that she was fantasizing.

Even though Teresa knew she was lucky to have her daughter around, she still had little time for her own child, what with taking care of the two boys. They had to be her top priority, for if Teresa failed in her duties, she and her daughter would suffer the consequences. But she knew many methods of stealing time with her child. Without a doubt, her best opportunity was at mealtime.

Since the mistress' newborn was about the same age as Winnie, she would sometimes hold and cuddle them both, suckling one at each breast. "You two gonna be a fine pair," she often told them. "My Winnie will get to know all the good things right along with you, Bertram. One day, when her father sees her, he will feel proud to know that this child is his daughter."

CHAPTER TEN

"Emanuel. I'ze goin' call dis baby Emanuel," Bell said to herself. She had pondered endlessly, trying to choose just the right name, one that was deserving of a God-sent child. She had heard somebody say that name was from the Bible.

"His name gon' be Emanuel," she told Nanna.

"Dat's a fine name. F'om de Bible," Ole Nanna said approvingly.

Bell had managed to find herself a relatively peaceful corner in the cabin, away from all the other smaller children who stayed there during the day. She kept a close watch on her little one, making sure that none of the older, mischievous children did him harm.

Bell looked at all the little faces of the children whom she'd never bothered to get to know. It was best to not form an attachment; a child here today may be a child sold elsewhere tomorrow. She looked at her own cuddlesome little baby and was seized with fear. What if her child were sold? What if he were sent to some distant place where she would never see him again?

"If anybody tries ta do dat," Bell said aloud, "dey gon' hab ta kill me first."

As she rocked her son back and forth, Bell began to hum softly. Effortless, soft sounds sprang forth as she broke into song:

> *I sangs to yo'*
> *'cause yo' makes me happy*
>
> *I sangs to yo'*
> *'cause yo' makes me sad*
>
> *I sangs to yo'*
> *'cause yo' makes up fo' all dat I lost*
> *and some dat I neba had*

Curious, some of the children moved in closer when they heard Bell's voice. It had been a long time since she'd sang for anyone. She once loved to sing and be happy and make others feel good. But time had changed all that. Over the years, Bell had transformed from a friendly, outgoing child into a withdrawn teenage girl.

She'd never known her parents, who died when she was young. She didn't know exactly what caused their deaths, but she guessed they'd just worked too long, rested too little, and aged too fast. Her brothers and sisters had been sold when she was a tiny child, so she hardly remembered them. Ole Nanna was the only family she'd known. She told Bell her many stories about the great homeland across the water, just as they had been told to her when she was younger. According to Nanna, her mother had been on the great ship that crossed the water. Her mother's mind had been cursed and she would awaken at night, screaming about the hardships inflicted upon her during the journey. Bell wondered sometimes if Ole Nanna's mind was cursed for she, too, moaned and groaned in her sleep. Sometimes Nanna's cries would awaken Bell and she would crawl over to the old woman and hold her until she settled back to sleep.

Unlike most other slaves, Ole Nanna had tried to form a bond with her past. As a younger girl, she had been very inquisitive of other slaves who had made the voyage on the great ships. She would talk with them for hours, asking questions about the motherland. Now she was middle-aged by plantation standards, and those who had told her stories about Africa had died or been traded. Yet, she continued to nourish the stories. It was her inquisitiveness that had earned her the know-how to work with medicinal roots and herbs. For every ailment she had a treatment; sometimes they worked, sometimes they didn't. Nanna's children had been sold or were dead, so all that she knew she tried to pass on to Bell, in whom she found an attentive student.

Bell often thought of the neck piece Nanna wore. It had been given to her by her mother and one day Bell knew it would be hers. It seemed to be Nanna's only tangible link with her past and she wore it with pride, never removing it. On many occasions, Bell sat and listened to the story regarding the neck piece, just as Nanna had heard it from her mother. Bell remembered every word, but what stood out most was the promise Nanna made. "When I die, dis neck piece be yo's," Ole Nanna would tell her. "It gib yo' de strength and wizdum to guide yo' life and make no mistakes."

"Waa, waaa, waa, waa, waa, waa-waa-waa!" Bell pushed her nipple toward Emanuel's mouth, and with each vigorous suckle she could feel the baby's midsection grow tighter and bulge as it filled with milk. Soon the child was asleep again, resting securely in his mother's arms. Bell reveled in the contentment that she saw and felt in this small living creature. Nevertheless, her love, her pride, her joy were tempered by the realities of slavery. A wave of hopelessness swept over her. Kill him! Kill him, she thought, so he will never know the pain of his birthright! She knew that kind of thing happened, but she certainly couldn't do it. Still, she vowed, there could be no more children.

The plain truth was that this child was not the result of an act of love, rather the greed that was so much a part of the slave system. He was a living testament of how little control the black man had over his own existence. Her baby, like his father, would yearn for, but be denied, the God-given right to freedom.

Emanuel would never know the priceless feeling of tilling his own soil, growing his own fruit and vegetables, or raising his own animals to slaughter for fresh meat. This man-child could never stand on his own land and filter plain dirt through his fingers and say, "This is mine." Her son would not be able to cut down the great trees around him to fashion into shelter, and sit by a blazing fire at night to soothe his aching, sore muscles into readiness for the next day's labor and say—"This is mine!"

Bell's child would always be a slave. That's why she wanted no more.

Before long, Bell was up and about, her strength slowly returning. She knew that she'd soon return to hard work. Already she had taken more time off than usual, but this was permissible if a woman bore a strong, healthy boy. This was the master's way of encouraging fecundity among slaves, but it mattered not to Bell. Not a day had gone by since her son had been born that she hadn't asked Nanna, "When yo' gon' do it?"

"Stop pesterin', chile," was Nanna's usual reply. "Soon!"

On one of the last mornings before she had to go back to work, Bell watched as Nanna fried a slab of fatback for breakfast. The grease crackled and popped in the worn-out skillet in a way that was teasing to a hungry stomach. The fatback, along with a piece of ho-cake, would serve as breakfast.

Bell sat quietly as Nanna tugged at the tough outer skin of the piece of meat before she settled down to devour the meal.

When Nanna appeared to have been satiated, Bell posed her question again.

"Nanna, when yo' gon' do it?"

Ole Nanna sucked her fingers clean and leaned the chair in which she sat against the wall. She fixed her eyes straight ahead and began to speak. "Ma used ta tell me many thangs and many stories 'bout life 'cross de water. Ma use ta say dat de greatest day in de life ob a young boy and girl wuz de day when dey wuz allowed to be man and woman. On dat dey evathang mus' change. Dey mus' walk like dey is a man or a woman, dey mus' look like dey is a man or a woman. After dat day, dey got ta set aside all selfish thangs an' evathang mus' be done in de bes' int'rest of evabody.

"De boys separated fom de girls fo' three days and three nights. Dis time de girls is taught de way ob de woman and de boys is taught de ways ob de man. Dey taught to 'spect each other and de woman is taught de man is ha brotha and dat whatever she do fo' a man is to make him a stronga brotha to care fo' hu and to protec' hu. De man is taught dat de woman is a sista. Dat time he taught dat, in de belly o' my sista lies de pasta ob all life and dat ta protec' a sista is ta protec' life."

Nanna looked straight into Bell's eyes. "Why do yo' want to shut yo' pasta?" she asked.

"Don't want no mo' chilluns fo' de massah," Bell told her.

"When dat pasta's shut," Nanna warned her, "it's shut fo' good!"

"I knows dat. Don't want no mo' chilluns dat can't breathe

wid'out de massah's say-so, or eat wid'out he say-so," Bell said emphatically. "Don't want no mo'. Maybe it best dat ma pasta be closed."

"Listen, chile, it ain't gon' be dis way always. It ain't. One day de Lawd gon' see dat we all is set free. I got da faith He will. It ain't gonna be dis way always," Nanna countered.

"Maybe so, but it dat way now. Don't want to gib dis kind of life to no chile o' mine. Is yo' gonna help me, Nanna? Is yo' gonna help?"

Nanna could see the relentless desperation in Bell's eyes. She reached out to caress Bell as if she were her own child.

"I helps yo', chile," she said sadly. "I helps yo'."

"When? When yo' gon' do it?" Bell asked.

"Saturday night. Den yo' got a day ta git well since dey ain't no work fo' Sunday."

Bell was filled with much apprehension that week. Each day, she watched as Nanna brought one peculiar item after another into the cabin—herbs, leaves, roots, pine cones. One day, she even returned with a hollowed-out sugar cane pole. Bell couldn't help but wonder what Nanna would do with it, but she knew not to ask.

As the week grew shorter, Bell's apprehension gave way to fear.

But she reminded herself that this was something she must do. Saturday arrived, and Bell figured Nanna wouldn't do anything during the daylight. She was right. It was late when Ole Nanna approached and instructed her to lie down, with legs pointing toward the fireplace. Bell could feel the heat from the fire on her thighs as Nanna exposed her body from the waist down.

"Kin yo' bear de pain?" Nanna asked. "It will hurt an' yo' can't make no commotion dat'll wake up nobody."

"Yes'm," Bell replied. She knew there would be pain, but she also knew that any sound heard beyond the confines of the cabin would lead to discovery and punishment. Bell tried to take her mind off what was about to happen by focusing on the nearby pile of material that Ole Nanna had accumulated over the past few days. Then she couldn't help but wonder what the items were for, so she shifted her gaze to the crackling flames in the fireplace.

In the center was a pot from which steam rose. "Go on an' do what yo' got ta do," Bell told Nanna. "I kin bear it."

Bell lay quietly as Nanna began her meticulous preparations.

One part of her wanted to watch; the other wanted to turn away, fearful of what was to come. From time to time, she braved quick glances in Nanna's direction. Bell saw her place a handful of pine tar in a wooden saucer which she hung over a steaming hot pot filled with pine needles and medicine roots. Next, she sprinkled coal oil soot over the melted pine tar and watched closely as the concoction slowly changed from golden brown to black. By this time, the room was filled with a minty aroma as Ole Nanna removed the heated roots from the pot, cutting one of them in two. Then she lifted the saucer of pine tar from the fire and sat it in front of her. By now the roots had cooled enough so that Ole Nanna could squeeze their juices into the pine tar mixture. She used the remaining roots to stir her potion until it cooled.

Nanna was ready to begin. "Open yo' legs wide," she instructed Bell.

"It gon' hurt now?" Bell asked.

"Yeh, it gon' hurt some, but don't yo' make a sound. Here, put dis in yo' mouth." She handed Bell a scrap of cloth from an old blanket.

Bell opened her legs and Nanna knelt between them. Eyes squeezed shut, hands flat against the dirt floor, she braced herself for the pain. It started immediately, and Bell bit into the cloth as hard as she could. She felt a heavy object pushing against her pelvic organs as Nanna whispered instructions to her.

"Raise yo' legs, gal," Nanna told her. "Raise 'em up." Sweat rolled across Bell's brow as she struggled to follow Nanna's orders. Another searing pain jolted her writhing body, tossing her head from side to side. At that moment, Bell regretted the torture to which she had subjected herself; yet, she knew this had to be done.

Suddenly, everything came to a halt. The pushing stopped; the pain subsided. Relieved, Bell tugged at the cloth that had muffled her cries. She opened her mouth wide to take in deep gulps of fresh air. The pushing began anew, catching her off guard. A searing pain shot through her stomach and she was unable to suppress a loud groan. She had once thought there could be nothing more painful than childbirth, but this was ten times worse. Bell tried to sit up just as another pain gripped her, slamming her back down. Back arched and fists clenched, she prepared for the next assault. This time, it was over.

Bell lay spread-eagle on the floor, nearly oblivious to her surroundings. Her only thought was of Massah Littlejohn and what her punishment would be if he ever found out what she had done.

Convinced that it could be no worse than what she had just been through, Bell managed a brief smile before falling off to sleep.

Aimlessly, Kathryn's pen stroked the air as she nervously tried to find the right words to express her feelings. Long ago she had begun to use her writing talents to express her loneliness and despair. For no special reason, her mind reflected to the trip from England and the hanging that occurred several months ago.

Remorsefully, she began to write:

Yon stars so bright,
You enlighten the darkness, the night
Tell me what is true between the
black and the white
Tell me what is true,
Tell me what is true.

She read her poem as she tried to dissect its meaning. After a while, she emerged from her entranced state, only to wish that she could stay there forever, but she knew better. Out of loneliness and desperation, she flung herself on the bed, stuffing her face into a pillow that muffled her sniffles. Her mind was rolling endlessly with thoughts of what she had written the day before. The words clouded her mind so that she could not think clearly. She pondered her thoughts of the previous day:

> *My life seems to have ended already, for my position, I find, does not allow me to be myself. I am but a statuesque figure to be controlled and manipulated by male counterparts who represent all power and authority. You see, this is an accepted part of Southern tradition. I can speak but not be original. I can think but not be heard. I am but a flower that must not bloom too brightly. Surely, such a life will take its toll on me.*

CHAPTER ELEVEN

After months of rapidly declining health, Kathryn's father died in May 1834. A few days later, the Charleston aristocracy turned out to pay its last respects to the wise old politician.

Joining them were members of a special delegation from the South Carolina legislature.

Now that Kathryn's father was gone, many of the state's political elite felt it was only right that William succeed him as a member of the South Carolina leadership. After all, he had the proper training in law and was already versed in politics.

Many were impressed with his successful negotiation of a liaison—however tentative—between South Carolina and certain foreign countries in the event secession became a reality. But, more important, Sir Edward's son-in-law was a member of the Charleston aristocracy.

William was thrilled at the prospect of being a political leader, and eager to make another contribution toward protecting the interests of Southerners. He knew the tariff issue, nullification crisis, and talk of secession had only been shelved temporarily, and the discord between the Union and Southern states would resurface. And he was especially distressed by the anti-slavery movement, which was alive and incendiary. Fueled by fiery rhetoric, abolitionists were rapidly gaining a worldwide audience. Disturbing changes were already under way: Slavery had already been abolished in the British West Indies.

William, like most Southerners, felt threatened. He believed there was only one recourse—to fight, to the death if necessary, in order to save the prized institution of slavery. To counter the abolitionists, agents like William were dispatched to spread pro-slavery rhetoric in the South and the North. The campaign included the denunciation of female abolitionists like Maria Weston Chapman, and calculated efforts to orchestrate brutal attacks against anti-slavery agitators. For Southerners, the course was as clear as the mission.

William now spent even less time at home, and had it not been for Kathryn's efforts, the plantations would have shown acute neglect. She pleaded with him to attend to affairs at home before taking off on long trips, but to no avail. Kathryn felt she had no one to turn to—until she thought of David. She wasted no time drafting a letter to him.

Dear David:

Perhaps you heard that my father passed away several months ago. My reasons for writing are directly related to the untimely event. William, as well as many of his counterparts, has taken to the road in an effort to confront the new wave of anti-slavery activity in the North. He is rarely at home and the burden of managing the two plantations has fallen on my shoulders. I find myself inept and oft times unheeded in giving commands to the field servants. Reluctantly, I have concluded that it is a job for a man.

If it is at all possible, will you consider returning to Charleston to permanently manage my father's dwindling plantation, Echo Holler, and perhaps help me at Lakeview?

Kind regards,
Kathryn

David read the letter in the presence of a friend. His thoughts quickly centered on Kathryn instead of the plantations.

"Think about it; it would give us a base in the South, one that we sorely need—and you would go with the full support of our society," his friend said.

David sat quietly for a moment. "Since I left Charleston, I have never even considered returning to make it my home. My brother and his associates think of me as a drunken, irresponsible good-for-nothing, who spends all his worthwhile time in chasing drink or ladies. The thought of returning permanently curdles my blood," David said thoughtfully.

"Well, the task is not an easy one," his friend responded.

"Charleston will be the last stronghold of Southern thought. Friends and allies in our cause will be few to none. Reports of felonious assaults by Charleston's aristocracy on any male with innuendo of anti-slavery activity are increasing. Moreover, the Mississippi legislature has passed a law offering a reward of $5,000 leading to the arrest of any person circulating anti-slavery literature. This kind of organized assault against our interests must be stopped. Our organization has no base in the Deep South and to be caught would mean certain death by lynching, at best. Someone like you could establish that base for us. You have roots there and would fit right in. But, it is dangerous. I know what I'm asking of you, the organization knows and will be grateful regardless of what you decide. Just think about it."

David was far less worried about endangering himself than he was about the lifestyle he'd have to assume, one that he now loathed. And of course, there was Kathryn . . . Could he resist falling deeper in love? He honestly didn't know.

Still, William was away so much, David pondered. What if something happened while he was gone? That's it, he decided, I'll give it a try.

"All right, I'll return to Charleston. But I'll need someone I can trust to help with our work," David said. "That person could serve as my overseer. He would have to be one of our allies if I am to be successful."

"What about Tom Baldwin?" said the friend.

"Perfect!" David exclaimed. "He has had experience running a plantation and he's familiar with Southern lifestyle and tradition. His activity with our society is unknown to anyone but ourselves, and he's white. No one would suspect him. Also, I'll need four or five free blacks to pose as slaves. If you can get these people, I think I can make it work. Do you think he will agree?"

"Consider the matter taken care of," David's friend assured him. "I'll see to it that he returns to Charleston with you in whatever capacity is needed. As for the free blacks, I know of many who would be willing to work as your allies."

Within a month's time, David and his entourage were heading to Echo Holler. As promised, he was accompanied by Tom Baldwin and three free blacks who had willingly accepted the position of slaves in order to help the cause.

As he approached Echo Holler, David could see why Kathryn

had written to him. The grounds were in shambles; shrubbery grew unchecked and dead tree limbs dotted the lawn. Even the house was in need of a coat of paint. But David could still detect glimmers of the mansion's former majesty.

David and the overseer entered the house where they were greeted by Ole Claud, Sir Edward's house boy of many years. Although he was old and stiff, he made an effort to step lively in David's presence. "Claud, Mrs. Littlejohn told you of my arrival, I trust. This is Tom Baldwin. He will be my overseer. Get someone to put those slaves I brought along with me in cabins," David instructed the servant.

"Yes, Suh," said Ole Claud, who sensed that the appearance of these new faces would rejuvenate what otherwise was a dying plantation.

"I'll be going to pay my respects to Mrs. Kathryn."

Jonathan met David at the door of his family's mansion.

"Massah David, come on in," he said, smiling broadly. "I'll fetch Miss Kathryn."

"Thank you, Jonathan." Though he was standing in his own home, David chose to wait in the foyer much like a visitor who had never been there before.

He was there for only a few moments before Kathryn began to descend the spiral staircase. They greeted each other cordially.

"David, I'm so glad you could come," Kathryn said as she kissed him gently on the cheek.

"Kathryn, you get lovelier every time I see you. How have you been?" David inquired.

"Just tolerable, thank you. With William being away so much, at times, it has been hard. But, with you here, that all will change for the better, I'm sure." Kathryn grabbed David's arm to guide him to the parlor, where they both settled into overstuffed wing chairs.

"Where is my dear brother? Does he know about this little arrangement?"

"No," Kathryn said, "but with him being away so much and my father's plantation virtually falling apart, I don't believe that he will argue too much. But you let me worry about your brother. Tell me about yourself. What have you been doing? Are you married?"

How odd of her to ask me that, David thought. She knows how I feel about her.

He decided to play along.

"No, I'm not married," David said, looking directly into her eyes. "And, when I do, you'll be the first to know."

Then he stood, signaling the end of their short visit.

"Well, I'd best be going. There is a lot of work to be done."

Kathryn decided not to protest. "Good-bye, David. Thank you for coming to my rescue. All of my father's records are locked in the study. Ole Claud can show you where they are."

Kathryn walked David to the veranda where she watched him mount his horse. "I guess this makes you my boss," he said as he took the reins in his hands.

"I'd rather think of it as an agreement between family and friends," she told him.

He would never consider Kathryn as mere family or friend, David thought as he set out toward Echo Holler. He wanted more than that.

David assumed his duties at Echo Holler with a vigor that most Charlestonians didn't know he possessed. He started by pressing the slaves into service. The yards were cleaned and manicured; fences mended; horses shod; and equipment was stored, oiled, and cleaned in readiness for next year's crops.

Baldwin and the free blacks who had accompanied David set the pace, which was hard, but fair—new experience to the old plantation slaves. Resting time was just as sacred as the time for work. Only a half day's work was expected on Saturday and nothing but menial jobs were to be performed on Sunday. Each cabin received extra food allotments. The slaves quickly found joy in working for this new massah and they didn't fear his presence. Preoccupied with their good fortune, few of them had time to notice the extra log cabins being built alongside the lane that led up to Echo Holler.

The year 1836 marked the end of Gen. Andrew Jackson's stormy second term. He had survived the onslaught of the nullifiers, led by John C. Calhoun, and the matter was temporarily laid to rest.

He had temporized, but not answered, the issue of Texas's entrance in the Union. And he survived the last attempt by his archenemies, Daniel Webster, Henry Clay, and John C. Calhoun, to put his administration into disrepute by censuring him and the doctrines of his administration. This last-ditch attempt at revenge against "Old Hickory" had failed and many Southerners, like William, were dismayed.

Once again, William's political efforts had taken him away from home. And this time, had it not been for David, the plantation might have met with ruin. Initially, William felt threatened by David's presence in his home, after all David, by all rights, had just as much right to the property as his older brother did. But when William first learned of the arrangement between David and Kathryn, he had flown into a rage. Finally, he had to yield to the facts: Kathryn could not manage the two plantations alone. William's only recourse was to demand that the plantations be assumed under one name—his. Kathryn and David complied. By January 1837, the year that Martin Van Buren took over the presidency, the court records of Charleston officially designated the separate lands once recognized as Lake-view and Echo Holler as one, and they were now referred to as Lake Holler. William Littlejohn II was listed as the proprietor.

Staunch members of the aristocracy like William saw little hope for Southerners under Van Buren, whom they thought of as a pawn of Andrew Jackson's. Many of them, like William, continued their pro-slavery effort by talking with various interests throughout the North and by keeping the right people in state government.

In February 1838, William traveled to Massachusetts in an effort to counteract abolitionist efforts. While there, he learned that an abolitionist was to appear before a legislative committee for the Commonwealth of Massachusetts. He became even more interested when he learned the speaker was Angelina Grimke.

William knew her well. Not only were they both from Charleston, but her father, like his, had been a prominent planter, and they had socialized in the same circles during childhood. But no more; she and her sister had permanently marred their place in Charleston's society with their anti-slavery rhetoric. Moreover, two years earlier, Angelina had published her *Appeal to the Christian Women of the South*, in which she had strongly refuted the argument that the Bible supported the practice of slavery.

And now this bold, cocky female was about to stand before a legislative body to spew forth her blasphemy! William was there when Angelina delivered her speech. It was all he could do to contain himself as Angelina spoke:

> *More than 2,000 years have rolled their dark and bloody waters down the rocky, winding channel of time into the broad ocean of eternity. Since woman's voice*

was heard in the palace of an eastern monarch, and woman's petition achieved the salvation of millions of her race from the edge of the sword. The Queen of Persia, if Queen she might be called, who was but the mistress of her voluptuous Lord, trained as she had been in the secret abomination of an oriental harem, had studied too deeply the character of Ahasureus not to know that the sympathies of his heart, could not be reached, except through the medium of his annual appetites. Hence we find her arrayed in royal apparel, and standing in the inner court of the king's house, hoping by her personal charms to win the favor of her Lord. And after the golden scepter had been held out, and the inquiry was made, "What wilt thou, Queen Esther, and what is thy request? It shall be given thee to the half of the Kingdom?" Even then she dared not ask either for her own life, or that of her people. She felt that if her mission of mercy was to be successful, his animal propensities must be still more powerfully wrought upon the luxurious feast that must be prepared, the banquet of wine must be served up, and the favorable moment must be seized when, gorged with gluttony and intoxication, the king's heart was fit to be operated upon by the pathetic appeal, "If I have found favor in the sight, O King, and if it please the King, let my life be given at my Petition; and my people at my request." It was thus, through personal charms and sensual gratification, and individual influence, that the Queen of Persia obtained the precious boon she craved—her own life, and the life of her beloved people.

The audience was mesmerized by the force and skill with

which this plain, unassuming woman delivered her message. As they sat in earnest anticipation of her words, William fought to contain his rage, abhorring Angelina Grimke's reprehensible message.

Mr. Chairman, it is my privilege to stand before you on a similar mission of life and love; but I thank God that we live in an age of the world too enlightened and too moral to admit of the adoption of the same means to obtain as holy an end. I feel that it would be an insult to the Committee were I to attempt to win their favor by arraying my person in gold, and silver, and costly apparel, or by inviting them to partake of the luxurious feast, or the banquet of wine. I understand the spirit of the age too well to believe that you could be moved by such sensual means—means as unworthy of you as they would be beneath the dignity of the cause of humanity. Yes, I feel that if you are reached at all, it will not be by me, but by the truths I shall endeavor to present to your understandings and your hearts. The heart of the eastern despot was through the loves and propensities of his animal nature, by personal influence; yours, I know, cannot be reached but through the loftier sentiments of the intellectual and moral feelings.

Let the history of the world answer these queries. Read the denunciations of Jehovah against the follies and crimes of Israel's daughters. Trace the influence of woman as a courtesan and a mistress in the destinies of nations, both ancient and modern, and see her wielding her power too often to debase and destroy, rather than to elevate and save. It is often said that women rule the world, through their influence over men. If so, then may we well hide our faces in the dust and cover ourselves with sack cloth and ashes. It has not been by moral power and intellectual, but through the base passions of man—this dominion as woman must be resigned—the sooner the better; in the age which is approaching, she should be something more—she should be a citizen; and this title, which demands an increase of knowledge and reflection, open before her a new empire.

I stand before you as a Southerner, exiled from the land of my birth, by the sound of the ash and the piteous cry of the slave. I stand before you as a repentant slaveholder. I stand before you as a moral being, endowed with precious inalienable rights, which are correlative with solemn duties and high responsibilities; and as a moral being I feel that I owe it to the suffering slave, and to the deluded master, to my country and the world, to do all that I can to overthrow a system of complicated crimes, built upon the broken hearts and prostrate bodies of my countrymen in chains, and cemented by the blood and sweat and tears of my sisters in bonds.

William could not control his anger any longer. While the speaker continued, he leaped up amid a silent and spellbound crowd. He cast a long, hateful stare in Grimke's direction.

Desperately, he wanted their eyes to lock upon one another so she could see how much he loathed her. But Grimke continued, undaunted, unyielding, and unaware of his presence. William made his way to the aisle, turned for one last look at this defiled woman, and stormed out of the legislative hall.

CHAPTER TWELVE

The sun was hot on the left side of Emanuel's face.

Whenever he could, he would ease his hand to his cheek—he knew he dare not move more than one limb at a time—and quickly rub his burning skin. The moisture from his sweaty palms was soothing. Then he began to feel equal discomfort over his left shoulder and back—an intense stinging that caused him to twinge and twist his upper body in an effort to get relief. From time to time, beads of sweat would form under his armpit and roll down his left side, leaving a moist, cool trail that brought on an itch. The stinging that inevitably followed caused him to raise his hand and wipe away the moisture with one quick swoop.

But the greatest discomfort came from the gnats. They landed on the corners of his mouth, causing an annoying tickle that stimulated every sensory nerve ending in his body. He blew at them from the side of his mouth, causing them to flee a short distance, only to return to tickle the hairs in his nostrils or to play a "betcha-can't-trap-me" game with each eyelid. Then they buzzed in his ear, producing a tuning fork-like sound that destroyed all powers of concentration.

Emanuel, along with other boys of similar age, endured this afternoon of torture while serving as "backers." Their task was to stand with their backs to the lake and hold clean, dry towels for swimmers. Looking directly at the swimmers was an unpardonable sin and to drop one of the towels to the ground was almost as bad, and certainly an offense deserving of punishment.

Emanuel hated this day with a passion and couldn't figure out what bothered him most—the sun, the gnats, or the sweat.

No doubt it was a conscious effort on the part of Master and Mistress Littlejohn to flaunt the natural beauty of their plantation by having lakeside parties once or twice a year during the hot summer months, despite the dreaded fevers which caused most to seek more urban surroundings. The event in the summer of 1840—like all the others—was listed on the Charleston social calendar, and all but the infirmed elite were there. Guests would come from great distances to take off their clothes, put on swimsuits, and dive into the refreshing lake waters for the occasion. Some would float idly to the center of the lake in boats. Others would attempt to swim the width—most of the time unsuccessfully; still others simply sat along the side, dipping their toes in the water as they shared conversation about their favorite subjects—politics, money, horses, and slavery.

Handsomely attired slaves circulated among the guests, distributing a never-ending supply of food and drink.

None of the festivities were supposed to be seen, much less enjoyed, by the backers. The task of holding towels and drywear for hours at a time while the hot sun, gnats, and sweat gradually took its toll was theirs. This time, while Emanuel suffered through the chore, an idea came to him. It wasn't the best idea he'd ever had, but he was going to try it anyway.

Slowly, he dropped the towels he was holding and bent over to retrieve them, knowing full well that someone would see him. He was right.

"Hey, nigga boy, pick up those towels," yelled a drunken male voice from the direction of the water. "You can't even hold towels right. Pick them up, I say!"

By now, everyone in the vicinity of the incident was paying attention and laughing—except the other slaves, of course.

"Hey, William, is this the quality of slaves you have on your plantation?" another anonymous male voice crowed. "They can't even hold towels. How can they pick a decent load of cotton during the day?"

Again, there was laughter from the guests.

By now, the prodding had prompted William to act. Though drunk, he swam swiftly across the lake, reaching the water's edge in seconds.

"You son of a bit . . . , " he muttered, "I'll fix you."

But as William attempted to climb out, he slipped and fell backward. Furious, he dug into the water and lifted a handful of mud, which he hurled at Emanuel. The guests, now convulsed in laughter, soon joined in and pretty soon all of them were heaving mud at Emanuel's back.

His plan had worked; the cool mud was the closest he could get to a refreshing dip in that lake. Emanuel dutifully tolerated his "punishment" while gaining some relief from the burning hot rays of the sun. Still, William's drunken words kept rolling over and over in his head—"son of a bitch." Emanuel didn't know what a son of a bitch was, but he felt it must have been something ugly. It didn't matter, though, because the eight-year-old slave had decided long ago that he didn't like Massah Littlejohn at all.

Realizing that his relief from the searing heat was only temporary, Emanuel pondered other ways to distract himself. He began to mumble a song that, to him, suited the occasion:

> *Dere's mud on ma back*
> *Dere's mud on ma back*
> *While white folks had dey fun*
> *Me a standin' in de sun,*
> *and, dey's mud on ma back.*
> *Gnat, gnat, gnat, gnat*
> *dere's mud on ma back,*
> *back, back*
> *Gnat, gnat, gnat, gnat,*
> *Dere's mud on ma back, back . . .*

Once he grew bored with singing, Emanuel contented himself with watching two squirrels scamper among distant trees. He marveled at the little creatures' speed as they went 'round and 'round the tree, one after the other, up and down. From limb to limb they jumped with astounding confidence. At times, Emanuel thought the squirrels were playing, and at other times they displayed warlike seriousness. Finally, the squirrel being chased proved victorious and pulled away from his adversary. When he was assured of a safe distance, he looked back toward his tired pursuer perched on a distant limb, shook his tail, and rolled his forepaws triumphantly. Emanuel listened as the swifter squirrel issued a verbal challenge to his playmate for another round, a challenge the slower animal ignored.

By now, Emanuel was even more tired and running out of ideas to make the time pass. Hunger pangs gnawed at him; even the not-so-palatable meal of ho-cake and fatback would be a welcome treat, he thought. Then he imagined himself lying down and sleeping forever, or at least as long as he was allowed.

Sometimes, when they both were especially tired, he would massage his mother's back after she massaged his. If she was in a particularly good mood, she would also sing to him. Emanuel enjoyed his mother's singing, but she did it much too infrequently. Sometimes after a song, she would hug him so tightly and for such a long time that he could hardly breathe.

Maybe it was to hide the tears in her eyes, he thought. But he knew they were there.

At long last, it was time for Emanuel to return to his cabin. Too exhausted to run, he trudged home slowly. The trek reminded him of the last time he'd come home with skin so sun-torched that he wouldn't allow his mother to touch him. On that occasion, she simply sat back and wept. Then she tried to sing, but her emotions overwhelmed her voice. Emanuel tried to calm her down by asking a question.

"Why don't yo' eva' sang to nobody but me?" he inquired.

His mother fell silent. She looked deeply into his eyes and rubbed each side of his face tenderly, her voice quivering with emotion as she tried to talk.

"Yo' s'pose ta sang 'cause yo' is happy. Yo' s'pose ta sang 'cause yo' is sad. I's a slave an I ain't s'pose ta hab de right ta be neither."

At that moment, more than ever before, Emanuel felt Bell's hopelessness and despair. He knew that, somehow, when she touched him and rubbed him softly, she was trying to give him all she had to offer—her love and her strength. It was as if her soul, plus everything she had in her being, everything she held valuable, was in her fingertips, and she wanted to bestow it upon him.

"Don't I's make yo' happy?" he had asked sadly.

"Yo' do. Yo' makes me very happy. Dat's de reason I sangs ta yo'. But it's fo' yo' and only yo', 'cause dat's all I's got ta gib' ya and nobody kin take it away."

Upon arriving at his cabin, Emanuel decided to try to conceal his pain and fatigue. He ate what was available—all the while conscious of his mother's keen eyes on him—and immediately lay down to sleep. It wasn't long before his mother joined him.

As he thought about the events of the day, it was all he could do to keep from crying aloud. He felt hate, hate for Massah Littlejohn and all he stood for, hate for everybody like him, and he wanted revenge. But what kind of revenge? What could he do?

That night, Emanuel didn't sleep very well. He dreamed of big mud balls being thrown at him by giant gnats. Upon awakening, he realized how silly his dream was. As the dream faded, Emanuel faced a sobering fact: He wanted to do something to hurt Massah Littlejohn. But what? The water, he thought, the water!

He eased from underneath his makeshift coverings, being careful to not wake Ole Nanna or his mother, and crept out of the cabin into the night. Crickets serenaded him, and the gleaming stars and full moon lit his path toward the big house. As he made his way around the side of the house to the front yard, he could see gentle flashes of light bounce along the lake's surface.

Heading toward the water's edge, he felt in good company as an occasional lightning bug drifted in front of him.

Emanuel was not afraid. He took comfort in a mystical, symphonic bliss generated by the sounds of the night—the whistles of the crickets, the squeaking of bats all set to the base rhythm of the hooting owls. He tried to listen to each sound; for reasons unknown to him, it was important that he distinguish them individually.

Upon reaching the lake, he walked slowly along its perimeter. It didn't take long before the memory of what had happened earlier that day flooded his mind. He envisioned white folks splashing and frolicking in the water. He remembered the hot sun and the mud balls. Inside, he boiled with anger.

Eagerly, Emanuel approached the pier, stepping carefully onto the wooden surface and walking as close to its edge as he possibly could. Then he dropped his pants, took out his penis, and urinated in the lake. Emanuel shook his organ back and forth vigorously to ensure that he fouled as much of the water as possible, then he jerked the last few drops of urine from his penis and returned it to his pants. Turning to leave the pier, he felt vindicated.

Emanuel often wondered what it was that black folk had that kept white folks from wanting them in their lakes or swimming ponds. How well he remembered Massah Littlejohn saying, "If niggers are going to take baths in white folks' water, they'll have to do it downstream. Fortunately though, most of them are temperamentally disinclined to bathe."

Well, Emanuel thought, whatever it is that we have, I hope I left some of it in that lake so white folks can catch it. Satisfied, Emanuel began to run a little faster toward his cabin.

He arrived to find Bell and Ole Nanna still sleeping. Quickly, he lay down on his pallet with his hands folded behind his head. Too excited to sleep, he listened to Nanna's snoring; it was loud—like a pig rooting for food. A smile crossed his lips as he thought about what he'd done that night, and that brought to mind one of Ole Nanna's favorite sayings:

"Boy, ya got ta be able ta listen to de night and love quiet 'cause when de day of judgment comes, fo' de fust time in dey life, men will have quiet, and quiet will make no sounds."

Emanuel had heard lots of distinct sounds. He wasn't afraid of the night anymore.

The next day, after Bell left the cabin, Emanuel seized the

opportunity to ask Ole Nanna some questions. He always looked forward to quizzing the old woman; she had an answer for everything, and sometimes she could tell the best stories.

"Why de white folks don't want niggas in dey water?" Emanuel asked Ole Nanna as she went about her work.

"Guess it 'cause dey thank some of de black gon' run off," she replied as she continued to work, being careful to not look at the boy. She had always felt Emanuel was different, smarter than most, and she was afraid for him. Afraid that his burning desire to know would cause him to seek answers that whites didn't want him to have. She knew the best way to handle his questioning was to give a nonchalant answer. Never let him know he had struck a nerve.

"What's wrong with being black?"

"Nuthin' that I knows of."

"Then, why dey keep us out of der water an' away from dem?"

This time, Ole Nanna stopped to look Emanuel straight in the eyes. She had accepted slavery for what it was—an act on the part of the powerful to suppress the will of the weak. But she always felt in her soul that suppression was only temporary.

Emanuel, she felt, had to accept himself and what he was. In that moment, she wanted to plant a seed in his mind that would grow long after she was gone. Ole Nanna nearly tumbled to the ground, and Emanuel feared that she was sick. She knelt before him and grasped his shoulders. At first, she looked weak about the eyes, but she quickly developed an unwavering stare.

"Yo' lis'n to yo' nanna, boy. Yo' lis'n good! Dey ain't nuthin' wrong wid bein' black or no other color. Yo' hear? Dey ain't nuthin' wrong. De same Lawd made us all. Yo' got ta be prideful of what yo' is or yo' ain't worth a handful o' dirt an' yo' ought not to be born. Yo' gots ta be able ta see inta thangs, and I don' made ma own reason. If'n a man ain't nuthin', yo' don't pay him no 'tention. None at all. If'n yo' an me an all dese odduh black niggas ain't nuthin', den why dey pay us so much 'tention? Why de white folks spen' so much time tryin' to fin' us if we runs away? Why? If'n we ain't nuthin', why dey spen' so much time sendin' all de way ta Africa to git mo' of us—if'n we ain't nuthin'. Dat's a long way ta go ta pick up nuthin'. Why, boy, yo' got ta ask yo'self, why? De reason, I don' know, but it ain't because yo' ain't nuthin'. Cause if'n yo' was nuthin', dey wud leab yo' 'lone."

Emanuel wished Ole Nanna wouldn't hold his shoulders so tightly. But he knew to not say anything because she couldn't hear him; she always seemed to be in some kind of trance when she talked that way. Most of the time he didn't understand what she was saying—like now. But sometimes at night, when he was about to go to sleep, he could figure some of it out. This time, as Ole Nanna continued, she revealed something he hadn't known.

"I don' seen dat fire in yo' eyes, dat same fire was in yo' pa's eyes, and it got him lynched. De Lawd knows dat I hope dat don' happen ta yo'! But if'n it does, it don't look like Ole Nanna gon' be live ta see it. Thank de Lawd. But no matter what yo' be, be proud of what yo' is 'cause if'n yo' is nuthin', nobody cares, an' yo' got ta be somethin' ta git as much 'tention as us niggas gits."

"Yes'm," was all Emanuel had to say. He knew not to ask another question.

That night, Emanuel had much to contemplate. The pieces were falling into place. Most of the other boys in the slave yards had lost any hope of finding out who their fathers were or where they were. Most of them had been lynched, had ran away, or been sold.

Time and time again, ever since he realized he was supposed to have one, he had asked the question of his mother.

"Where's ma pa? Don't he live here?"

Her reply was always the same. "He don' gone away."

She would never say more. But through random yard chatter, when grown-ups thought he wasn't listening, he had learned that his father was murdered. Today, he had learned how. Now, all he needed to know was by whom.

Wilhelmina, or Winnie, as she was called, was now a pretty little eight-year-old. Long, curly locks of jet black hair framed her cherub face. Her skin was deceptively white in color, with but a hint of a dark hue evident only upon close inspection. She was as dainty as any purebred white child could be, and her mother seized every opportunity to remind her daughter of her special looks.

"Winnie is my very own precious little girl—just as pretty as any little white girl could be," she often told her.

Teresa would comb her daughter's hair and fashion it in the styles she'd seen her mistress wear. Then she would place a small mirror before her daughter.

"See how pretty you are," she cooed.

At this age, Winnie had full run of the house and plantation yards, just like her ever-constant companion, Bertram. However, Bertram was forbidden to enter the slave yards, and so was she.

Neither child fully understood why, so when the chance arose for them to sneak among the slave cabins, they seized it. But once was enough; they decided they didn't like the squalor and odor of excrement that prevailed. Thereafter, they had no problem confining their activities to the beautiful plantation yards.

One of their favorite pastimes was playing on a swing suspended from one of the trees in the front yard. Each of them would take turns pushing the other until the rider reached frightful heights and screamed in mock terror. Sometimes Robert, the older brother, would play with them, but he never developed the closeness to Winnie that Bertram did, and was quick to remind Winnie that she, too, was a slave. Though she didn't understand the meaning of the word, Winnie knew it hurt to be called one.

Pretty soon, though, she would immerse herself in frivolity with Bertram and forget what had happened.

The end of a wonderful morning of play and fun was often marked by a special treat: gingerbread. Winnie and Bertram both ate until their stomachs bulged tightly, then would eat more—if Teresa would allow it. Afterward, the pair was separated so Bertram and Robert could retreat to the parlor. As near as Winnie could understand, the boys were directed to play a game wherein they were required to call out numbers and words from a book at the insistence of their mother. At first, Winnie wanted to play, too, and protested loudly. But this was the one time her mother spoke so harshly to her that she soon forgot about interrupting them.

"Winnie," she would say, "if you goes and messes with Bertram while he is with the Missus, I'll beat you till you turn black."

So Winnie accepted the fact that she couldn't spend this time with Bertram. Like Winnie, Bertram didn't understand the separation. Unlike her, he chose to not accept it—at least not totally. Every chance he got, he would bring along the books from which he and Robert received their instructions and teach Winnie everything he could remember. And he made Winnie promise on her life that she would never tell that she, right along with him and Robert, was learning her numbers and how to read.

CHAPTER THIRTEEN

Early on, Emanuel realized his life had a routineness that did not particularly suit him. Almost every day, he arose just before dawn and ate fatback and ho-cake for breakfast. From early morning until sundown, he did chores, then returned to his cabin with Ole Nanna and his mother for food and rest, only to repeat the same thing the next day. Almost any event or occasion that altered the routine was welcomed.

Although he was only eight years old, Emanuel sensed there was about to be an extraordinary change in his life—an unwelcome one. He knew it would involve Ole Nanna. During the past year, he had watched her grow steadily weak. She had long since relinquished her duties of caring for slave babies to Bell.

Emanuel missed her stories about Africa and her philosophy of life. These days, Ole Nanna said nothing to anyone. Her arms and legs had grown so stiff that they couldn't be straightened. Large sores developed on her feet and backside that left a pungent odor in the cabin most of the time.

Emanuel watched with ambivalence as Bell attempted to care for her, praying for her to live, refusing to accept her impending death. Emanuel loved Ole Nanna very much and had known her as a proud, strong individual. Although he dared not say it to his mother, he felt she would be better off dead; then she could go to heaven. He had heard her speak of the place so often that he wondered what it would be like up there. Nanna assured him that he'd find out one day because most all niggas were going to heaven because it would be the first time that they would know life and freedom. But, she added, there's a lot of white folk that's gonna have to do a whole bunch of praying to make it. She never mentioned any names.

One evening, Emanuel walked into the cabin at the end of the work day, like he always did. But this time he found his mother lying across Ole Nanna's chest, She sobbed deeply, and each muted cry seemed to send her body into spasms. Emanuel looked at Ole Nanna's lifeless frame and was suddenly seized by fear and deep-seated emptiness that he thought would never end. He had known others in the slave yard to die but never anyone so close.

Bell finally regained her composure. Reaching around Ole Nanna's lifeless neck, she removed the neck piece that the older woman had always worn. It was Bell's now; Ole Nanna had promised it to her on the occasion of her death. Gently, she pressed Ole Nanna's eyelids closed. From somewhere deep inside, a slow moving rhythm seemed to burst from her, erupting into a mournful song:

> *Smoke cloud, smoke cloud;*
> *Lawd, send down dat smoke cloud.*

An intense frown fell across her face as her eyelids closed tightly, damming the stream of tears that moistened her cheeks.

She continued her sad song:

Lawd, send down dat smoke cloud fom heab'n
dere is an angel dat's on huh way
de journey is long, huh soul, O, so willin'
Lawd, send down dat smoke cloud today.

I want yo' ta ride dat smoke cloud ta heab'n
I'se gonna meet ya dere someday
I want yo' ta ride dat smoke cloud ta heab'n
One day yo'll show me the way.

When yo' smoke cloud lands in heab'n
Gib yo' 'spect ta de grace ob God
and if dere 'nuff time fo' him ta
Lend yo' an ear,
tell him dat life down here sho' is hard.

Bell's voice trailed off into more sobs, but her song became a permanent part of Emanuel's soul. He would never forget it, or the occasion that prompted its creation.

Through tearful eyes, Bell finally saw Emanuel standing in front of her.

"Come here, Emanuel," she said, voice trembling.

Slowly, he overcame his trepidation and walked toward his mother. He tried to not look at Ole Nanna's face.

"Yes'm."

"Ya got ta feel Nanna and say good-bye ta huh. She done gon' on ta de Lawd na."

Terrified, Emanuel moved his hand toward Ole Nanna's arm, but he would only touch her with one finger. He felt that too much aggravation of her lifeless body would cause her to awaken, and that would surely scare the life out of him.

"Now yo' go tell de 'seer dat Nanna's done died so he kin tell

Massah Littlejohn. Den yo' go tell ol' John an' some o' de rest ta come hep me wid de body."

For once, Emanuel was more than eager to do as he was told.

"Yes'm," he replied.

Hurriedly, he ran off to find Big Sam, the overseer. He found him near the stables, grooming his horse. Big Sam was the only black man Emanuel ever saw riding horseback about the plantation. Everybody else walked or was driven on wagons. For as long as Emanuel could remember, Sam had been the overseer at Lake Holler. He was a large, muscular man whose appearance alone was threatening enough. In the presence of Massah Littlejohn, he could be as grueling a taskmaster as any white man. In his absence, he saw that the work was done. Yet, he respected the inhabitants of the slave yard. Perhaps he never felt above his position as a slave or maybe he understood that leniency on his part would only lead to his being replaced with someone even more harsh. In any case, he did his job to the satisfaction of all concerned and was considered the overseer.

Emanuel stood a little ways away from him, a little intimidated by his massive presence, as he presented the news.

"Ma say ta tell yo' dat Nanna done died."

Sam finished grooming his horse before he approached the Big House to tell Massah Littlejohn. There was nothing new about this ritual. He was not reporting the death to Massah Littlejohn with any expectation of sympathy but rather to clear the way for whatever funeral service that was to be held.

When Sam knocked on the door, Jonathan the butler answered and led him to Massah Littlejohn, who was seated in the study, reading a newspaper. He hardly looked up when Sam entered the room.

"Massah Littlejohn, Ole Nanna done died and we needs to git her buried," Sam said.

"Ole Nanna finally died, huh?"

"Yassah."

"Well, see that she gets buried tonight," William said. "Any kin can leave the field early. But git it done today. Tomorrow is another workday."

"Yassah, Massah Littlejohn."

Sam turned to leave the room.

"By the way, Sam, this ought to leave Bell kinda lonely some at night. There ain't been no steady man with her since I hung that shiftless husband of hers years ago. Maybe you can make her produce some nigger babies."

Sam had stopped in his tracks to listen to his master's dialogue. He had heard it all before.

"Yassah, but Bell ain't had no results from my lovin'," he said simply. "Lawd knows I tried. Yassah, I sho' did."

Indeed, Sam and Bell had been lovers on several occasions. Not because she wanted it that way but because the easy solution to the problem was to accept the advances of the men that Massah Littlejohn pushed on her, and relish knowing how frustrated he had to be over her inability to breed more field hands for him.

After a while, Sam had felt demeaned by his futile efforts and his advances had weaned to almost never.

"Massah Littlejohn, you know, I believes dat woman's done had roots worked on her and she ain't gon' nevah hab no babies," Sam said.

"Well, maybe you are right, but don't stop trying. I've tried many a time to sell her off, but just as soon as a prospective buyer asks how many children she has had and I say one, they look at her like she has some kind of disease," William said bitterly.

"Yassah."

"I guess I'm stuck with her now. She's about to be too old to sell and now I guess we need her in Nanna's place to watch the nigga babies in the daytime."

He paused a moment.

"See to getting Nanna buried tonight, Sam. You may go now."

After Sam left the room, William sat back in his chair while he fumbled with his pipe. He was contemplating what Sam had said about the roots. Married thirteen years and no children. Maybe someone had worked roots on Kathryn. After so many years and not even a hint of pregnancy, he was willing to believe anything. And now, he and Kathryn had grown more distant. What with him spending so much time away from Lake Holler, at pro-slavery conventions and the like, it was only on rare occasions that they made love.

Then, there was his brother. Even he admitted to himself that without David's presence, the plantation would not have done so well, perhaps not even survived. But whenever the three of them dined together, although infrequently, the ease of conversation between Kathryn and David triggered thoughts of jealousy. He wondered if they saw each other while he was away.

Moreover, he wondered if they made love.

From past experience, Emanuel knew it would be pitch dark before the body would be ready for burial. He also knew the preburial ritual was not to be witnessed by children, and he was grateful for that. Nevertheless, he couldn't help but wonder what was going on inside the shack where this old woman, who had had such an impact on his life, had died. Never before had he known of death in his own home. He wondered if he would now be too frightened to enter it alone.

As the other slaves waited, the old women of the slave community prepared and washed Ole Nanna's body for burial. It was thought that an unclean body would not be allowed to make the holy journey to heaven. After the body was scrubbed clean, it was moistened with oil, which was subsequently rubbed off. The women chose a frayed but clean dress in which to dress Ole Nanna's body; tradition dictated that whatever dress or robe that was clean and not worn at the time of death would become the burial garment. If there was none, and often there wasn't, then a clean burlap sheet would have to do.

For the most part, the mood was somber. But like many times before, the women began a funeral chant as they finished preparing Ole Nanna's body. Their voices could be heard all the way to the Big House. Emanuel had heard that the white folks had become so familiar with the sounds that they called them "death moans."

If the dead person was highly respected in the slave community, the front door of the cabin was taken down and used as a burial bed. Surprisingly, Massah Littlejohn had never challenged this odd custom, even though it meant doors had to be replaced.

Such was the ceremonial last rites given to Ole Nanna, who died old before she was fifty-five years of age.

At graveside, Emanuel could hear a nameless voice pay homage to Ole Nanna in the dark of night with a final prayer:

> *"De Lawd giveth an' de Lawd taketh away,*
> *Lawd, put a powa'ful han' on dis woman's*
> *brow an' let de weight of yo' han' shadow*
> *dis woman's vision from all evil as she*
> *makes huh way ta ya promise lan'."*

An occasional mournful plea would escape into the night air as individual slaves envisioned their own plight. The speaker continued:

*"Lawd, we know dat life on dis
earth ain't been too good ta us all
de time, an' all we's got ta say
'bout dat is let yo' will be done,
but now, Lawd, dis here soul done
made huh way down here and she deserve ta see de odduh side. She
done dreamed 'bout dat promise
lan'. She had kindness in huh
heart, Lawd, an' prayer ta clear huh
vision. Sho' huh de way, Lawd, an'
let huh path go unhindered, but most
of all, let yo' will be done.
Amen! Amen!"*

After the funeral, Emanuel's trepidation took over again and he felt uneasy in the cabin where he had spent his whole life. The thought of being there alone or even sleeping on the other side of the room away from his mother was unbearable.

He was afraid to go to sleep. He snuggled close to his mother, who had already curled into a fetal position. How could she go to sleep so fast, he thought, but he knew that sorrow had been so much a part of her everyday life that she would not allow it to consume her. Still, he had to think of some way to awaken her without revealing his fears.

"Ma, where'd de dead folks go?" he asked.

"Heab'n," Bell replied, her voice heavy with fatigue. "Dey goes ta heab'n. At least, good ones go dere."

"Will Nanna go ta heab'n?"

"Yeh, dat sho one woman dat gon' go straight ta heab'n."

Realizing how frightening a death in the house must be for a little child, Bell rolled over to face Emanuel. She pulled him close to her body.

"How she git dere?" he asked, wide-eyed.

"What all dese questions 'bout?"

"How Nanna git ta heab'n?"

"If'n I tell yo', yo' got ta git ta sleep. All right. De night when evabody done gone ta sleep, de Lawd will send down a cloud dat works like white smoke. Dat cloud so white dat it look like one o' Missy Kathryn's fresh-cleaned sheets. Dat cloud will cover Ole Nanna's grave an' suck Ole Nanna right out ob de groun' an' carry huh right on up ta heab'n. I know dis is true 'cause I done had a vision. I had dat same vision when yo' pa done died. She won' hab ta worry 'bout nuthin' no mo'."

Silence once again crept into the room and with it came the return of Emanuel's fears. He snuggled even closer to his mother when he realized she was about to go to sleep. He had heard the sounds of night many times, but tonight they seemed especially eerie. Try as he might, he couldn't fight the fear; he had to keep his mother awake somehow. He thought of another question.

"Ma." He nudged Bell a little but got no response.

"Ma."

"What, 'Manuel?"

"Where'd yo' git dat song?"

"What song?"

"Dat smoke cloud song, dat yo' sang when Nanna died."

"I don' know. I made it up, I guess. Songs jes comes inta ma head an' I don' know where dey comes from. Been dat way fo' as long as I 'member."

"Den why don' yo' sing dem songs out loud so evabody kin hear?"

"Dem songs done been put in ma heart fo' me. Without dem I couldn't make it thew de day. So I keeps dem fo' me an' de ones I love and dat's all. Na, hush up an' go ta sleep."

Emanuel had one more question—the most important of all.

135

"Ma."

"Emanuel, if'n yo' don't hush up, I's gon' tell Nanna ta come down here an' haint cha."

"Ma."

"What, Emanuel?"

"Who done kilt ma pa?"

Bell sat straight up in the bed, looking Emanuel directly in his eyes.

"Who don' tol' yo' dat somebody kilt yo' pa? Ain't anybody kilt yo' pa but his own stubborn head. Na, yo' hush up! Hush up, I say!"

Emanuel was crushed. He thought he had a right to know what had happened to his father. Now, he felt abandoned and it no longer mattered whether the "haints" got him. Sobbing loudly, he scrambled away from his mother to the opposite side of the bed. Bell was now near tears also. She realized how much she had hurt her son. Bell reached for Emanuel and pulled him toward her, wrapping him in a loving embrace.

"Don' cha worry, Emanuel. Ain't no haint gon' git ma 'Manuel," she said over and over again. Soon, they both fell asleep.

CHAPTER FOURTEEN

At ten years of age, Emanuel was thin and lean and in no way spectacular. But he did have a knack for putting forth the most docile face when confronted by an elder, a talent that any mischievous little boy found useful.

One day, Emanuel was given the task of delivering the supper meat to the Big House—a freshly killed chicken whose neck had been broken by a quick twist. He headed to the mansion with the feathery animal in tow, its limp body dragging the ground. Blood and salivary juices drained from the dead bird's mouth. He paid no attention to the noxious secretions as he ascended the back stairs. Emanuel entered the kitchen without knocking, since he knew Big Gertie would be close by to accept the bird.

"Big Gertie, me got dis thicken," he yelled.

"Boy, git dat nasty-ass chicken out o' ma kitchen fo' I wrings yo' neck!" Big Gertie screamed.

"Dey told me ta bring dis thicken in here," Emanuel responded defensively.

"Well I's tellin' yo' ta git dat nasty-ass bird out o' here. Na git!

On de back porch! Go on!" said Gertie, waving her arms in a fanning motion.

Big Gertie was a tall, brown-skinned woman whose girth made her wobbly on her feet. To Emanuel, it seemed her large lips were always fashioned in a sardonic smile. She was by far the biggest, fattest person on the plantation—a testament to the fact that she constantly sampled her own cooking. Emanuel knew he could outrun her if he had to. When she walked, her bare feet slapped against the floor, causing her hips to vibrate vigorously. When provoked, she adopted a ferocious look, one that mischievous little slave boys knew well.

"Na, yo' sit down dere," Gertie said, leading Emanuel to a bench on the back porch. Then she went into the house and returned with a pail of water that she sat in front of Emanuel.

"Na, yo' pluck dat stankin'-ass chicken clean and git all dat blood and chicken shit off, den bring it in de kitchen while's I goes and cleans up dis mess yo' dun made on de flo'."

Gertie turned and walked away.

Holding the chicken by its feet, Emanuel submerged it in the water for several minutes to soften the feathers. When he finished, he held the dead chicken aloft. The odor from the raw, fresh meat was a bit noxious, so he conjured up the smell of crisp fried chicken with potatoes, his favorite meal. But Emanuel knew that if there was any meat on his table tonight, it would only be fatback.

"Me don' cleaned dis nasty-ass thicken," Emanuel muttered.

"Big Gertie gon' cook dis nasty-ass thicken, an' de white folks gon' eat dis nasty-ass thicken and me don't git none."

He continued to hold the chicken over the bucket so all of the water would drain from its skin and not mess up the porch.

Again, he entered the kitchen and offered the chicken to Gertie.

"Here dat thicken; me cleaned him ta de bone."

"Gimme dat chicken," Gertie said gruffly, "an' yo' git."

Emanuel felt a bit let down. He had done a good job on the bird and he'd hoped Gertie would offer him a piece after it was fried.

As he turned to leave, he heard a musical sound coming from somewhere in the house. He had heard the sound before from the yard and would often sneak up to an old oak tree near the house, hoping to see its source. But he was too short to peek inside the nearby window, so he had to content himself with listening to the music. He was always extra careful, making sure no one noticed him malingering about the house as the soft musical tones swelled in his ears.

Now, the sounds rang out louder than he'd ever heard, and he decided to find out where the music was coming from. He watched from the back porch until Gertie's back was turned, then he eased his way back into the kitchen and hid behind the pantry door until he could make his way into the house. Never had he been beyond the kitchen, but he had to follow the music.

Emanuel crept beyond the kitchen into the dining area. He looked back at Gertie to confirm that she had not discovered him.

She was busy dismembering the chicken.

He turned toward the music, which was now accompanied by a soft, feminine voice. He was certain that it belonged to Missy Kathryn, for surely no other person in this world could be blessed with such a beautiful voice—except his mother, of course. As he moved down a hallway, he glanced at large portraits of men and women he'd never seen. He looked down at a floor that seemed too clean and shiny to walk on. All around him were furnishings unlike any he had ever known.

Suddenly, Emanuel had reached the room from which the

music emanated. Quickly, he secured a place behind the nearest wall.

When he thought about Gertie discovering him there, he almost urinated. But he was determined to see and hear everything he could because he was convinced he'd never get another chance to do so. For a moment, he forgot himself and was completely absorbed in the music.

He peeked around the wall, catching a glimpse of a big black box with long legs and white teeth. The mistress was sitting on a stool with her back to him, producing the pretty sounds by pressing down on the teeth in the middle of the box. Emanuel was astounded and grew more attentive as the music progressed. Though the lyrics were foreign to him, he liked what he heard.

He watched as Missy Kathryn's fingers shifted from one end of the box to the other. Never had he seen fingers move so fast. So engrossed was he in the music and the big box that Gertie's arrival came as a complete surprise. But the feel of her heavy hands on his shoulders quickly brought him back to reality.

Grabbing his ear, she yanked him toward the kitchen. Emanuel was so terrified that he was unaware the music had stopped. All he could hear was Gertie's words.

"Yo' li'l imp, whatcha doin' in da house?"

In the kitchen, Gertie released his ear, then raised her right hand high in the air while holding on to Emanuel with her left. He wrenched away from her and raced to the opposite end of the cooking table. They both stood their ground, then Gertie moved toward the back door, where she stood and waved her massive hands.

"Yo' li'l nigga boy, yo' come here or I'll beat yo' half ta death!"

Emanuel remained motionless—safe, or so he thought. He looked Gertie straight in the eyes, watching her anger mount with each passing second. Her lips and jaws were clenched so tightly that he thought she would surely explode. At last, Gertie could stand it no longer. She rushed toward the table as fast as she could, lunging at the boy as he extended his body backward, just out of her reach. Gertie was so off balance that she almost fell to the floor. She hit the sturdy oak table, which made a loud scraping sound as it slid under her weight. Then Emanuel heard something that scared him even more.

"What's happening in here, Gertie?" Missy Kathryn asked from the doorway. "What was that noise?"

Gertie turned. Her eyes full of revenge, she said, "Dat li'l nigga don' snuck in dis kitchen."

She was too embarrassed to tell the whole truth, that her inattention had allowed the mischievous child to enter the room. This was her kitchen and she liked to feel in complete control. Now, her domain was threatened. She decided to make up a lie.

"He don' snuck in dis kitchen and he don' tried to steal dat fried chicken," she said, pointing at several pieces of the meat she had fried and spread out on a platter.

Emanuel could feel nothing but contempt for Gertie. This woman, who was a slave like him, was deliberately telling a lie.

Bowing his head, Emanuel didn't bother to protest. He thought briefly about running but knew that would be pointless.

They hung little slave boys who tried to run away.

"What is his name?" asked Kathryn.

"Dat's Bell's boy. Only child. Neva did know a nigga woman dat couldn't hab but one baby. He name 'Manuel."

Kathryn placed her hands on the boy's shoulder, then lifted his face. She smelled so sweet that he could hardly believe it. Her touch was soft; her waist was so small that Emanuel thought it would break if she bent over too far. Never had he been so close to her. He dared not look above her waistline. Still, he could tell how lean and well-proportioned she was, especially compared with Gertie.

"Emanuel, why did you try to steal the chicken? Are you hungry?"

Emanuel finally looked up at her.

"Me didn't steal no thicken," he said. Then his fears began to mount. This was the mistress of the whole plantation. She was pretty and delicate and married to the white master whom Emanuel knew would not take kindly to having her agitated. This is the end, he thought. My head is gonna be chopped off just like the chicken's, for sure.

Kathryn saw the boy's tongue protruding through his teeth as he mispronounced the word "chicken." Instantly, she recalled the black man with the forked tongue. She almost felt a kinship between herself and the boy. Kathryn glanced over at Gertie.

"I'll bet he is hungry. He's so thin and frail that a good meal would probably do him some good," she told the slave woman.

Emanuel's eyes widened in amazement. For a second, he thought he was dreaming. He said nothing.

"Gertie, find a nice big piece of fried chicken and give it to him. Give him some bread to go along with it."

Gertie started to protest.

"Missy, dat li'l nigga don't deserve . . . "

"Do as I say, Gertie," Kathryn ordered. "Give Emanuel the chicken and bread."

"Yes'm," Gertie said reluctantly. From the platter, she picked up a nice breast bone, thick with crisp, moist white meat, and handed it to Emanuel along with a piece of bread. Emanuel couldn't remember when he had been so happy. He glimpsed Gertie's eyes as she handed him his supper. They were filled with revenge and hate, something he had never seen in another slave, for another slave.

"Now Emanuel, when you want something, you must learn to ask for it," Kathryn said. "Now run along."

"Yes'm," Emanuel said. He hurried through the back door.

Hunger gnawed at him, but he didn't bite into his priceless meal; he simply placed it in his pocket as he ran toward his cabin.

Kathryn watched Emanuel scamper from the kitchen, protecting the meal like it was a piece of gold. She smiled to herself when she thought of how he'd pronounced "chicken" with a "t." Perhaps, she thought, the problem was the late development of his front teeth.

Again, his speech impediment stirred the haunting memories of the trip from England and the black man, to whom she remained indebted. Giving the chicken to the boy was her attempt at repaying her debt. Oh, how silly of me, she thought, a piece of chicken for a life. There's no comparison. For the rest of the day, she tried to put the thought out of her mind. But every time she thought about the snaggletoothed little boy, she also remembered the black man with the forked tongue.

Mounting clouds of dust stuck to Bell's sweaty skin like honey to a piece of bread. The stiff burlap cloth from which Bell's skirt was made added to the problem. Nevertheless, she continued to swing her broom at the cabin's dirt floor. For some reason, the dirt appeared cleaner to her after it was swept.

Emanuel saw his mother's familiar repetitive swings as he approached the cabin. Ever since he could remember, his mother had performed this useless task. He surmised that the objective of cleaning was to remove dirt, and there was little difference between the swept and unswept kind. But he had to live with the practice since Bell gave little room for argument on the subject.

When he was around, Bell sometimes insisted that Emanuel help by moving the pile of swept dirt in front of the door. To him, this was a witless task, not to mention an embarrassing one if witnessed by the other children. When the sweeping was over, she would always dust the fireplace and hearth until not a grain of dust was left. Afterward, Bell would bring in the quilt or blankets that she'd hung outside in the sun.

Bell had always put great emphasis on taking care of what was hers. More than once, Emanuel had challenged his mother about the seemingly senseless task of sweeping dirt.

"Boy, dis ain't much o' nuthin' what we got here," she always replied, "but it all we got, so ya' got ta keep it best yo' kin."

When Bell finished sweeping this time, Emanuel approached her with his prize. He knew that a piece of crisply fried chicken, even if slightly crushed from being inside his pocket, would be a welcome addition to the dinner table and he wanted to share it with her.

"Look what me got, Ma," he said as he lifted the chicken breast from his pocket. A large, greasy spot now took its place alongside the dirty, assorted patches on the front of his pants.

"Boy, where'd ya git dat piece o' chicken?"

"F'om de Big House," he told her.

Bell's right hand landed heavily against Emanuel's face.

"Ain't I don' tol' yo' ta stay away fom inside dat house?" she shrieked. "And naw yo' don' started stealin'."

Emanuel stared up at his mother.

"But me didn't 'teal it," he said as tears curved around the corners of his tightened lips. Dropping the chicken on the freshly cleaned dirt floor, he went to lay down on his pallet in the corner.

His mother began to have second thoughts about striking him, especially since she hadn't heard the whole story.

"Where'd yo' git dat piece o' fried chicken, Emanuel?" she asked, struggling to control her voice.

"De missus gib it ta me. Missy Kathryn gib it ta me. Me didn't 'teal it," Emanuel said quietly.

Bell knew he was telling the truth, but she still launched into a lecture.

"Meddlesome li'l boys gits sol' away to dem slavers," she warned, her voice trembling with emotion. "Yo' all I got, 'Manuel. Yo' all I got in dis world. Nanna don' died. Didn't know ma ma and pa. Massah Littlejohn don' kilt yo' pa. I ain't got nobody but yo' and if yo' gits sol', I ain't got nobody. Most anytime, deys takin' li'l boys yo' age f'om here an' dey ain't seen no mo', an' I don't won't dat ta happen ta yo'. I wants yo' ta be here wid me til' yo' grown an' kin make yo' own way. So stay away f'om dat Big House."

Emanuel had heard it all before, except the part about his father. He wanted to know more, but one look at his mother's weary face told him this wasn't the time. Besides, he had plenty to think about. He lay on his pallet, wearing a passive look on his face. But inside, a fire that could only be extinguished by revenge began to burn. The truth had come to light because of a piece of chicken. Never had his mother hinted at what had happened to his father. He had found out on his own that his father had been killed. Lynched! Now he knew who did it.

"One day I will kill de massah," Emanuel said under his breath. "One day I will."

Bell picked up the piece of chicken. After brushing away some of the dirt, she put it on a platter with a piece of fatback and ho-cakes. Emanuel joined her as she sat down on the floor with the food. She placed the platter between them, clasped her hand in her lap, and offered an apology to her son in the form of a prayer.

"Dear Lawd, we thanks yo' fo' de
grace and kindness dat yo' don'
bestowed on us. Dere is a new piece

o' meat on dis table tonight an'
whilst de devil in me made me 'cuze
ma li'l boy o' stealin', de rest o'
me knows dat dis meat wuz sent by
yo', Lawd. I gibs yo' tanks.
I ask his fo'gibness. Amen."

Emanuel listened to his mother's words. She usually made him pray along with her, but tonight she didn't. When she finished, she picked up the piece of chicken and pulled close to half the meat away from the bone. The biggest piece she left intact and offered it to Emanuel by holding it in front of his face. He was almost always hungry, but at the moment he didn't feel much like eating. He looked at the piece of meat then at his mother, whom he knew was starved. But he also knew that if he didn't eat his, she wouldn't eat hers. He took the chicken and began to eat it slowly, savoring each luscious mouthful. His mother did the same. As they ate, they occasionally glanced toward one another but said nothing.

That night, Emanuel's head was filled with many questions.

Why did Massah Littlejohn kill his pa? He knew there was no way he could approach his mother for answers and he could think of no one else in the slave yards he could turn to. He wished Ole Nanna was living. She could give him the answer; she had the answer for everything.

Emanuel decided that his father's death must have been related to the fact that his pa, too, was a slave. He had heard talk in the slave yards of other slaves—mostly men—being lynched. He had not yet come to grips with this thing called slavery. To him, a slave was a person who had a master, a white master. But why the lynchings? Why the killings? He had to find out more about it.

Then his mind slowly drifted back to the day's earlier events. What was that big black box with the white teeth? For months, he had heard the beautiful sound that came from it. More than once, when he had an excuse to go near the Big House, he had stopped by the window to listen to the music. But not until today had he seen the instrument from which it was produced.

What was the big black box called, he wondered. Tomorrow, he'd ask his mother. He couldn't do so tonight, not after her emotional outburst. He had not forgotten her orders to stay away from the Big House; nor did he forget that he hadn't responded to that particular demand. Emanuel knew that, given a chance, he would return. He had to see the black box again.

He awoke early the next morning before sunrise as his mother moved around in the cabin, and rose without any prompting. As always, the smell of fatback and ho-cake filled the air. He knew that was all they got, so he didn't complain. Besides, his curiosity helped quiet his hunger pangs this morning. He simply had to ask his mother about the box.

Had Bell not been rushing to prepare for all the young'uns who'd soon be left in her care, she would have noticed that something was amiss.

"Ma, me ask sumpin?"

"What?"

Slowly, he began to speak. He knew his mother didn't like questions of any kind, but this time Emanuel's curiosity overpowered his will to keep quiet.

"Me wuz at de Big House, me saw dis great big box dat had white and black teeth. De Missus touch de teeth an de box make music lak when yo' sangs. What dat box is?"

After last night, Bell decided to go easier on her son.

"De box is a peeanna an' it make de music like me when I sangs. But yo' mus' neva try ta touch a peeanna 'cuz dey may bite if nigga boys touch it. It bites dere fangers right off. Dat's whut dem teeth is fo'."

Emanuel remained calm as his mother shared this startling revelation. If he had believed one word of it, he truly would have been disappointed. But he doubted something that could make such beautiful sounds could do harm.

Peeanna. The word became implanted on his mind.

"Wher' de peeanna come f'om?" he asked.

Bell knew her attempts to instill fear hadn't worked.

"I don't know 'cept some white man made it, I guess."

Knowing that further conversation would only fuel his curiosity, she decided to bring it to a halt.

"Eat dat food! Don' ask no mo' questions."

Emanuel obeyed. His mind was already far away from this little one-room shack, away from the stale ho-cake and tough, greasy meat, away from the slave yards that were the harbingers of so much work. His mind was on the piano and the beautiful music it made.

As always, he had more questions, but he knew there would be no more answers that day.

CHAPTER FIFTEEN

April 9, 1843

Dear Auntie Mame,

Why must it be that every time I stain your pages my heart carries the tone of unhappiness. This seems like such a poor use for, if not an abuse of, a diary. I can find no logic in my attempts to record in private my own unhappiness. But, I do. Again, I must say to you that without your willing companionship, by now, I would most certainly be of unsound mind.

At times, I feel the greatest contempt for my husband. I share his bed but not his thoughts; I share his life, but cannot participate in his will to achieve. Yet, at other times, I feel that it is he who should have contempt for me, because I am the one who remains barren. But I find myself existing in a society that will not allow measurement of a woman who cannot bear children. Pretentiousness prevails above all else. God knows that I have tried to consummate that part of my marriage. It would seem, however, that that particular blessing in life is not for me.

But pretentiousness has no bias and indeed it has its role for me. I can't help but believe that my husband finds contentment with the practice of concubinage, even here in his own house. In this society, the kindly ladylike approach is to look the other way and say nothing. Every day that I exist, I am finding this more and more difficult and uncomfortable.

As she wrote in her diary, Kathryn had to stop repeatedly to wipe the tears from her face.

Only once before had she been so lonely, she thought, and that was when she was nine years old and bound for England. She remembered little about her cruise except for how terrified she was. However, in England, she soon found comfort with her aunt, Madame Bartholomew. Later, she would find even more satisfaction in her studies of the piano, her primary interest for several years.

Her tears nearly dry, Kathryn suddenly remembered one cheerful instance that she could share with her aunt.

On yesterday, I had a rather surprising experience with one of the younger slave boys. The scenario to the unknowing eye would have suggested that the little boy was hungry and after a piece of chicken from the kitchen. Indeed, this was the suggestion offered by my maid-servant, Gertie. But I think not. I believe that the youngster crept to the innermost parts of the house searching for the music that he heard on the piano.

Yes, I'm almost sure of it. You see, if I am not mistaken, and I don't think that I am, I have discovered this boy hidden behind the big oak tree outside the music room, listening to me play the piano. I believe that I have seen him move his limbs to the beat of the music.

Quite by chance, on one occasion, the boy was so engrossed in the music that I believe that he forgot to be on the lookout for my observance of him. When he realized my discovery of him he scampered away like a frightened rabbit.

I find it unusual, if not extraordinary, that the one person in this area, of an uneducated class, who shows interest in the classics and the music I would so love to teach and share with all of Charleston, is a lowly slave boy. I have no reason to believe that he would understand anything more than the most basic music which so often seems to usher his people into shouting frenzies.

Even so, it might prove strategic to find the boy duties within the confines of the house. I could use a good fan boy. The hot days of April are almost unbearable. In any case, it seems that the boy will be of little good in the yards since he himself has designated as his prime duty to listen to me play the piano. That's it, I shall have him be my personal fan boy. I can imagine that he would approach the job with much vigor, especially if I play while he fans.

At last, Kathryn smiled.

CHAPTER SIXTEEN

As often as not, William and Kathryn slept in separate bedrooms. Tonight he lay atop his bed, fully clothed. Hands clasped behind his head, he stared at the ceiling. His thoughts centered on trying to decide what to do with his future, specifically whether he should throw his hat into the political ring. He had little experience, but he reasoned he was as capable as anybody else. After all, it was the Northerners and President Van Buren that allowed for the Depression of 1837. Banks had declared bankruptcy at an alarming rate in Northern states. To say the attitude on Wall Street was one of hysteria was to be kind. Stocks dived to the point of worthlessness. In New York City, real estate depreciated by some $40 million, and some 20,000 workers were laid off their jobs. If that was not enough to jolt the nation into realizing it needed new leadership, anti-slavery sentiment was increasing, largely due to the relentless efforts of a former president and current member of the House of Representatives, John Quincy Adams.

William realized his pro-slavery advocacy throughout the North had been met by an increasing anti-slavery effort.

Abolitionist journals and newspapers such as *The Liberator, Emancipator, Philanthropist,* and *The Evangelist* continued to grow. For whatever reason, all factions of the Union were crying out for a change. The medium of that change was to be the Whig Party, whose slogan was "Every breeze says change. The cry, the universal cry, is for change." With the chant, "Tippecanoe and Tyler too" still on their lips, the American people swept William H. Harrison into the White House along with his second-in-command, John Tyler. One month later, the nation mourned Harrison's untimely death, and Tyler became president.

Southerners like William agreed that the Whig Party's offerings were the lesser of two evils, but they were far from satisfied with those. Maybe the time was right for a new leader—with Southern interests at heart—to emerge.

William felt the need to share his thoughts with somebody before he made a decision. He ruled out Kathryn immediately; they no longer communicated well and, besides, she was a woman.

Maybe I could talk with David, he thought. We have never been close, and that may be more of a reason for him to respond candidly.

William decided to pay David a visit first thing in the morning.

David looked up from his writing table as his brother strode into the study. He was finishing up a letter to a friend in Philadelphia.

"Why, dear brother William, what a surprise! It isn't often that I have the pleasure of a visit from you," David said.

"All right, David," William said brusquely, "you can cut the pretense. There is no reason for you to be overjoyed at seeing me. May I have a drink?" William said as he settled into a nearby chair.

153

"Sure thing, it's still your plantation," David replied. He directed the house boy to bring refreshments.

"Now, dear brother, to what do I owe the honor of this visit?"

The servant returned quickly with drinks for the men. William took a sip and looked at his brother.

"I'm not here for trouble, David, I simply want to talk, or mention something, about my plans and I need someone to listen.

"Not Kathryn, because I'm not so sure a woman would understand."

"Well, what's on your mind?" David asked.

"I'm thinking of running for Congress in the 1844 elections."

"That's great! But I don't understand what that has to do with me."

"Nothing," William said. "I just wanted to share my decision with somebody."

"Oh, I see," David replied.

"It will mean even more time away from the plantation . . . I'm away so much as it is. I'll admit that I had reservations about your returning to Charleston, not to mention your taking over the day-to-day operations. But you've done a good job. I couldn't have done better myself. I don't really feel that I'll be missed, and it will give me a chance to do some of the things I've always wanted to do."

"If you are successful," David told him, "it will mean that you will have to move to Washington."

"Yes, I know."

"Have you spoken to Kathryn about this?"

"No, no, I haven't," William said, "but I believe she will give me her full support. She can come to Washington with me and return to Lake Holler as she wishes."

"Well, well, big brother. Looks like you've got it all figured out. You can depend on me to keep Lake Holler running in your absence."

David paused.

"Funny, isn't it?"

"What do you mean?" William inquired.

"You know, how life can reverse our roles over time."

William was now truly puzzled.

"I don't understand what you mean."

"Well, now you will be the prodigal son of sorts and I will be sending you the stipend!" David said with a touch of vengeance.

At first, William didn't know how to take his brother's statement, but bickering with David somehow didn't seem so important anymore, so he managed a halfhearted smile.

"I guess you are right."

William stood.

"I'd best be on my way to Charleston if I'm to return by tomorrow."

"You are going into Charleston now?" asked David.

William nodded.

"Perhaps you can drop a letter off for me at the post office. It will take me just a minute to finish it."

"Sure will," William said. "I'll wait on the veranda while you complete it."

William left a few minutes later with David's letter in hand. From the porch, Tom Baldwin watched as William rode off in his carriage, holding one of David's familiar envelopes.

He met David on the porch.

"Was that one of the special letters?" Tom asked.

"Yes, it is."

"But, Boss, is that wise, knowing your brother's beliefs and all? He'll surely read it."

David smiled.

"Tom, that's the beauty of it all. He will read every word and not understand one bit of the message. I even took the liberty of not sealing it too tightly so he can re-paste it without much difficulty. Even if he researches the background of the member to which the letter is being sent, he will find nothing."

David massaged Tom Baldwin's shoulders as he directed him into the house.

"Come, my friend, let's have an early-morning toast to the continued success of our venture."

William was barely past the new slave cabins, alongside of which grew the most beautiful roses, before he broke the seal of the letter and began to read.

> *Dear Friend, Elijah Pennymaker:*
>
> *I hope that my thoughts and these few printed words will find you well. You will be glad to hear that I have been nurtured into the finest of Southern gentlemen, and I find myself liking the position and status accorded me. Much to the surprise of all Charleston, my brother included, I have found myself, and no longer do I spend a life of frivolity such as when you knew me in Philadelphia. I am studious in every way and I follow my records so that not a ledger falls out of balance, nor a bill goes unpaid. I would say this to no one but you, but I feel that much of my success is due to lack of fellowship with the spirits of the bottle.*
>
> *Before I close, I should like to take the liberty of inviting you to visit Charleston at your leisure to see for yourself. If I must say so myself, I deem myself a credit to*

the beautiful plantation I serve.

A friend forever,

David Littlejohn

P. S. Would you believe that right in the courtyard of the plantation, right up to the month of November, the roses are in full bloom?

It was weeks later before Elijah Pennymaker received the letter. He smiled as he read the message. He would have to send a directive to all the stations to be on the alert for a shipment—a shipment of escaped slaves. They would arrive in Philadelphia not later than November.

BOOK THREE

CHAPTER SEVENTEEN

Early on this April morning, the cool breezes were already giving way to stifling hot air. On the first day that Emanuel was to begin his duties within the plantation house, Gertie had already apprised him of his duties. It was the Missus's habit to practice early in the morning before the air became hot and unbearable. He was to see to her every need during this period.

At the moment, there was nobody in the room but him. And, of course, there was the piano. He had memorized the instrument after his earlier brief encounter. He remembered the big white teeth in front of the big black teeth and that there were more white ones than black ones. He wondered why. So many times he had pictured this big box-like frame as he'd tried to fall asleep. He wondered how it produced the pretty sounds that now rang out in his head almost continuously.

Every day since Gertie had caught him in the Big House, he found himself mimicking the sounds with his mouth. He growled to make the low-pitched sounds of the base notes. He hummed softly, in the highest tone his vocal chords could produce, to mimic the higher tones. What would happen if he pressed the pretty white teeth, he thought. He dared not . . . not yet.

Briefly, he remembered what his mother had said about the piano biting off little slave boys' fingers. It took only the few moments that he had alone with this great instrument to realize that it was not designed to do harm. Whenever he got the chance and was certain of not being discovered, he would have to touch it. It was just that important to him.

Missy Kathryn entered the room. She seemed to not notice him, but he couldn't help but notice her. How he wanted to take a long look at this magnificently beautiful woman, but he knew slaves were not to stare at whites, nor look them straight in the eye.

"It's going to be another hot day," she said to Gertie, who'd followed her into the room.

"Yes, Ma'am, it sho is."

Neither she nor Gertie looked at or said anything to him.

But this time, Emanuel didn't feel out of place because he had been ordered there by Missy Kathryn. She had asked for a fan boy and, more important, she had requested him. He was elated, and thought that there could be no greater event in his life than to have a job that would allow him to hear and be near the piano.

"Gertie, would you get Emanuel a peacock feather?"

"Yes'm."

Gertie ambled out of the room and soon returned with a large multicolored feather. Emanuel knew quite well how to use it as he listened to Gertie's quick instructions.

"Na yo' stand ober dere by dis winda, boy, an' yo' fans dis cool air on Missy Kathryn. Don't yo' move till she tells yo' ta."

He did as he was instructed. Standing there, he watched as the Missus raised the seat of the piano stool and began to fumble through all sorts of papers. He saw all the lines and funny symbols as she sat before the piano and discerned that somehow all those funny marks told her what sounds to make, or what tooth to touch. His arms grew tired as he fanned the air, but he knew he couldn't stop until he was told, even if he wanted to—which he didn't.

The Missus was turned partly away from him so that he faced her back. This suited him fine because he could look directly at everything and no one would notice. His eyes, for the most part, were glued to the piano keys as he watched the Missus's nimble fingers dance from one end of the instrument to the other. Until now, Emanuel watched and listened to the many sounds: high-pitched, low-pitched, and others somewhere between.

He had never heard this type of music in the slave yards; he had never heard his mother sing it. Did he like it? Yes. Because it came from the piano!

That night, he lay awake till the early-morning hours.

Gertie had made a makeshift bed in the pantry behind the kitchen, which served as his bedroom. There were shelves from the bottom of the floor all the way to the ceiling and each row was lined with jars of food. Looking at the pantry, he couldn't help but remember the many times he had been hungry.

Why did this have to be, he thought, with so much food available in this house? More than once he remembered his mother eating only bread, and giving him some along with a tiny piece of meat. He also wondered why she always prayed before each meager helping. But Emanuel learned very early that not saying the blessing meant being denied a meal. How well he remembered his mother's voice as she sang a prayer:

"Lawd, me and ma boy sits grateful befo' dis small 'mount o' food dat yo' hab sent ta satisfy de hunga in de stomachs. Not gonna ask why de 'mount so small or de

*taste so bitter. I pray, Lawd, dat whateva' de 'mount or
how bitter de taste, dat yo' accept ma tanks fo' dis.
Amen."*

Emanuel eased off his bed and walked slowly past the shelves
and stood under a small window. Again and again, he picked up
a jar and held it close to the window to examine it in the
moonlight. He identified beans, corn, okra, tomatoes, peaches,
apples, rice, and flour. There was barely enough room in the
pantry for all of the food. Again, he thought of his mother and
how her prayers would be answered if she had a fraction of this
food. He decided then and there that the Lord must have put him
in this room for a reason, and that reason was to get his mother
some food.

Maybe Ma was right, he thought, maybe the Lord does answer
prayers.

Emanuel returned to his bed, where he began devising a plan.
Once a week, he would sneak one or two jars of food to his
mother. Each time, he would bring the jars he had taken—
washed, of course—to store among the empties he had noticed
on one of the shelves. His mother would no longer have to give
her food to him anymore. He would see to it that she had some as
often as he could.

As he tried to will himself to sleep, his thoughts turned to the
sounds he had heard that day. Soon, he was humming the music
just as he had heard it. Today, for the first time, he had been up
close and alongside the piano. He had heard the Missus play, had
watched her nimble fingers touch the teeth. His ears had listened
to unfamiliar music that rang out clearly in his mind as if he'd
composed it himself. He had heard a name, a name somehow
connected to the music the Missus played. The name was
Mozart.

The Missus had said it after she finished playing the new music.

"Mozart's genius will surpass the length of time," she'd said.

Who was this Mozart, Emanuel wondered. He remembered that there was some writing at the top of the page with all the funny symbols and marks. More than ever before, Emanuel wanted to know how to read and write. But he couldn't nor could his mother, who had taught him a few letters of the alphabet and two or three words like "and," "the," and "God." He had seen one of the letters that he was taught, the letter "o," but there were other letters he did not recognize. Emanuel decided that whatever it took, he was going to learn the rest of the alphabet so he could know what the words and funny symbols on the paper meant.

Emanuel struggled to remember two words before he drifted off to sleep. What were they? What were the words she had used for the paper the music was written on? He pieced them together in his head and tried to say them before falling asleep. Finally he remembered.

"Sheet music," he mumbled. Then he fell into an anxious sleep.

Emanuel awakened a short time later, eagerly anticipating the new day's session. But on this morning, there was no music.

As near as he could figure, the Massah had returned that night and was sleeping late; the music would be too much of a disturbance. Emanuel wondered how such pretty music could disturb anyone.

Emanuel was deeply fearful of being around the master.

Although he lived on his plantation, he had only had a few encounters with this white man, and those were too many. These days, the mere mention of his name filled Emanuel's thoughts with hate.

You killed my pa, he thought, *and someday I'll kill you.*

When the master finally descended the stairs for breakfast, he hardly noticed Emanuel, much to the boy's satisfaction. As he and the mistress ate, Emanuel resumed his duty with the peacock fan. He felt a little more at ease in the household since his presence attracted so little attention. Emanuel acted as disinterested as he could, but by nature he was the type who would try to understand what was going on around him—including conversation—and he had excellent powers of recall.

"How was your trip, William?" Kathryn asked after a long silence.

"Nothing exciting. Speeches, dinners, conferences, the usual," William replied. "By the next election, I hope to be as well-known throughout the South as I am in Charleston."

"So you intend to proceed with this idea of becoming a congressman?"

"Yes, yes I do. You act as if you want me to give up the idea."

"Oh, I don't know. It's just that over the past few years, you and I have grown so very far apart and we hardly see each other now. And if you are elected to the Congress, we will see each other even less. There seems to be such little time to grow and revitalize what we once had."

"Kathryn, we have been through this before," he said wearily. "Now, my mind is made up."

"Yes, I can see that."

William didn't want to argue. He decided, after observing Kathryn's unhappiness with his decision, to change the subject.

"Gertie, would you bring the package that I brought Mrs. Littlejohn?"

"Yassah, I thought you'd neba ask," Gertie said as she disappeared from the room. She returned with a package containing sheets of music. Emanuel tried to watch as closely as he could as the Missus examined her gift.

"Oh! Beethoven! Where did you find these?" she asked, her eyes shining.

William was pleased with her reaction.

"It's supposed to be the very latest from England with most of the compositions destined to become classics. I made the purchase at Siegler's as I was browsing in Charleston. I thought you might like it."

"Ay! Beethoven. How rapidly he became one of my favorites. Do you know, William, that at one time I aspired to dedicate my life to the writing of beautiful music such as is written by the Bachs, Beethovens, Mozarts, and Handels of this world; but that was before I met you, of course, and certainly that became more of a dream than a reality . . . "

Kathryn's voice trailed off. " . . . just a dream."

Emanuel detected a bit of emptiness—something missing or incomplete about her life. But no matter, that was not his concern. However, the new name he'd heard was because it appeared to have something to do with the music. He listened attentively, hoping to hear it again.

"Beethoven died the year before I left England," Kathryn continued. "All of Europe was in mourning over the loss of such a great, talented musician. It was the topic of conversation at every tea and in the headlines of every newspaper."

She paused.

"I don't know why, but it seems that so many of our great composers die young."

Beethoven, Beethoven, Beethoven. Emanuel mumbled the name under his breath. Who was this man? Why did he mean so much to the Missus? Apparently, she only knew him through his music. Was music this powerful, this great that it was listened to from one country to another? So powerful that even after a person was dead, he and his music would be remembered. Why?

William's words interrupted his thoughts.

"There you have it," he said to Kathryn. "They die young, eccentric, reclusive men who spent their lives, their short lives, seeking the essence of life through an art form like music. The very idea bespeaks a certain, but necessary, amount of unhappiness and loneliness, don't you think? Surely, Kathryn, you can't compare that with what you have here."

"Well, William," Kathryn began, "if comparisons are in order, then it seems that loneliness is an agent of both worlds. I chose marriage and the life of a plantation mistress over a musical career because I met someone whom I love very much. But I think the loneliness that is felt by great artists and musicians is also felt by the wives of plantation owners. I thank God for such genteel pastimes to entertain myself with when you are away."

Kathryn's tone was now short and cutting. William had heard it before and didn't like it. It represented the kind of independent thought that a Southern wife wasn't supposed to have.

Long ago, he'd decided that it was a result of Kathryn's English tutelage. He'd also decided that if there was ever a girl child born of this marriage, she was to be reared in Charleston only, where good manners and breeding would be instilled from day one.

"What am I to do, Kathryn? I have a position of responsibility and leadership in this community. Moreover, it is my duty, along with all the other plantation owners, to protect our way of life. Your father and my father were willing to give their lives to build this noble way of life, and so am I."

"Yes," Kathryn said. "I agree with that. But what am I to do? Sit idly by and let emotions, forethought, pride, and anger about this beautiful countryside reside solely within the mind of the man? It's just that kind of reasoning that discouraged me, and I'm sure other women, from seeking careers in music or anything else. You see, our pride and anger is to be replaced by flippancy and nonchalance, the essentials expected in the makeup of a well-bred Southern lady. Well, I maintain that we have emotions about this great Southern land that we nurture and live on. We ought to be heard. But we have no voice."

William viewed Kathryn's position as nothing more than defiance, and it made him angry.

"A true, well-bred Southern woman from Charleston would know her proper place. It is not your place to make political decisions or fill the offices of government, but it is your God-given duty to make the decisions of home and bear children.

"It is not your right to decide who shall fill public office, but rather your duty to direct the house-slave in the common duties of home as suits his abilities. It is not your place to exact or enforce the laws of the land, but rather to provide for and see to the comfort of the male members of the gentry. Any well-bred Charleston woman would know that this is her place and not have to be told."

By the time William had completed his fiery discourse, he had stood and angrily stormed out of the room.

There was nothing left for Kathryn to say and, at this point, no one for her to say it to. But she knew that if William's words were supposed to be an accurate description of a true Southern lady, then she did not fit the mold.

After their confrontational breakfast, Emanuel noticed a change in Missy Kathryn's attitude toward her husband, and that the distance between the two was growing.

There was another change that pleased Emanuel even more: the burgeoning relationship between him and Missy Kathryn. One morning, the mistress sat at her piano, staring into space. Then she turned toward Emanuel.

"Emanuel, put down the fan and come sit here beside me," she ordered.

Emanuel was stunned at first and thought he was surely hearing things. He kept his place, feather in hand and eyes cast at the floor.

"Emanuel," she repeated, pulling the feathers to get his attention. "Put down this fan and come sit here beside me."

There was no mistake. This was no dream, he thought. But this white woman is going crazy.

Slowly, he did what he was told. He perched on the very edge of the stool, as far as he could get from Missy Kathryn without falling on the floor. She put her arms on his shoulders and pulled him close.

"Emanuel, that's such a nice name. Where did you get it?"

He paused a moment while looking at his feet.

"Me ma says ma name come fom de Bible. She say 'cuz I's special."

"And that you are," replied Kathryn. "How would you like to learn to play the piano?"

Emanuel was so startled that he even looked up from the floor, his eyes and mouth stretched wide open.

This white woman has surely lost her mind, he thought.

After a second or two, he managed to respond.

"Me?"

Kathryn nodded.

"Yes, you."

From that day on, Emanuel's life took a 180-degree turn and his relationship with Missy Kathryn would never again be one of just slave boy and mistress. It also became student and teacher.

During the first lesson, Gertie stumbled into the room. She was so shocked at what she saw that she hurried to the other side of the piano.

"Missy Kathryn! What dat li'l nigga boy doin' sittin' beside yo'? Let me knock him off dat seat fo' yo'."

"You will do no such thing,'" Kathryn replied. "I'm going to teach Emanuel to play the piano."

This time, Gertie was shocked into speechlessness. Then, she felt a searing hatred for this little boy who was about to be given privileges in a house that was under her control.

Jonathan heard all the commotion and entered the music room to see what was happening.

Kathryn turned to them and issued a stern order.

"When Master Littlejohn is out of this house, which seems to be most of the time nowadays, I shall teach Emanuel to play piano, as best I can. If Master Littlejohn hears one word about this from you or anybody else, I'll have you both flogged. Do you understand?"

"Yes'm, Missy Kathryn," said Gertie.

"Yes'm, Missy Kathryn," said Jonathan, displaying a wide, toothless grin about this turn of events. For most of the day, Jonathan was elated, and he saw to the comfort of Missy Kathryn and Emanuel without having to be asked.

Emanuel's first lesson was a simple one. Amongst other things, he learned that the black and white teeth were called "keys."

Winnie developed much envy for Bertram's relationship with his father. She often wondered what they said to each other behind the closed doors of the study. There were few secrets between Winnie and Bertram, but he never talked with her about his conversations with his father. She felt it was one of the few things Bertram held sacred, so, after a while, she stopped asking him to tell her what went on.

Winnie became more and more curious about her own father.

First of all, did she have one? She had accepted the fact that she was a slave and she had noticed that not too many slaves seemed to have fathers. One day, she approached her mother about the subject as she sat darning socks for Bertram and the master.

Winnie had always felt that her mother was a beautiful, brown-skinned woman. Surely, there must have been a man in her life at some time.

"Ma?" said Winnie.

"Yes, Winnie, what is it?" asked Teresa.

"Do I have, uh, have I ever had a father?"

"Yes, you had a father. All li'l children have had fathers or they wouldn't be here," Teresa said.

"Tell me about my father. Why isn't he here?"

"He would be if he could, Winnie, but he can't."

Teresa had nurtured her own fantasy about her relationship with William. It was one that satisfied all her needs for love, and was so real to her that she nearly jumped at the chance to talk of it to anyone who would listen.

"Your father was a proud, good looking white man who sat on a horse in such a way that it would make you fall humble to your knees at the sight of him, and he loved me. I know he did, and if this mean old world had given him and me a chance, we would still be together," said Teresa.

"Does he know about me?" Winnie asked. "Does he love me?"

"Sure he does. He is the one that found this place for you and me. He wanted to see to our comfort and make sure that nothing would ever happen to us. If he could, I know he would come get us and take us away with him and care for us."

Winnie was mesmerized.

"My father. He sounds like such a good man. I would like so much to know him," she told her mother.

"Yes. He was a good man. A good white man. That means that

you have half-white blood, and don't forget it. Who knows? Maybe one day you'll meet up with a fine white buck who ain't ashamed of a colored girl."

But Teresa issued a warning, this time in little-used slave dialect.

"You just remember that you wants you a white man—dat takes baths and sleeps on clean white sheets. You ain't fo' those nigga mens and don't have nothing to do with them 'cuz they ain't no good and they ain't got nothing. You remember that."

"Yes, Ma'am," Winnie said dutifully.

Teresa leaned over to caress Winnie's silky, long strands of hair.

"You know a body has to look mighty close at you to know whether you nigga or white. You inherited your father's skin color and I'll bet up north, nobody would even know the difference. Maybe one day you'll git to the North and find you a nice, white man that will take care of you."

But Winnie wasn't interested in the future.

"Ma, tell me more about my pa."

"Child, you done been around Bertram so much you even sounds like a white child—talk and all."

Teresa finally began to answer Winnie's question.

"Oh! There ain't much else to tell 'bout him 'cept he sho' loved him some Teresa and, oh, dat man sho' liked to use cotton in a funny sort of way."

"Cotton? What did he do with cotton that was so funny?" Winnie asked, puzzled.

That question finally brought Teresa out of her make-believe world.

"Na you hush up and stop asking me so many questions. I ain't never gonna git finished with this sewing if you keep talking."

For the rest of the day, Winnie wondered what her mother had meant when she'd talked about the cotton. Maybe I'll find out one day, Winnie mused. She probably could, if only she had some clue as to her father's whereabouts.

CHAPTER EIGHTEEN

Late one night, Emanuel lay on his cot with his eyes closed, jerking his foot back and forth to a silent rhythm. The room was dark, except for a brief hint of light from the small window over his bed. Suddenly, he heard a knock at the door. Before he could speak, the door opened and Jonathan entered. He had something long and white in his left hand, and a second object of some sort in the other.

"Jon'than," Emanuel said, "what's wrong?"

"There ain't nothing wrong," Jonathan assured him. "As a matter of fact, things been more right around here since you come into this house than they ever been before."

Jonathan positioned himself at the end of Emanuel's cot. Then he took a match from his pants pocket and lit the candle he'd brought.

Emanuel was completely puzzled.

"What yo' doin'?" he asked.

"What I'm about to do is give you your first reading lesson," Jonathan said. "You must promise that you will never tell anybody, and that includes old big mouth Gertie. Can't learn the piano if you can't read."

Emanuel was pleasantly surprised. Though Jonathan's words were a bit slurred and his voice raspy, Emanuel was suddenly aware that he sounded kind of like white folks when he talked. It never occurred to him that Jonathan spoke that way because he knew how to read.

"Me promise," said Emanuel.

"No, it is 'I promise'," Jonathan said. "Say it, Follow me. Together, now . . . "

"I promise," they said in unison.

"That's better," Jonathan said with a nod of approval. "Good."

Then Jonathan revealed the second object in his other hand: a book with faded covers.

"Whud book is dat?" asked Emanuel.

"It's a reading speller," replied Jonathan. "I've had this old book hidden away for years. It's what I used to learn to read and after tonight, it will be yours."

They huddled together close by the candlelight and Jonathan began his lesson.

"Now, repeat after me," Jonathan said. "A, B, C, D, E . . . "

Night after night, when everyone else was asleep, Emanuel and Jonathan would meet to read from the speller. To Jonathan's surprise, Emanuel was not only a willing student but a very capable one. On occasion, when his meetings with Jonathan ended early, Emanuel would pretend to fall asleep while Jonathan was in the room. After he left, and Emanuel was sure that everyone, including Jonathan, was asleep, he would practice his reading alone.

For Emanuel, nighttime quickly became a wondrous period that opened up the worlds of words and music.

In his mind, he'd create little rhymes to bring the alphabet to life. He worked diligently at learning new words one at a time.

Music. M-u-s-i-c, he thought.

Piano. P-i-a-n-o.

Mozart. M-o-z-a-r-t.

On the few nights that he grew tired of reading, Emanuel would sneak into the music room and sit on the piano stool, silently mimicking what he had learned from Missy Kathryn that day. He could hear the notes ringing out in his head. Already, he knew the sound of each note and the pitch of every key by heart.

He was soon introduced to chord structure and the sounds of notes played in combination, and quickly memorized the dominant chords.

With his newly acquired reading skills, plus instruction from Missy Kathryn, it wasn't long before he knew all the major scales and chords.

No matter what he did—be it his daytime chores or his nighttime reading lessons—music played a recurring role in his thoughts. Phrases like *tonic chord, dominant chord, first and second inversion* seemed to have a bewitching hold on him.

Quietly, as he went about his duties, he moved his lips to form such words as *adagio, largo, diminuendo, arpeggio,* and *legato.* Such strange, pretty words, he thought. Missy Kathryn told him that the meaning of the word *piano* was *soft.* To Emanuel, that seemed an insufficient definition for such a beautiful, majestic instrument. "Soft and sweet," "soft and pretty" were more appropriate descriptions of his beloved piano.

At one point, Emanuel became so engrossed in his thirst for musical knowledge that he grew discouraged with his progress, which he thought was lagging. Every time he mastered one technique, Missy Kathryn would come up with another that was more difficult. Late one night while in

Jonathan's company, he shared his frustration with his old friend.

"I don't guess I'll ever be able to play the piano like Missy Kathryn or know all the music there is, will I, Jonathan?" asked Emanuel.

"Not with an attitude like that you won't," Jonathan said disapprovingly. "You are doing a fine job and the Missus has said as much."

"Has she?" Emanuel asked. "Has she, Jonathan?"

"She certainly has," he replied. "You have talent beyond most folks when it comes to playing the piano. I know, the Missus knows, even old Gertie knows. You are blessed with a talent, boy, and you must use it and never be discouraged."

"Doesn't everybody have some talent?" Emanuel asked.

"I reckon they do—for something, I guess. But most people spends their whole life looking for the one special thing that they can do and they never finds it. I s'pose that's what happened to me. I kept looking and looking for my talent and I never found it, yet."

Jonathan looked a little sad.

"Maybe you didn't look in the right place," Emanuel said. He felt sympathy for his friend.

"Maybe so, but I sho' did try," Jonathan replied. "I ran away every chance I got 'til I done got so old that I can't run no more and 'til ol' Massah Littlejohn pulled every tooth out of my head, trying to make me do right. That's the reason my mouth is as bare as an ol' skin't rabbit. But I can't say it wasn't fun experiencing a little freedom. I got no regrets."

Emanuel wasn't so sure.

"Don't seem right to me," he said.

"What don't seem right?"

"Why nigga folks got to be slaves."

"I don't know if I can answer that, Emanuel."

"Well," the boy said again, "it just don't seem right."

Jonathan struggled to come up with an answer. Finally, he spoke.

"Don't you worry none; one day us colored folks gonna be free as a bird. I know we are. It ain't natural. It just ain't natural to keep a man born with freedom in his heart all tied up so's he can't do nothing for hisself. If you takes an ol' dog and ties him up, he keeps on trying to git aloose and when he stops tryin', he ain't no good. The white man expects niggas to stay tied up, but at the same time keep his spirit up when it comes time to do. And we just like that ol' dog. If you keep us tied and we gits away and we git caught and tied up again, after a while we gives up and then we ain't much good no mo'. Just like that ol' dog."

The whole thing still seemed so unfair to Emanuel. He decided to change the subject.

"You know what?" he asked Jonathan. "You promise and cross your heart to die that you won't tell nobody?"

"I promise."

"My ma kin sing better than anybody in the whole world, but you promised not to tell nobody," Emanuel said.

"I won't tell," Jonathan promised.

"Ever since I kin remember, when we were alone she would make up little songs and sing to me. But she would only sing to me and Ole Nanna when she was alive. Sometime I use to feel real bad when something happened, and just to hear her voice would make me feel much better inside."

Jonathan smiled.

"I didn't know that Bell could sing," he said. "She kept it a secret all these years."

"You promised not to tell."

"I know. It'll be yo's and my secret," Jonathan promised again.

"She say dat her voice is hers. It don't belongst to the Massah or nobody else and that's the only thing she can call her own and she only gonna use it when she wants to," Emanuel added.

"You love yo' ma very much, don't you?" Jonathan asked.

"Yeh, she all I got," the child replied.

After Jonathan left his room that night, Emanuel lay back on his cot, staring into the darkness. In an effort to stay awake, he replayed all of Jonathan's words in his mind. Later, when he was sure everyone was asleep, he would raid the kitchen, gathering whatever small parcel of food Gertie was sure to not miss so he could take it to his mother.

It was after midnight. David was bending over an injured escapee who lay on the ground near one of the cabins. The black man's clothes were all but torn away and the front of his body was covered with blood and nearly stripped of all its skin.

Maybe he'd committed the crime of running away, or had defied his master some other way. Whatever the reason, the penalty for his actions had been the treadmill—a round, wooden wheel that revolved against the front of his body while he was suspended in the air with his arms tied to an overhanging apparatus.

"How bad is he?" asked Tom Baldwin.

"Looks pretty bad," David replied. "If he lives, it will be a long time before he can travel."

"Look at his toes, his knees, his chest, and forehead, all on the front of his body. You know what that means?" Tom asked.

"Yeh. The treadmill. Damn it. How could anybody do this to another human being?"

"I guess that's the problem, David," Tom replied. "They aren't considered human beings by most. Just animals that happen to walk on two legs."

Tom squatted beside the wretched slave, cradling his head in his arms. He moaned in agony before taking his last shallow breaths.

"Well, David," Tom Baldwin said quietly, "looks like we won't have to worry about this one. He's dead."

Kathryn was especially lonely today. Again, William was away on one of his political campaigns. She dispatched Jonathan to fetch her carriage so she could pay a visit to what was once her father's plantation. As Kathryn prepared for the short ride, she tried to convince herself that this was an innocent trip. She knew better. She wanted to see David, talk to him, feel his presence. This would entail meaningless inquiries about the plantation, which she knew was in fine shape. But such conversation, however meaningless, was more than she had at home.

For the first time, Kathryn noticed the slave cabins that had been built along the main entrance to the mansion. How odd, she thought, that David would put them in such a conspicuous location.

As Kathryn's carriage pulled up to the front porch, the house boy opened the door and stood at attention.

"Good morning, Missy Kathryn," he said.

"Good morning, Claud," she replied. "Where is Mister Little-john?"

"He's in his study, Ma'am. Come wid me and I'll let him know dat yo's here."

"Oh, that's all right, Claud," Kathryn said. "I want to surprise him. You go about your work and I'll kind of sneak up on him."

"Yes'm," Claud replied, then he disappeared.

Kathryn walked around to the study and entered, but David wasn't there. Instantly, she was struck by the memories that came rushing back as she stood in the room. It had been her father's favorite place—a place where he could be alone or talk plantation business, or politics. She had enjoyed the many occasions when she'd sat on her father's knee and listened to him tell stories. It didn't seem important or odd then, but she almost never saw her mother in this room, and if she did, she never sat down or stayed any length of time. Now Kathryn was a plantation wife with her own husband and while she had freedom at her house in William's absence, it was considered improper for the mistress to disturb the confines of the study. She often thought the chambermaid had more freedom in this room than the plantation wife. Now that she was fully grown, she wondered whether her father—if he were still living—would permit her to spend time in his study.

Kathryn began to browse and soon made her way to the sturdy oak desk that her father had used for so many years. She spotted his familiar inkwell and pen next to a stack of newspapers.

Kathryn moved in for a closer look. On top of the stack was William L. Garrison's *Liberator*. She wondered how it made its way to—of all places—the desk of a plantation owner. Charlestonians considered the possession of such abolitionist material an act of treason. Slowly, Kathryn extended her hand toward the paper.

"It's not nice to peruse someone's desk without permission," said a voice from behind.

Kathryn whirled around to find David leaning calmly against the door to the study, hands folded in front of him.

"I was just reminiscing," Kathryn said quickly, "the desk . . . my father's . . . you know."

"Yes, I know," David said. "I have friends in the North who keep me abreast of those dreaded abolitionists. To fight your enemy, you must know him. Don't you agree?"

Though David hadn't mentioned the paper by name, Kathryn knew what he was talking about.

"Whatever you do, don't let William see that paper," she said. "He would just as soon lynch anyone he saw reading it as he would to ask them why. He hates it with a passion."

David walked past her. When he reached the desk, he picked up the paper and threw it down on top of all the others.

"It's a piece of worthless junk," he said contemptuously. "I have to agree with my brother, for once. So, why did you come over here?"

"Oh, I don't know. It's been a while since I was over for a visit," Kathryn said.

"Exactly, three weeks and two days." David paused. "Social call or business, or maybe you just wanted to see me?"

Once again, Kathryn admitted to herself that she'd come to see him. Somehow, he made her feel alive. But what she would admit to herself and to the rest of the world were two different things. Kathryn began to feel a bit uncomfortable, as if her visit was wrong. She became aware of how close David was—so close, that she could feel his breath on her neck. He placed his hands on her shoulders to turn her toward him, but Kathryn extended her arms to break his hold. Once free, she took a few steps back.

"I have to go now," she said abruptly.

David was disappointed. He had felt her longing for him, of that he was sure.

"Kathryn," he said as she walked toward the door, "is it so hard for you to say that you miss me and want to see me? Is it that hard?"

She turned around.

"No, it's not hard. As a matter of fact, it would be very easy to say such things. That is the reason I must go."

Once again, Kathryn turned and walked into the hallway.

"Damn," said David. He was determined to not let her go. Racing to the hallway, he grabbed Kathryn's arm and turned her toward him again.

"Now tell me," he said gently. "Tell me you miss me as much as I miss you."

"David, it's not right. Where would this go? I'm married."

"I know you're married to my brother. But where is he?"

He didn't wait for her to respond. "I'll tell you where. He's off on some self-imposed political responsibility to save the world for the South; and you are here alone."

"David," Kathryn cried out, "don't."

"Go on," David shouted as he shook Kathryn by the shoulders, "tell me you miss me. Tell me that the reason why you stay away is because you can't stand to be so near. Tell me!"

"It's true. It's true," she said, her eyes filled with pain.

"So now you know and what can we do about it?"

Kathryn wrestled out of David's grip. Quickly, she opened the door and flew down the porch stairs and into her carriage.

Now her tears flowed freely. She felt like a lonely maiden whose lover was thousands of miles away in some foreign land. Only Kathryn's love—her husband's brother, no less—was just next door. And that made it all the worse.

Later that day, Kathryn composed a letter to her aunt.

October 1843

Dear Auntie Mame,

There seems to be an unpardonable situation developing in my life. Holding true to values and to my Southern-bred instinct, I am a reluctant, but wanting participant in a trilogy that can only lead to disaster for all. Today, I almost embraced and caressed my hus-

band's brother. My desire for him goes much deeper than I should ever have permitted, but so does my love. What shall I do? He is a man of mystery and possessing what some would call a double personality. On the one hand, he would have one believe that he is carefree and flippant, with an aggression toward the bottle; on the other, he has evolved into a responsible southern gentleman, capable of holding two plantations together and functioning. Perhaps it's wrong of me to judge, but I think there are secrets in this man's life that are yet to emerge. No matter, I must be honest with you and tell you that I love him.

Now I must change the subject. Thinking about the matter only depresses me.

Do you remember the little slave boy a while back who displayed so much interest in my playing the piano? His name is Emanuel and he assumed his duties as my fan boy quite well. But beyond that I took the liberty, in secret of course, to take it upon myself to give this youngster instructions in playing the piano. My longings to teach had been frustrated, perhaps by other concerns with my marriage. Nevertheless, in a moment of rebellion, I placed the little fellow at my side and started his instruction. I am astonished and delighted at this boy's talents, for they not only equal, but exceed, the talents of whites, regardless of age or background. His immense talent scares me because I know of nothing that he can do with it. Nevertheless, my rebellious attitude has resulted in many pleasurable moments at the side of this little boy at the piano.

My thoughts about this cruel and unjust system of slavery are changing tremendously. What other talents lie suppressed by dark skin color in the thousands of slave yards throughout the South? What other capabilities exist unnurtured because of the pull of the plow or the dig? From where I sit now, it is an unpardonable act to even suggest that the abilities are the same between the two races. While genius and skill are nurtured amongst the whites, they are equally oppressed amongst the blacks.

But, there appears to be a remarkable new vibrancy taking place in the North. An old word with new exaltation has come forth and that word is abolition. More importantly, there are many women in the forefront of the movement, two of whom originated from Charleston, the Grimke sisters. To mention their names amongst polite Charleston society is to risk punishment.

Abolitionist societies are springing up like weeds. As soon as one is dissolved or battered, another springs forth. It appears that our educational institutions are now feeling the thrust. A few years ago, some students walked out of Lane Theological Seminary in Cincinnati in an abolitionist effort. Later, they formed their own institution and I am pleased to report that, from the first day, they opened their doors to children of slave parentage. Needless to say, such undertakings only encourage my surreptitious efforts to teach perhaps the first colored maestro. That's all for now.

With affections,
Kathryn

P. S. Initially, my intentions were only the basics, but with his abilities, I don't believe a team of horses could keep him away from the classics!

 186

CHAPTER NINETEEN

"**M**ama! Mama! Wake up!" Emanuel shook his mother vigorously.

He had brought her a jar full of freshly canned peaches. He knew she would be hungry; field slaves were always hungry.

"Mama! Mama! Wake up! It's me, Emanuel."

His mother began to come around slowly, and started stirring a little faster when she saw the jar of food.

" 'Manuel?" she asked. "What is yo' don' brought me?"

"Just a jar of peaches, a little bread, and some meat. It's all I could git without ole Gertie missin' it. Here, let me open dem, I mean, them peaches," he said as he twisted the lid off the jar.

The slave yards were a world of negatives and restraints.

You can't do this . . . you can't do that, but whatever you do, it's for the benefit of the master. Emanuel's eyes were now open to a new world—a world of thought and learning, and now that the introduction had been made, there was no turning back.

Emanuel knew his mother had noticed he'd corrected his speech. His actions had sent a strong message: I'm going to take on the challenge of the white man's world. The parcels of food sent yet another message: No matter where I go or what I become, I will never forget that you are my mother and that it was in you that it all began.

Bell was fully aware of the dangers and risks Emanuel was taking. In the past, she had tried to discourage him from bringing food, but the more she scolded, the more he brought.

Now, she simply admonished her son to be careful. The food was welcomed. She especially enjoyed the canned fruit—peaches, apples, pears, apricots, and blackberries. And he always brought smaller parcels of bread and meat, maybe an ear of corn or a nice tomato. Before she took one bite of the food he'd brought, though, Bell would place it before the hearth. No matter how voracious her appetite, she would say a blessing.

> *Dear Lawd,*
>   *Fo' some reason yo' don' seen fit to pervide me wit morsels ob food dat eva'body can't git, don't know why, but it don' happen't. I trus' dat it's yo' will.*
>
>   *Me boy's takin' awful risk bringin' me dese here vittles. I hopes yo' won' see it as stealin', but if yo' do please forgib 'im an' place all da blame on me. Watch 'im, Lawd, guide 'im, Lawd, gib 'im de sign like yo' gave da night he was bon'. Show 'im de way.*
>
>   *Amen.*

Emanuel was a bit bewildered by his mother's prayer ritual. But he knew she was just as determined to bless the food as he was to bring it. Still, he didn't understand how she could have so much faith in the Lord. You couldn't see him or touch him, and he did little to ease the trials and tribulations of black folks. But he knew his mother's faith was unshakable. He wondered if he could ever have that much faith in some Lord.

He sat on the dirt floor in front of his mother, watching her devour the food. Being hungry was such an unnecessary part of being a slave, Emanuel thought. Bell offered some of the food to him, but he declined. Living in the Big House had afforded him the privilege of regular meals. Besides, he didn't know when he would be able to sneak out more.

As he watched his mother gobble down the food, he realized he felt sorry for her. Before moving into the Big House he had never known such a feeling. He remembered Missy Kathryn, how clean she was—how she smelled of sweet perfume, how dainty and soft her hands and feet were. Emanuel wondered how his mother would look with all the dirt and grime washed off, freshly bathed to remove the pungent odor that signaled the presence of a field slave, wearing a clean dress with a lace border. He knew that for his mother, this could never be. But he would see to it that his mother didn't go hungry all the time.

Emanuel watched his mother run her finger along the rim of the now-empty canning jar and stick it into her mouth to suckle.

" 'Manuel, how you like bein' in dat Big House wit all dem white folks?" Bell asked. "You been up dere all dis time."

"I like it fine, Ma, 'specially 'cause me, I mean, I'm a learnin' to play de piano," said Emanuel, remembering the tutelage offered him by Jonathan and Missy Kathryn.

"But 'Manuel, whatcha gon' do when yo' knows how ta play? Yo' is a slave. And fo' as I know dey ain't nobody lookin' fo' slaves dat play de piano," Bell said.

"Maybe not, but still it makes me happy and one day I'm gonna learn to play all the pretty songs like you use to sang to me," Emanuel replied.

"Jes so long as yo' don't tell non o' dem white folks dat I sangs," Bell reminded him. "Ma voice belongs ta me, nobody else."

Emanuel tried to change her mind.

"I bet Miss Kathryn would love to hear you sang. She's a nice lady."

"No, boy," Bell said firmly. "Don't yo' say a word ta dem."

Emanuel concurred with a nod of the head.

"I jus' don' know 'bout yo' learnin' ta play dat thing," Bell continued. "White folks don't like uppity smart niggas. Dems de ones dat gits folk kilt."

"But I'm good at it, Mama. Missy Kathryn says I'm the best she's ever seen."

"Dat's what I's afraid of, dat yo' gon' be good at it," Bell confessed. "But what it gonna git you 'cept a noose aroun' yo' neck? White folks jes don't like uppity smart niggas dat can do what dey do."

Emanuel sought to reassure her.

"Don't worry, Ma. I'll be careful. 'Sides, Miss Kathryn told Jonathan and Gertie dat she would lynch them both if she heard a word 'bout her teachins'."

Bell shook her head.

"Still, jus' don' seem right. Yo' know what dem field hands calls yo'? Dey calls ya 'Piana' and dey treats me like I'm some-body special. All 'cuz dat prophecy when yo' wuz bon'."

"What prophecy?" Emanuel asked.

"De one dat says yo' somebody special 'cuz yo' wuz bon' on de same day as de Lawd and Sav'ur Jesus Christ an' dem ol' slave women belieb it, and when dey git up near de Big House, up near whey yo' use ta hide, dey start ta git a happy feelin' in dey feets and dey starts ta jerkin' and a sangin'. Dey oughts ta be ashamed."

Emanuel smiled a little.

"Piana," he said, "dey calls me P-I-A-N-A."

"Everyone o' dem ol' women, an' de young'uns, too," Bell said. "Every time I heh's dat word, Piana, de fear ob God strikes me. I feel it in ma bones. It'll be de ruin of yo'. I knows it. I kin feel it in ma bones."

"I wish you wouldn't worry 'bout me," Emanuel told his mother. "I'll be all right. You'll see. Besides, I would rather be dead than not learn to play. Dat's how important it is to me."

"It's dat impo'tant ta yo', 'Manuel?" Bell asked as she looked him straight in the eyes.

"Yes'm, it is."

"Eben if'n it kills yo'?"

For a long moment, Emanuel and his mother were quiet. Then Bell pulled her son to her in a long, firm embrace as she whispered in his ear.

"Then yo' learns ta play dat piano as best yo' kin an' yo' mama will be prayin' fo' yo'," Bell said. "Yo' know I'll bet yo' gonna hab a nice, pretty voice ta go 'long wid dat piana pla'in jus' like yo' mama."

"Do you reckon I will?" Emanuel asked. "Do you believe I'm gonna have a pretty voice, too?"

"I reckon so. I can tell, even now, yo' voice is a pretty one. Dat Missy Kathryn gon' teach yo' de piano an' I'se gonna teach yo' ta sang. Dat'll makes yo' a mighty big knot on de tree. Come on, le's do a song."

They sang.

"I'll sing ta yo' 'cause yo' makes me happy.
I'll sing ta yo' 'cause yo' makes me sad.
I'll sing ta yo' 'cause yo' makes up fo' all
dat I lost and some dat I neba had."

"Well, look who the wind don' blew in. If it ain't William Littlejohn. How have you been?" asked Sadie Meyers, a once-beautiful lady with jet black hair and large breasts that commanded attention. She was wearing just a little too much makeup, but this was the accepted way of dress in the bordello that Sadie ran—heavy on the makeup, little to no clothing.

"How are you, Sadie?" William inquired.

"I'm surviving, thanks to good customers like yourself. What will it be tonight? The second or third floor?"

You know the answer to that, Sadie. In all the times that I have been coming here, have I ever changed?"

"No, I guess you haven't," Sadie admitted. "Just thought you might like a different variety tonight. Come on, let me get you a drink before you go up. It will warm you up," Sadie said as she grabbed William's arm and pulled him toward the bar.

"So how is the little wife these days?"

William had had several drinks before his arrival and was feeling a bit loose.

"For a lady of your outstanding social position and character, that question is in very poor taste. But anyhow, she is fine, at least the last time I saw her. I haven't been home in six weeks."

Sadie nodded.

"I hear you're getting to be a big political figure."

"All the way up to governorship one day," William said. "Who knows, maybe even the presidency."

"How nice. Did you ever get that son that you always wanted?"

By now, the liquor had started to take a toll on William's speech.

"Ssssadie, you knows you have a w-w-way of stinging a man's ego right where it hurts and I . . . I think before you ask me another embarrassing question, I'm going to the th . . . third floor."

William staggered off, bumping into other customers as drunk as he was.

"Come on," he waved to Sadie, "maybe you had better help me up the stairs."

Sadie led him to the third floor. All the girls on that floor were black, and those not already busy were standing naked in the hall.

"Jennie," Sadie called out, "take care of Mr. Littlejohn tonight. He is a very special customer."

"Yes'm," Jennie replied, as she curled his arm about her neck and helped him to her room. Once inside, William began to undress with her help, stopping momentarily to throw a ball of cotton on the center of the bed.

"Wake up, 'Manuel."

Bell was shaking her son furiously. She knew he had to go back to the plantation house before anyone discovered his absence.

"Wake up, boy. Yo' gots ta go."

Emanuel yawned and attempted to turn back over onto the bed.

Bell tapped his face lightly with her open palm.

"Wake up, boy."

Finally, Emanuel woke with a start, realizing where he was.

He had been in the plantation house only a matter of months, but he already felt out of place in his mother's shack. His life had taken such a different turn, for the better, he hoped. When he saw his mother's ragged clothes and dirty face, he felt a little guilty because he wasn't here to share some of the misery. Then, he remembered how he could help. Only from within the plantation house could he sneak parcels of food to her. He felt a little better about staying where he was.

Before walking out the door, Emanuel picked up the empty jar that he'd left on a previous visit. Then, he looked back at his mother. He knew that she was about twenty-six years old, but she looked much older. Emanuel wanted to hold her close and tell her how much he loved her, but that would not change a thing, he thought.

"Yo' say yo' learnin' ta read?" Bell asked.

"Yes'm. Jonathan is teaching me."

"Dat's fine. I 'memba ol' Jonathan to be a fine man, not like most slaves dat libs in de Big House dat gits de big head."

"Why'd you ask about de readin'?" Emanuel inquired.

"Oh, no particular reason," she said. "Jes wanted ta know."

Emanuel closed the door behind him as he walked out into the cool, early-morning air. The predawn darkness shielded him as he started to run toward the plantation house. He had to dust himself off and clean himself up before anyone else woke up, so no one would know he had been out. After entering the Big House, he did just that and hurried to his cot. Emanuel could hear Gertie up and about in the kitchen. He closed his eyes, knowing it wouldn't be long before Gertie would enter the pantry to awaken him for help in preparing breakfast.

Rachel Robards had a perplexed look on her face as she watched Bertram and Winnie from the window. They were hard at play in the yard, an almost inseparable pair. She had been against allowing Teresa to keep her child from the beginning. But it was her husband, James, who had the last say. Perhaps he'd had a brief reflection on some verses in the Bible that extolled the virtue of keeping mother and child together, she thought.

Now, day by day, she was growing more and more intolerant of the children's relationship. It was unnatural for a white boy to have such an affection for a slave child, even if the slave child looked white. There was little doubt in her mind now that Winnie's father had been white. Probably, some worthless vagabond, she thought, the kind that was the essence of white trash.

Her patience with the relationship between her son and Winnie had been severely tested this past Sunday, when they'd had out-of-town visitors for dinner. Upon seeing Bertram and Winnie together, a guest replied, "What a beautiful son and daughter you have, Mrs. Robards."

Rachel was flabbergasted to the point that she choked on her food and excused herself momentarily from the dinner table, whereupon her husband corrected the error. Meanwhile, Rachel stormed over to Winnie's mother.

"Teresa, either you keep that child of yours behind closed doors under lock and key, or I will see to it that she is removed from my presence permanently."

Teresa was frightened out of her wits; she knew very well what Rachel had meant. She escorted Winnie to their quarters, whereupon she whipped her while admonishing her at the same time against being seen again until the visitors had left.

Winnie accepted her punishment and cried herself to sleep.

Her understanding of what had happened was not to come until later.

Bertram retaliated by losing his appetite and did not return to the dinner table. Instead, he went to his room as self-imposed punishment for what had happened to Winnie. He would not be seen or heard from for the rest of the day.

CHAPTER TWENTY

Kathryn had always preferred plantation life over that of residing in Charleston. Her visits there were few and usually precipitated by special occasions. Like her father, she risked staying in the country and coming down with the fever during the summer rather than spending time in the city. And having David nearby was yet another reason to maintain year-round residence on the plantation.

Music and managing the household helped keep Kathryn busy. And of course, there was Emanuel, whose progress amazed her. So taken was Kathryn with his abilities that she committed herself to honing the little slave boy's talents even further.

On the plantation, few questions were raised about her music pupil because few were around to ask. Kathryn knew she could always take him to Charleston to continue his tutelage, but the risks of discovery were greater there. In Charleston, too many people spent their days going from house to house on visits—a practice Kathryn found unbearable and intrusive.

William, when he was not on the road trying to build upon his career in politics, was as likely as not to stay in Charleston at his town house. He had all the servants he needed, and had ceased worrying long ago about the day-to-day business of the plantation. He knew David and Kathryn would see to that.

Kathryn often wondered what their father would have thought about such a drastic change of events.

Life in Charleston was busy and exciting, full of near-daily brushes with new and important personages. For William, it made for a much more strategic vantage point to nourish political aspirations. His ambitions were no secret, and under such conditions, William's wife was expected to take care of the plantation. So, few questions were asked about Kathryn's frequent absences from his side, especially with 1844 being an election year.

At times, Kathryn did enjoy the spontaneity and excitement of city life. But by and large, her activities there were restricted to conversations with Charleston's female elite, and she found the social life full of pretense.

During her days on the plantation, Kathryn found solace as she wrote in her bedroom, played or taught music in the music room, or read in the parlor. She developed an unquenchable thirst for the printed word and found delight in the independent thought expressed by women writers. She would go to almost any length to get the latest books. In David, she found a willing cohort who'd bring her the latest literature whenever he traveled to Boston, Philadelphia, or Baltimore.

Over time, David and Kathryn came to realize they had a camaraderie cemented by a thirst for knowledge and reflection on all points of view. They never questioned each other's beliefs on political issues, slavery, abolition, or emancipation, but it went without saying that their inquisitive interests in free thought would not be acceptable amongst polite Charleston society. They kept their reading interests hidden from others; in fact, David was more than happy to provide a hiding place for Kathryn's literature.

Kathryn realized with much anxiety that there was an uneasiness brewing within her soul that was being nourished by the new breed of women writers. She read all the available works of Angelina and Sarah Grimke, including Angelina's *Appeal to Southern Christian Women.* She thought the premier works of Frances Trollope, *Domestic Manners of the Americana,* a bit too harsh, obviously vindictive, but stimulating. She avidly searched for the writings of Harriet Martineau and could never forget her statement that, "The personal oppression of the Negroes is the grossest vice which strikes a stranger in the country."

Nor could she forget another of Martineau's declarations, " . . . the most savage vices that are now heard of in the world take place in the southern and western states of America."

It was no surprise that Kathryn's broad reading selections had affected her own writings. She was no longer marginal or obsequious but more inclined to be opinionated and forceful. Her writings no longer reflected the women who knew and kept to their rightful places; they were now likely to scold and be critical of the status quo. She often wondered what David would say if he saw them. Though she felt certain she had no fear of reprisal from him, she made sure her diary was kept under lock and key.

Kathryn's hunger for literature was matched only by her hunger for music. Her infrequent visits to Charleston always included a stop at the local music store, where she found new music to take back home for Emanuel.

Without realizing it, Kathryn's new feelings and thoughts were influencing the way she taught Emanuel. She became more demanding of the boy and would accept nothing short of perfection. Her doubts of his abilities had long since vanished and she pushed Emanuel to the limit, making him master the basics in record time. His illiteracy had been only a minor obstacle that was overcome through her tutelage and Jonathan's surreptitious aid. After one year, Emanuel had command of the alphabet and numbers, could read most common words, and had a musical vocabulary equal to any white student. Kathryn believed repetition was the key to perfection, so she insisted Emanuel play the same tune over and over again until it satisfied her ears. Then, and only then, would she move on to something else.

Generally, the lessons would begin in early morning before the sun's heat became a hindrance.

"Now, sit, Emanuel," Kathryn would instruct her young student, "and first let's do our finger exercises. Straighten your back and don't stoop."

Emanuel always thought the finger exercises silly; he had long since mastered every major scale and almost never missed a key. His timing meshed perfectly with Kathryn's, and he was eager to move on to a musical composition. No matter, the finger exercises were just as ritualistic as his mother's prayers.

"Make the notes sing," Kathryn would tell him. "A smooth transition from one sound to the other, Emanuel. Make the notes sing out smoothly. Now keep up with me."

Emanuel would oblige her. First, the C-major scale, then G-major, F-major, A-major, E-major, then the same for the minor scales until each had been done. After that, they would move on to chord structures. After all the major chords were reviewed, only then was it time to play a melody. Sometimes, Emanuel's fingers were so tired after these preliminaries that he didn't know if he could go on. Then he'd wonder how Missy Kathryn's delicate, soft fingers could take such abuse and remain so pretty.

After a brief rest, though, Kathryn would press on.

"Emanuel, let's do our first melody," she'd say.

He always felt relief when he heard her say those words because now he could play the music that almost constantly rang out in his head. His favorite piece was the first one he'd ever learned, "My Country 'tis of Thee." The song moved him, and its words rang out cryptically in his mind, arousing passions that were not supposed to be felt by slaves of any age.

My country 'tis of thee;
sweet land of liberty,
of thee I sing.

Land where my father died.
Land of the pilgrims' pride.
From every mountainside,
Let freedom ring.

As often as not, even after the music had stopped, the words continued to resonate in Emanuel's mind—"Let freedom ring." He always wondered why Missy Kathryn wanted him to learn such a song. But it didn't matter; it was one of his favorites and would remain so.

To Emanuel's delight, the lessons always came to an end with Missy Kathryn performing impromptu renditions of some melodies she had heard the slaves sing. He thought her mimicry of the tunes complimentary, and he smiled with amazement when she performed in a voice so unlike the gruff, low-toned sounds that he had heard in the slave yard. He smiled before dissolving into loud giggles at the sight of Missy Kathryn contorting her face as she mimicked the tones. Emanuel was no longer afraid to laugh or be himself around his mistress; he no longer felt as if he was stepping out of place by striving to master everything she was willing to teach him. Besides his mother, he could think of no one whom he loved more than Missy Kathryn.

Emanuel spent the rest of his days toiling at chores that seemed to be multiplying—Gertie's way of wreaking vengeance, no doubt. But each night precisely at midnight, he would awaken and make his way quietly to the music room, where he would stealthily touch the piano's keys. He managed to not produce one sound, yet the imagined tones rang out in his heart and mind.

He was living in a dream world. His mother and all that he had ever known were within shouting distance, but his world and his outlook on life were too different to be believed. Why was all of this happening to him, Emanuel wondered. Why would Missy Kathryn want to waste her time with a slave? Maybe, he reasoned, it had something to do with what the field slaves were always saying—that he was special and was born blessed. His move to the Big House prompted a major change in his old quarters. Now, regardless of what was going on, his appearance there would cause all activity to stop and he would become the center of attention.

Other slave children his age expressed delight at just touching his skin; then they would scamper away, giggling with delight, like squirrels that had happened upon some nuts.

The elders would assemble and begin to mumble to themselves.

"I members when dat boy wuz bon'," they'd say. "I know'd he wuz a sign. He a bless'd chile f'om de Lawd."

When they occasioned a word with him, all but his mother would address him as "Piana." Only Massah Littlejohn himself commanded more attention in the yard. This caused some consternation on Emanuel's part. His only interests were music and the piano; he didn't want to be revered as blessed or special.

Emanuel began to withdraw from all peer worship and finally

restricted his visits to the yards to nighttime, when he would slip food to his mother.

But it was inevitable that Emanuel had to accept his special place amongst his own kind. No one—except Gertie—would be denied this special messenger from heaven. Every single one of them awaited the message, never doubting it would come. Meanwhile, they would wait, and keep a watchful eye on their blessed one.

One particular morning, Kathryn and Emanuel sat side by side, as usual, at the piano stool. He had completed his finger exercises and scales and was playing some of the pieces he had learned. Neither he nor Kathryn had any way of knowing a rider was approaching. Jonathan and Gertie were at the back of the plantation house, and couldn't announce this impending arrival.

Only the field slaves could see what was about to happen as they picked from cotton rows that led up to the edge of the grounds.

Two elderly slave women, as they reached the end of the cotton row, began to sing a message:

De sun up dere is a shinin',

Then they would dip down behind a cotton bush as if to continue work, only to stand up again quickly.

On de rider down here, dat's a comin'.

They would dip and stand again.

Now I'se sho dat he don't know,
Soon he'll be knockin' at de front doe.
De sun up dere is a shinin'.

Emanuel was the first to realize what was about to happen.

"Somebody is coming, Missy Kathryn," he said, interrupting his playing. She had barely noticed the message, and had passed off the song that the two women sang as just another field-hand melody. Suddenly, they heard knocking at the door.

"My God, Emanuel, you were right." She didn't know who to expect. Emanuel stood, and Kathryn began to play the same song he had played. By this time, Jonathan had returned to the house to answer the door.

"Emanuel, pick up the fan quickly," she said. Emanuel did as instructed, and started to stir the air with it.

Jonathan entered the music room with David in tow. Kathryn stopped playing immediately.

"David, how nice to see you," she said brightly. "What brings you all the way over here so early in the morning?"

"I thought I would bring the ledger of last month's bills and receipts, and since it was such a nice morning for a ride, well, here I am," he told her. "You will be happy to hear that we expect a double yield in the rice crops this year. Big profit."

"Thank you for saving me a trip," Kathryn said. "I'm sure everything is in order. Can I get you some breakfast, coffee, or tea?"

"Yes, tea, thank you."

"Emanuel, have Jonathan bring in some tea and then you may go about your chores," Kathryn said.

"Yes'm," Emanuel replied. He resented the intrusion by Massah David, especially when he noticed the sparkle it brought to Missy Kathryn's eyes.

Emanuel left and passed on Kathryn's instructions to Jonathan, who returned to serve a pot of tea to his mistress and her guest.

As he sipped from his cup, David felt a sense of completeness about him that only surfaced in Kathryn's presence.

Watching her gracefully lift the cup to her lips, he knew she felt the same way. But as always, they placed the proper restrictions on expressions of how they felt toward each other.

Even in the vast music room, with its array of furnishings and decorations to distract the eye, they'd always find themselves gazing at each other. Sadly, nothing could be said aloud, but their eyes relayed the messages from their hearts.

David broke the silence. "Any word from my brother?"

"Yes," Kathryn answered. "He has business of some urgency and he wants me to come to him since he can't seem to get away."

"Are you going?" David asked anxiously.

"Yes, I thought I might. It's been a while since I've been to Charleston. It would be nice if we're seen together on occasion."

As she spoke, Kathryn hoped David could tell her relationship with William was now based on propriety, not love. But she could never say that aloud either.

"I see."

"Maybe I'll take the ledger with me so that he can see how well we have done managing Lake Holler."

David nodded. "Well, I do hope you will miss me a little," he told her.

Slowly, Kathryn rose to her feet. She said nothing as she escorted David to the front door. But as he mounted his horse, Kathryn told him what he so desperately wanted to hear.

"Yes, David," she called out from the piazza, "I will miss you very much."

David rode off with but one thought on his mind: Now, more than ever, he wanted Kathryn to be his—and his alone.

William was in Charleston for his latest political and antiabolitionist rendezvous. Lately, he had grown unsure of whether he was making any headway toward building a political following, or decreasing abolitionist activity. His uncertainty led him to reach an important decision—one whose success would be determined by a meeting he was headed to with Barfield Chambers at the Jockey Club.

Loud chimes from the bells of Saint Michael's Cathedral signaled the two o'clock hour. He was on time. Inside, William greeted his colleague and friend. A tall, conservatively dressed man of sixty years, Barfield was clearly someone to be reckoned with. All of Charleston knew him as the president of the city's most prestigious law firm.

"Barfield, how have you been?"

"Fine, thank you. Just fine. And how was your trip?"

"Not encouraging, I'm afraid," William admitted, "but still there is reason for hope, I suppose."

Barfield spotted a pair of high-backed chairs with soft, cushioned seats.

"Let's sit down and have a drink while we talk," he told William.

A waiter quickly placed two tall glasses filled to the brim in front of them.

"William," said Barfield, "let me come right to the point. Have you given any consideration to the offer I made you before your last trip?"

"Yes, Sir, I have. I've given your offer a lot of serious thought."

"Good, then I hope you have come to the right decision for both of us."

"I think I have," William responded. "I have decided to accept your offer."

Barfield was pleased. "Outstanding, my boy. I knew all along that you would make the right decision."

"Thank you, Sir."

"Don't sir me," Barfield scolded him gently. "You are now a junior partner in the law firm of Chambers, McGill, and Faust. A junior partner, but that will improve with time. Here is a toast to our association; Chambers, McGill, Faust, and Littlejohn. I must say that it has a certain ring to it, and I might add that you have the blessings of my partners who will be elated to have you aboard. I am proud of you, my boy."

"Thank you, Barfield," replied William. "You know, of course, that I haven't practiced law since my days in training, and I bring little or no experience."

"Yes, we realize that," Barfield said with a wave of his hand, "but that's not important. We will teach you everything you need to know and if you are as bright as we think you are, you will catch on fast."

"I'll give it my best and try to earn my keep," William said.

"Now there is one other thing," Barfield warned him. "We don't want you to redirect your life's goals too much. One of the reasons my partners and I are so interested in you is your political aspirations, and we believe that you have the necessary talent to go far, and we want to be a part of that."

"But I have not run for any major office or won any election," William noted.

"You will, my boy, you will. The law firm of Chambers, McGill, Faust, and Littlejohn will see to that."

The old barrister paused for a moment to retrieve his pipe from an inside jacket pocket.

"I need not remind you how important this next election is," Barfield said as he prepared to light his pipe. "A win for Clay will be another blow to the South that I doubt we can withstand."

William felt completely at ease with political talk. Since his father's death, he had given his all to learn as much as he could about politics and government, in anticipation of one day entering this volatile arena. He suspected this conversation was more than casual dialogue on Barfield's part and that his friend was employing old lawyering tactics to feel him out.

"I could not agree with you more," William responded. "James K. Polk will better serve the interests of the South. Although he is aligned with the Jackson faction, he can, I believe, be prodded into reducing the tariff as well as reclaiming Texas as a slave-holding state."

Barfield was pleased again.

"Well said, William, very well said. Indeed, Polk is not ideal, but it seems that he is all we have. It's of critical importance that we begin to nurture one of our own, a true-bred Southerner to the bone with Southern ideals and beliefs, a man who will carry to the White House all of our interests and not just a few pacifying exhortations; that man could eventually be William Littlejohn II."

Barfield's voice grew ominous.

"But let me warn you now, my boy. You must be careful not to commit political suicide. That is precisely what happened to John Calhoun. Think of how much more effective he would have been toward protecting the interest of the South had he become president. Furthermore, he was but one step away when he resigned the vice presidency. He was an impetuous fool who sacrificed the crowning of his brilliant political career by prematurely invoking his wrath of the Jackson camp with that Eaton affair, such a petty reason to lose face with your immediate superior."

Though William had heard his friend's warning, his attention had focused on Barfield's reference to him as being presidential material. The very idea sparked a glimmer of hope, leaving him more than elated.

Barfield raised his glass in a toast.

"To the future. To the success of our partnership and realization of our common aspirations. Let's hope that I can be, shall we say, more patient than Mr. Calhoun was."

Kathryn arrived at the town house at No. 6 Church Street. It was late Friday afternoon, and the long carriage ride had been tiresome. A gentle breeze detached rust-colored leaves from their trees.

Kathryn surveyed the house as she ascended the stairs. In her eyes, the stately dwelling couldn't compare with the beautiful, white-columned plantation house at Lake Holler. The redbrick town house surrounded by a spiked fence seemed crude and lacking in warmth. Kathryn didn't like this place. Although the two-story mansion was huge, she felt tightly closed in. Kathryn also realized she hated the town house even more when William was present, not so much because of its crudeness, but because it was here that he cheated on her. She remembered the first time she had heard the lustful whimpers of his sex mates through a locked door leading to the servants' quarters. Maybe it was someone else with the slave girl, she had thought. But who? No male servants were present that day.

On another occasion, she had watched from an upstairs window as he exited the slave girl's room. Kathryn had been devastated but said nothing to him.

"How are you, William?" Kathryn asked as she embraced him quickly and planted a kiss on his cheek.

"Better now that you are here," William responded cordially.

"You look great as always."

"Thank you for your flattery, but I must look a mess," Kathryn said. "Actually, the trip was tiresome. Perhaps I had better clean up a bit before dinner."

"That will be fine," William responded. "I will have Dancy prepare the table. Would you care for a cognac before dinner? It will help you relax."

"No! No! Thank you. I'll just go get refreshed and meet you at dinner," Kathryn replied.

"Do hurry," William said eagerly, "I have some great news that I would like to share with you."

"I won't be long," Kathryn called out as she climbed the stairs.

Later at dinner, Kathryn and William sat at opposite ends of the table. A three-pronged candelabra sat in the center of the table, providing the room's subdued lighting. Its presence alerted Kathryn to what William had on his mind, and she was not in the mood. She searched her mind for an alternative to William's plans.

"I hear there is a lovely play at the theater, and I would love to go," she told him.

William looked disappointed.

"I was kind of hoping that we could spend some time together, alone I mean," he said, "but I guess we will have plenty of time when we return. What's the name of the play?"

"*When Betsy Ross Made Old Glory* is the name," Kathryn said.

"It sounds like revolutionary type material," William remarked.

"Yes, it is," Kathryn said. "It's a patriotic play, centered at the core of the American Revolution and the origin of the American flag. I hear that there is the most wonderful musical score in it, and I would like to see it very much."

"Well then, that settles it," William replied. "We will go."

Kathryn was genuinely pleased—and relieved.

"Oh, what did you have to tell me?" she asked.

William tried to sound matter-of-fact.

"Oh, it's nothing. Barfield Chambers offered me a position with his law firm and I accepted."

So accustomed was she to not having William around that Kathryn truly didn't know what to feel. Still, she knew how important this was to her husband, so she responded with a perfunctory smile.

"That's fantastic. What about your travels?"

"I'll have to give it up for the most part. But I will be closer to home. Of course, I will have to spend most of my time here in Charleston, and you can stay here most of the time, too," he said.

"William, if I stay here, then who will mind the plantation?"

"I hadn't thought of that," William admitted. "Well, you can still spend some time here anyway."

Kathryn felt relieved that William had accepted her reason for not staying with such ease. There must be an ulterior motive for him to even ask, she thought.

Later that evening, Kathryn and William attended the play at the Dock Street Theater. As far as Kathryn was concerned, the production was a hit; it contained far more music than dialogue. But it did not keep her thoughts from straying to David. She imagined him sitting next to her instead of William. How special such a moment would be. Then she remembered she'd once felt as strongly about William as she now felt about his brother. My God, she thought, what happened?

William watched the entire play in ambivalent silence until the cast launched into the finale, a song called "One Land United."

As he watched the curtain close, William felt certain the sponsors were of the Unionist faction. Another effort to unite all Charlestonians under one banner, he thought.

A full moon lit the path for Kathryn and William's slow carriage ride home. William's advances, along with the unseasonably warm weather, left Kathryn uncomfortable. She passed up his offer to ride to White Points Garden on the excuse that she was tired. She had hoped that reluctance on her part would cause an early end to the evening, but as she'd feared, William entered her bed later on in an amorous mood. He made gentle, measured approaches toward her, placing delicate kisses on her cheek and the nape of her neck. Kathryn could feel the warm air from his nostrils and mouth as it tickled her skin in the most blissful places. For a moment she forgot herself, but she soon remembered that this was not David. This was his brother, her husband, a man for whom she no longer had any passion. She could not relax, nor enjoy his lovemaking. But dutifully, she surrendered to his wishes. When he was done at last, she rolled over, praying for sleep to come.

Emanuel awakened feeling exuberant and well rested. He decided to spend time practicing the piano before he had to begin his scheduled duties. On his way to the music room, he detoured through the kitchen in search of whatever leftovers he could find. He already knew that in Missy Kathryn's absence, Gertie didn't cook for anybody but herself. Emanuel felt her presence as he gathered the food. He turned. Sure enough, she was there— with a bedeviled look in her eyes. After he finished the leftover bread and jelly, he walked out of the kitchen toward the music room. Gertie followed, stalking him like a mother following a child to a secret place of mischief.

Emanuel placed some sheet music he'd brought with him against the piano stand and began his ritualistic finger exercises. He'd planned to follow the exercises with a new tune, Columbia, the Gem of the Ocean. Missy Kathryn had introduced him to this piece before she'd left for Charleston. Emanuel liked the sound and wanted to perfect it.

As he prepared to play the new piece, a heavy hand gripped his shoulder and shoved him backward to the floor. Emanuel quickly found himself on his back, looking up at Gertie.

"You little black nigga, yo' thanks yo's somethin' special," she said. "Yo' git yo' butt off'n dat piano an' yo' gonna do some work like a nigga s'pose ta do."

Emanuel was furious. Had he been larger, he would have fought. But Gertie was such a big woman.

"I'm gonna practice my music," he said, staring straight at her hateful face.

"Yo' ain't gonna practice nothin' roun' heah," Gertie hissed. "When de Missy ain't in dis house, yo' got ta learn how ta keep yo' place. Yo'se a little nigga an' yo' place is in de fiel's or some place workin', not pla'in no white folks' piano."

"But Missy Kathryn says it's all right," Emanuel shot back.

"Missy Kathryn ain't heah," Gertie said as she struggled to reach Emanuel. He scuffled away from her.

"Come heah, yo' li'l black nigga," she screamed. "Don't run from me."

Gertie began to swing wildly at Emanuel, who was still trapped on the floor. For the most part, he was safe; Gertie's girth prevented her from bending deeply enough to reach him.

The old woman's ruckus soon brought Jonathan running. He stopped in the doorway behind her, watching her "attack" on Emanuel. Slowly, he eased up on her, lifted his right foot off the floor, and planted it squarely on Gertie's rear.

"Aaahhhhhh!" Gertie screamed in fury and pain. She whirled around to face Jonathan. His anger, she saw, clearly matched hers. Gertie then made the mistake of opening her mouth to speak.

Jonathan's right hand came crashing down across her face.

"Now you keep yo' fat ass quiet and don't say another word or

I'll knock yo' to kingdom come," Jonathan barked.

Gertie lunged. Jonathan stepped aside quickly and the woman stumbled past him. This time, he slammed his hand into her back as hard as he could.

"Woman, don't play wid me," he yelled. "Emanuel, git off dat floor and git to practicing yo' music."

Emanuel had never seen Jonathan this way. Quickly he got up and sat at the piano stool, where he sat and watched as Jonathan smacked Gertie again across the face. The force of his blow propelled her backward onto the sofa.

"If'n you ever touch that boy when he is practicing his music, I'll cut yo' throat with one of them butcher knives. Do you heah me, woman?"

Gertie acknowledged him with a nod of her head. She'd do anything to avoid more of Jonathan's wrath. Only once before had she seen him so enraged: the day Emanuel's father was lynched.

That day, she'd even heard Jonathan threaten to kill Massah Littlejohn with a butcher knife while the white man slept. In time, of course, Jonathan calmed down, but Gertie didn't think for a moment that he had forgotten his threat.

Jonathan wasn't through with Gertie.

"Who are you to decide what a niggar's place is?" he shouted. "You ain't nothin' but a niggar yo'self. And it's niggars like yo' dat's the reason we ain't gonna never git nowhere. Every time one of us tries to take a step forward, you takes two steps back. 'Cause yo' ain't nothin', yo' thinks nobody else kin be nothin' but slaves fo' white folks. Now yo' listen to me good. Fo' the first time in a long while I gots me a reason to live and dat's to see dat boy doin' something dat most white folks say he ain't s'pose to do, and I'll kill anybody dat tries to stop him. Now, yo' understand me?"

The look on Jonathan's face convinced Gertie that he was the devil himself. She was more frightened at this moment than she'd been when she was torn from her mother's arms on the auction block. Gertie rocked forward until she gained enough momentum to rise from the sofa. Jonathan readied to do battle once more, but Gertie was no longer a threat. With her hand against the right side of her face, she walked silently out of the room.

Jonathan's anger dissipated almost instantly. He even managed a faint smile.

"Now you can practice in peace," he said to Emanuel. "Gertie won't mess with you no mo'."

But Emanuel sensed Jonathan's lingering frustration with Gertie.

One slave trying to pull another down . . . like a bunch of snakes crawling all over each other. Nobody gets nowhere. Emanuel felt exactly the same way.

For a while, Emanuel sat on the stool without touching a key. As he gazed out the window, tears welled in the corner of his eyes. He felt a little insecure, not because of Gertie and what she had done, rather because of Jonathan and all the field slaves who looked up to him. It was as if all of them had transferred all hope for personal gain and achievement to him, and he didn't know if he could live up to their expectations. Such a large burden, he thought, but his alternatives were few. He had started this thing and he had to finish it.

As he began to play his new piece, he sang the words softly, as he remembered them from Missy Kathryn's lips:

> *O, Columbia the gem of the ocean*
> *the home of the brave and the free . . .*

He practiced until his fingers grew numb.

 214

It was midmorning on Monday when Kathryn prepared to leave for Lake Holler. William tried to convince her to stay, but she insisted that there was no one to take care of the plantation.

She had seen her name listed in the *Charleston Courier* as one with mail remaining at the post office. After bidding good-bye to William, she directed her driver there and picked up a parcel.

Once on the road, Kathryn opened the package from Auntie Mame. She was always glad to hear from her godmother, and she felt her companionship on many occasions when she had written her most private thoughts in her diary. She found a letter inside.

My dearest Kathryn,

I trust this letter will find you in the best of health. I know you think of me and I hurry to tell you that I am well. Somehow the deterioration imposed by time has managed to still leave me functional. Too, my fingers have stiffened and the mere act of writing can be unbearable.

And how is the little boy of whom you speak so fondly in your letters? If he is at all as talented as you were, then he is truly gifted.

I must warn you that there are those in Charleston who would find what you are doing as nothing less than hideous.

Be careful. Be happy.
Love,
Auntie Mame

P. S. Here is a gift I think that you and your little friend will appreciate as well as enjoy.

Kathryn held a book in her hand. What a lovely, thoughtful gift, she thought. It was Beethoven's *Musical Memoirs for the Piano*. Kathryn thumbed through the pages to arrive at a brief overview of what works were presented. There was *Sonata in G, La Marmotte Op. 52, No. 7, Walzer, Fur Elise,* and *Bagatelle in C, Op. 119, No. 2.*

As she read the titles from his works, music began to play in her head. The work before her was by the great master himself. And now, she would teach Emanuel—she had no doubt of his abilities, but she also wanted him to feel the music, to hear the message translated into rhythmic vibrations that would soften hardened souls and mend broken hearts. This had been Beethoven's challenge, and he had met it.

CHAPTER TWENTY-ONE

Emanuel's fingers danced artfully across the keyboard, producing a mesmerizing sound. He had grown more confident of his ability and talent as he dissected the works of Beethoven, a master craftsman whose music was filled with emotion. The realization that his musical ability was equal to that of his white counterparts, according to Missy Kathryn, boosted his confidence even more. The more he played, the more his obsessions grew. It was as if this new kind of music had set him free—creatively, that is.

Upon Missy Kathryn's return, his morning practice sessions resumed. His mistress taught with a renewed vibrancy. Long ago, she had also been hypnotized by the force and fire of Beethoven's mastery. She taught his music with much more vigor, and was far less tolerant of mistakes. But Emanuel didn't care, so eager was he to learn all there was about the man and his music.

"Who was this Beethoven?" Emanuel asked one day as they sat practicing the piano.

Kathryn turned to face her student, who longed to know so much. It was as if she couldn't teach him fast enough.

"He was one of the greatest masters of piano," Kathryn replied. "He was born in Vienna in 1770. It was rumored that, like you, at a very early age, he exhibited great musical talent."

"Was he a slave, too?" Emanuel asked naively.

The question caught Kathryn off guard. Not once since Emanuel had come to live in the Big House had this word been uttered between them. The brutal realization of his situation, for a moment, made her want to cry, but she kept her composure.

"No, he was not a slave. He was a white man, although it is rumored in Europe that he had Negro blood," she said.

"Oh," the boy responded.

Kathryn sensed disappointment in Emanuel's reply. His simplistic response implied that there was no hope for him to use his talent because he was a slave.

"Emanuel, did you know that not all Negroes are slaves?" Kathryn asked.

"Everybody I know is."

"Yes, that's true, but that's because you live on a plantation. In the cities there are Negroes who are free, and up north, there is no slavery."

"Where up north?" he asked.

"Everywhere up north. Can I tell you a secret and you must promise never to tell that I told? You promise?"

"Yes'm," Emanuel said eagerly.

"One day all slaves will be free," Kathryn said. "I feel it. I know it will happen, but I don't know when."

The thought of being free had never occurred to Emanuel. It seemed to brighten his spirits some. He turned to face the keyboard. Automatically, his nimble fingers danced across the keys as he played Beethoven's *Fourth Piano Concerto*. Missy

Kathryn was silent as she looked on in utter amazement. T'was true. She didn't know when all slaves would be free, but she knew this one would be, even if she had to stake her life on it.

Late that night when all was quiet and everyone was asleep, Emanuel eased softly from his cot. He gathered a small bundle of food that he had previously hidden in the pantry, plus a jar of canned peaches, then quietly exited the house through the back door. He was off to see his mother.

The night air had a refreshing coolness; this time, Emanuel did not run but walked at a relaxed pace. He had grown accustomed to these nighttime excursions and he had little fear of being caught. On one occasion, Big Sam, the black overseer, had discovered him just as he was about to enter his mother's cabin, but he knew he had little to fear because Big Sam only exercised his authority in front of Master William. When no one was around, he saw no evil.

The sounds of the night owls and crickets brought back memories of when he used to live with his mother and roam the slave yards at night. How things had changed for him. He was darker and had developed into a thin-faced, skinny boy who showed signs that he would one day be tall. On every visit to the cabin, his mother remarked how much he had grown, even if the visits were but a week or two apart.

He gently bumped against his mother's door. Emanuel knew she would be hard to awaken because she was always so tired, so he continued to knock until he heard noisy squeaks that signaled the door was opening.

" 'Manuel?"

"Yes'm. I brought you some food."

Always, the mention of food brought her to full wakefulness. She let him in, taking the jars and placing them on the hearth at the fireplace. There was little light to see. Emanuel took a small candle from his parcel.

Bell said her blessing before she began to devour the food. As always, Emanuel didn't eat.

As Bell was about to finish her meal, she looked up at Emanuel.

"Seems like I gits mo' hungry eba day," she told her son.

"Yes'm."

"'Manuel, I want ya ta do somethin' else fer yo' ma."

"What?"

"I wan'cha ta teach me ta read dis."

"What is it?"

"Da Bible. Ole Nanna gabe it ta me befo' she died. Git close ta dat candle,"she said, motioning to her son.

Now Emanuel understood. He was a little surprised at his mother's request. He didn't know what to say.

"Well, yo' told me yo' learnin' ta read. Naw sho' me. I know my A, B, C's, all de way to Z an' I knows some words like *the*, *and*, *them*, and *Lord*. Teach me some mo'," Bell ordered Emanuel.

"Where do you want to start?"

"Start from de begin'n. Heeah."

Bell pointed to some words. Emanuel read for her first, then they plodded along, word for word. Emanuel enjoyed learning to read and he had done so easily. He found his mother to be a willing student, hungry for knowledge of the Bible. Together, they read.

In the beginning God created the heaven and the earth. And the earth was without form, and void; and the darkness was upon the face of the deep. And the spirit of God moved upon the face of the waters.

Bell asked for no explanation of what Emanuel had read; Emanuel wasn't certain that he could explain anyway.

Meticulously, they rambled through the unfamiliar words. "And God said, Let there be light and there was light."

When it was time for Emanuel to leave for the Big House, his mother kissed him on the cheek; she had never done that before.

Emanuel also noticed that she had a smile on her face. He had never seen that either.

After Emanuel was gone, Bell lay on her cot to rest before the morning chores had to be done. She didn't hide the Bible in the corner where she'd always put it. This time, she placed it under her head, below a makeshift pillow. Pride now replaced some of her fear for Emanuel. And she even had a newfound sense of fulfillment that came from knowing she, too, could learn to read.

William Littlejohn concentrated exclusively on the paper that he held before his eyes. It was the morning edition of the *Charleston Courier*, dated June 17, 1845. It confirmed what he had already heard: Andrew Jackson was dead. Like a dead carcass that sends its smell across the land, news of the death of Jackson, whom some considered the greatest president who ever lived, spread across the countryside like a stench, preceding the printed facts by days.

"Andrew Jackson died at the Hermitage at 6 o'clock p.m. on Sunday, the 8th," William read. "His funeral took place on the 10th at 11 o'clock. He died quietly, calmly and with entire resignation, with full confidence that he was prepared for a better world."

William assumed a pensive mood as he lay the paper down. He knew Jackson as a reckless individual before he had assumed the number one post in the Union but a man who held steadfastly to his beliefs, ideas, and morality, even if it meant his own destruction. It was he, and he alone, who had repelled the last great thrust of the nullifiers to secede from the Union. Yet right up to his death, he commanded the respect of his friends and foes alike. At best, William felt ambivalence toward the man, but even he could not deny him his rightful place in history as a great American hero.

For the better part of June, there were reports of the many posthumous ceremonials designed to honor the death of Gen. Andrew Jackson. President Polk set the standard for all ceremonials when he ordered all government offices closed and military personnel to wear mourning dress for six months.

On June 27, a funeral procession began at President's Square and proceeded up Pennsylvania Avenue to the Capitol. All of the key government officials attended along with numerous citizens, the military, and diplomatic corps. At the Capitol, George Bancroft, secretary of the Navy, gave a two-hour speech commemorating the greatness of Jackson.

William felt a need to be that important to the American public, and he was inspired to approach his work with all the vigor he could muster. There was little time for frivolity.

The burning issue of the day continued to be slavery and what to do with it. William could think of no better issue with which to make a name for himself. A quote from Governor Hammond attributed to the works of a Mr. Grosvener best summed up William's thoughts on the issue. The governor had once said "that he had twenty objections to the abolition of the slave trade: the first was that it was impossible—the rest he need not give."

At work, in cases any way related to the question of slavery or the proper demeanor of the slave or the free black population, William made sure he was the attorney for the prosecution. Arson attempts, presumably by unhappy members of the black population, were becoming ever more frequent in Charleston. It was the case of the City of Charleston vs. a free man, an ex-slave named Casey, that William used to increase public scrutiny of his talents and abilities.

Casey had been an industrious kind of individual who belonged to a kindly master. He served his master well as a domestic and was allowed to sell goods in the marketplace to earn extra money. He was frugal with his pennies and eventually saved enough money to purchase his freedom, at which time he decided to change his duties to those more suitable for a free black. So, he became a barber by trade and continued to do well.

One fateful evening, Casey left his barbershop and began walking home. He chose the route around the perimeter of White Point Gardens, knowing very well that he could not enter after a certain hour. Yet, he saw little harm in walking around the gardens. The moist, cool air that blew across the Ashley and Cooper rivers was unseasonably refreshing. There was no one directly about, so Casey reached into his pocket and pulled out a cigar to smoke. If there had been whites about, he would not have done this because it projected an air of arrogance. He stopped for a moment to light up. Just as the end of the cigar ignited, two Charleston policemen jumped him from behind and pushed him to the ground.

"You started that fire uptown, didn't you, nigga?" one of the officers said as they both stood over him.

"What fire? I don't know nothin' 'bout no fire," Casey protested. "I ain't been uptown."

The officers persisted.

"You like to see fires burn, don't you, nigga? Makes no difference whether it's a cigar or a building, does it?"

"I don't know what you are talking about," Casey said.

"Get up!" the other officer barked. "It's off to the guardhouse for you."

Casey knew there was little hope that the policemen would listen. He offered no resistance as he was carried off to the guardhouse.

Later, he was given his day in court in front of a large crowd. His attorney did little arguing in his defense against the prosecutor, William Littlejohn. To Casey, William's entire case rested on God's irrefutable majesty in deciding the fate of all men, and that God meant for men of African descent to be enslaved.

"It is He (God) who is all powerful," William told the jury in his closing remarks. "And he will not allow his children to change the master plan or foil his designs and, for certain, when we tamper with the natural course of things, the results can only be disastrous and punishing such as in the case of this former slave, now a free black, called Casey. A fire, maliciously set by his indelicate hands that could have reduced all of Charleston to ashes . . . "

The crowd shouted its approval of William's words. Casey's attorney did muster a weak objection, but even that was quickly overruled. Casey never got the opportunity to say he was nowhere near the area that burned that night or that he had never had any malicious intent toward anybody. He knew that, at best, his case was hopeless.

During the predawn coolness of the second Monday of October 1845, Casey was hung by the neck until dead.

William was sitting at his desk when his law partner, Mr. Chambers, entered the room.

"You handled that jury brilliantly, William," his colleague said.

"Thank you, Sir," said William.

"You did not have a speck of evidence against that nigga

except that he could light a cigar, and you got a conviction. Brilliant!"

"It was pretty easy, you know," William confided. "It was what the jury wanted. It was what the community wanted. From time to time, you've got to do something to let the free niggas know that they must stay in their proper place. This was just the right case for that."

Chambers pulled out his pipe.

"You are right. Now if we could find a simple solution to keeping the slave population in their place. You hear about more and more runaways every day. Somebody has got to be helping them," Chambers said as he twirled the pipe between his teeth.

"I agree," said William. "But there isn't a simple solution. Our slaves escape from right under our noses and get to the northern states. When they are found and carried to the courtroom to be processed and returned to their rightful owners, those damned abolitionists interfere and set them free again."

"There is no doubt that we have got to persuade the Congress to exact a more stringent fugitive slave law than the one passed in 1793, which seems antiquated at best," Chambers said. "And I'm not so sure that even that will be enough. William, my boy, the South is upon hard times and I can foresee times getting even harder."

William leaned back in his chair.

"Well, I wish I had the answer, but I don't," he said. A look of concern crossed his face. "What else can we do?"

The old barrister would never allow anyone to think he was without all the answers.

"There is but one last resort," he declared.

"What's that?" William asked.

"Secession."

David Littlejohn had followed the case of Casey with deliberate interest. Intuitively, he knew what the outcome would be, and that there was little he could do without revealing his true motives. But he also knew there was one thing he had to do: get Casey's family out of Charleston. His brother had done an excellent job of arousing public sentiment against Casey, and the trial and punishment would be used as a warning to all the other free blacks. And when Charleston's aristocracy had vindication on its mind, as far as blacks were concerned, one's innocence was never perceived as a possibility. Some of the anger would extend to Casey's family, perhaps resulting in re-enslavement of his wife and children, if not worse.

Casey was survived by a wife and four children; the youngest was two years old, the oldest was nine. David knew that Mrs. Casey would not be up to trusting anyone with a white face, so he sent Tom Baldwin, along with one of the black female confidantes, into Charleston to persuade the widow to leave town. She was told that she should trust them, and that they would ensure her safe passage to the North.

Mrs. Casey had no one else to turn to, no friends or relatives who could help her; she knew she had to let these strangers decide her future. Secretly, she kept a knife in her possession. If her decision turned out to be wrong, she would slay all her children, and then herself.

Winnie was showing early signs that she would mature into a beautiful woman. Her hair was long and curly—the curls being about the only sign of her Negroid heritage. Winnie's skin was smooth and unblemished, with a mild tint that made her look like a white person with a year-round tan. Her cocoa-brown eyes enchanted even the casual observer. At thirteen, Winnie's figure was well-proportioned; even her breasts possessed a womanly fullness. Though Winnie was pleased with her looks, she was even more pleased to catch Bertram gazing her way amorously. Rachel, Bertram's mother, realized their childish friendship had grown into an early infatuation, and had it not been time for Bertram to go away to school, Winnie would have certainly been sold in order to avoid any connubial interest.

Bertram tried to give the impression that he was disinterested in Winnie, so as not to provoke his mother to sell her. In private, they had already mastered every technique for escaping and spending time together alone.

On Bertram's last day before leaving for school, he and Winnie made plans for their last evening together. They agreed to wait until everyone was asleep, then slip out of the house and meet behind the corn crib. Bertram made it out of the house quietly, without awakening anyone. But when Winnie attempted to get out of bed, her old straw mattress caused so much commotion that she roused her mother.

"Where in the world is yo' goin' child, at this time of the mornin'?" Teresa asked.

"I couldn't sleep," Winnie replied quickly. "I was just getting up for some fresh air."

"I'll bet that fresh air is Bertram, ain't it?"

Winnie knew it was pointless to lie.

"Yes'm," she said slowly.

"Well, you better hurry, child, he ain't gonna wait for you all night," Teresa told her daughter. Teresa still engaged in her fantasies. Perhaps, she reasoned, there was a way that Winnie and Bertram would somehow make it together. After all, Winnie was light enough to pass for white. They could go north, and no one would know.

"I'll keep an eye out for old Miss Rachel," Teresa said, "and you hurry and come back as soon as you can."

Winnie said nothing as she left the room and headed to the corn crib. She found Bertram sitting on the ground, waiting patiently. They'd had many previous secret encounters, but this one was different. Quickly, they embraced each other with all the tenderness and love of those much older than them. Then they released each other, pausing to engage in a loving stare. Before either of them knew it, their lips met in a kiss that began as an inexperienced battle between two tongues. It was their first.

Reluctantly, Bertram broke away. The look on his face told Winnie he had something important to tell her.

"I love you, Winnie," he said.

"I love you, too."

"I promise that I'll think of you every day and every night in my dreams."

"You promise?"

"I promise," Bertram assured her, "and when I get old enough, I'll come and take you away. We'll run away someplace where Mother will never find us."

"Until that day comes, I'll wait," Winnie said breathlessly. "I'll wait as long as I have to."

Shortly after daybreak, Winnie watched from an upstairs window as Bertram boarded the carriage that would take him away.

Slowly, tears dampened her face. She had never known life without Bertram. During the past few years, his mother had made it a point to keep them separated, but in spite of that they had always managed to meet secretly. Now, he was gone; only God knew for how long! She vowed to keep her promise to love him and wait for him, always.

CHAPTER TWENTY-TWO

Talents seen, talents hidden
Talents grow, talents forbidden
O' non-existent life, o' black son
What is your purpose, what is your design
Why grow thee so tall and dark if not to be seen,
Why grow thee so strong if not to be felt.
But grow thee not tall, dark or strong
You are not here, but non-existent.

Kathryn thought a moment about the poem she had written, her tribute to Emanuel.

She could find no justification, no reason to keep this boy's enormous talents hidden, yet she had no choice but to do it. Years ago, she had taken him under her wing, more to humor his mischievous qualities than to nourish any talent he might have. Much to her surprise, she had happened upon a child just as capable as any other, and more capable than most. He just happened to be black. He devoured the compositions of Thalberg, Gottschalk, Ascher, and Verdi. He memorized and emulated the works of Mozart and Beethoven. The more Kathryn became enamored of the full scale of his talents, the less tolerant she was of his oppressed status. Such talent was meant to be nurtured to the fullest, but even with her tutelage, this couldn't happen on the plantation. Perhaps it was then that she first had thoughts of helping him escape, but her thoughts quickly gave way to selfishness. She knew not having him around would be almost unbearable.

Oftentimes, she found herself gazing at him admiringly, just as if he were her own son. Now fourteen years old, Emanuel was a thin, dark-skinned boy of about five feet nine inches in height. He had a crop of woolly hair atop his head, and a thin peach-fuzz of a mustache adorned his full lips. When he walked, his toes pointed slightly inward and he had a slight bow in his legs.

Already, women took notice and their perception was that he had the makings of what would be a handsome man. Emanuel realized what women thought of him, but he was inclined to shy away from the oohs and aahs of the younger slave girls in the yards.

William's thoughts of selling him at a profit were curtailed when Kathryn stood her ground firmly and negatively. At those times, Emanuel made it a point to stay out of his way. He hated William's intrusion but gained some satisfaction from fantasizing about some sort of vindictive act against his master.

Nevertheless, he tried to be subservient and, thus, less noticeable. This wasn't altogether easy for him, since he was approaching William in height. Having to look up to a servant was a real thorn in William Littlejohn's side.

As soon as Master Littlejohn was out of the house, Emanuel resumed his practice schedule, but things were different now. Before, practice was a privilege; now it was a requirement placed upon him by Missy Kathryn. She pushed him to his limits while trying to make up for the restraints of plantation life. Emanuel consented willingly and continued his habit of rising late at night, practicing the piano silently while musical thoughts filled his mind. Now his reasons for late-night play were different. He was crafting his first composition dedicated to his mother and Missy Kathryn. Under the secrecy of darkness, he worked, note by note, sound by sound. Even if someone else had been in the room, they wouldn't have heard anything because the sound played only in Emanuel's head.

"What is a concert?" Emanuel asked Missy Kathryn one day as they rested briefly between practice sessions.

"A concert is a performance by a great musician or any orchestra, either alone or together, where music is played for an audience," replied Kathryn.

"What's an orchestra?" inquired Emanuel.

"An orchestra is a group of musicians that play many different kinds of instruments together," she replied.

"Have you ever been to a concert?"

"Oh! many times, in England."

"Was it exciting?"

"Very much so." Kathryn had a reminiscent look about her. "Oh! How I enjoyed them and there were many."

"Is England the only place that you can go to see a concert?"

"No," replied Kathryn. "There are concerts right here in Charleston, oftentimes sponsored by the Saint Cecilia Society."

Emanuel didn't know what the Saint Cecilia Society was, but he had read the name in the *Charleston Courier*. He and Jonathan discerned that this society must have something to do with music.

"Tell me more about the concert. How was it done?" inquired Emanuel excitedly.

Kathryn knew how relentless he could be when he wanted to know something.

"Each orchestra has a leader, who directs them. This man is called a maestro and he walks onto the stage with his baton in his hand, steps up to the podium, and bows before the audience after his introduction. Then the featured musician comes onto the stage. If he is a pianist, he sits at the piano stool. The maestro acknowledges his presence, turns toward his orchestra, and taps the podium lightly with his baton to gain their attention. All of this is done in such grand style. Each musician, the maestro, and the featured musician, wears a black, swallow-tailed coat with the whitest of white shirts fitted with a bow tie and then finally, the ecstatic moment arrives when the pianist begins to play."

Emanuel was now dreaming of places he had never been and music he had never heard. But reality intruded all too quickly.

"Have you ever seen any Negroes perform a concert?"

"No, Emanuel," Kathryn said slowly. "No, I haven't."

That night, Jonathan visited Emanuel in his room. As usual, they read over old newspapers that they'd managed to confiscate. Jonathan would never let anyone else know he could read, not even Missy Kathryn.

"Jonathan," Emanuel began, "have you ever heard of any black musicians?"

"No, can't say that I have. No more than the few fiddlers and banjo players that you run into in the slave yards."

"No, not that kind, I mean the ones that play at concerts before audiences."

"Well," Jonathan replied, "it will be a cold day in May before you ever hear of such."

Jonathan saw Emanuel's facial expression change. "But you know, like they say, there's a first time for everything. Who knows, maybe one day you will make it to the North, where you can be free, and God only knows what might happen after that."

Jonathan knew that a bit of realism was in order. He didn't want Emanuel to be discouraged, nor did he want to build his hopes up too high.

"There's just some things that white folks won't let us do and I guess that's just about everything that requires thinking and not working. I've always kept it in my thoughts that a man is a failure if he lives to realize that he stopped trying. If you knows what you want out of life, son, then you got to keep working for it, even if you died trying. That can't be as bad as not trying at all."

A sense of hopelessness began to engulf Emanuel as he looked at Jonathan in silence. Jonathan sensed his young friend's despair and decided to cheer him up. He walked toward one of the pantry shelves and reached behind its contents to bring out a jar of peaches. He handed the jar to Emanuel.

"Here is some peaches that I saved for your mother," Jonathan said. "I added a little extra sugar."

"How long have you known?"

"Since your first trip, years ago. You always seems to carry more peaches than anything else, so I figured your mother must like them."

Emanuel watched Jonathan as he turned and walked out the door. He lay back on his cot to try to fall asleep before the morning.

The following day, Kathryn greeted Emanuel with a question.

"Emanuel, how would you like to go into Charleston and see a real orchestra playing classical music?"

Emanuel hesitated. He knew his position outside of the house was that of a slave. How could it be that he could ever hear a real orchestra? Finally, he answered her with a simple "Yes, Ma'am."

Kathryn went on to explain that the Saint Cecilia Society was giving its annual ball and that the music and musicians were the best that Charleston had to offer.

"I can make arrangements for you to be one of the servants. You will have to have a formal coat, but that's a problem we can solve upon arriving in Charleston."

At that moment, Jonathan announced a visitor. Missy Kathryn instructed Jonathan to bring the guest into the parlor. Emanuel knew there could be no lessons now and he assumed a servant's position. David entered the room.

"How are you, Kathryn?" he said.

"Very well, thank you." She instructed Emanuel to leave the room.

"Can I offer you some coffee or tea?"

"Oh, no, no thank you," he replied as he sat down beside her. "My brother asked me to accompany you to Charleston for the Saint Cecilia Ball next week. I came to see when I should come by for you."

"Anytime after dawn on Monday will be fine. How nice of William to arrange it so that we can spend time together," said Kathryn.

She and David now fully acknowledged their love for each other but had agreed to stop their desires short of physical contact. They had decided it would be unwise to let their relationship get out of hand.

"This will be the only time that I could hope that the distance between here and Charleston were greater. You must know how hard it is for me to stay away from you."

"I feel the same about you, David, but what can we do about it? Nothing! We must content ourselves with what brief moments we have together. There can be no other way."

"I know," said David. He quickly looked about the room to make sure no one was watching, then leaned forward and kissed

Kathryn on the lips. She made no attempt to refuse him as their mouths met for a brief moment. There was no embrace.

That night, Emanuel placed food for his mother into a small sack. Like countless other times, he quietly tiptoed from his pantry bedroom and eased down the back steps into the night air.

It was only a short walk from the Big House to his mother's shack, but their worlds seemed an eternity apart.

On this February night, his breath chilled to a visible mist against the bright moonlit sky. He felt warm in the heavy wool coat that Missy Kathryn had provided for him. Many times he had tried to give the coat to his mother, but she refused, realizing that such a luxury item was much too conspicuous and would cause suspicion.

As he approached his mother's cabin, he could see heavy, thick smoke coming from the chimney. He was not alarmed. This had happened before and it usually meant there was someone else in his mother's cabin.

He began knocking on the door.

Bell was there before the third knock, cracking the door just enough to show her face. A brief burst of heat escaped into the night air. Bell's face and clothing were moist with sweat.

She put one finger before her lips and made a shushing sound. Emanuel knew he was not to enter his mother's cabin tonight; moreover, he was to say nothing.

Bell could see her son's face clearly from the light produced by the fireplace. She felt a brief surge of pride as she marveled at this tall, thin black boy, the only thing in this world she could call her own. Moreover, he had fulfilled the predictions at his birth that he was special. His mastery of the piano dominated every fireside chat. Thoughts of Piana occupied the minds of just about every slave in the yard. He had become the reason to exist, to keep trying.

When she heard them refer to Emanuel as "Piana," she was more certain that her son deserved better than this, but who was she to question why. Was it not Jesus himself who was born in a manger, only to be hanged on the cross at age thirty-three? Before she learned to read, there had been many tears, many fears, many questions. But now, the word of God was within her and he would show them both the way.

Because she, like the Virgin Mary, bore a special son, because she could read, because of her mastery of the Bible, because of her knowledge of medicines and herbs, Bell was given a special place in the slave yards. She was the doctor for the sick, the counselor to those troubled, the preacher for those needing spiritual guidance, the nanna for all the children, the midwife for all births, and she was also the one to whom all the fertile young girls came to try to prevent pregnancy. Another young girl had needed her services tonight, and that was why she could not allow her son to enter the cabin. She longed to embrace him, kiss him, and tell him how much she loved him, but now was not the time.

"Gib me de sack; now hurry back to de Big House befo' dey misses you," Bell ordered Emanuel before closing the cabin door.

Emanuel had learned to not question his mother in these situations, and was familiar with welcomes such as the one he'd just gotten. Years before he remembered vaguely how Nanna had spent much time instructing his mother about herbs, medicines, childbirth—and more important, how to prevent it. He hoped the young girl, whoever she was, would survive the ordeal. He knew that some had not.

Bell had altered her procedure since Emanuel had taught her how to read. Before she did anything, she and the helpless and often very young girl would kneel before the hearth while she read from the Bible and prayed. Her favorite verses were Matthew 5:3-12:

> *"Blessed are the poor in spirit: for theirs is the kingdom of heaven . . . "*

Bell had no remorse over what she did for those helpless, often immature young girls. When there was a pregnancy, she tried to abort it and then attempted to prevent a subsequent occurrence. She perceived her abilities as a gift from God. Again, she did not ask why.

CHAPTER TWENTY-THREE

After only a few miles of travel, Emanuel had already gone beyond the boundaries of the first fourteen years of his life. He belonged to Lake Holler and had spent all of his days there, amongst the great magnolia trees and huge live oaks whose long braids of Spanish moss dangled like unkempt hair. As he looked farther down the road, somehow he felt that this mass of forest trees, wildflowers, and bushes would open at the end of his journey and reveal a startling new world unknown to most of his kind.

He was sitting so close to the driver of the carriage that their bodies touched, but their thoughts were so different and few words passed between them. Emanuel observed the man's slumped position and reasoned that the toils of slavery had broken his spirit as well.

As mockingbirds and thrushes darted amongst the trees, Emanuel knew their treble tones had a special meaning for him, for they, too, must have known of his great love for music. The long flat squawks of blackbirds and the hoofbeat of the horses added the base clef to this forest symphony. In his mind, Emanuel applauded their performance just as Missy Kathryn had said an audience would applaud a great performance by a large symphony orchestra.

Kathryn and David sat alone inside the carriage, oblivious to everything but each other. Moments like these were few and far between. Soon they would be in Charleston, where William was, but right now, they wanted the ride to continue forever. Their bodies were turned ever so slightly toward each other so that Kathryn's knee pressed against David's thigh. Despite their longings, they managed to maintain restraint, exchanging only soft, gentle kisses. Then, they held hands as they made small talk about the plantation.

David had always wondered what Kathryn's reaction would be if she knew what part he played in the escape of slaves to the North. Somehow he felt in her an ally but didn't take her in his confidence as much for her own safety as well as the security of his underground activity. To be discovered meant a long jail term, at the very least, and if the prevailing temperament was too violent, one could end up on the wrong end of a rope. He didn't want any harm to come to Kathryn. Still, he decided to find out more about her sentiments on the subject of slavery.

"We've been very fortunate at Lake Holler," he said.

"How do you mean?" Kathryn inquired.

"We've had fewer slave escapes than any of the surrounding plantations and we've had good crops to show for it."

"Well, maybe so," Kathryn said, deciding to not commit herself. She had always felt that David was not the typical plantation taskmaster, but, somehow, he got the job done.

"It's still hard for me to see you as the typically harsh, bruising slave master, who seems to be the rule around here," Kathryn told David. "Even William has no sentiments when it comes to a slave. I have never been able to see you in that light, in spite of the good job you are doing."

"It's simple," David responded. "You can get more out of a well-rested and well-fed body than you can a tired, malnourished, discontented one. I don't believe in the whip or the lash."

David paused, trying to make sure he didn't sound too sentimental. "Unless, of course, it's absolutely necessary."

"Nobody can argue the point in view of your success, not even William," said Kathryn. Her attention turned to Emanuel, who she could see atop the carriage. His talent had made such an impact on her that she dreamed of him performing before the most sophisticated of European audiences. She pondered what David would say if he knew she had taught Emanuel to play the piano.

Reticence engulfed her. Though it was noticeable to David, he said nothing. Kathryn's feelings about Emanuel's predicament were becoming more and more disturbing; she had seen and felt Emanuel's growing intolerance of enslavement. His instincts told him this was not his rightful position in life. His talent and abilities had triggered a yearning to do more, see more, learn more. Kathryn had never once regretted the tutelage she had offered this slave boy; she had not forgotten her debt to the black man with the forked tongue.

Emanuel had jumped at the chance to go to Charleston, even with the risk of being around William, whom she knew he hated.

Maybe he was thinking of escape, she thought. If he was, she had already decided that she would help.

They arrived in Charleston at dusk. Emanuel's reaction to seeing the city for the first time was one of subdued excitement. The carriage entered on one of the city's largest streets.

Emanuel looked as far in the distance as he could see, and there was still no end in sight. The roadway must have been as long as Lake Holler was large, he thought. It seemed amazing to him that the oak, palmetto, and cypress trees sprang up between the pavement brick, almost in perfect alignment. He saw the name "Meeting Street" on a sign at one of the corners. He remembered seeing it mentioned frequently in the paper that he and Jonathan read, and he knew there were important buildings on this street.

The steady jolting of the carriage and loud clapping of the horses' hooves on the cobblestone roads drew Emanuel's attention to the pavement. He wondered how many slaves it had taken to position those stones.

Rows and rows of homes and buildings of various sizes lined the street. The houses were familiar to him because they had downstairs and upstairs piazzas, just like at Lake Holler. What was odd to him was that all the piazzas faced the same direction.

People sat out on some of them, looking out over the street. He dared not look up, but he spotted them with his peripheral vision.

Emanuel noticed that the wrought iron fences and gates surrounding many of the houses were all soot black and ornamented with circles and curves. Maybe the gates were to keep the slaves from running away, he thought.

He saw the beautiful gardens that adorned many of the houses. The flowers were out of season, but the evergreen bushes were alive and colorful. He imagined that in early spring the buds from the plants would burst open with life and intrigue the onlooker with many different colors. The air would be filled with a sweet fragrance not unlike that emitted by a field of honeysuckle. He thought of his favorite flower, the Mexican rose, Missy Kathryn had called it. There were many planted outside the windows at Lake Holler and he checked them daily when they were in season to see if they had undertaken the ritual of changing from white to pink-ish red.

The carriage turned a corner before stopping in front of a white-columned house that seemed much smaller than the Big House, perhaps because the yard was so small. The commotion from the back of the carriage told Emanuel that this was where he would be staying. Like most of the others, this house was surrounded by a wrought iron gate. Again, he wondered why.

Emanuel stepped down from the carriage to help the driver unload the luggage. He saw William exit the front door of the house and walk toward the buggy. He was all smiles and seemed happy to see Missy Kathryn as they embraced and kissed. He then greeted his brother.

"Thanks for coming in with Kathryn, David. I'm always afraid that she will run into some kind of scalawag when she comes alone."

"Don't mention it," David said. "I enjoyed the ride and a chance to get into the city. Who knows? I might meet someone as beautiful as Kathryn and take her for my wife."

Kathryn's fixed smile disappeared when she heard David's words.

"I should think it is about time, dear brother," William said. "You certainly have settled down and proved us all wrong about your destiny. Wouldn't Father be amazed? You are successfully running two plantations and I'm practicing law in the city. He wouldn't believe it in a thousand years."

"Yes, it is a pity he isn't here to see this, isn't it?" David asked.

"Well, let's go inside," William said, "Emanuel can help the driver with the bags."

Emanuel always felt the need to be on guard in the presence of most white folk, but that was especially true when William Littlejohn was around. The old driver seemed to have the perfect solution: He said nothing and did what he was told. It was almost as if he weren't there. For the duration of Missy Kathryn's stay in Charleston, Emanuel and the driver would be added to the servants' pool.

Inside, Emanuel became so intrigued by a piano tucked away in a corner of the parlor that he barely took notice of the other servants: two maids, a cook, and a butler—more than at Lake Holler. He wondered why there were so many.

The butler's name was James. He was courteous and all smiles, eager to do the bidding of his master. Emanuel hoped he would be a source of information about Charleston.

There was Sukie, the cook. Emanuel would learn that she rarely looked up but busied herself in her own little world that was pretty much restricted to the kitchen.

Dancy appeared to be older than the other servants. Her peculiar habit of mumbling aloud, either alone or in company, would quickly become apparent to Emanuel, who would come to think that she must have been a bit touched.

But Lettis, the second maid, was the most beautiful black woman Emanuel had ever seen. The other servants were in no way spectacular, but this woman was magnificent. Almost immediately, they caught each other's eye. Emanuel felt urges in his pants that made him very self-conscious. He hoped no one noticed.

Lettis had jet black hair that was long and well groomed; her skin was a smooth mahogany. She had full, inviting lips and sensuous, large eyes. The bodice of her dress revealed the deep chasm between her large breasts. Emanuel felt his heart pounding.

She didn't look the part of a servant; she was too beautiful and elegant. What was she for, thought Emanuel.

He would became suspicious of Lettis's function when he

learned that she slept alone in the cellar beneath the main house while the other servants slept out back in the two-story servants quarters. Emanuel, James, and the reticent driver were to sleep downstairs; the other women would be upstairs.

Lettis wasted no time extending him an invitation for a visit, but Emanuel declined the offer. Her mere presence caused sensations that he didn't understand.

His thoughts were on the other events of the day. He was especially intrigued by the funny way his new acquaintances talked; he had never heard any slave speak that way. Because of his musical background, he had less trouble than others understanding the highly resonant, rapid speech. That made him remember Lettis's words.

"Hey, pretty boy," she had said in a commanding voice, "you come lay with me tonight."

His thoughts went wild over what might have happened.

Kathryn had long ago run out of acceptable excuses that would deter William's efforts at lovemaking. At most, she only saw William once or twice a month. During their encounters, she imagined that it was David who was smothering her lips with moist kisses; lifting her gown; massaging her breasts, buttocks, and thighs; penetrating her and methodically pounding her form into the soft mattress. Tonight, once it was all over, she felt defiled and cheated. Why was she being so faithful to a man whom she knew made no effort to return the respect? Besides, she was in love with someone else. She turned her back to William and discovered a small mound of cotton on the bedside table. She didn't bother to ask what it was for.

Wednesday morning blossomed into a bright day with a glowing sun set against a clear blue sky, offsetting the chill in the air. The weather was well-suited for Charleston's most famous time of the year—the beginning of race week. There would be daily races, parties, and celebrations of every kind, followed by the Saint Cecilia Ball. At this time of year, all of Charleston was filled with energy and excitement.

Between functions, there was time for strolling along the beautiful streets and grounds, or just talking, because one was too full to do anything else after a heavy meal. The food was varied and abundant—eggs boiled or scrambled; bacon fried crisp and brown, giving off a tantalizing aroma; other meats of all varieties: plump sausage, shrimp, fried oysters, mounds of white hominy; breads: yeast rolls, corn muffins, biscuits; fruit: strawberries, apples, oranges, pears, figs, and bananas.

Emanuel helped Sukie with breakfast this morning. He had never seen so much food prepared for one family's meal in his life. There was so much that there was little time to do anything but eat, which was just what Kathryn, William, and David did.

Behind closed doors, the servants ate as heartily as the masters and the mistress. Guests were to be expected, as visitation was a part of the holiday ritual. Each household was prepared for drop-in visits from either local members of the Charleston elite or visitors from out of town.

William's senior partner, Barfield Chambers, was the first such visitor. He was accompanied by another man named William Pennison Porter, whom everyone in the room knew.

"Mr. Porter, it's a great pleasure to have you in my home," William said. "I'm very happy that Barfield could bring you over."

They walked into the sitting room where David and Kathryn were. "Mr. Porter, this is my wife, Kathryn, and my brother, David. Barfield, I believe you have met everyone."

"My dear Kathryn, you get more beautiful every time I see you," replied Barfield. "And you, David, how are things at Lake Holler?"

"Just fine, Sir. Everything seems to be in order."

"Barfield, just hearing your compliments is more than enough reason for me to visit Charleston more often," Kathryn said as she embraced him affectionately.

"Now, if you gentlemen will excuse me. You must have things to talk about. Nice to see you, Mr. Porter."

"The pleasure was all mine, my dear."

This was the first formal introduction of W. P. Porter that Kathryn, David, or William had had. But they knew he was a senator from one of the parishes. He seemed courteous and relaxed, yet possessing an aura that suggested he was a man of authority.

"Mr. Porter, Barfield, David come. Let's sit in the drawing room and have an early morning glass of sherry," said William.

Lettis brought in the refreshments that included tea and coffee. Her presence captured the attention of everyone in the room. Though her dress was plain and conservative, her shapely body and smooth dark skin drew lascivious glances. All was quiet until she left.

"That was William's maid," Barfield Chambers said, with an emphasis on the word "maid." He and Mr. Porter began to laugh.

David's expression did not change, but William grimaced slightly while drinking his sherry. He decided to change the subject.

"It would seem, Mr. Porter, that our Northern friends leave but one alternative, if we are to preserve our Southern traditions and way of life."

William was feeling his way, but his questioning was fueled by a desire to know where the South Carolina legislator stood.

"And what might that alternative be, Sir?" replied Mr. Porter. His disposition had suddenly become solemn, as if he were delivering a speech before the U. S. Congress.

"I don't think that it's any secret that there are more of us who feel that complete and total separation of the Southern from the Northern states is the only way the South can protect its institutions and way of life."

Mr. Porter's face grew hard as a statue's.

"As you already know, I'm sure, there are political notables— Rhett, Bennett, Cheves, to name a few, who are actively working toward that end."

David had sat quietly up until now. He wanted to add a new wrinkle to the conversation without revealing his position.

"You must also realize that there are those, Joel Poinsett, for example, who outwardly oppose any action supporting disunion. He and his followers believe slavery to be too unprofitable in the farming districts, and that its presence is gradually waning in states like Maryland, Virginia, and North Carolina, not to mention its virtual absence in the North."

William looked at David in astonishment. Until that moment, he had been completely unaware of his brother's political insight. He quickly turned his attention to Mr. Porter.

"My feelings on this subject are as firm as the idea of liberty and freedom can be," replied Mr. Porter. "The question now is how much must the South sacrifice? How much must we compromise before we are given our just say-so in this nation that we are at least one-half responsible for? It's imperative, in my view, that if we are to feel a part of this great nation, our just rights must be recognized and our constitutional equality asserted. I fear, gentlemen, that the issue of compromise has been forced upon us once too often and there are many who are willing now to openly resist. The tariff issue has been with us too long and it needs to be settled with all haste in a manner that's soothing to the Southern states. The slavery issue, as it involves any newly acquired western territory, is the most serious point of contention in any future debates between the North and the South. Should the pendulum shift in favor of the North and we lose the balance of slave versus free states in the western area, then the Southern position will be severely weakened."

Mr. Porter's words held everyone spellbound. They knew that perhaps he, more than anyone else present, had some inkling of what was to come of the cold war between the North and South.

"But," Mr. Porter continued, "there is one last issue that must be settled expeditiously, and with all of God's speed, and that is the problem of runaway slaves who find themselves in the protective custody of the North. Gentlemen, I am not at liberty to say much at this point, but I shall say this: before next year's end, my sources inform me that a bill will be passed in the Congress of the United States that will assume enforcement of the Fugitive Slave Act, making it mandatory for the North to return known runaways to their rightful owners."

Mr. Porter's last statement ignited a mood of elation, as if a major battle had been won in some great war. William, Barfield, and David all stood in applause. Every face, except David's, wore a smile.

Kathryn stood silently at the window. She tried to bring her eyes to focus in the distance where the Cooper River silhouetted against the luxuriant sky. But for her, the window was a mirror, and in her mind were images of her and David. They were holding each other tightly in a warm embrace, her arm around his back and his across her shoulders. She listened to his words.

"Kathryn, I love you so much. I don't know how much longer I can stand being without you, sharing your presence but not your love, feeling your warmth but not holding your body close whenever I need to. Tell me you feel the same."

Kathryn was in her own little dreamworld—the one she had created to make her predicament tolerable. She imagined herself responding to David.

"You know I do. My love for you is so strong that to think or dream of you gives me almost enough pleasure—I hunger for you all my waking moments."

She and David, together, standing toe to toe as their lips met and fused softly as one—an ephemeral kiss, to last, forever.

"Kathryn!" the door swung open abruptly as William entered.

"You had better hurry and get dressed. It's time we leave for the races."

Just like that, Kathryn's dream world quickly dissolved into the present.

"Yes, I'll hurry," she replied.

The races were held at the Washington course on the perimeter of Charleston. The event was certainly the most popular of its kind for Charlestonians as well as for visitors from Virginia, North Carolina, and Georgia. Many of them had brought their fastest steeds along in hopes of winning the handsome purse offered by the Jockey Club, sponsor of the event, to the winners of the one-, two-, three-, and four-mile races. A steady procession of spectators streamed into the race track: tour wagons for those without horse or carriage; others making the long trek by foot; and the elite, who rode in private chauffeur-driven carriages.

William sat in his carriage beside Kathryn, peering out the window at the determined pedestrians. Race week had been the annual holiday occasion of note in his life since as long as he could remember; he had missed only a few. During his father's time, one or two of the favored horses always came from his stables, but after his death, there had been little time to care for a prized racehorse. Now, a passion that lay dormant for years was resurgent in William. He didn't just want to enter the races; he was determined to have the winners of the major race come from his stables. He was aware that his law partner, Barfield Chambers, had one of the finest stables of horses in Charleston.

He also knew that an outright purchase of a horse from Barfield was out of the question. To win a bet fair and square was his only chance. The stage had already been set a few days back.

Every word of his conversation with Barfield was still etched in his mind.

"William, I've never been one to shy away from a fair wager, no matter what the risk. You appear to me to be an excellent gambling patron, not afraid of the risks," Barfield had said.

"What sort of wager do you have in mind?"

"Well, just a little wager on the horse races that are coming up. Now it's no secret that you have had your eye on some of my prize horses. What about a little side bet just between you and me?"

William had grown accustomed to the shrewdness of his partner and didn't want to seem overly anxious.

"What kind of wager do you have in mind?"

"I'll stud my best stallion with any mare in my stables and you get the first two sires—stallion or mare, against old Echo Holler plantation."

William knew the stakes were awfully high for what Barfield was offering, but he also felt that he could win. He hesitated only for a moment.

"All right, what's your deal?"

"It's simple. You are to study the entries of all the races on the roster. Choose your winner from each race and prepare a list; also, you must present the time of the winning heat. We will hand this list over to a mutually agreed upon fellow Jockey Club member. At the end of the last race, the man who has chosen the most winners will take all. In the event of a tie, the man guessing the winning time, or coming closest to it, wins all."

William pondered the offer for a while. He knew he could not tell Kathryn about this wager. He also knew his yearnings for a good racehorse overpowered reason.

"I'll accept your wager on one condition," William said.

"What is it?"

"I can choose any one horse presently in your stable plus the yearling of any sire that I choose."

They both agreed; the wager was on.

David sat on the opposite side of the carriage, alone. Occasionally, as if under the power of some magnetic force, his glances met Kathryn's. For brief moments, the sparks were there between them, just as if William didn't exist. In their hearts, he didn't. Both recalled their earlier ride to Charleston. Never had they been alone and in each other's company for such a long period, and they knew they were desperate to repeat the experience. As Kathryn sat waiting to disembark from the carriage, she composed a poem:

> *Carriage ride, a race to be*
> *Fret fool beside me, lover 'cross from me*
> *O' destiny air the truth, wilt thee,*
> *Lover beside me, fret fool across from me.*

This first day of the event commenced with weather perfect for horse racing. There had been a drought, but the field was well cared for by stewards who watered down an otherwise crusty and dry track. Everyone of note in the city was in attendance and the smiles and laughter of the women in attendance set the tone for an elegant, exciting event filled with anxiety and gaiety.

The first race was over quickly, the heat won by a mare called Bostona with a time of 7:50 minutes. William and Barfield compared notes. Both had chosen Bostona, with similar times, 7:49 and 7:50 respectively.

A horse named Millwood ran the first and second heats of the second race with the fastest time at 3:47½ seconds for a two-mile run. By the end of the day, Barfield and William felt a bit at ease; the wager remained any man's to win.

Rosalie, a six-year-old mare, was such an obvious standout on the second day of racing that Barfield and William concluded the second day would end like the first—a draw. And it did, with both picking the horse to win the second race as well.

The second race day was even more of a social event because it was followed by the ball. No doubt there were a few who did not return to the races every day, but all the city's notables were present at the ball, one of the most prestigious social events of the year.

Emanuel, along with James, William's butler, had been allowed to hire themselves out as waiters. Emanuel had never been in the company of so many rich, dressed-up white folks in his life. His fears and shyness were soothed by the music which, of course, was his main interest. It was extremely hard to show disinterest, especially when he heard a style of music with which he was not familiar. He later learned that what he had heard was called a *polka*. He also imagined himself at the keyboard as the band played a waltz by Mozart. He could feel Missy Kathryn's eyes on him, but knew he dared not look at her.

On one occasion during the evening, Emanuel had to serve his master. Although he went unnoticed, William unnerved him to the point that he forgot all about the music. He had heard William talking to three or four men about his disdain for the heretofore unheard-of-habit of smoking cigars in front of the ladies at the race track's salon. He thought such impropriety was hideous and archaic and certainly a point of discussion by the rules committee at the club.

The party ended before dawn and Emanuel made his way home to the town house. As he walked the path behind the house to the servants quarters, Lettis emerged from her cellar room. She wore only a loose-fitting nightgown.

"Why don't you come on down here and stay with me tonight, handsome?"

"I'd best not do that," Emanuel shyly replied. He was glad the darkness concealed the throbbing organ in his pants.

Lettis, being older and more experienced, was not one to continue taking no for an answer. With a firm grasp, she took Emanuel by the arm. She felt the strength of his muscles and imagined the energy trapped in his youthful body. He was a man-child; she sensed his stored passion. It wasn't often that she got to sleep with her own kind, and she knew Master William would be with his wife tonight.

"Now, you just come on," she said, steering him toward her room and all but dragging him across the threshold. As the door closed behind them, the candlelit room set the tone for the romantic interlude that was to follow.

Every twist of Lettis's body heightened Emanuel's desire. As her gown slipped to the floor, he noticed how smooth and soft her skin was. He desperately wanted to know what it would be like to touch her.

Lettis's breasts were full like ripe fruit. She stepped behind him, allowing her nipples to brush across his back. Emanuel felt a sense of warmth and safety, like a suckling babe. Lettis's slender waist accented the roundness of her hips and thighs. Emanuel delighted in the beauty of her form but was still not fully aware of the pleasure she would bring. He finally accepted the fact that he did not want to leave.

His only desire was that time would stand still as Lettis undressed him. The light of the candle illuminated their forms as they began to press, hold, and massage each other. Emanuel's obvious inexperience unleashed an animal-like passion in Lettis.

She led him to her bed and laid him down on it. She was hungry for the company of a black man and didn't try to hide it. Lettis wanted to please him—give to him willingly what was so often demanded of her by Massah William.

Emanuel experienced her body in a way he had never known before. As Lettis blew her warm breath along his neck, she swayed from side to side, letting her breasts brush across Emanuel's chest. He felt his penis throbbing.

Lettis ran her hands through his thick, woolly hair as she tongued his earlobe, moved across his cheek to kiss his lips, then over to the other earlobe. Hungrily, she crawled down his body from the nape of his brown shiny chest to his flat, muscular stomach, tickling his navel with her tongue. Then she held his privates in her hand. Each of his virgin throbs sent jolts of electricity through her body, heightening her arousal.

Emanuel lay as still as he could, yielding totally to Lettis's guidance and erotic tutelage. Her skill was obvious as she hypnotized him with soft scintillating kisses and stimulating caresses. She crawled atop his frame and launched into motion. He could only lie limp on the bed.

She embraced him, then opened her warm thighs, inviting him to enter her. Once again he was moved to another plateau of pleasure as he crawled on top of her.

Eagerly, he began to counter her every move as he assumed

command. They kissed and grabbed each other ardently. Her inner warmth ignited him and their bodies moved in unison—a connubial dance. They mesmerized each other with frenzied, chaotic jerks that grew and grew in momentum. Then, Lettis mustered the strength to push Emanuel off her. Playfully, they tossed, turned, and rolled about the bed in search of the most erotic position.

They found it, and Lettis's soft body cushioned his thrust as their erotic rhythm grew. He felt his body quicken like a clap of thunder, then quiet like the calm after a summer storm, as their erogenous rhythm ended in bursts of tiny explosions.

Lettis lay beside him, slightly curled in his arms. There wasn't much time; the sun was coming up. Emanuel glanced at her moist brown skin. Neither of them had bothered to cover themselves, not that it mattered to him; he was proud of his manhood. For the first time, he knew who and what he was.

He was a man. His identity was complete.

William tried to use the covers to shield his face from the rising sun that peeked through the windows. He felt dazed and groggy from his late-night partying. He could hear Kathryn's soft breaths beside him as he pulled himself out of bed. As he reached to close the curtains, he saw a figure on the walk leading from Lettis's room.

William rubbed his eyes to clear his vision. A surge of anger energized him. Emanuel! He became infuriated at the thought that both he and a nigga slave shared the same wench's bed. He had not felt this degree of anger since he first looked in the face of Buck after his capture. William was seething as he thought of what punishing tactic he would use to exact revenge.

He had always warned his concubines that they were not to sleep with nigga men.

Quietly, he eased on his pants and a shirt and went downstairs. He knew Emanuel would have to enter the house soon to begin his duties, so he waited near the back entrance.

"You black son of a . . . ," he shouted, then raised his foot and kicked Emanuel in the groin. Searing pain erupted throughout Emanuel's body as he fell to the floor, clutching his privates. He had never known such agony. Emanuel could barely hear the words of his master.

"You stay out of the cellar room, boy! If I so much as see you near there again, I'll hang you just like I did your worthless nigga pa!"

His anger spent, William turned and headed back up the stairs. I've got to find a way to get rid of that nigga, he thought. Don't understand what Kathryn sees in that damn good-for-nothing anyway. I'll find a way, in spite of her.

Emanuel remained motionless on the kitchen floor, Massah Littlejohn's words momentarily numbing his pain. So this was the murderer of my father, Emanuel thought, shamelessly offering a full confession.

At first, Emanuel had hurt so badly that he wanted to die, but he knew he had to live to avenge his father's murder.

Something startled Bell out of her deep sleep. A seizure-like jerk had her awake and sitting up, looking about the empty shack, trying to discover some reason for her anguish. Inside she felt afraid—not for herself but for Emanuel. Something had happened, but there was nothing she could do except hope he was alive and that she would see him again. She tried to pray but couldn't; she felt so hopeless. Finally, she muttered a few words aloud.

"Lawd," she begged, "please bring mah chile back ta me."

The final races took place on another gorgeous day.

Multitudes of the local populace, as well as visitors from afar, filled the stands.

There were many smiles and much gaiety. The beautiful ladies, all dressed in the latest fashion, were the only distractions from the race that was about to begin.

William and Barfield sat beside one another, each conjuring up in his mind a victory for his chosen horse, yet fearful of an inevitable defeat. They entered this last series of races tied.

In a matter of minutes the wager would be decided.

As soon as it was announced that Bostona, Shark, and Rosalie were starting in the race, the gambling amongst most males became more fervent. Another Jockey Club member assisted William and Barfield, keeping their lists of winners on his person.

"Now then, Sirs," the aide said to them, "it seems very likely that both of you may have chosen the same horse as winner, since this has been the trend up to now. In the event of such an occurrence, I shall ask you to write down the time in minutes and seconds you think necessary for the winner to complete the race.

"The winner, of course, will be that person guessing the number of seconds or closest to it."

Each man followed suit.

"Gentlemen, be so kind as to set your watches."

They did as instructed.

"Now, gentlemen," the aide said, "exchange watches so that each of you will hold check on the other."

The horses barged out of the gate with jolting force. All eyes were on the three principle contenders: Bostona, Shark, and Rosalie. Each horse ran so well and effortlessly that halfway through the race it was hard to predict the winner. Then the field began to separate with Shark dropping back to a long-shot third. It was a two-horse race right to the finish until Rosalie assumed a comfortable lead to win. The crowd roared in excitement and pleasure.

The aide could hardly hear himself when he stood to announce each man's choice.

"Sir Barfield Chambers, Rosalie. Sir William Littlejohn, Rosalie."

It all came down to each man's recorded time.

"Gentlemen, the official time of the first heat was five minutes thirty-one seconds. Mr. Chambers, Sir, please stand and announce Mr. Littlejohn's predicted time in seconds," instructed the aide as he handed the older man a slip of paper.

"Five minutes and thirty seconds," said Barfield.

"And you, Sir, Mr. Littlejohn."

A big grin spread across William's face as he read Barfield Chamber's predicted time of five minutes and twenty seconds.

"Gentlemen, let it now be known that on the twelfth day of February 1849, the wager between the parties Littlejohn and Chambers was won by William Littlejohn. Sirs, you may settle the wager in private."

William felt enormously relieved. He had not bothered to tell Kathryn that he had bet her father's lands against a prize horse. Now, there was no need. He had won.

With all the gentlemanly reserve that he could muster, Barfield approached William to concede his defeat.

"You have your choice of any horse in my stables now or any to be born over the ensuing year," he told William. "I have only a gentleman's request that you make your choice as soon as possible to spare me any prolonged anguish over my loss."

Having said this, Barfield walked away.

William soon made his choice—a yearling: a shiny, black colt that he called Trumpet. He fully anticipated the day the horse would answer the call of the horn with a win at Charleston's Race Day. It had to happen. He would see to it by personally helping to train the colt. This would mean spending more time at Lake Holler plantation, away from his law practice, away from Lettis, and more time with Kathryn.

Somehow, the thought of being with Kathryn had lost some of its appeal. What excitement there had been during their marriage had long since dissipated, and he doubted that involvement with other women would change just because he was going to spend more time at home. Oh, well, a matter of little concern for the moment since he could always bring his conveniences home. He had certainly done it before.

BOOK FOUR

CHAPTER TWENTY-FOUR

"Winnie, you get up now," said Teresa. This time, there was no need for lengthy poking and prodding; Winnie was instantly out of bed and on her feet.

"Yes'm," she replied, turning slightly away from her mother so she could not see the smile on her face. Quickly, Winnie moved toward the face bowl where she doused her face with fresh, cool water. She dried herself, then glimpsed at her reflection in a small mirror on the nightstand. She was pleased with what she saw.

Yes, she thought, I'm as pretty as any white girl that I have seen. I'm sure my father would be so proud of me.

Winnie's nose was perfect: not too pointy, not too wide, but delicate and well suited for her pouty lips. She prided herself because her hair flattened to her head in long, glistening strands when wet, just like Mistress Robard's, the lady of the house. Winnie had watched her every move, and during private moments she would practice walking like the mistress with a straight back and short, ballet-like steps. This was so unlike her mother, whose stride was more purposeful and less graceful.

Winnie had to practice acting like a lady because one day she would be one. In fact, she felt her time had come; she was about to receive payback for all the years of emulating white women. Today, Bertram was returning home.

"Come on here, child. Get your face out of that mirror," her mother said. "We've got a lot to do to get ready for Massah Bertram. He's comin' home today."

Winnie had never been beyond this plantation in Natchez, Mississippi, where she had been born, but she was certain that this had to be one of the most beautiful in the world. It lacked nothing in its natural ornamentation. Many species of birds flew among the tall trees; beautiful flowers of all colors were in full bloom, making this wondrously happy day even more beautiful.

She, along with all the plantation household assembled on the front lawn, soon saw a carriage approach in the distance. Suddenly, Winnie felt as if one of the butterflies that floated around the flowers had somehow lodged in her stomach.

The driver reined the horses in front of the house. Two handsome, well-dressed men chauffeured the carriage. Instantly, Master and Missus Robard were at the carriage, embracing their sons.

"Oh! This is the happiest day of my life," said Mrs. Robard. "I've waited for this moment for so many years. Welcome home, Robert," she said as she kissed her oldest son on the cheek.

"Welcome home, Bertram," she said as she kissed him, too.

"My, you have grown so. Now, let's go into the house, out of this hot sun, and have some refreshments." The young men escorted their mother up the steps.

Bertram caught Winnie's eye as he passed. It was the longest, sweetest moment of Winnie's life. She could see that this mischievous, unrestrained boy had grown to be a tall, handsome young man, and she knew that he would be at her side, holding and caressing her, the first chance he got.

That night, assured that her mother was asleep, Winnie eased out of bed as quietly as she could. Every squeak of the floorboards and the old straw mattress caused her to fear that her mother would awaken. But she could wait no longer; she had to see Bertram. Even if her mother woke up, she knew she would just have to tell her the truth.

Winnie reached Bertram's room, carefully turned the doorknob without knocking, and entered. It was almost as if Bertram knew she was coming. He immediately opened his eyes and pulled back the covers of his bed so she could lie beside him. As soon as she was in reach, his hands were touching and probing her most intimate spots. Winnie did not resist. It was her first sexual experience, but she could sense that it was not his. Still, she thought he was a little rough, but dismissed it. Winnie realized Bertram had not uttered a word other than her name, but that was all right. She knew they would talk after they finished their lovemaking. Winnie relaxed, giving herself completely to Bertram.

She eagerly awaited an orgasm that never came, but she knew Bertram had, as she watched him experience his final orgasmic thrust.

Though she hadn't enjoyed this experience, Winnie felt satisfied that she had pleased Bertram.

"You better go now," he ordered her. Knowing that Winnie expected a more affectionate tone, he added, "before my parents awaken and find you here."

Was that all, Winnie thought. She knew there was plenty of time before daybreak. Again, she felt butterflies in her stomach, but for different reasons. She wanted to cry out to show her hurt.

But she was somewhat encouraged when Bertram said he would see her again tomorrow night.

The next night started just like the one before until Winnie pushed Bertram aside.

"Bertram, you haven't said more than two words to me since you returned home. I want it to be like old times again, when we used to talk and laugh together."

He looked at her.

"What is there to talk about? I've been places that you can never go and I've seen things that you can never see because you're a . . . you're a slave girl."

Winnie could see her dream turning into a nightmare.

"I was a slave when we knew each other as children," she responded. "It didn't seem to matter then."

What had happened to the free-spirited, nonprejudiced boy whom she had grown up with?

"Well, this world will never let you forget what you are, and that's a slave, so we might as well make the best of it," replied Bertram as he pulled her down on the mattress. Winnie was so stunned by his words that she didn't have the will to resist.

Before now, being a slave had not made a whole lot of difference. She had always had a great deal of self-esteem, but Bertram had just destroyed that. Preoccupied with her thoughts, Winnie didn't notice when Robert entered the room. Before she could move, Bertram held her down as he exchanged places with his brother, who was even rougher than Bertram. With every thrust, Winnie felt a searing, sharp, agonizing pain. She wanted and tried to fight off her aggressors, but the two of them had a secure hold on her arms and legs. She could not let this continue. Physically defenseless, she did the only thing she could: She screamed, a bellowing, shrill cry certain to awaken everyone in the house. A heavy hand clamped firmly over her mouth and her assailants froze, listening for any signs of discovery.

But it was too late. The door burst open.

"What is going on here?" Mistress Robard exclaimed as she looked on in utter horror. "Oh! I feel faint."

Her body grew limp. As she began to crumple to the floor, her husband appeared out of nowhere and caught her.

Within minutes, Mistress Robard was fully revived. Winnie had never seen her so angry, so unforgiving. She demanded that Winnie be removed from the plantation the first thing in the morning. By this time, Teresa had arrived and was begging for her daughter's sake. She told them she would do anything if they would just let Winnie stay. Her pleas were ignored. At sunrise, she was told, Winnie was to be sold to any slave trader offering a fair price—under the condition that she was not to remain in Natchez.

Months after Massah Littlejohn's assault, Emanuel's life seemed to have taken a turn for the worse. The master was spending more and more time at the plantation, overseeing the training of his new horse, Trumpet. He supervised everything: getting the horse used to people, the bridle and saddle, even the trotting exercises. No matter what was on the training schedule, Massah Littlejohn took responsibility for seeing that it was done correctly, or at least to his satisfaction. Emanuel had never seen him take such a strong interest in anything. Even though it was summer, when most whites moved to the city to get away from the scorching heat, the mosquitoes, and the dreaded fever, Massah William returned regularly to oversee the training of his horse, much to Emanuel's dismay. This meant less available time to practice the piano, lest he be discovered. Emanuel didn't know what was worse—to be beaten by the master or just having him around all the time, keeping him from practice.

Bell noticed the change in Emanuel's mood and attitude on one of his nighttime visits to her cabin.

"Why de sad face, 'Manuel?" she asked. "You ack like somebody done run away wid yo' arm or yo' leg. Wha's de madda?"

"Massah Littlejohn is in the house most all the time now," he answered, "an' I hate that white man."

Emanuel was tempted to tell her of the incident in Charleston, but he didn't want to worry her.

"The more he's around, the less I can play the piano. Missy Kathryn, she's unhappy, too. I can tell it. When she's with Massah David, she smiles like she's happy. When she's with Massah Littlejohn, she acts like she's sick all the time. Seems he just makes everybody unhappy."

"Well, 'Manuel," replied his mother. "Sometimes yo' hab ta speak yo' troubles to de Lawd. It neba eva was meant fo' a black chile to hab no learnin' an' play no piano. Now, see, all it's done is made yo' unhappy. What good is it fo' yo'?"

Emanuel always cringed inside when his mother spoke that way. It seemed to him that white folks were supposed to have everything now and black folk would only get theirs when or if they got to heaven—and it would take a whole lot of praying to do that. Emanuel tried to restrain his anger.

"Seems to me that if I'm not s'pose to do it, then why did it happen? Seems like all black folks s'pose to do is pray while the Lawd and white folks does everything else. It ain't right."

"Now yo' hush up that kinda talk fo' de Lawd smacks yo' lips together so you can' speak anotha word," Bell warned him. "The Lawd will make a way. Yo' got ta belieb dat, an' dat's all I knows."

To respond seemed useless. As he sat looking down at the dirty floor, he made up his mind that he wasn't going to wait on the Lawd. He would find his own way.

♦♦♦

During the ensuing weeks after her dismissal from the Robard plantation, Winnie's life quickly evolved into one of despair. In Natchez, she was purchased by a greedy slave trader who knew that such beauty as hers would bring a good price in any port or city.

To Winnie, this was a new world with new experiences, indeed a new life that she had to become accustomed to. Hunger, filth, and fatigue to the point of exhaustion were all her new acquaintances, ones that she vowed to rid herself of, whatever the price.

She was passed from one dirty hole after the other, usually with women of similar condition, or at times with slave men who used her unusual beauty as an excuse to gaze lustfully. She had to thank God for the leg irons and chains that restrained them all—including her—to the steamboat, for surely, she would have been raped at will by her comrades in misery.

One day on the ship, Winnie had fought her natural urges but could restrain herself no longer. She maneuvered herself onto a small bundle of hay. As best she could, she raised her filthy dress over her buttocks and let the water flow. Her urine was hot and bore a strong ammonia smell. The itchy discomfort of the water flowing down her leg was no match for the relief that came as she reduced the swelling bulge in her lower abdomen. The women sensed her unfamiliarity with the situation. The men, on the other hand, smirked in satisfaction, as if to say, "Now you are one of us; no better, no worse."

She ended up at an auction in New Orleans. Despite her battered appearance, the traders could see her obvious beauty and signs of her rearing as a house slave. There were many bidders for her services. Eventually, she was purchased by a Mr. Montclaire to assist his wife with a new baby and the housekeeping. It didn't matter too much to Winnie where she went, as long as she could lie down someplace and sleep. She was exhausted from the boat ride and the trek by foot to the auction site, where again, she had been placed in heavy chains.

Her duties at the Montclaires began almost immediately. She was given only enough time to bathe and change into clean clothes before the newborn was handed to her.

"Now, you must not allow her to cry. It irritates me," were her initial instructions from the Missus.

Winnie cradled the baby and lowered herself into a rocking chair. She hummed softly and rocked steadily, hoping the child would sleep so that she could get some rest. God forbid that she dropped the baby while she slept! But she knew there was no way she could stay awake much longer.

A smack to the face startled her.

"Stay awake, you little wench," the Missus screamed. "I won't allow you to drop my baby."

Winnie roused herself as much as she could, her body so numb with fatigue that even the smack to the face triggered little emotion.

It was soon apparent to Winnie that no matter how hard she tried, she could not satisfy the Missus. Winnie knew why. The Missus had caught her husband gazing at Winnie once too often. After only a few weeks, she once again joined the ranks of the slave chain gang. This time, things were different. While at the Montclaires, she had managed to get some rest when everyone else was asleep and the baby was quiet. She felt a little better, stronger.

Winnie tried to not let her thoughts stray to Bertram. He was like all other white men, she told herself, he would be of no help. She longed to see her mother again but knew that was hopeless. She remembered her mother's admonishment . . . white men, clean sheets, soft beds. Now, it looked like she did not have a choice. Whatever came her way, she would have to accept.

Winnie and her companions had boarded ship at the Gulf of Mexico. The rumors were of only one destination, Charleston, South Carolina. Charleston, Winnie thought. She had heard the place mentioned in conversations at the Robard plantation, and she grew more apprehensive. She became frantic when, just before their arrival, she was separated from the other slaves. She was bathed, her hair was combed, and she was given a clean dress. At first, Winnie felt odd when they put her in front of—and chained her separately from—the others. Then, she realized what was about to happen. All of the preparations meant one thing—auction.

William, like most of the Charleston plantation owners, assembled in the square near the auction area. The whole affair was managed much like a bazaar; there were vendors of various types strategically located amongst the sites where horses and carriages, as well as slaves, were sold to the highest bidders. But the event of the day was the slave auction.

This was the start of the cotton-picking season, when the large plantations needed every available hand to gather the crop.

Hundreds of slaves—infants, older children, men, and women—were brought before the auction block and put on public display.

Victimized by what most in attendance considered to be a natural fate, they were each pushed into the arena and, once sold, roughly ushered out.

The affair proceeded with one human animal after another being brought before a stolid-faced auctioneer, spitting out words so fast that they were unintelligible except to the experienced ear:

"Now-what-am-I-bid-fer-this-genteel-wench-with-the-lighter-skin-and-long-black-hair. . ."

Winnie heard the words spoken about her. She, like her companions, stood motionless. She wanted to get the whole thing over with. This was her second auction in a matter of weeks, but she had already adjusted to the crudeness.

By far, she was the main attraction of the day. Earlier, the crowd had been abuzz with carefree chatter; now all was quiet as each man silently registered a winning bid.

"Gentlemen, the bidding starts at $200. Who's going to match it? Well-bred, she is. You can see that, and a bit of a looker," said the auctioneer.

"$200," shouted a lone voice.

William was mesmerized by this slave girl's youthful beauty and knew he had to have her, no matter the price. She would more than fill the vacancy in his cellar at Lake Holler. He said nothing, allowing the preliminary bidders the chance to eliminate themselves.

"Three hundred dollars."

"Three hundred dollars is the new bid. Do I hear $350?" asked the auctioneer.

Careful to not look them in the eye, Winnie stole glances at the crowd of mostly men, catching sight of their lascivious smiles and lustful gazes. She tried to console herself by remembering what her mother had said: white men, soft mattresses, clean sheets.

"Four hundred dollars," someone called out from the crowd.

"Four hundred dollars going once; $400 going twice."

"Eight hundred dollars," interrupted William.

The crowd gasped and was now abuzz over this large bid for a slave—a female slave at that.

"Eight hundred dollars," replied William again.

"Nine hundred dollars," said an unrelenting bidder.

"Going once! Going twice!"

"Twelve hundred dollars," announced William.

The crowd was stunned into silence. Never had anyone heard of such a price for one slave.

Deliberately slowing down to leave time for any other bids, the auctioneer said, "Going once, going twice; sold to William Littlejohn."

Whenever Master Littlejohn was away from the plantation, Emanuel would double his practice time. His introduction to the classics had been thorough and wanton. Missy Kathryn was now content to sit back and watch Emanuel perform. Only occasionally would she stop his play to offer instruction. He had all of his preferred pieces memorized.

Mozart, without a doubt, was his favorite; to Emanuel, his music awakened all the emotions. When he needed to vent his anger or express his emotions to the extreme, he played a piano adaptation of the *G-Minor Symphony*—a strong, stormy piece. For more thoughtful, enchanted moods, he preferred the piano adaptation of the *A-Major Symphony*. Emanuel's adept fingers brought Mozart's music—and seemingly his spirit—to life, and for those oh-so-short moments, they embraced as one.

Beethoven inspired Emanuel to be spontaneous and original. Like his mentor, Missy Kathryn, he needed Beethoven's impromptu ways to help him play with the much-needed freedom he and Kathryn both lacked. Any one of Beethoven's thirty-three sonatas allowed Emanuel to explore the passions of free men. He felt it his privilege to do so.

Emanuel's body was now alive with new yearnings and desires; Missy Kathryn and Lettis had been the instruments of his learning, but the gifts had been granted by God and he alone controlled them.

Emanuel's body resided on Lake Holler Plantation, but his soul was as ubiquitous as the elusive air around him. His thoughts, his yearnings, his emotions could never again be harnessed. He sensed something was about to happen and responded with fear and wanderlust.

Bring on the new, he commanded silently, let the clavier call out to the unknown.

CHAPTER TWENTY-FIVE

Today marked William's return from his trip to Charleston and, as always, the house slaves made ready for his arrival. Even Gertie hurried to complete her chores; for reasons no one understood, she was always elated when Master William came home.

Jonathan could care less that Massah Littlejohn was coming home. In fact, he wished his master would never return but knew that was just as unlikely as his being made a free man.

For Kathryn, William's homecomings always triggered a state of depression. She never played the piano during his stay, nor did she allow Emanuel to do so.

For years, Emanuel had feared Massah Littlejohn's returns.

Lately, though, his fear had given way to hatred and a clear realization that a disastrous fate awaited the two of them.

Subconsciously he was prepared and poised to exact his revenge.

He often thought of the Bible verses that told the story of David and Goliath. Well, he was David, but, as of yet, he had no sling.

Still, he would avenge his mother's and Missy Kathryn's suffering and his father's murder. For a long time, he had thought his only reason for being in the Big House was to learn to play the piano; now, thoughts of vindication were urging him on.

A yard slave called out as Massah Littlejohn's carriage appeared in the distance. Everyone in the house, including Missy Kathryn, came out, the slaves poised to help unload their master's luggage.

Massah Littlejohn's driver soon stopped the carriage alongside the front porch. Behind the carriage was a wagon filled with new slaves. Inside were five men, all of whom appeared to have not slept in days, and one girl, who appeared to be equally as tired. When Emanuel saw her face, he became instantly mesmerized; she was the most beautiful girl he had ever seen. But all too quickly, Massah Littlejohn broke the spell, barking out orders about his luggage. Startled, Emanuel made an awkward move and fell right on his face. He jumped up, and was relieved when he realized the girl had seemed to not notice his untimely accident.

After he and Kathryn engaged in a perfunctory hug, William issued another order.

"Gertie," William said, "the new girl's name is Winnie. She will be my new maid for my study. Show her to her quarters."

Emanuel had not experienced such passionate zeal and happiness over anything since Missy Kathryn asked if he wanted to learn to play the piano. This beautiful, angelic girl would be living and working in the same house under the same roof—with him. His body began to tingle, his stomach churned, his heart trembled, and his toes curled. He had to come to know this girl!

He had to fully investigate these new emotions. His introduction to manhood had been all-informing; but now, he was in love.

He knew it! He wanted it! He liked it!

That night Emanuel could not sleep; in fact, he didn't want to. He wouldn't allow such a basic, human necessity to rob him of moments he could spend thinking of Winnie. He paced the pantry-bedroom floor, all the while gazing out the small window that was the only source of light in the room. He looked forward to morning when he could begin his day so he could see her.

Later, when the first hint of early morning light appeared, he heard a soft knock at the door. Without waiting for a reply, Jonathan entered, and Emanuel noticed that the older man moved a lot slower than he used to.

As always, Jonathan sat down to catch his breath before he began to talk. Emanuel was happy to see him. He always enjoyed their conversations. Besides, now there was something extra special to discuss.

Jonathan's voice was slowed by a constant hoarseness and the effort he had to put into speaking. "You feel good and happy now, don't you?" he said.

Emanuel tried to appear as if he didn't know what Jonathan was talking about. "I feel so-so, no different than before."

"Come on, 'Manuel, ever since that girl got here yesterday, you've been moping round here like a pregnant cow," replied Jonathan, before a short burst of violent coughing forced him to stop talking and cover his mouth.

"Are you all right?"

"I'm fine," Jonathan said, still coughing ". . . just this damned cough."

After Jonathan's coughing subsided, Emanuel began to speak, expressing his newly acquired emotions.

"She's the most beautiful person I have ever seen. I've never felt this way about anyone in my life. I mean, I've never had this funny feeling about a girl."

Jonathan replied like a father talking to his son, "I know, there is a first time for everybody."

"Is that true? Everybody gets this feeling?" asked Emanuel.

"At one time or other. Now, 'Manuel, you be careful."

"I know. I'm a slave boy. I don't have the right to be in love."

"No! That's not what I mean," said Jonathan.

"What do you mean?"

"Massah Littlejohn. That girl. She is for him."

"You mean . . ."

"Yes! When Massah Littlejohn brings these girls and puts them in that room, they is for him. He been doing it ever since he was a young buck. When I saw what was about to happen with you, I thought, I'd better warn you."

Emanuel was crushed. Then he remembered Lettis, the cellar room in Charleston, and the altercation he had had with Massah Littlejohn. Of course, he was going to make her another Lettis.

What can I do, Emanuel thought as he helped Jonathan get up off the bed and watched him leave. I have to do something!

Kathryn had her concerns, also. Of course, she had known of William's many other escapades. She had grown to not care, but this time was different. This girl was so young and pretty indeed! Furthermore, she, too, had noticed Emanuel's reaction and was elated for him. Kathryn felt she must intervene this time, yet, she didn't know quite how. For the moment, she knew William was out of the house overseeing the training of his horse. After all, the races were only months away, so she decided to start getting to know this girl.

She called Winnie to the bedroom upstairs.

"Winnie, come sit beside me on the bed, I want to talk to you."

"Yes'm."

"How old are you?"

"Sixteen, Ma'am."

 278

"Where did you come from?"

"Natchez in the beginning," said Winnie. She tried to sound unlearned, like a slave girl was supposed to be. "After that, one plantation or one slave hole after the other."

"Did you have family?"

"Just my mother. Her name was Teresa. She all I had . . . 'fo I was sold."

"You must miss her very much."

"She all I had," Winnie repeated as tears welled in her eyes.

"My husband is kind of a strange man. He may ask you or make you do things for him. Womanly things. Have you ever been with a man before?"

"Massah Bertram and Massah Robert, they . . . I guess I'll do what I have to do. I'se tired of bein' shipped from one dirty hole to the next. My mother used to always say white men, soft mattresses, clean sheets. Missy Kathryn, I don't mean to hurt nobody, dat includes you, but I'm a slave girl and guess I'll just have to do as I'm told all my life."

Kathryn realized this young girl had been beaten into submission and would now do whatever it took to survive. She could feel no anger toward this girl. She remembered her boat trip from England many years ago and the evil captain and the ugly black man with the forked tongue. When she had met William, she thought he would be her savior. But now, William was the evil captain and a lonely, frightened slave girl was to be his victim.

This time, Kathryn would have to be the hero. She turned to Winnie. "Maybe not, Winnie," she told the girl. "I shall do all I can to help you and keep you safe while at Lake Holler." Missy Kathryn brushed Winnie's tangled hair off her forehead with her hand. "You know what I think? There is a handsome boy about your age who is living in this house who is becoming very interested in you."

"You mean dat clumsy boy? I ain't never had nothing to do with no black nigga man before.'"

Winnie's word's took Kathryn by surprise. She tried to keep her composure.

"Oh, I see," she said quietly. "I assure you this one is very nice."

"Seems to me if he is a slave just like me, he can't do much for me."

"Maybe. Maybe not. We shall see. You better go now before William returns."

Kathryn could see through the wall that Winnie was trying to build around her. Sometime in her life, probably recently, the seeds of mistrust and cynicism had been sown deeply. But the tremor in her voice revealed the truth. Winnie was afraid— afraid that somehow in this house, like the others, she would be used and abused, afraid to give of herself and show any emotion because to do so was a sign of weakness.

Perhaps she was right, Kathryn thought, there could be little reason for a beautiful Negro girl in the South to have faith in anyone.

It was that evening, after supper, before Emanuel had a chance to speak to Winnie. They were alone in the dining room.

"I've been wanting to say something to you ever since I first saw you yesterday," Emanuel said nervously.

Winnie had also taken more than a second look at Emanuel.

She thought he was handsome, but like her—a slave. She had never known a black man in her life whom she could call a friend; she only knew there was a certain magnetism that had to be squelched.

"What on earth could you have to say to me?" Winnie asked coldly.

"Just what's your name and . . . "

"You know my name," she said abruptly. "It's been used by everybody in this house all day to fetch me."

"All right, I know your name," Emanuel said. "I'm just trying to make conversation. Get to know you."

"And once you know me, then what?"

Emanuel decided that the polite approach was getting him nowhere. Momentarily, that strong, mischievous personality of years ago surfaced and he walked around to the side of the table where Winnie was. He clasped his hands behind his back, leaned forward just a little, and looked right down into her eyes.

"Now listen to me, lady," Emanuel said, stretching out the word "lady." "I want to get to know you 'cause you are the most beautiful girl I've ever seen in my life. I've never loved any girl before and no matter what I have to do or how hard I have to try, I am going to make sure you are the first."

Winnie realized Emanuel's head-on confrontation was a scare tactic. She started to retaliate in kind, looking straight into his eyes. But retaliation turned into intrigue. She saw the sharp, determined glint in his eyes. She wanted to touch his smooth, black, glistening skin. She loved the way his mustache petered off into scant, new furry hair that adorned his handsome face. Her stomach felt queasy and light. She had pains, love pains.

"Now you're a slave and I'm a slave and everybody in this house seems to know why I was brought here and it wasn't to clean off the dinner table," Winnie told him. "We will both end up hurt and unhappy . . . like always."

"Maybe you're right," Emanuel conceded. "But I'm not hurting now and I'm happier than I've ever been in my life and I like it."

At that moment, Gertie burst into the room.

"What y'all doin' in heah?"

She turned to Emanuel.

"Boy, don't you overstep yo' ground or Massah Littlejohn'll have yo' neck," she said before leaving the room. Gertie did not look once in Winnie's direction.

"Well, who does she think she is?" inquired Winnie.

"She thinks that she is something special in the eyes of Massah Littlejohn, I reckon. She has hated me since I first set foot in this house. But enough about big fat Gertie. Why don't you let me show you around this place tonight after midnight when everyone is asleep?"

"Well, I don't know," Winnie said. "You're just going to make something happen between us, aren't you?"

"Come on," Emanuel teased. " 'Fraid you'll miss ole Massah Littlejohn if he comes a knocking?"

"One day he will, you know. Both you and me are powerless to do anything about it."

"Yeh, I know," Emanuel said. "Let's worry about it when it happens. I'll see you at midnight."

Strong rolling waves slapped at the lake shore. The night was breezy and atypically cool for September. Maybe this is the first sign of fall, Emanuel thought. He and Winnie left the house separately as agreed, to meet at the lakeside. He arrived first and chose a spot far enough from the Big House so no one could see them. When he saw Winnie approaching, he realized the eagerness in her step, and his heart began to pound faster and faster. When she was within arm's length, he reached out and pulled her close. Instantly, their lips met as they caressed each other firmly. The kiss was soft and succulent, sending tremors and tingles from head to toe. Their souls blended as they sought a world far from this place, away from slavery, bigotry, hatred, far away where they could exist as lovers without having to hide or resort to secrecy—far away from William Littlejohn.

When the kiss was over, Winnie buried her head in Emanuel's muscular chest. She kept her eyes closed as she recounted her mother's admonishment—white men, soft beds, and clean sheets.

282

Oh, Mother, Winnie said to herself, how wrong you were!

The feelings that Winnie aroused in Emanuel were new and exciting to him. He wanted the whole plantation, all of Charleston, the world, to know of his first love. He especially wanted his mother to know, but Winnie refused his offer to go to Bell's cabin. It was late and she was afraid of discovery, especially from telltale Gertie. She returned to the plantation house, and Emanuel went to visit his mother.

Emanuel felt no remorse over awakening Bell. He felt that his happiness would be her happiness. He wished he had brought food, but he simply hadn't thought of it this time.

" 'Manuel, somethin' wrong?"

"No, I just wanted to talk to you."

Bell looked at Emanuel's empty hands, then felt a little embarrassed. She had grown to expect food during those late-night visits, but she didn't want Emanuel to think she was not happy just to have him come see her.

"Well, sit," she told Emanuel. "What yo' want ta talk about?" Emanuel hesitated. He had never talked to his mother about such things before, never told her about his experience with Lettis.

"You ever been in love before?" he blurted out.

Bell smiled briefly. Her son was a young man now, though she had never really thought of him in that way. Slavery only allowed for general differences—big slave, little slave, strong slave, weak slave. Little was said about emotions; slaves were all supposed to feel the same.

For a moment, she felt reminiscent of her first and only love with Emanuel's father. The horrible ending brought her back to reality.

"Yo' got ta 'member dat yo' a slave an' dat any slave dat falls in love got ta be ready fo' anything," Bell told Emanuel.

283

"Yo' got ta be ready fo' de day dat de love is taken way. De white man don' want no love 'tween his slaves. He wants babies ta work his fiel's as soon as dey git big enough, an' dat's all."

Bell could see the disappointment on Emanuel's face. She knew she had never encouraged many happy moments in Emanuel's life. But this was perhaps the most important happy moment in his life and she wasn't going to ruin it. She placed a hand on each shoulder and looked him square in the face.

"'Manuel, yo' be happy wit dis love of yo's. It's dat new girl at de Big House, ain't it?"

"Yes'm."

"Yo' love dat gal a whole lot, don' yo'?"

"Yes'm."

Inwardly, she felt such a relationship could only lead to more pain, but she tried to be encouraging.

"Bet dat gal all in love wid ma han'some boy too, ain't she?"

"Yes'm. We love each other."

"Yo' 'member dis what I say, it takes three seconds to say I love yo', but it takes a lifetime to prove it. Most folks seems ta be sayin' more dan dey is a provin'."

On the way to the Big House, Emanuel remembered all that his mother had said, and he realized the fears she had and the ones she did not mention.

That morning, Kathryn accepted an offer from William to ride over to see David. She had not seen him for weeks and felt the need to do so, even if she and David could not talk freely. He, and only he, comforted her just by being in her presence.

There was more than a physical distance between Kathryn and William as they rode in the carriage. Perhaps she, more than William, realized the widening gap between them. And now, there was Winnie—young, afraid, and helpless to resist any of her husband's demands. Kathryn had decided she would do whatever she had to keep Winnie from harm, at least until she could arrange for Emanuel and Winnie to escape. This, she had determined, was the only solution, and there was no one she could trust except Jonathan.

William greeted David cordially as he stepped onto the veranda.

"How are things with you, David?"

"I have no complaints. And dear, beautiful Kathryn. Good morning." David's greeting had a conspiratorial hint to it that only he and Kathryn could detect. She acknowledged David's greeting with a smile. William seemed to not notice any of this.

"David," he said, "I need to talk to you about a very important matter. It won't take much of your time."

"Sounds urgent."

"Well, it is, sort of."

"Have a seat. I'll have lemonade brought out."

"None for me," Kathryn replied. "I'll just take the time to stroll around the old home place."

"Of course," David said, "I know you must miss this place."

"Yes, yes, as a matter of fact I do at times," replied Kathryn.

She had recognized William's statement about "a very important matter" as her cue to leave. She opened her parasol and began to stroll around the grounds.

"All right, William," David said. "Must be pretty serious business for you to ride over to see me personally."

"It is. I've lost a dozen or so more slaves over the last two weeks. That's a total of forty over the past six months. How many have you lost?"

"Last count, none."

William had a bewildered look on his face.

"That's awfully peculiar," he said. "Every planter that I know of is losing some slave runaways."

David realized he had to raise himself above suspicion.

"Maybe my slaves don't have a reason to run away," he said defensively. "They get proper rest and food and I don't allow whippings. If you and the other planters tried to be a little more humane, then perhaps you wouldn't have such a problem."

David could see the anger in his brother's face when he finished. His reply to William had left the older brother speechless.

William couldn't stand being outdone by anyone or their methods.

He had a mind to become even more of a tyrant to his slaves just to prove his method was the right one.

Oblivious to the two men's conversation, Kathryn ventured over to the horse stables. As a child, this had been one of her favorite places. Unlike most women of her position, she enjoyed the smell of hay and horses that lingered in the barns. She stepped carefully so as to avoid the manure. As she walked, she thought she saw something through the large planks in the barn.

"Who's in here?" she called out. There was no answer. She was certain she had seen someone in the small tool area. Her curiosity aroused, Kathryn approached the door, lifted the latch, and opened it. There must have been five or six slaves all huddled together—men, women, small children. Furthermore, she realized some of them were from William's plantation. Before she could utter a word, she heard William call out to her.

"Kathryn. Where are you?"

She raised a finger to her lips and made a shushing sound. She had never seen so much fear on so many faces at one time.

Quickly, she turned and left the stables before William could enter, composing herself as she made her exit.

"Here I am," she replied, standing outside the stables.

"I'm ready to return home now," William said.

"So am I. It's so hot and stuffy in that barn."

She turned to David, who seemed a bit apprehensive as he stood beside William.

"You know, David," she said to him, "I must commend you; the old place is just like Father left it. I really enjoyed my walk, but I'm afraid I snagged my dress in the old toolshed in the barn."

She smiled a little as she looked into David's face.

"You might get one of the boys to clean it out a little."

David knew she had to have seen what was in that shed, yet, she said nothing. In fact, it appeared she was trying to keep William away from the barn. His apprehensions began to subside.

"Whatever you say, Miss Kathryn." He had never called her that before.

Kathryn finally knew why David had never seemed like the rest of the planters: He was helping slaves escape.

Here was her answer. He would help her get Winnie and Emanuel to freedom.

She was elated.

William and Kathryn's departure was a blessing for Emanuel and Winnie; they could spend more time together.

Winnie gleefully kissed Emanuel in front of Gertie as they stood in the kitchen.

"Did I tell you last night that you are one beautiful black man?" she asked teasingly.

"No less than a hundred times," he said with a laugh, "and you are the most beautiful woman I know."

They kissed again.

"Come with me," Winnie said as she grabbed his hands.

"Where are we going?"

"I want you to play for me."

"Play for you? How did you know . . . "

"Jonathan told me. Will you, will you please play the piano? Just for me?"

"Well," Emanuel said in mock hesitance. "I've never had much of an audience before."

"If you are as good as Jonathan says you are, then you will do fine."

"All right. But first, you must go into the music room and sit while I get ready."

"Get ready!"

"Please," Emanuel said. "Now, do as I say."

Emanuel walked off to his pantry room. He had memorized Missy Kathryn's stories about the great music halls in Europe and how the pianist, in his most formal outfit, would sit and play for hours, and how great audiences would register their approval with long applause. He had known that, for him, there could be no great music halls or great audiences and long applause. But now there was Winnie and no audience of any size could be more important to him. Today, more than any day before, he wanted to show off his talent. He put on his swallow-tailed coat, shirt and tie, formal pants, and shoes that he had worn in Charleston.

Deliberately, he strutted into the music room. As he lowered himself onto the piano stool, he flipped his tails outward.

He began to play Douce, convinced it had been composed for a moment like this. Winnie stood and walked to the side of the piano. She was amazed as she listened to Emanuel's rendition of Hayden's *Concerto in E Flat Major*. She didn't know what it was, only that it was the most beautiful piece of music that she had ever heard. She was stupefied.

Emanuel continued, but soon the music without words was no longer enough. All of his emotions surfaced as he began to sing:

It takes three seconds to say I love you
A lifetime to prove
But I do, Oh, Lord, I do.

It takes three seconds to say I love you
A lifetime to prove
But I do, I do, Oh, Lord, I do.

Your hair is so pretty
your face so divine
It's hard for me to believe
that you are mine.

Your kiss is so heavenly
your lips o' so sweet

It's hard for me to believe
that you belong to me.

I love to hold you
in my arms o' so tight
And now in my life
everything is all right.

No one can take you away from me
To have for themselves
A sight I couldn't bear to see.

Winnie, my love
I pledge my life to thee
I'll fight for you, die for you
Or spend a life filled with glee.

Winnie's eyes were filled with tears. She believed that what she was experiencing was real love and she was enjoying every minute of it. She shed tears of joy and happiness, the latter she had known only superficially. Winnie made no attempt to say anything; she knew of no words that could equal the beautiful music Emanuel had dedicated to her. But her face told the story.

Silently, she pledged her life to Emanuel—the first black man she had ever known.

The field slaves closest to the house grew still when they heard Emanuel's beautiful voice. Over the years, as his mastery of the piano increased, he had become even more special to them.

One of the slave girls ran to fetch Bell, dragging her over to the window to hear what was going on. Although Bell was immensely proud of Emanuel's accomplishments, she would never admit it.

"Missy Bell," the young slave girl called her, "ain't dat de most beautiful playin' an' singin' you eva heard?"

"I guess so," Bell said hesitantly.

"I know what wrong with Piana, now."

"What?" Bell asked.

"Piana be in love. It dat new girl. She be a pretty li'l thang."

Bell said nothing. She was a little jealous. Emanuel's visits had become less frequent, and when he came he moped about like a sick puppy. Moreover, Bell's fears were ever increasing.

Emanuel had talent that could never be revealed to his white master, and now he was in love, in love with a young, pretty,

290

light-skinned Negro girl whom Massah William had probably purchased for his own pleasures.

There was going to be trouble, Bell could feel it. There was no place for love amongst slaves. It could only lead to pain.

Bell walked away. Her tears had dried up years ago and that made her crying undetectable.

CHAPTER TWENTY-SIX

Barfield Chambers appeared pensive. He had asked the secretary to send William to his office first thing. Barfield did nothing as he sat at his desk, awaiting William's arrival. He eyed the mounting stack of papers on his desk, but as far as he was concerned, other matters were more urgent.

William entered Barfield's office.

"Good morning, William."

"A good day to you, Sir. Mrs. Singletary said that you wanted to see me. She said that it was urgent."

"Yes. Yes. Sit down, my boy, and don't look so long-faced. It's not quite that bad."

William sat down.

"I don't have to remind you of the rather perilous times that we live in, in terms of our relations with the North."

"No, you don't. There have been few more urgent moments in the history of the South."

"If California is admitted to the Union as a free state, we will lose that delicate balance that has kept us from the warpath against those Northern sympathizers."

William listened almost dispassionately. He knew whenever Barfield launched into these tirades over anything concerning the North and the South that he wanted something. In his own time, and only his own time, would he tell him what it was.

"Yes, Sir," William replied.

"I'm convinced that whatever the course set in Congress for California will decide the fate of New Mexico and Utah and God knows what other territory as well. If those territories enter the Union as free soil, then the scales will forever be tilted in favor of the North."

"Yes, Sir, I agree, and might I be forward to ask whether you have some plan?"

"As a matter of fact, I do," Barfield said. "I've been in touch with John Calhoun by letter and he assures me that the South needs the most strong-fisted lobbying effort that she can muster. Furthermore, he wants as many prominent, well-known Southerners as possible to line the galleries of the Senate and House to exhibit a show of strength and concern over these current trends. He wants them as soon as possible. He has arranged for a gallery seat for someone from this office at the Senate congressional hearings until a favorable decision is made pertaining to all of the South's concerns. I would go myself, but I'm afraid, like Calhoun, my age is catching up with me. Can you represent us? Your departure will have to be as soon as possible."

"Yes, yes, of course," William said. "I'll leave at once."

"Good! Excellent! I knew I could count on you. I'm sure Kathryn will understand, and give her my love, will you?"

"Certainly," he replied. There was nothing for Kathryn to understand. Since Winnie had entered the house, Kathryn had given him a lot more attention, but he knew things were not the best between them. Moreover, he welcomed the chance to sit in on the congressional hearings. Of equal concern to him was the passage of a more stringent Fugitive Slave Law. All total, he had lost some forty to fifty slaves—escapees to the North, and he wanted them back. Moreover, he wanted the North to be made to send them back. It was time that Northerners were forced to stay out of Southern affairs. They had their gall to even think it was right to offer sanctuary to slave refugees. Yes, he would go, and he wanted his presence felt.

Soon after William's departure, David paid Kathryn a visit.

She felt both exuberant over seeing him and traitorous because she had to conceal her feelings for him in William's company. Long ago, she had admitted to herself that William's lovemaking did not satisfy her. But submitting to him was a tactful move designed to divert his attractions from Winnie. So far, it had worked.

Kathryn and David greeted each other cordially in the piano room.

"Good morning, Kathryn," he said. "I just thought I would drop by to see if everything was all right since William was away."

"How nice. I hope you are well."

"Yes, I am, thank you."

"How would you like to escort a desperately lonely lady, who just happens to be dressed for the occasion, for a walk along the lake?"

David bowed.

"The pleasure would be all mine, m'lady," he said.

"Emanuel, please fetch my shawl," Kathryn said.

Winnie and Emanuel were standing in attendance, and David noticed Winnie for the first time. Were it not for her simple, cotton dress—an undeniable insignia of enslavement—David would have mistaken her for a white girl.

Emanuel brought Kathryn her shawl. He started to return to his appointed spot when he heard Missy Kathryn speak.

"Emanuel, you may resume your practice. I would like for you to play something special for me. Let's see, Beethoven's *Fur Elise* will be fine, thank you. Winnie, will you please go with him?"

Emanuel had no choice but to look at her like she was crazy.

No one off the plantation knew of his talents.

"You mean play the piano, Missy Kathryn?" Emanuel asked slowly.

"Yes! I mean the piano," she replied with a smile of confidence that removed all of Emanuel's fears.

"Yes, Ma'am!"

David had a curious look on his face. Waiting on the porch, he could hear the entire conversation. What he had learned had astounded him, because he realized he and Kathryn had even more in common: They both had something to hide.

"Revelations and confessions, an appropriate pastime for today, wouldn't you say?" Kathryn appeared at his side and took his arm. "Shall we begin our walk?"

They were well beyond the plantation veranda before Kathryn spoke again.

"It was you that helped all those slaves escape, wasn't it?" Kathryn asked abruptly.

"Yes," David said simply. He knew there was little use in lying.

"All those planters and your brother running all about the Carolinas looking for escaped slaves and you had them sitting right under their noses," Kathryn giggled approvingly.

"Yes. You won't tell, will you?"

"No, of course not."

They stopped momentarily. He faced her and kissed the back of her hand lovingly.

"Somehow I knew I could trust you."

Kathryn looked into his eyes, detecting a hint of fear. She touched his face with her hand, then rubbed it gently. There was no reluctance on her part and she didn't care who saw her.

"Dear, sweet David," she said tenderly, "you needn't worry. From this day forward you have an ally. I want to help you. I must help you, because . . . because I love you so much."

She rose to her toes and kissed him long and hard.

"I love you," she said again when their lips parted.

"I love you, too, Kathryn, and I know you must know that. But will we have to be a secret forever?"

"No! No! I promise you."

They resumed their walk. Again, there was silence until David spoke.

"All those years, spending the hottest of summers on this plantation. You did it for him, didn't you?" inquired David.

"You mean Emanuel?"

"Yes."

"At first, for Emanuel, but then later on, when you moved back south, I wanted to be near you."

She thought for a moment, then continued.

"You know, he is an extraordinary talent. I know on the surface it must seem that I did the teaching and that's true, but the real truth is that there was very little teaching to do. Such a gift, such talent should never be harnessed and re-stricted by any means and certainly not by a system as crude and cruel as slavery; and for that reason, and that reason alone, I must see to his escape—if it's the last thing I do. David, will you help me?"

"Yes, you must know that I will," David said.

"Now, there is both Winnie and Emanuel," she continued.

"They are so much in love. The first time they laid eyes on

each other, it was like a thunderbolt hit them both at the same time. But there can be little happiness for them here."

"Don't worry your pretty self about it. We will get them to safety and freedom," David told her. "I promise."

"I know," Kathryn said. "I don't doubt you one bit. It's just that I'll worry until it's all over with."

David was already pondering the method of escape.

"It's too short of a notice to get them out before winter sets in," he said. "But you know, I have a plan that just might work. With Winnie looking the way that she does it just might . . . It'll take me a while to work things out, but . . . come on, I'll tell you what we are going to do."

They walked back toward the plantation.

While William was away, Emanuel visited Winnie's bedroom in the wine cellar at will. He knew full well that what he was doing was an offense punishable by lynching.

Winnie hated her bedroom. It was so far away from where anyone else slept. She felt alone, and enjoyed having Emanuel sleep with her. There, they had a private little world all their own, but it couldn't last and they knew it. Escaping, running away was a daily part of their conversation. Emanuel's love for Winnie overpowered his reluctance to leave his mother and Missy Kathryn. Maybe if he could escape, he could return later for his mother, he thought.

During their time together, Winnie restricted all of Emanuel's efforts at lovemaking to heavy petting. It wasn't easy, but Emanuel understood. Winnie feared pregnancy almost as much as she feared Master Littlejohn. She made Emanuel promise to not make love to her until they were free. That was the only way she could assure herself that there would be one less child to enslave. But her fears and anxieties were mounting day by day.

Master Littlejohn would return for Christmas. She knew too well that the privacy of the cellar bedroom was for a purpose, but she also knew she would die before she would let William Littlejohn touch her.

The 1849 Congress recessed briefly for Christmas and New Year's. William returned home to celebrate with his wife. There were no children. No sons. William felt the void. Had he grown sterile? There was one way to find out, he thought: Winnie.

It was late night, New Year's Eve. In two days, William was to return to Washington to hear the Senate debates. His time with Kathryn was routine—nothing exciting or special, but he still felt like celebrating. William was a bit anxious over his departure. Starting after supper, he drank more than the usual.

He and Kathryn had little to say as they sat in the parlor before a roaring fire. At the stroke of midnight, they kissed each other ceremoniously to usher in the new year; still, there was no denying that the affection was gone.

Kathryn had dedicated her first thoughts of the new year to David. William's thoughts were on the pleasures of the evening that would follow. He couldn't wait for Kathryn to go to sleep. As soon as she did, he descended the stairs with drunken unsteadiness and entered the wine cellar.

He lit a candle and looked at Winnie, who had heard his arrival and pretended to be asleep. He began stroking her gently, massaging her whole body. Though she had known this day would come, she was still terrified.

"Massah Littlejohn, Suh! What are you doing here?"

"Take off your clothes," he ordered. "You and me gonna have some fun."

She sat up in bed and slowly began to disrobe. He did the same but much faster and clumsier.

298

"Hurry up, gal, git those clothes off, I don't have all night." He walked to the dresser as if he knew what he would find, and pulled out a bundle of cotton that Gertie had put there earlier. He lay down beside her on his stomach.

"Rub me. Massage me all over with this."

He put the cotton in her hand. By now, Winnie was almost hysterical. William, his name is William, she thought. My father was named William, a white man. Then she remembered her mother's words: "That man sho' did like to use cotton in a funny sort of way."

What was she to do? She couldn't let him do this to her, not her father! Not the same man that her mother had tried to convince her was a good white man who would take them away from the cruelties of slave life if he had the chance. Not the one source of all her hope for so many years. This was the man lying beside her, ready to use her like any other slave master would use his black mistress. It was all more than she could bear. She threw the cotton to the floor and began to scream.

Emanuel was the first to hear Winnie's shrieks. Instantly, he pulled on his pants and ran toward the wine cellar. At the top of the stairs, he paused. Massah Littlejohn was standing with his back to him, hand high in the air, about to strike Winnie. The same devil that had murdered his father and viciously attacked him was about to assault his woman.

Emanuel lunged forward, landing on the floor next to a startled William. He spun his master around, away from Winnie.

Pow! One strong blow to the stomach, followed by another. Then he kicked him in the groin as he crumpled to the floor. Emanuel took William's neck in his hands, squeezing until he felt someone pulling at his back. It took all the strength that Jonathan, Gertie, and Missy Kathryn could muster to pry him loose from William. Once they were apart, William was more embarrassed than beaten, more drunken than sober—the picture of guilt. Defeated, he fell back in a drunken stupor. Nobody except Gertie attempted to assist him.

"Come on! Come on, you two! You've got to get out of here." Kathryn started pulling and tugging at Emanuel and Winnie.

"Jonathan! Quickly, get the horses and wagon ready. No, we'd better use the carriage, it's faster. Saddle Trumpet and tie him to the carriage. Now, go, hurry! Hurry! Winnie and Emanuel, you come with me. Come on, hurry!"

This was it. Kathryn and David had already devised a plan of escape for Winnie and Emanuel, but it was supposed to have been initiated once William had left for the congressional hearings.

Fate had altered their plan.

They followed her to her bedroom. There, Kathryn dressed as they waited. She packed a small bundle of clothing—shoes, dress, hat, underwear, and stockings and makeup.

They descended the stairs quickly, and headed straight to the carriage that Jonathan had waiting for them. Emanuel had but one regret: He had not said good-bye to his mother. He turned and looked toward her cabin, silently whispering his good-bye. There was no way Emanuel could know his mother was awake. She had felt there was trouble and knew Emanuel was leaving forever. As Emanuel said his silent good-bye, so, too, did she.

"Massah William! Massah William! Y'all got ta wake up now. Dey gonna git away," Gertie said excitedly.

"Go away! Leave me alone!" replied William, his arms flailing.

He's too drunk, Gertie thought. It will have to wait 'til morning. Then I'll tell Massah Littlejohn everything that's been going on in this house since that nigga boy come in, and that sassy little gal, too.

The trip to Lake Holler was rapid-paced. Soon, they were at

David's front door. Emanuel and Winnie were frightened out of their wits, and stopping at this plantation where Massah Little-john's brother lived didn't help the situation. But Emanuel trusted Missy Kathryn, and since he did, he followed and Winnie followed him.

At last, David opened the door. He could see that something must have happened.

"Come in, quickly," he said as he motioned to them. He could see the reluctance and fear on Emanuel's and Winnie's faces.

"Come on in Emanuel and Winnie, it's all right."

Then he turned to Kathryn.

"Maybe you had better tell me what happened."

"Emanuel and William were fighting," she said. "William was intoxicated. Emanuel found him with Winnie and she was screaming and one thing led to another . . . Oh, my God, it was awful."

Now in tears, Kathryn embraced David and continued.

"We have got to get them out of here before William sobers and Gertie tells him everything."

"I know. I know. They are safe here. Nobody has any suspicions of me. Now calm yourself. It will be all right. Did you bring everything we need?"

"Yes."

Emanuel was not surprised about Missy Kathryn and David; he had known about them for years. But he couldn't believe what they were saying. So it was David all the time, Emanuel thought, helping the slaves escape. He finally felt at ease, only to become concerned again when Tom Baldwin entered the room. He knew the man was David's overseer.

"Is there trouble? I heard all the commotion and I thought I had better come see what was happening," said Tom.

"I'll give you the details later, Tom. This is Emanuel and

Winnie. I told you about them. We are going to have to put our plan into action a bit sooner than I thought."

He was silent for a few moments.

"But first things first. We've got to get you back to Lake Holler before William awakens and Gertie spills her guts and tells everything she knows. That wagon is too slow."

"I thought about that and I brought Trumpet along in a saddle," Kathryn told him.

"Excellent! Tom, hide Winnie and Emanuel in the usual place. They will be safe here until tomorrow night when we move them to the Jones station. But first, get me the fastest horse in the stable," David said.

"I'll have him ready in a second, boss."

"Kathryn, I can't allow Gertie to know about me and what I'm doing. Once we get to Lake Holler, can you control her?"

"I've been doing it for all these years, "Kathryn declared confidently.

But as she realized what was about to happen, she was about to lose Emanuel probably forever, her emotional fabric was torn to shreds.

She turned and took one last look at the black slave boy that she could only perceive as her only child.

"Let's go, then," David said. "I'll escort you back to Lake Holler. We had better hurry. Winnie and Emanuel, just stay here until Tom returns. And don't worry, we haven't lost an escapee yet and we don't intend to start with you."

Emanuel now felt safe, but Winnie was frantic. She remembered the dirty slave holes, chain gangs, and slave cartels.

But this time, she was with Emanuel. He had fought for her and had won the battle. She wanted to be in his arms because there she felt secure, so she embraced Emanuel, burying her head against his chest. Raising her mouth to his she covered his lips with victory kisses. Then they both prayed silently. If there was a God in heaven, they asked that he help them be together. Help us to find freedom, or let us die together, they said. The gentle thumps of their hearts transcribed the message between them.

Kathryn and David were well on their way back to Lake Holler. By the time they arrived, the sun had established its dominance over the sky. It was a clear day, and the realities of what had happened that evening seemed to dawn with it.

"I'll unsaddle the horse and dry him off," David said. "You hurry to the house. Maybe you can sneak in the back way."

"I love you, David," Kathryn said as she exited the barn.

Kathryn entered the house through the back way. She came upon Jonathan in the hall.

"Where's William?"

"He's still down in the wine cellar," Jonathan said. "Old Big Mouth just went down to check on him."

"Come help me, Jonathan, I've got to get upstairs without them seeing me."

"I'll keep watch," said Jonathan.

"If you see anyone coming, stall them until I'm safely in my room."

Once she was safely upstairs, Kathryn quickly changed into her night clothing. All she could do now was await her confrontation with William.

Desperately, Gertie continued trying to rouse her master.

This was her chance to get back her kingdom—at least inside the plantation house—to rule as she pleased.

That nigga gal and that nigga boy had changed everything, but revenge would soon be hers. Massah William would see to that.

If only she could awaken him and get him on his feet.

"Massah William, yo' gots ta wake up! Wake up!" She shook him vigorously as she spoke.

Slowly, William began to awaken. He managed to sit up on the side of the bed, his face buried in his palms.

"Gertie! Gertie! What happened here?"

"Don' cha know, Massah William? Dat nigga 'Manuel done hit you."

"What?" Slowly he remembered what had happened the night before.

"Dat boy done hit you," Gertie said again. "I knowed it wuddin' right what Missy Kathryn was doin'. I know'd it wuddin' right."

"Gertie, what are you talking about? What wasn't right?" William asked, giving her his full attention.

"The piano, Missy Kathryn been teachin' dat boy ta play de piano all dese years."

"No wonder she was so attached to that nigga. Well I'll fix his hide. Here, Gertie, help me upstairs."

William's hangover was slowly being replaced by anger. A nigga gal had refused him, a nigga boy had hit him. It was more than he could tolerate. He would fix them and fix them quick.

Once he and Gertie made it up the stairs, William ambled unsteadily into his bedroom. He could see that Kathryn was asleep, or seemed to be. Clumsily, he made his way about the room, looking for fresh clothes. His noisiness gave Kathryn the excuse she needed to act as if she was just awakening.

"What are you doing?" she asked.

"I'm looking for my clothes."

"Your bags are already packed."

"I need clothes to find that nigga houseboy that hit me. I'll fix his hide."

"You'll do nothing of the kind!" she informed him.

"What did you say?"

"I said you'll do nothing of the kind," Kathryn said, her voice filled with defiance.

"And who's gonna stop me?"

"I am, William Littlejohn. If you so much as put one foot out that door with the intent of hunting down Emanuel and doing the same to him that you did to his father, then you're going to have to kill me first. If you don't kill me, I'll spread the word all over Charleston about the proud aristocratic William Littlejohn who beds his own slave girls, and how he got beat up by one of his slaves because of it."

The fire in Kathryn's eyes told William that she meant every word. His thinking was clear enough for him to realize what would happen to his reputation if word got out.

"All right!" he said menacingly. "I have to get back to Washington anyhow, but there will be another day and that day will be mine, I promise you."

Kathryn saw no remorse in his eyes for what he had done to her, no guilt for having been caught with another woman. Her feelings did not matter to William. It was his stupid pride that was wounded—and that did not matter to her. Her heart belonged to David now, and the only other thing that was important was seeing Winnie and Emanuel to freedom.

Her only satisfaction on New Year's Day 1850 was that William left the plantation a day early.

CHAPTER TWENTY-SEVEN

Emanuel and Winnie were given their traveling instructions, which they committed to memory. Emanuel heard David refer to each point of stopover as a station. They were now at station number two. During the night, they had secretly been carried into a cellar warehouse. All Emanuel knew was that they were somewhere in Charleston. The hoofbeats on the cobblestone streets were unmistakable, and reminded him of his past visit. But, oh, how different the circumstances, he thought.

There were others in the room, all runaway slaves who were more afraid than not of what their newfound freedom would bring.

No one said anything. Each person found his own small nook and settled down, as comfortably as possible, to sleep.

Winnie lay her head on Emanuel's chest and was soon asleep.

Emanuel knew everyone in the room had taken a second look at her.

After all, except for her clothing, she looked like a white lady; the success or failure of their journey to freedom hinged on that fact.

It was time to sleep. Emanuel secured his embrace of Winnie before closing his eyes. As of tonight, he was in training. He would teach himself how to think like a free man. Still, behind every thought, every smile or glimmer of hope was a strong visage of his mother, whom he had left behind. She remained a slave and he meant to return one day for her.

He slept, dreaming of places Missy Kathryn had spoken about.

Their journey to freedom would end in Philadelphia, "free soil."

From there they would proceed to Boston or Canada; the choice was theirs.

Warmly and with loving tenderness, he held Winnie close to him as his dream brought him back to this cellar room. He unleashed his imagination and the room was transformed into a great dance hall. The occupants were not escaped slaves but patrons—free black men and women. In the center of the room was a grand piano which Emanuel played while everyone danced. He recognized faces from his past. There were Tilda Lee and Shadrach, the best dancers on Lake Holler's plantation, doing the rooster. With hands on hips and arms flapping back and forth like wings, they swept the floor rhythmically. Their feet interchanged positions in a skipping fashion, and their heads bounced back and forth like roosters plucking corn off the ground. The crowd's oohs and aahs urged them on to dramatic swirls and limbering twists and turns that were their trademark. Every few moments, someone from the crowd would give a shout.

"Play dat music, Piana! Make dat rooster crow!"

Then, the music in his dream grew softer, and Emanuel saw himself and Winnie high atop a soft, white cloud. They were beyond the troubled land from which they had come, holding each other close and kissing softly, a long lingering kiss made more urgent by the touching of their bodies. They were making sweet love, the clouds shielding this private moment.

Emanuel's dream was interrupted by a hand on his shoulder.

"Wake up! Wake up!" a voice said. "It's time to go."

Now it was time to continue their journey to freedom.

Kathryn had forsaken any intent of wifely duties or obligations to her husband, who had left for Washington in defeat.

She entered David's plantation house without knocking. The houseboy directed her to the bedroom where David was toweling himself after a bath.

"David," she said.

"Kathryn."

The greeting was tentative. Kathryn closed the door and removed her shawl. She walked to the edge of the bed.

"Did everything go all right?" David asked.

"Yes, everything went just fine."

David draped the towel around his neck and walked toward Kathryn, who was filled with nervous excitement. She had forgotten this feeling that she had known only once in her life—on her honeymoon. She couldn't help but look at David. Such a muscular, handsome man, she thought.

"You made provisions so that Emanuel could get a bond on arriving in Baltimore?" she asked, never taking her eyes off him.

"You know that Negroes must have a bond to pass through . . ."

"Yes, I know," David said as he gazed at her. "He will have his bond and Winnie has her ticket."

They were close now. David reached out and unbuttoned Kathryn's dress.

When she was completely naked, Kathryn grasped the towel from around David's neck and pulled it to the floor.

"I love you, David, and I want to spend the rest of my life with you."

"I love you too, Kathryn, and we will be together, I promise."

They moved to the bed. David looked at the soft, curvaceous beauty who lay before him. Then, they began to make sweet love.

Cuddling and kissing passionately, their bodies became one as they moved to a state of tranquility.

Before this moment, they had both built a cocoon around their emotions, protecting themselves from William. Today, they no longer needed one.

As they lay in each other's arms, Kathryn penned a poem in her mind:

> *Sweet dove, fly again*
> *Crippled wing without flight*
> *for so long.*
>
> *Pitiable bird, lame emotions*
> *Alive now, swift! Swift! Swifter! Fly again.*
> *Pierce the head winds of my willing soul*
>
> *Land gently, quietly,*
> *flutter thy wings, never to be*
> *crippled again.*
> *Never to be lame again.*

Winnie felt a bit fearful, worried that somebody might recognize her even though she was in disguise. After all, it was here in Charleston that she had gone on the auction block. Now here she was at the train station, dressed like a white woman, made up like a white woman, and talking like a white woman. She had an affliction, an eye disease—one made worse by light. She had to wear a black band across her eyes in daylight. Her servant, Emanuel, was to serve as her guide.

Emanuel stood behind his mistress, bags in hand. He looked obsequious because he knew that was what white folk wanted. Inside, he was afraid—more afraid than he had ever been in his life.

Winnie did the talking, reviving the accent she had learned from Bertram and Mistress Robard. She approached a ticket agent.

"Kind sir, here are the tickets and a promissory note for my servant's bond that he will need in Baltimore."

"Thank you, Ma'am," replied the agent. "Here you are. Everything seems to be in order."

"Oh! One other thing, kind sir. Would you please see that I am seated near the baggage car where my boy servant will be just in case I need his services?"

"Yes, yes, of course. I'll speak with the conductor."

Winnie wasn't through. "Oh! One other thing. Please alert the conductor to pull the shade down by my seat, then I can remove this God-awful mask."

"Yes, Ma'am."

"Thank you for your kindness." She took a very modest hold of Emanuel's arm with one hand and, with a cane in the other, they boarded the train where she took a seat in the rear.

Emanuel was placed one box car over with the freight. There was no seat; he either had to stand or sit on the floor. A white worker who smelled as if he needed a bath eyed him.

"You stay in that corner, boy." He said nothing else.

Emanuel smiled to himself when he thought about the way Winnie was teasing the ticket master. It seemed so easy. He was just one train ride from freedom.

The trip was uneventful. They first stepped on free soil in Philadelphia. Much to their surprise, a small crowd awaited their arrival. David had mentioned that someone would meet them at the train station, but they didn't expect the twenty to thirty people who were present, shouting cheers of adulation and joy. The crowd was mixed—blacks and whites who in no way tried to hide the reason for their celebration. Immediately they burst into a chant:

> *Welcome to freedom!*
> *Welcome to freedom!*
> *Welcome to freedom!*

Their apprehensions eased, Emanuel and Winnie finally realized what had happened. They had escaped! They were free! No tipping and bowing. Belated smiles crossed their faces as they clung to each other in a long embrace.

"I love you."

"I love you, too."

"Will you marry me?"

"Yes! Yes! I want to have a whole house full of free black babies for you. I love you!" Winnie replied ecstatically.

The daring escape was reported across the country. Every Northern abolitionist boasted of the story of Emanuel and Winnie.

There were smiles on their lips and mockery in their hearts as they envisioned Southerners' reaction.

The escape was the topic of conversation in every slave hut and shanty throughout the South. Whispers carried the news from slave to slave, cabin to cabin, plantation to plantation. Emanuel and Winnie were saints blessed by "de Lawd himself."

The old *Liberator* printed this article:

DARING ESCAPE FROM CHARLESTON SLAVE PLANTATION

Two persons of Negro descent, one man of dark complexion, another, a woman so light that she could be mistaken for white, dared test the strength of the shackles that bound them to their southern way of life.

Without hesitation at a predetermined time, just as the sun's earliest rays situated themselves, right out in the open for all to see, those two bravados approached a ticket agent at the Charleston train station while pretending to be a crippled mistress with her lone dedicated slave. They purchased tickets to ride a train right into the midst of this great free-soil, like errant homing pigeons that decide that freedom is in the opposite direction. No questions were asked by their unsuspecting victims.

It is highly plausible that the southerners involved were inexplicably deceived by an imperious vanity of their own that allows for a common belief that those of colored hue have not the innate courage or intellectual abilities to perform such a feat. At least, in this instance, we must thank God for that kind of perpetual ignorance.

Emanuel is about 18 years of age and his companion and wife-to-be, the same. Both are remarkably well-educated, considering the situation from which they came. Furthermore, Emanuel is well-versed in the play of the piano—talent from which all our ears shall benefit in time.

"Imperious vanity my ass!"

William succumbed to the fury that he had tried to suppress since Emanuel and Winnie's escape.

"Imperious vanity, is it! When I catch that nigga I'll string him up from the highest tree in Charleston."

William was about to tear the paper from which he read the article. Then he realized that article was his only lead to Emanuel's whereabouts.

"We'll see who has the last laugh, nigga piano player. I should have known all along. My own wife teaching a nigga how to play . . . those damned music books she used to buy all the time, not for herself but for a nigga," William mumbled. It was all he could do to control himself.

I'll make her watch this time, he thought. He had never insisted, nor had he wanted Kathryn to watch any of his previous lynchings of slaves, but this time she was going to watch every moment, he would see to it. His revenge would be sweet, but for the time being it would have to wait.

The congressional hearings were under way and they were the talk of the day. Not since the nullification controversy of years past had there been issues before the Congress of the United States that so directly affected the future of the South, if not the entire Union. Already a bill had been introduced in the Senate and sent to the Judicial Committee that would provide for the more effective execution of the Fugitive Slave Law. Everyone awaited with hopeful anticipation the scheduled speech of Henry Clay.

The Southern response and attitude was to be voiced, as always, by J. C. Calhoun; following that, Daniel Webster was to speak. More than any others, these three men reigned as the articulators of the Constitution. All were in the twilight years of great and distinguished careers; yet, perhaps for the last time, they were to face each other and do battle with words as only they could do.

Shortly after reciting their marriage vows on free soil, Emanuel and Winnie were advised to move farther north to Boston—the home of the abolitionists. They did so willingly.

There, the atmosphere was one of apprehension over the current congressional meetings and the possible reactivation of the Fugitive Slave Act. For this reason, the two fugitives were advised that it would be safer in Canada or perhaps England. Emanuel refused to go farther. He shared his reasoning with his wife.

"Winnie, this is as far north as I can go. But I have no right to make you stay if you want to move to a safer place."

"My place is with you, Emanuel. Don't you dare try and get rid of me."

"You know I wouldn't . . . "

"I understand why you don't want to move on."

"Do you?" asked Emanuel.

"Yes, I do. It's your mother, isn't it?" Winnie asked solemnly.

"Yes. Someday I have to return and bring her here with us and then we can go anywhere we want."

Emanuel could see that Winnie was sad.

"Don't worry, Winnie, I'll find your mother, too."

"No! No!"

"Why? I don't understand."

"We will have to leave my mother right where she is, in the midst of her own fantasy world. Long ago, she stopped facing reality and started making up lies about my father and how kind he was and how much he loved me. Lies, all lies."

Winnie had told Emanuel that William Littlejohn was her father.

"Would you have felt better if she told you the truth about your father, that he was white and mean and didn't care?"

"No, I guess not. But please promise that when you decide to go after your mother that you will tell me first. Promise, please!"

"It's a promise," Emanuel said.

They stood so close that their foreheads, then their lips, touched briefly.

"I love you, Winnie."

"I love you, Emanuel, forever."

They kissed for a long while. Totally relaxed in each other's arms, neither of them wanted to admit their growing apprehensions over what the future held for them.

CHAPTER TWENTY-EIGHT

Tuesday, February 5, 1850. The Senate galleries were filled to capacity. A subdued but steady noise arose from the assemblage as most chose to pass the waiting moments by talking to whomever was nearby. Others sat quietly in hopeful anticipation that the moment would soon arrive—an auspicious, eloquent occasion, highlighted by a contest of wills, between the greatest orators of the time.

The senators sat near the speaker's podium. They were poised and courteous in appearance, but every face reflected the gravity of the situation at hand.

Immediately behind the senators stood an audience of richly attired women who were relatives or other supporters of the men who would carry on the proceedings. Their sweet smiles and dainty decorum added an air of ebullience to an otherwise stodgy atmosphere.

William was in the gallery. His soul was filled with anguish and apprehensions over the decisions that would be made at these hearings. He didn't talk to anyone. He only wanted to dissect the words of the speakers. Just as much as any senator present, he knew the gravity of what was about to happen. He, too, anxiously awaited the arrival of the speaker of the hour.

Henry Clay was the first to address the Senate gathering. He was a great statesman bearing the charisma and character necessary to mend the widening schism between the North and South. Pacification personified, he had been absent from the Senate for seven years. He had journeyed from Kentucky, as that state's representative, to address the Senate and negotiate his third compromise. This man alone was responsible for originating the conciliatory approach that would soothe sectional differences threatening to tear the Union apart. Like a mediator in the middle of a war zone, he had to deliver a plan cautiously and propitiously that would not arouse rancor on either side. There was little doubt in anybody's mind that Henry Clay was equal to the task before him.

The issues were clear in the mind of Clay. Undaunted, he stood before the elite body he was to address. Even at age seventy-three, he was perhaps the tallest man in the room. His calm, serious attitude along with his firm, erect stance commanded the silence of his audience. Over the course of a few hours, he delivered a vigorously powerful, clear-headed speech that so entranced his audience that the spell could not be broken—even when he asked a senator for a pinch of snuff.

His opening statement had set the stage for one of the greatest oratorical presentations of his time.

"Mr. President, never on any former occasion have I risen under feelings of such deep solicitude. I have witnessed many periods of great anxiety, of peril, and of danger even to the country; but I have never before arisen to address any assembly so oppressed, so appalled, so anxious . . . "

That evening, William returned to his room early. He had grown weary from having to stand during most of the speech given by Clay. Now, worn and exhausted, he totally surrendered his body to a deep sleep and entered his dream world. He dreamed he was magistrate over some great tribunal and was outlining his resolutions before his legislative body, just as Henry Clay had done a few days prior to his historic speech.

ITEM: Be it resolved! California was to be admitted to the Union without any restriction or compulsion as to slavery.

ITEM: Be it resolved! There was to be no restriction or conditions as to slavery in the territory acquired from New Mexico.

ITEM: Be it resolved! The western boundary of Texas was defined far short of its expectations.

ITEM: Be it resolved! The government would assume the indebtedness of Texas if the state would accept the proposed boundary.

ITEM: Be it resolved! Abolishment of slavery in the District of Columbia and Maryland without the consent of the people and without compensation to slave owners.

ITEM: Be it resolved! Abolishment of the slave trade in the District of Columbia.

ITEM: Be it resolved! The northern states would honor

*the Fugitive Slave Act of 1793 and make it the law of
the land.*

*ITEM: Be it resolved! The power of Congress to inter-
fere with trade in slaves between the states was restricted.*

William's sleep became more and more tortuous. He grew
short of breath and broke out in a cold sweat. He twisted and
turned until, finally, he thrust himself upright in bed and awakened.

Darkness blanketed the room and brought him back to reality.
His dream had turned into a nightmare and he had envisioned a
war zone with guns shooting, cannons blasting, and men standing toe to toe fighting to the death, bare fisted or with knives or
bayonets.

Fully awake now, his trepidations eased. He lay back, hands
folded behind his head, staring off into the darkened space. In his
mind he reviewed the key points of Clay's speech. Although the
theme was conciliatory, the actual substance of the speech was
palliative for the South. The concessions were heavily weighted
in favor of the North. It seemed that, more than ever before, the
South had to show a united front, even if that meant secession.
There was but one faint glimmer of hope: John C. Calhoun, the
author of *Southern Opinion*, would have to be heard.

But at best, his was just a dim light at the end of a dark tunnel.
His body, weak and frail from the consumption, would not
tolerate the length and breadth of these proceedings. Bedridden,
Calhoun missed Clay's speech and most sessions prior to that. It
was rumored that when it was time for him to speak, he would
have to have someone else read his statement or there would be
no statement at all.

On February 28, 1850, Judge Butler formally requested of his Senate colleagues, on behalf of John C. Calhoun, that he have the privilege, because of medical reasons, of having his statement read by a friend on the following Monday. Without even a motion, there was total concurrence. For the first time since December 3, 1849, when this Thirty-first Congress had begun its sessions, William Littlejohn had occasion to smile. Having someone read Calhoun's statement was better than none at all. The South's voice had to be heard. Like everyone else in Washington, William knew that, for the most part, Calhoun had spent his time playing hide-and-seek with death. If he could hold on just a few more days, he would again rob death of its moment.

Calhoun entered the Senate floor a few minutes after twelve on March 4, 1850. So feeble was he that he had to have the assistance of Gen. James Hamilton of South Carolina. There was not an empty seat in the chamber. William was in the gallery. As he looked around, he noticed a lack of gaiety and excited chattering. The festive air of the previous proceedings was gone, replaced by a solemnity and show of respect for a great statesman.

Only the grim straight lips served as a reminder of the old Calhoun. Ceremoniously, the likes of Webster and Clay greeted their old adversary with reverent esteem before he sank into his chair.

James M. Mason of Virginia read Calhoun's speech, the context of which came from Calhoun's famed "Disquisition on Government." Calhoun, now a ghostlike figure, was weak, soft, and fragile, but his words were as hard, unyielding, and unrepentant as ever. William Littlejohn and the rest of the Southern constituency felt exhilarated by the uncompromising exhortations that crossed another's lips but could only come from Calhoun's heart.

"I have, Senators, believed from the first that the agitation of the subject of slavery would, if not prevented by some timely and effective measure, end in disunion . . . The agitation has been permitted to proceed, with almost no attempt to resist it, until it has reached a point when it can no longer be disguised or denied that the Union is in danger. You have thus had forced upon you the greatest and the gravest question that can ever come under your consideration—How can the union be preserved?"

William Littlejohn was hypnotized by the message of his fellow Confederate. He listened to Calhoun's discourse explaining how bureaucratic manipulation had unequally divided the spoils of the nation in favor of the North. He denounced the ordinance of 1787, the Missouri Compromise, the Wilmot Proviso, and the protective tariff as corroborating evidence of disproportionate gain. He mentioned slavery as the key issue and that "Every portion of the North entertains views and feelings more or less hostile to it." He explained the relations between the white and Negro races in the South as "one which cannot be destroyed without subjecting the two races to the greatest calamity, and the section to poverty, desolation, and wretchedness; and accordingly they feel bound, by every consideration of the interest and safety, to defend it." He touched upon the inevitable subject of disunion: "It is a great mistake to suppose that disunion can be affected at a single blow. The cords which bound these states together in one common union are far too numerous and powerful for that. Disunion must be the work of time."

William surveyed the chamber to gauge reaction. Calhoun sat motionless as he heard his words stun his adversaries and soothe his cohorts. Webster grasped at every word by leaning forward in his chair and Clay was equally attentive. William, along with the rest of the assembly, heard the pulsating finale on how the Union could be salvaged.

"The North has only to will it to accomplish it—to do justice by conceding to the South an equal right in the acquired territory, and to do her duty by causing the stipulations relative to fugitive slaves to be faithfully fulfilled—to cease agitating the slave question, and to provide for the insertion of a provision in the Constitution, by an amendment, which will restore to the South, in substance, the power she possessed of protecting herself, before the equilibrium between the two sections was destroyed by the action of the government. There will be no difficulty in devising such a provision—one that will protect the South, and which, at the same time, will improve and strengthen the government, instead of impairing and weakening it.

"It is time, Senators, that there should be an open and manly avowal on all sides, as to what is intended to be done. If the question is not now settled, it is uncertain whether it ever can hereafter be; and we, as the representatives of the states of this Union, regarded as governments, should come to a distinct understanding as to our respective views, in order to ascertain whether the great questions at issue can be settled or not. If you, who represent the strong portion, cannot agree to settle them on the broad principle of justice and duty, say so; and let the states we both represent agree to separate and part in peace.

"If you are unwilling we should part in peace, tell us so, and we shall know what to do, when you reduce the question to submission or resistance. If you remain silent, you will compel us to infer by your acts what you intend. In that case, California will become the test question. If you admit her, under all the difficulties that oppose her admission, you compel us to infer that you intend to exclude us from the whole of the acquired territories, with the intention of destroying, irretrievably, the equilibrium between the two sections. We would be blind not to perceive, in that case, that your real objects are power and self-aggrandizement, and infatuated not to act accordingly."

William, like most of the other members of the Southern constituency, with the exception of Henry S. Foote of Mississippi who openly repudiated much of Calhoun's speech, felt their position was adequately stated.

Daniel Webster, the last of the great triumvirate, spoke on March 7. He captured his audience with his opening statement: "Mr. President, I wish to speak today, not as a Massachusetts man, nor as a Northern man, but as an American, and a member of the Senate of the United States. . . . I speak today for the preservation of the Union. Hear me for my cause."

After Daniel Webster's speech, William felt there was still reason for hope. Webster had tactfully soothed, but not healed, the wounds opened by Clay and Calhoun. His speech, although pointed and sectional, had been respectful and to some degree conciliatory.

William's departure from Washington was premature. On March 31, John C. Calhoun died. His death sent shock waves throughout the congressional community as well as the South. William was aboard ship along with many Washington delegates to accompany his body to Charleston.

Along with his family and a parade of followers, William was at the graveside of John C. Calhoun. Perhaps as much as Calhoun's death, the unexpected death of President Taylor in 1850 fueled the fire of settlement and compromise as much as anything. After all was said most Southerners believed, like William, that their gains had been little and that the Fugitive Slave Law was their only profit. It was more than legal for Southerners to go north to recoup escaped chattel; the South wanted the citizenry of the North to aide and abet the effort.

William received the names of one Mr. Hughes and Mr. Knight, reportedly the best slave-catchers of the day. He made arrangements to have them meet him at his town house in Charleston. The two men were smartly dressed in business suits and clean-shaven so as to suggest that theirs ranked among the most honorable of professions. Their appearance plus the fact that they were punctual made William feel these were men of quality who could be trusted. The taller of the two did most of the talking; the other relentlessly chewed a plug of tobacco.

"Mr. Hughes and Mr. Knight, I'm glad that you could come," William said with a serious, stern look on his face. "Please come in."

"Mr. Littlejohn, we appreciate the invite," Mr. Hughes said. "I trust that you can use our service in some way."

"Yes, I believe so. Let's go into the parlor and talk. I'll have a servant bring refreshments. Anything special?"

"Mint julep for me," said the talkative man.

"Straight whiskey," said the other.

The servant at hand walked away to fetch the beverages. William began the conversation as they all sat down.

"Gentlemen, I'll come right to the point. You men have been referred to me as two of the best slave hunters in the business. I trust my information is correct."

"We've had no complaints from our other customers."

"Well, then, perhaps you can be of service to me." At that moment William removed a copy of the *Liberator* from his pocket.

"Here, read this," he said, pointing to the article about Emanuel and Winnie.

The men accepted their drinks from the servant as they began to read the article. William waited to see if Mr. Knight, the shorter of the two, was going to dispose of his tobacco before he drank. He never did.

"Looks like you've had the wool pulled over your eyes by a half-breed and a full nigga," the taller man said.

William took offense but managed to remain calm. His response hinted at condescension.

"We shall see, how did you put it, just who has had the wool pulled over his eyes; and that's where you come in. I want you to find my slaves, both of them, and bring them back to me . . . alive and unharmed."

"Gonna cost you a little more to bring these niggas back alive and unharmed," Mr. Hughes said.

"I am prepared to pay your price."

"Well, Sir, you've got yourself a deal. My partner and me will be off to Boston at first light. According to this here newspaper that's where they were last heard from. Oh, by the way, that'll cost you extra—it being Boston, the extra distance and all. There's a whole bunch of them abolitionist fellas up there and they protects them runaway niggas like a man would a good horse."

"I'll pay you one-half of your money now and the other when you complete the job," William interjected. "You shouldn't have too much trouble, what with passage of the Fugitive Slave Law."

"Well," Mr. Hughes said, "I wanna tell you that there ain't no curse word in the English language that'll explain what them Yanks thinks of yo' Fugitive Slave Law. But don't you fret none, we'll git them niggas for ya. If they's alive and on this Earth, we'll git 'em.'"

The servant escorted the two men to the door. William was so repulsed by seeing the shorter man drink around his tobacco that he felt nauseous and left his drink untouched.

CHAPTER TWENTY-NINE

"**I**'m going to have a baby."

"A baby," Emanuel responded groggily as he lay half asleep, nestled close to Winnie.

She sat up in bed and shook him, then repeated herself.

"Wake up! I said, I'm going to have a baby."

This time, the words sunk in.

"You're what?" Emanuel was up on his knees. "You're . . . you're going to have a baby?" he stammered.

"Yes! Yes, that's exactly what I've been trying to tell you all night."

"You're, you're with child? Oooh! Gooood gracious! You're going to have a baby," Emanuel repeated.

"Yes, for the hundredth time. You . . . " she said, jabbing her finger into his chest with each word, "are going to be a father. You know, like one of those little cute things that cries a lot," she said mockingly.

"Oh, my God. I never thought of myself as a father. I'm so happy!" Emanuel said. He reached out and embraced Winnie lovingly.

"Be careful, you don't want to hurt the little one that's between us now."

"You know that I could never do anything to hurt either one of you, you know that."

"I know." Winnie responded with an embrace of her own, accompanied by a long kiss.

"I love you."

"I love you, too, and I'm mighty proud to be carrying your baby."

They lay back on the bed.

"That means that you will have to stop working."

"Stop working!" Winnie responded. "Where did you get that great idea?"

"I don't want no wife of mine, who is with child, out having to slave for somebody."

"I am not slaving. I'm working." Her tone was a bit argumentative now. "I'm working to help abolish slavery, not to support it."

"I know. I know," Emanuel said. "I had hoped that my wife could have the privilege of having a baby without having to work.

"Slave mothers are back at work even before their pain has stopped."

Winnie tried to reassure him.

"I understand and I love you for your concern, but we are not in slavery anymore. We're on free soil and I'm working for pay because I want to. Don't you see? Our baby will have a much better chance the more money we have. When the baby is born, I'll stop for a while, but I want to return as soon as I can. Besides, it will work out fine. You work at the tavern at night and most of my speaking engagements are during the day or early evening."

Emanuel listened to what was being said, then silently acknowledged a truce by gently kissing Winnie's cheek. As he lay back on his pillow, he reviewed their life. He was employed as a piano player and maintenance man at a local pub. He had applied for the job after seeing a sign in the window and proved himself by playing. Initially, he had thought classical music would excite his audience. He did a rendition of Beethoven's *Piano Sonata No.14 in C-Sharp Minor.* The few women present seemed to enjoy it, but before he could finish the *adagio sostenuto,* there were harsh boos from the mostly male crowd. Quickly, he had to switch to more rhythmic dance music. The response from the crowd got him hired on the spot.

Winnie had finally given in to the urgings of the local abolitionist society.

"Such an eloquent speaker you are," the society's president said. "My dear, you should give strong consideration to joining our group and speak to the willing ear about the evils and crudeness of slavery. I assure you that there are many free-spirited men and women, Negro and white, who would love to hear your voice, and the pay is not bad."

Winnie was swayed by the financial rewards, and soon was quite often on the road, speaking on the horrors of slavery. She was good at it.

They had only the one room. A tidy, clean place with one chair, a bed, a small table, and wash basin. It would be plenty big enough for the three of them. Not as spacious as Lake Holler, but a sight better than the slave cabins.

As he approached the sleep stage, Emanuel's thoughts drifted some more. Got to save money for the new baby. Wanted to save enough to somehow free my mother and get her out of the South. Have to wait a little longer, I guess.

They both slept.

Emanuel worked out a deal with the owner of the tavern. After hours, when all the work was done, he could practice on the piano as long as he liked. This Emanuel did religiously. A burning desire to create his own musical piece was resurfacing. It didn't much matter what kind of composition—a symphony, concerto, sonata, or even an opera—so long as he was the composer. After all, there was no other way for him to express his musical talents.

He didn't like the tavern music he had to play night after night, but he found it intriguing that his audience enjoyed it so much. He made this duty much more tolerable by imagining himself center stage before a concert audience playing a great classical piece.

As he had tried to pen his first musical score, his thoughts were a culmination of all his varied musical influences—the lively, oft time ambivalent music of the slave yards; the stirring soft melodious solos of his mother; the stinging, multi-tempo, polyphonic classics of Missy Kathryn; even the loud, boisterous, invigorating tavern music. From these variant exposures, his task was to choose those special sounds and chords and arrange them uniquely in such a manner that the work would hold an audience's interest. Goals defined, he began to work. His body went through the many motions required of him at the tavern, but his mind was always on his composition.

As the pregnancy progressed, Winnie became less interested in her public speaking and more involved with the newborn-to-be.

"What will we name the baby?" wondered Winnie.

"Oh, I don't know. Haven't thought about it much," Emanuel admitted.

"Well, I have. If it's a girl, I want her to have a proud name that people respect. Something like Jessica. I heard Missy Kathryn say that was her mother's name."

"What about a last name? Jessica, Jessica what?" asked Emanuel.

"I don't know, never gave a last name much thought. Don't know if I ever had one."

"Me neither."

"Well I guess we can make it anything we want. Let's see, Davidson, Griffith, Carson, Stewart. I like Stewart, it goes well together with Jessica. *Jessica*," Winnie said emphatically.

"Anything but Littlejohn," Emanuel stated. "I ain't gonna name a child of mine after that man."

"Then Stewart it will be. That means that we are Emanuel and Winnie Stewart. It feels good to have a last name of your own choosing. I love you, Emanuel Littlejohn Stewart," Winnie said playfully.

"I love you, too, Winnie Stewart, but I'll love you a lot more if you do away with calling me Littlejohn anything."

"It's a deal."

"What if it's a boy?" Emanuel quickly returned to their former topic.

"There's no question about the name if it's a boy. I want him named after his handsome and talented father . . . Emanuel Stewart Jr., no, Emanuel Stewart II . . . "

"Why don't we stop wasting what little time we have together and worry about names when the baby gets here?" Emanuel said as he pushed her gently back on the pillow. "I know exactly what we should be doing right now."

CHAPTER THIRTY

Dear Auntie Mame,

I hope that I have not taken advantage of our love and friendship by calling upon your willing ear at the most disenchanting times. There is so much that I want to tell you, perhaps to seek advice from your now silent voice, maybe to air my innermost feelings and concerns. Whatever the case may be, let me thank you first for preparing the route of perpetual communication with you by giving me this most lovely book that hides some of the most intimate details of my life.

Perhaps I shall start with a more pleasant prelude this time. It represents a small beginning, but to my way of thinking, and I'm sure yours too, an important one. In 1848, the first Women's Rights Convention was held at Seneca Falls, New York, under the auspicious guidance of a daredevil reformer named Elizabeth Cady Stanton, who to no one's surprise has served her other functions as mother, wife and homemaker as well. She has persevered the criticism of the times and nourished the seed of hope for equality for women in all walks of life.

More than ever before, I feel the haunt of rebellion from within. There was a time when music would soothe my soul and satisfy all of my needs, but no more. I now have urgings to lash out at a system so unrestricted and good for some, yet so oppressive for others. Old cliches like it's not fair come to mind often. So you can see why it is so inspiring to me to hear of women coming together in conference to express their grievances.

They put forth these resolutions that were made public.

> *That such laws as conflict, in any way, with the true and substantial happiness of women, are contrary to the great precept of nature and of no validity.*

> *That woman is man's equal—was intended to be so by the Creator, and the highest good of the race demands that she should be recognized as such.*

> *That all laws which prevent women from occupying such a station in society as her conscience shall dictate, or which place her in a position inferior to that of man, are contrary to the precept of nature, and therefore of no force or authority.*

As I ponder these resolves, I must admit with all candor that I am the victim of double indemnity for I am certainly sympathetic and supportive of all the assertions pertaining to the rights of women and I pretend no reluctance toward supporting these same assertions in the name of our Negro slaves. But I must also admit to a cowardly instinct, for a public admittance to such a belief in the present day south falls just short of tyranny. But unlike me, there are newly organized female activists who carry the banner asserting the rights of women in one hand and also the banner for the abolition of slavery in the other. This extraordinary revelation is the source of much contentment for me.

With each passing day and with every event that further diminishes the hold that slavery has on this country, I am filled with new hope for my Emanuel and his friend Winnie. Hopefully by now, they are man and wife. They are now in the territory and I am most happy for both of them. Their whereabouts are unknown, but while this leaves much remorse within my soul, it is for their own good since in my husband's mind, their fate and destiny is to be damned. I must hope that Emanuel and Winnie reside far, far away from me; since it is within William's power and will, and he now has the right to do so by law, to fetch them like so many lost sheep. The manner in which Winnie and Emanuel made their escape left William an obsessed demonic fool—without reason. Were it not for the overseer, the plantation would have wasted into dust because now its maintenance is low on William's list of priorities. He lives for the drink; he rests little and possesses little devotion for anything but his horse. Even I have been cast aside and while such treatment is commensurate with my illicit wanton desire to be with his brother, it's hard for me to stand by and watch a man I once loved destroy himself, inside and out, with hate and drink.

Now the bitter but sweet truth comes out. There are so many emotions tearing at my spirit that sometimes I feel helpless and out of control of my own destiny.

Most of my time is now spent at my father's plantation with David. William has no admitted knowledge of our connubial existence or perhaps he remains so drunken that he can't realize the obvious. I am afraid that I don't handle deceit very well and were it not for David's need for secrecy, because of his cryptic anti-slavery activity, then I would face my husband with the truth, no doubt to be ostracized not only by him, but the sainted community in which we live also. So it appears that at least for the moment utmost secrecy is tres importante.

I don't know where it will all end, and my burden is getting harder to manage. But as always, it's now much lighter since there has been open and candid communication with you.

I love you and miss you, Auntie Mame.

Always, Kathryn

CHAPTER THIRTY-ONE

Emanuel Stewart II was born November 15, 1850. His complexion was of a lighter hue, like his mother's. He had long curly hair that concealed his face. When Winnie parted it, she discovered the most adorable round visage that she had ever seen.

"You're big and handsome, just like your father!" Winnie told the child. She loved holding him close and feeling his soft, spongy skin next to hers. When he cried, she turned to Emanuel.

"Sing to him," she demanded. "You have a beautiful voice, sing to him!"

"What shall I sing?"

"What about the song your mother used to sing to you?"

He needed little coercion as he held his son close, resting the tiny head on his chest, as he sang:

I'll sing to you
because you make me happy.
I'll sing to you
'cause you make me sad

I'll sing to you
'cause you make up for all that I lost
and some that I never had.

Except when the child was hungry, Emanuel's soft, soothing voice was all that was needed to calm the baby.

These were special times for he and Winnie. Quickly, their child became the center of their attention. Oftentimes, as they lay with the baby between them in bed, secret fears surfaced about their son's fate, but neither of them would darken the moment by saying a word. What would be his destiny? Would he be allowed to live on this Earth a free man? Would he have to spend the rest of his life answering for, or running because of, his color? Had they allowed their passion to replace reason and practicality? Would he pay for their mistake?

Before the birth of Emanuel II, Winnie pursued her duties with the abolitionist society almost casually. She was free and with the man she loved, and he loved her and that was all that mattered. Once her son arrived, she became more sensitive to the issues. What had been a mere job became an obsession. Her speeches became more fiery and demanding and less conciliatory.

Before, she had accepted the penalties of slavery as her destiny, a hideous birthright that only God could explain. Now, its existence was an inexplicable horror, and the only way a Negro could be safe from its wrath—regardless of his birth on free soil—was total abolishment.

Winnie's abolitionist cohorts soon became resentful of her newfound pugnaciousness, and began to offer criticism:

You must not be too outspoken and militant or you will repel our white, middle-of-the-road sympathizers here in the North. We are white and we are your friends and we understand fully your contempt for the institution of slavery. We share your pain, but we must effect gradual change through hush-hush type communication with the now committed, yet liberal Northern white populace.

Statements of such kind became a source of much irritation for Winnie, and she soon came to believe that Negro emancipation could only be achieved by Negroes. She became a disciple of Frederick Douglass, acknowledged spokesperson for the more than 3 million enslaved Negroes in the United States. Winnie read every published speech by him and felt no reluctance about echoing his sentiment. The highlight of her career was the day she shared the stage with him on the lecture circuit for the Massachusetts Anti-Slavery Society in February of 1851.

"Brethren," she began, "I am deeply honored today to share the podium with our most illustrious leader, Frederick Douglass. Like him, I, too, was a slave and also like him, I carry a message from the center of the hearts of millions of our enslaved brothers, sisters, aunts, uncles, mothers, and fathers. They say to you, do not forget us! They say to you that they do not forget that freedom is an automatic birthright for every man, woman, and child, granted by God.

"They say that enslavement and subjugation is the product of man's aberrant imagination and that any hint of ecclesiastical origins is mere pretense. In the South, its existence is symbolized willingly and openly by white men who designate themselves masters only because they have the keys to the cold, hard shackles that bind us. Yes! Brothers and sisters who plant your feet on free soil, do not forget us! Let the bonds between us be as strong as the iron chains that symbolize our condition.

"There are those who would have us believe that slavery is a necessary vituperation that will secure for people of color and black hue a place on the road leading toward eternal life. Non-sense! Perhaps there will be a road for Negroes and another for whites or maybe there will be just one road and the whites are to enter first. Nonsense! Any such self-serving allegations are atrocious to say the least and makes about as much sense as there being black and white air or my being able to separate the Negro part of me from the white part of me. We, as a people, must concentrate all our efforts toward eradicating humanity of this diabolical injustice, never to forget that many of our white brethren, as evidenced by their majority presence today, are at our side—openly and willingly. However, the major effort must come from within, and we must act to destroy the atrocities of human bondage ourselves. We must do it ourselves and any man or woman not willing to give his all, or even die for the sake of his children's freedom, doesn't deserve to have it.

"We have suffered enough. And if we are to suffer more, let it be because of our unrelenting effort to achieve total freedom. While my innate feelings tell me that unearned suffering is repulsive, the experience should have no color line or racial exclusivity. If suffering must be a part of life, let us suffer together for a common cause and a common good—just as our forefathers did against the British tyrants.

"Let us suffer together as we tame the wilderness and tender the soil so that it will bear us fruit and food for life.

"Let us suffer together as we fortress our lands and train the guard that will be necessary to ward off invasion by the enemy.

"Let us suffer together as we fell the trees so that their energies will feed the hearth to ward off cold nights and harsh winters.

"Let us suffer together as we bring to this land the gift of life that will sustain and secure human permanence on this earth.

"Let us suffer together as the sweat from the toil of the day moistens our skin as we erect beautiful homes, buildings, churches, and monuments.

"Let us suffer together as we try to envision and reaffirm the effort necessary to secure a bright future for all mankind, so that we can end suffering forever for all men, no matter what their color. Yes! Let us suffer together as we fight to end all suffering."

Applause, mostly from the black members of the audience, interrupted her. Winnie continued.

"And now the seeds of discontent are being sewn in other avenues. They tell me that two years ago, a Woman's Rights Convention was held in Seneca Falls, New York and it is good that its leaders have aggressively gone forward with a mandate demanding not only political and economic equality with men, but also the right to vote. As unequals to the power structure in this country, we Negroes, free and slave, must align ourselves with the efforts of those bold and brave women, and we can end this accursed oppressive system."

As Winnie spoke, many whites in the audience rose from their seats and left. She did not stop.

"Every moment that the black populace of this country remains overshadowed by racial hatred and oppression is another moment's delay toward reaching our goals in more productive areas, such as the arts and sciences. For with all its abilities, the human mind is sometimes weak and it cannot give concentrated effort toward more than one thing at a time. So errant and uncontrolled thoughts and actions make us all losers. The white man's mind, although free of restraint, loses because it directs its efforts toward the sacrilegious task of trying to harness another human being. The black man's mind loses because it is not granted its God-given right to expand, to think, and to express itself.

"In closing, let me remind you that I believe that full freedom for all races of men and for the sexes is the natural order of things and that this eventually will come to pass. To deny it, is not God's will."

"May I offer my congratulations to you, young lady," Douglass said to Winnie.

"Thank you, Sir."

"Come walk with me as we talk," he said, and they started to stroll.

"Don't be surprised if your invitations to speak at anti-slavery gatherings diminish from now on. You'll find that most of our white abolitionist friends would have us choose a more passive course."

"And you, Sir?"

"I agree with every word you said, but more importantly, I agree with your approach. All of our efforts to abolish the horrid institution of slavery have been stalemated, and I believe that the only way that we can renew the vigor is to Agitate! Agitate! Agitate!"

Winnie was relieved.

"Thank you, Sir. I was afraid for a moment that you would perceive my speech as too harsh."

"Never! No, never!" Douglass told her. "There is no statement against slavery that is too harsh. Remember that when certain times prevail, and you feel as I sometimes do."

"How is that?"

"Alone," said Douglass as he walked away.

One of the white abolitionist speakers approached Winnie. "A little strong, don't you think, young lady?"

"No, I don't think, Sir, that my speech was a little strong. But if it was, it certainly was not as strong as the chains that bruise

and maim my enslaved brothers and sisters, making them bleed
from ankles and wrists, and from whip lashes on their weakened
backs. Or perhaps you don't believe that Negroes bleed or can
bleed to dea . . . "

The white man cut her off.

"We must adhere to one issue. To ask total equality for the
black race all at once is more than even most Northern whites
will tolerate. We must move one step at a time. To even hint at
woman's suffrage is to add insult to injury. There are many
white sympathizers here and our presence should suggest that
we are familiar with the agony imparted on your race by their
enslaved conditions."

"Well just how familiar are you with it?" Winnie shot back.

"If there was someone beating you with the lash, would you
offer him your handkerchief to wipe the sweat he produced from
beating you?"

"Of course not . . . " the white man began.

"Then why must we move along with such moderation or use
methods more suitable to our white sympathizers when it's our
backs that are getting beaten. You see, kind sir, I believe, in part,
what Patrick Henry said. You see, I, too, have a regret. I regret
that I have but one life to live and if there is a force out there so
omnipotent that it won't let me live it, then at least let me die
trying."

Winnie walked away.

Emanuel could feel the presence of someone else in the room.
Though he felt as if he were being watched, he was not fearful.
He knew that Mr. O'Grady, the tavern owner, had a late night
visitor. As was his usual habit before working on his own
composition, he would practice the work of one of the great
masters. Like his mentor, Kathryn, he was capable of adapting

musical pieces meant for other instruments to the piano. This time, he chose Mozart's *Symphony No. 40 in G-Minor*.

Sitting tall, he imagined that he was clothed in full concert dress. He began the *molto allegro*, the first movement. His nimble fingers danced across the keyboard in rapid organized form, consistent with the tempo of this particular movement. He offered a swinging, fanciful interpretation of the opening statement, then advanced to a more sustained gaiety that embodied a vibrant lively theme, terminating in deep, hovering base tones.

Next, he moved to the *andante*. The rhythm was soft and soothing with a kind of skip to its beat. Emanuel thought this movement resembled a series of lullabies, calm and motionless.

He completed the *allegratte* and *allegro assai* in the otherwise silent room but heard in his head the sounds of a great orchestra with flutes, clarinets, violins, horns, and drums. At last, he finished, and heard a lone cheer in the tavern. The applause came from the stranger who had accompanied Mr. O'Grady.

"Thank you, Sir. I didn't know that anybody was there," Emanuel said halfheartedly, knowing that he was telling an untruth. He had taken full advantage of his secretive audience.

"A most beautiful rendition of Mozart's 40th symphony. Did you adapt the music yourself?" the stranger asked.

"Yes. Yes. I did . . . with the help of Kathryn, Missy Kathryn, I mean, my master's wife. I mean my former master's wife. She taught me to play."

"Indeed! Indeed, she did, and very well, too, I might add."

"Thank you, Sir."

"Cadbury is my name. William Cadbury and currently, I am the director of the Boston Orchestral Assembly. Mr. O'Grady here has been telling me about you and your magnificent talent. Quite frankly, at first, I didn't believe him, but you performed beyond expectation."

"Thank you again, Sir. I owe a lot to Mr. O'Grady for allowing me to practice."

"I have a proposition for you," Cadbury said.

"What kind of proposition?"

"A concert. How would you like to be the featured performer at one of our concerts?"

Emanuel couldn't believe what he was hearing.

"You're not foolin' me, are you?"

"No, I'm perfectly serious. Of course, it will take a little time to get you ready to perform before an audience. We will have to smooth out the rough edges. Decorum, the composition to be presented, things like that will have to be worked out."

Emanuel was elated and speechless. Finally, he managed to say one word.

"When?"

"We will have to decide on a time when I'm sure you are ready. I want the public to stand up and take notice. You will be the first. No other Negro has ever performed before such an audience, but I'm certain that you are up to it."

"I'll do my best."

"I know you will, my boy. I know you will."

It was almost dawn when Emanuel reached home. Winnie and the baby were sound asleep. At first, he thought it best to not wake her, but he couldn't restrain himself.

"Winnie. Winnie, wake up!" He shook his wife and whispered softly so as not to awaken the baby.

Slowly, Winnie came around.

"Morning, baby," she said, still half asleep.

"Winnie, wake up. I've got some good news."

"What? What is it?"

"I met this man tonight at the tavern. Mr. O'Grady brought

him. He heard me play and he wants me to do a concert with the Boston Symphony—as a guest performer!"

"Jesus! Emanuel, that is wonderful!" She wrapped her arms around his neck.

"I want you there with me on the front row. I'll have the audience pleading and begging for more. I'll play like I've never played before and . . . "

Winnie interrupted.

"I don't know if my being there is such a good idea."

"What do you mean? You not there? Why?"

"Emanuel, listen to me. I'm not the most popular person amongst liberal whites anymore. If they associate me with you, they may not appreciate you as much."

"Then I don't care. Don't you see? It's for you that I want to do this thing. I don't really care what anybody else thinks. I love you and my son. Maybe the rest of the audience will not like—because I'm a Negro, once a slave—the idea that I can play the piano, or maybe they will think I can't play well enough."

He held her close and looked directly into her eyes, his hands on either side of her face with only a hair's distance between them.

"I don't care. This is for you, my special lady. And the audience can come if they like."

They kissed—a long and passionate caress that ignited all the right emotional fires. The moment was theirs.

CHAPTER THIRTY-TWO

The *Boston Herald News* printed a feature article on the pianist Emanuel Stewart on April 27, 1851.

> *Emanuel Stewart, a recent arrival to the Boston area, gave an inestimable performance on this past Sunday before an audience of music lovers and concert attenders. He astonished and delighted the hundreds present with his play of the piano, flirting with the skirts of genius like any other seasoned veteran.*
>
> *The concert was given in two parts with a brief intermission in between. He opened with* Beethoven's Sonata, No. 14 in C Sharp Minor. *No doubt there was little hesitation in choosing this work as the first presentation because with it he enraptured and totally captivated his audience, and for the rest of the evening he toyed with their emotions and stimulated their passions at will—like the talented virtuoso that he is.*
>
> *There followed the* Sonata No. 8 in C Minor. *The opening movement was presented with verve and a*

lively concentration of effort unsurpassed by any kind of human endeavor. Then he eased into the second move-ment, the Adagio Cantabile, *so effortlessly, so naturally that he lulled his audience into a hypnotic state from which no one wanted to return. Then he stunned their consciousness and aroused them with his brilliant fin-ish—rondo allegro.*

The second half of the concert featured the works of Mozart.

And may I add that if reincarnation is at all possible, then Mozart now has a black face. This young pianist devoured Mozart's composition, almost as if his intent was to give his works a new birthright, and then he poured the charismatic sounds over a more than receptive audience.

He opened with the Concerto KV 271 in E-Flat Major. *If indeed, the first half was designed to demand the accolades of his audience, which he got, then the second half was designed to display the artistic mastery of his orchestra. In short, he played the concerto beauti-fully. He had complete control of the orchestra and elicited their accompaniment with the beckoning call of his fingertips. When he needed frivolous, gallant, excit-ing expression in the background, he had it.*

I find it impossible to account for this Negro boy's immense talents upon any hypothesis growing out of known laws of art and science. He was subjected to numerous tests at an audition for this performance and invariably, he came off triumphantly. Whether in decid-ing the pitch of component parts of chords, the most difficult and dissonant; whether in repeating with cor-rectness and precision any piece written or impromptu;

*whether in his improvisations or performances of com-
positions by Haydn, Mendelssohn, Handel, Chopin,
Bach, Mozart, and others no matter for what instrument the music was erected, he transformed all forms of
music into piano music with such power and capacity
that he must be ranked as one of the most gifted musical
phenomena of our time.*

Emanuel was so bedazzled, not by his exquisite performance
but the opportunity to give it, that he floated on air for days. For
the first time in his life he felt totally free and unhindered.
Nothing can stop me now! he thought. But that elusive, undefin-
able, impenetrable zone deep within continued to send signals
that would never allow him to get too far from his feelings of
impending doom. He wondered if Winnie had such feelings. If
she did, she also did a good job of not revealing them.

It was a beautiful night. The soft glow of moonlight illuminated Winnie's and the baby's faces. Emanuel leaned over and
kissed them both on their cheeks. He hadn't intended to awaken
Winnie, but she stirred.

"What are you doing still awake?" she asked groggily.

"Just looking at you and the baby."

She smiled.

"What a beautiful night. Look at that moon. It's so pretty,"
Winnie said.

"Will it always be this way, Winnie?"

"What do you mean?"

"Sometimes I get real scared that something will happen and
we will lose our freedom . . . our new life together . . . and our son
will . . ."

"Don't say it. Please, don't say it. I'll never let my son be a slave or lose his freedom as long as I've got life. Stop worrying."

"Maybe you're right."

"Now, there, let's enjoy what we have and not think any bad thoughts."

She desperately wanted to change the subject.

"Know what?" she asked.

"What?"

"Your concert last Sunday was the most beautiful concert I've ever heard."

"Well, it had to be, since it's the only one you've ever heard."

"I know that," she told him. "But a person can sense when something great is happening. You feel all funny inside. And I had that feeling when I heard you play. And the audience, they would have stayed all night had you continued to play."

"You reckon they'll want to hear me again?"

"I know they will."

"I've been playing piano since I was seven years old, but I've never had the feeling that I had that night. It was like my insides were filled with shooting stars that were all exploding, one right after the other. Everything came so automatic, so easy.

"Now I know what Missy Kathryn was talking about when she said, 'On stage before a great audience, you and the piano become one.' "

"Emanuel?" Winnie said.

"What?"

"Let's move the baby aside so I can show you how much I enjoyed the concert, you know, the proper way."

"What's the proper way?"

"Move the baby and I'll show you."

Emanuel did as he was told while Winnie slipped out of her gown. She didn't give him a chance to say anything. The kiss that followed was sizzling and aroused them both as she pressed down hard on his body, forcing him to lie back on the bed. She was in full control as she straddled his muscular body. In this performance, she was the maestro. They began to make sweet love.

Mr. Hughes and Mr. Knight read the newspaper article.

"Looks like we've got our man," Mr. Hughes said.

"Let's go get him, then!"

"No, no, just wait a minute. We've got the law on our side now. The right thing to do is to go down yonder to the courthouse an' git a warrant."

"Seems crazy to me. We right here in the midst of all these abolitionist and you gonna ask 'em to hand over a coupla 'scape niggas. Don't see why we just don't go an kidnap 'em like we always did."

" 'Cause the law says we don't have to," Mr. Hughes said. "Now, come on and stop actin' like a stubborn jackass."

On May 27, 1851, Judge Levi Castlebury issued a warrant for Emanuel and Winnie Stewart. The child's name was not mentioned in the document. No officer from the local police would volunteer to serve the warrant.

Word quickly spread about the two strangers, and a meeting was called at Faneville Hall to map out a strategy to thwart them. The audience was mixed, black and white.

"I say we tar and feather those two slavers and drive them out of town," came a voice from the crowd. The audience roared its approval.

"Now, gentlemen, please," said a voice followed by two knocks of a gavel. "We must have order. Please, sit and be quiet. These men are perfectly within their rights."

"Then change the law!" someone shouted, setting off the crowd again.

"Gentlemen, Gentlemen! Please sit down and be quiet. Please!" The group quieted.

"First things first. Somebody must warn Emanuel and Winnie. I suspect that the character of these men would prompt them to do anything to get what they came after, even kidnap the Stewarts just to avoid confrontation with us. It would be better if they were moved from their present address."

"I think I can help on both accounts. Winnie and I are very good friends and I would like to warn them, plus I have a small vacant cottage on the outskirts of town that would be ideal," said one of the sympathizers.

"Thank you, Mrs. Hilliam. Perhaps you had best be off whilst the rest of us map out a strategy. We wish you God's speed."

Mr. Hughes and Mr. Knight presented themselves at Emanuel's and Winnie's address.

"Looks like we gonna have to take matters into our own hands. These nigga lovin' Yankees ain't gonna help us none," Mr. Hughes whispered.

"Well, we've . . . "

"Shoosh! Not so loud. Somebody might hear you."

"I was saying we've kidnapped 'em before and I don't see no reason to change," Mr. Knight said in a hushed tone.

"I hear you. Now come on, let's kick this door down."

The men rammed their feet into the door, which gave way quickly. They rushed inside, only to find a tidy but empty room.

"Damn it!" Mr. Knight bellowed. "Somebody done warned them."

The men's commotion roused others nearby. Before Mr. Hughes and Mr. Knight could exit, they were surrounded by a group of men, amongst whom was an officer of the law.

"You two are under arrest for breaking and entering and

willful destruction of private property," the officer said.

"What the hell! We've got a legal and fair paper for the arrest of these two runaway niggas . . . "

"Oh, shut up, Knight," Mr. Hughes said, "Can't you see we been set up?"

The two men were marched off to jail.

"Thank you for your help, Mrs. Hilliam. Without it, we might be on our way back to a slave's life again," said a teary-eyed Winnie. "I don't want my son to ever know anything about slavery. I'd rather he be dead."

"Don't worry so much," Mrs. Hilliam said. "You have many friends in Boston now, all of whom will help, if need be. Soon this will blow over and you, Emanuel, and your son can get on with your lives."

"Thank you again. We'll be all right," said Winnie.

"Sure you will. You and Emanuel stay here in this cottage until it's safe. I'm sure no one will find you here," Mrs. Hilliam said as she left the room.

For a long while, Winnie and Emanuel didn't say a word. Then Winnie took her son from Emanuel and held him close to her chest, rocking back and forth. Lovingly, she kissed his forehead and cuddled him.

"Emanuel, we're going to have to leave Boston, you know," Winnie said, her eyes on her son.

"Yes, I know," Emanuel replied solemnly. He felt so diminished inside—beaten, angered, frustrated. For a short time he had known freedom, freedom to work for himself and control his own life, freedom to learn and create, freedom of scholarly pursuits heretofore denied him because of his heritage. The seeds had been planted. He knew his own abilities and talents now. All feelings of inferiority had been dismissed. Now he had a son, his own flesh and blood who depended on him for all the necessities of life. He was born free and would have to remain so, even if Emanuel's life depended on it.

"I know you want to remain here until you get your mother to freedom, but it just don't look like there is a way."

"There's a way," Emanuel said. "Just gonna take a lot longer than I thought."

"I hear Canada is a nice place," Winnie said.

"Sounds awful far away," Emanuel responded.

"It is an awful long way from here and even farther from slavery. I know someone who will help. If you'll just say you'll go there, I'll be off tomorrow to make some arrangements."

"Don't look like we have much choice, does it?" Emanuel asked sadly. "I'll watch after little Emanuel while you're away."

Winnie departed the next day.

"I love you, Winnie. You be careful, and don't let that temper of yours get you in trouble," he warned his wife.

"I'll be back soon as I can," Winnie said, "and we ought to be on our way tonight. Everything will be ready and don't talk to or tell anyone that you don't have to."

Mr. Hughes and Mr. Knight were back in their room at the U. S. Hotel.

"Wonder who paid that bail for us? Ten thousand dollars is a mighty big sum of money," inquired Mr. Knight as he squeezed a plug of tobacco into his mouth.

"Don't know. Don't care," said Mr. Hughes. "Just glad he did. Now let's get the hell out of here and find a place less conspicuous." They heard a knock at the door. Each man readied himself, pulling out guns.

"Who is it?" said Mr. Hughes.

"Messenger. I have a letter for a Mr. Hughes and Mr. Knight."

"Don't do it. Sounds like some kinda trick to me," said Mr. Knight.

"Maybe, but I'm tired a being pushed around. If that ain't a message boy, I'm gonna give him time to wish he was before I blow his head off."

Mr. Hughes unlatched and opened the door to view a harmless, frightened young boy with a letter. He took one look at the guns and grew even more terrified.

"I .. I . . . I . . . letter for Mr. Hughes and Mr. Knight!" he stammered.

Mr. Hughes grabbed the envelope and opened it. The boy bolted as Mr. Hughes slammed the door.

"Now who would be sending us a letter?" he asked as he paused to read it.

"Listen to this," he said. " 'Go to a small cottage across from the Belknap Street Church. There are people there that I am sure you would like to meet.' "

The letter was signed "Anonymous."

"Could be some kinda trick," said Mr. Knight, his right cheek filled with a plug of tobacco.

"It could be the same friend that paid the bail and I don't think he would shell out that kinda money if he wanted to do us harm," Mr. Hughes replied. "Come on, let's git."

The men stealthily approached the rear door of the cottage, scanning the area to make sure no one was around. In unison, they kicked the door down and rushed in. Emanuel, who was sitting at the kitchen table, started toward the nearby bedroom for the baby. Mr. Knight immediately stepped in his path.

"Well, looka here, Hughes, these niggas done had demselves a little nigga."

Emanuel stood ready for a fight.

"You dat nigga boy called Emanuel, ain't cha?"

As Mr. Hughes spoke, Emanuel dropped to his knees and delivered a blow to Mr. Knight's crotch. The shorter man doubled over.

"Git 'im, Hughes," he gasped, "that nigga done went down on me."

"I'll git the . . ."

Before Mr. Hughes could finish his sentence, Emanuel sprang to his feet and reached for the poker iron from the fireplace. He began swinging furiously at Hughes, making contact with his legs, buttocks, and back. One solid blow to the right side of the man's face had him down on the floor. Emanuel stood over him, holding the poker high in the air, ready to deliver the last lethal blow.

"Stop, nigga, stop! or I'll choke this young'un to death."

Mr. Knight had crawled over to the baby, and was gripping the child's neck so tight that he couldn't utter a sound.

Emanuel immediately dropped the poker. Now on his feet, Mr. Hughes began to beat Emanuel mercilessly. Emanuel knew he could not retaliate because that would mean certain death for his son.

The beating continued, and Emanuel lost consciousness.

"Stop it, Hughes, stop it!" Mr. Knight shouted. "We don't git paid if you kills him. You done beat the nigga so bad, we still may not git paid."

Knight's words, plus the pain from his wounds, caused Hughes to cease. He started to speak, but the pain in his mouth was too intense.

"Darn, that jaw looks broken!" Mr. Knight said. "You need a doctor."

Mr. Hughes shook his head defiantly. "Let's git dis nigga to Charleston. I ain't leavin' 'til I see him hanged."

Winnie returned to the cottage. The devastation she discovered told her the whole story. She stayed long enough to gather a few belongings.

Winnie knew exactly what had happened and where her family would be taken. She knew that they were not dead—yet. She knew what she had to do.

She told Mrs. Hilliam what happened and of her plans to return to Charleston. Winnie's plans sparked a heated exchange between the two women.

"Really, my dear Winnie, that is the most foolhardy idea that I've ever heard," Mrs. Hilliam told her.

"Maybe so, but it's what I have to do. Everything that is important to me was taken to Charleston and I intend to get them back or . . . "

Mrs. Hilliam finished the sentence for her.

"Or die trying, and die you might. But what good will that do? If you're dead, who will fight for their freedom above the Mason-Dixon? Don't you see, Winnie, you can do much more from where you stand. You've got an audience now; at least some people will listen to you."

"I've made up my mind. Are you going to help me or not?" Winnie asked sternly.

"Winnie, don't you see. You don't even have the law on your side. That darned Fugitive Slave Law gives slave hunters the right to confiscate runaway slaves."

"Answer my question," Winnie demanded, "are you going to help me?"

"Well . . . well . . . all right! Your mind is already made up, no use in trying to change it," Mrs. Hilliam conceded. "How will you do it?"

"I'll go back just like I came—as a white woman. If I could

borrow one of those fine and frilly dresses of yours, I'm sure I won't be recognized as a Negro."

"I've got just the dress for you," Mrs. Hilliam said wearily, "and with a little makeup here and there, when I finish with you, they won't know you from the Queen of England."

CHAPTER THIRTY-THREE

Winnie's return to Charleston was unhindered. Charleston was unchanged, but how different she felt from the last time she was here. She had tasted freedom and she liked it. If there had been innate, obsequious feelings before, they were long since buried. She had returned for a purpose—to try to secure freedom for her husband and her son. She had no doubts about their whereabouts or the reason for their abduction.

She carried a serious facade on her face and uninhibitedly, she looked at the whites whom she passed square in the eye. There was no concern that she would be recognized as black. When they spoke, she spoke. The agent at the train station directed her to the stables. She was going to rent a carriage and return to Lake Holler.

Where once there was fear, there was now determination. Where there had been skillful, wily maneuvering, there was direct, overt action guided by instincts and emotions that could only be nurtured in a woman who had lost her loved ones. Either she was going to get what she had come for or she would die trying. No more enslavement! No more subjugation! No more penalty!

In the middle of her gut, there was a deep feeling of emptiness that overshadowed the realization that she had never driven a carriage before. Courteously, a stable hand had helped her into the buggy and she skillfully guided the horse due south, just as if she had done it many times before.

William Littlejohn let his revengeful attitude grow and grow. At the right time, vengeance would be his, and there was no power on Earth that would keep him from enjoying every minute of it. Deep within his soul, he felt that nothing had gone his way of late.

John C. Calhoun—the voice of the South—was dead. His oh-so-sweet wife--whom he hadn't made love to in months—spent more time at her father's plantation than her own; he speculated that there must have been something going on between her and his brother David. Oh, what the hell, who cares? And then, there was the Compromise of 1850, but there was no compromise for the South, only mediocre concessions except for the Fugitive Slave Law which gave slave holders the right to apprehend and return their human property to the South, and this he had done. He had lost two slaves, he had confiscated two slaves. He felt a great deal of satisfaction and tomorrow morning at ten o'clock, he would pour out all his wrath on one captured slave, Emanuel. Just like his father, years before, he would be hanged by the neck until dead. He had his men disseminate fliers all over the county. Everyone was invited. Vengeance is mine, saith the Lord.

Well, not this time. Impervious vanity, I'll show that black nigga what impervious vanity really means. It was noontime. He had his first drink of the day.

That morning, Kathryn received a special letter from William, revealing that Emanuel had been captured. She was so frantic that she didn't know what to do. The letter also told of a baby—the captured slave's baby. It was a boy.

"Oh, my God, Emanuel has a son, born free and now he, too, has been brought into this hell hole called slavery," Kathryn bemoaned. As she continued to read, she became hysterical almost to the point of fainting. The words her husband had sent to everyone in the county pounded at her brain relentlessly as she read: "You are invited to witness the legal hanging of a slave called Emanuel, tomorrow at ten o'clock in the morning."

"David! David! Where are you?" Kathryn screamed as she ran through the house in search of him.

"What is it, Kathryn? My God, slow down! Now, what is it?"

"Here, read it."

"Tomorrow, tomorrow at ten o'clock."

"Yes, I see." David was pensive but in full control. "Less than twenty-four hours, doesn't give us much time."

"You've got to do something. I'm not going to let him hang Emanuel as if he were a criminal." The tears fell freely onto her face as she spoke between sobs. "We must help him."

David was still pensive. "There was no mention of Winnie. They must not have captured her. I wonder where she is."

"I don't know, but if she is alive, she'll be back. I know she will. See there," Kathryn said as she wiped her eyes and pointed at the letter. "They have a baby now, they have a son who was captured, too."

"You're right, unless I miss my guess, she either died trying to prevent their capture or . . . but there would have been some kind of word by now, you'd think. She probably is on her way here."

"I know she is. What will we do?"

"I don't know yet, I don't know. I'll think of something.

Whatever it is, it will have to be done under the cover of night. The whole county has been alerted. We'll just have to wait 'til dark."

"I'm going to talk to William. Maybe I can talk some sense into him."

"No! No! You stay here and get things ready just in case."

The yard hands stopped what they were doing on the day they saw Emanuel returned to the plantation. His body was robbed of its strength by the apparent beatings and lack of food and water. They helped him off the wagon as Hughes and Knight told William Littlejohn the whole story.

"Shackle and chain him in the guardhouse and give him water and food. I want him strong and alert when I stretch his neck, just like I did his daddy. Carry the young'un to Bell," William ordered some of the slaves in the yard.

"Give us enough time to clean up a bit and we'll stand guard over this nigga 'til you takes the rope of his stretched neck. See what he has done to the side of my face," said Hughes.

William observed the injury with little concern before turning to enter the plantation house.

"Pass de word, Piana's back, beat ha'f ta death," said one slave to the other.

"Pass de word, Piana's back . . . "

"Pass de word, Piana's back . . . "

"Pass de word, Piana's back, beat ha'f ta death."

Bell was utterly destroyed inside. All hope was gone. At least there was some compensation for her loss this time. She had a grandson. She held him close and rocked him back and forth. The child was exhausted and hungry. He was a strong little fella—she knew that because he had survived the trip. She tried to control her grief by praying and talking to God. Her mind was far from this Earth. Whatever was to happen was in God's hands and all she could do was pray.

The slaves did as they were told, but before the guard was set up by Hughes and Knight, they fed and gave water to Emanuel, then they tended his wounds with their own special poultices.

Emanuel was imprisoned in chains and under guard by Hughes and Knight. Bell wasn't allowed to see him, but no matter, they had communicated through the spirit for years. She knew his anguish. She heard his thoughts: I'll be all right, Ma, take care of my son for me, Ma. She, in turn, sent a message: Don't you worry, now. God is with you and let his will be done. I'll take care of my grandson, just like I took care of you.

It was late afternoon. Winnie's carriage turned onto the road leading to the Lake Holler plantation. As she reined her horse onward, she remembered her mother's story about how she left this very same plantation. She imagined seeing the wagon on the other side of the lake and William Littlejohn giving her mother a last loving glance. But over the years, Winnie began to know how illusory her mother's mind could be. Those things that she didn't have and wanted bad enough were committed to a world of make-believe. She described William Littlejohn, her father, as a kind, loving man. She knew this was a lie, but she had staked her life on the hope that somewhere deep within his soul, he could find enough compassion for her, his daughter, to grant her one request—let her husband and her son go free.

A yard hand helped her from her carriage. Jonathan was the first to spot her from the porch. He was startled when he recognized her. "Winnie," then as an afterthought, he said, "Miss Winnie?" She was as fine as any full-bred white woman, and years of accustomed behavior would not allow him to treat her any less.

"Miss Winnie, what is you doin' here?"

"Hello, Jonathan. I've come to talk to Mr. William about releasing my husband and my son."

"Miss Winnie, is you crazy? If you ain't, that man is. And he ain't of the mind to release nobody."

"Jonathan, I have to try. You see, I have one advantage, the man is my father and maybe he'll listen."

"Yo' father, What you talking about, girl?"

"Teresa, many years ago, Mr. William's concubine. She was sent away pregnant by him."

"Blow me down and pick me up again. That's the reason all those questions you needed to ask?"

"Yes, now please show me to his whereabouts."

"Yes, Ma'am! But I thinks this is a big mistake. He'll just as likely hang you as he is Emanuel tomorrow."

"Please, Jonathan."

"C'mon."

Inside the study Jonathan said, "Mr. William, you've got a visitor."

"Who is it?" he said. He was having another drink.

"Here she is." Jonathan closed the door behind him after Winnie entered.

William was surprised almost to the point of sobriety. He had a half-smile on his face as he walked toward Winnie. "Why, you little bi . . . "

"Mr. William, I've got to talk to you."

"Talk to me. I don't have to say anything to you except maybe thanks for coming back on your own and saving me the trouble of having to send slave hunters after you."

Winnie didn't back down. She held firm and looked him

straight in the eye as she slowly said, "You owe me and I want you to listen and I'll never ask anything of you again."

William, like Jonathan, was enthralled by Winnie's looks. She didn't talk like a slave, she wasn't dressed like a slave, and she was beautiful. Perhaps it was because of the liquor, but he wanted to hear what she had to say. He took another drink as he said, "Why do I have to listen to anything from you, nigga?"

"Cause you are this nigga's father."

William's face turned red as a beet. He choked on the drink that was already in his mouth. He had to cough several times to clear his throat enough to respond. "What did you say?"

"I said you are this nigga's father."

"What are you talking about? Thanks to a beautiful but barren woman whom I used to call my wife, I can safely say that I can lay claim to no progeny." He had a trancelike expression on his face as he added, "No sons or daughters."

"Well, maybe your slave women weren't so barren. At least one wasn't. A pretty black woman named Teresa that you sent away from here about nineteen years ago because she was pregnant. Yes, Mr. William Littlejohn, you have a child whether you claim me or not. But don't worry, I'm not here to collect on the family name; I'm simply asking a favor of you, and I'll stay out of your life forever." She was weeping somberly as she said, "Please, I beg of you, give my son and husband back to me."

The initial shock of her statement didn't last long. William replied, "You must be out of your mind. Tomorrow, I'm gonna stretch that nigga's neck from here to Boston, Massachusetts, so all them damned abolitionists can see it. Just like I did his daddy."

William's drunkenness was even more obvious now as he called out, "Gertie! Gertie, you come here!" When Gertie entered he said, "You take this Winnie girl down to her quarters and show her the proper dress for a slave."

Winnie jerked away as Gertie tried to hold her. She had no intention of trying to escape. She could hear William Littlejohn as she walked out of the room. "I don't have any sons or daughters." She also heard the glass and liquor bottle tinkle as they met.

Kathryn entered the study unannounced. William looked up but didn't rise from his seated position. Looking in her direction was his only acknowledgement of her presence. "What do you intend to do with Emanuel?"

"You know what I'm going to do. The same thing I did with his worthless daddy. The same thing you do to all uppity niggas. I'm going to lynch him. And you can watch."

Kathryn was not surprised at his statement. "I've never asked you for anything so important to me as what I'm about to ask you now. Please don't do it. Let him go for my sake. I'll do anything you ask."

"Why should I? You left this plantation to live at your father's plantation under suspicious circumstances, to say the least, where my brother. . . my own brother. . . just happens to live. And now you want a favor from me."

"Yes, I do."

"Don't hold your breath."

"But why? Isn't it really me you want to hurt because I pinned you down to a plantation life you never really wanted, not to mention the most horrible sin of all—not only did I not give you a son but no children at all. Isn't that what this really is all about?"

He took a drink before answering, "What difference does it make now?"

"You want to exact vengeance by taking the life of a harmless but talented black boy whose only mistake in life was being smart and capable. If it's me you want to hurt, then I shall concede to any punishment that you lay before me, but leave the boy alone. I plead to you as your wife."

"Wife! My wife left me in both mind and body a long time ago. I don't have a wife. Do you understand me? I don't have a wife! Now, take that back to your plantation and my brother, unless of course, you want to stay around for the whipping at six o'clock."

"No, please don't," Kathryn responded hysterically. She didn't know what to do, but she couldn't leave now. There wasn't enough time to send for David. She had to remain here; maybe she could stop it. Distraught, she ran from the study. She saw Winnie hidden safely from William's view. She had been eavesdropping.

"Missy Kathryn . . ."

"Shush! William will hear you. Let's go to the cellar where we can talk."

Kathryn closed the cellar door.

"Now we can talk."

"I heard everything Mr. William said. You've got to stop him, Missy Kathryn. You've got to stop him."

Kathryn embraced Winnie as she said, "Oh, Winnie, why did you come back to this? They didn't capture you."

"When they took Emanuel and my son, they took everything that is important to me. I thought I could reason with Mr. William."

"I don't know what made you think a thing like that. William Littlejohn doesn't have a reasonable bone in his body."

Winnie hesitated, then spoke slowly. "I thought. . . I thought . . . that since he is my father. . ."

"Your what? Winnie, what are you talking about?"

"Mr. Littlejohn is my father."

"How do you know?"

"My mother told me. I'm sorry, Missy Kathryn. I shouldn't have told you, you being his wife and all."

"Now, Winnie, you listen to me. You tell me everything. It may be our only chance for saving Emanuel's life."

"Well, my mother's name was Teresa. She was a house woman before I was born."

"I remember Teresa, just after William and I were married."

"Well, after she got pregnant with me, Mr. William sent her away and then he brought me at an auction, not knowing who I was. Of course, you know the rest."

Kathryn was flabbergasted. Such a remarkable turn of events. . . almost unbelievable. . . but then very believable. The light-skinned, almost white, Negro girl with curly hair. There was even a slight resemblance.

"Missy Kathryn, have you seen my baby? Is he all right?"

"No! No, Winnie, I haven't, but he will be all right, I'll see to it. I promise."

"Please, if anything happens to me and Emanuel, please get my baby back to free soil. Here, on this paper, is the address of some friends in Boston who will take care of little Emanuel." She paused. "He'll beat Emanuel to death, won't he?"

Kathryn embraced Winnie, who gave in just a little to the emotional strain by crying. Over her sobs, she heard Kathryn's words.

"No, no! He won't beat him to death. . . at least not today, he won't. You see, William had his pride and respect injured by a slave; and moreover, a slave that I grew to love as a son and sheltered like a son—a son that I could never give William. This made William hate Emanuel more. Now, he must exact revenge.

It isn't enough for him to punish Emanuel. He must exact the penalty of death in front of an audience of his peers, and that won't happen until tomorrow, and not even then, if I can help it. Now, promise me that you won't try to see Emanuel or the baby. David and I have a plan and you must be ready for anything tonight. Promise me!"

"I promise."

"Good, now rest if you can. There's going to be a lot of fast travel tonight if our plan works. I'm going to the barnyard to see if I can stop the whipping."

By six o'clock, Hughes and Knight had Emanuel tied to the whipping post. The food and water that were being secretly given to him by the other slaves was helping him regain his strength rapidly. He knew he could take the beating. He worried most about his son and his wife. He felt better not seeing his mother or son or his wife in the crowd that had gathered.

William Littlejohn had come. He was gloving the hand with which he would grip the whip. Emanuel looked his captor straight in the eye, no longer avoiding his gaze. He remembered the verse from the Bible. . . when I became a man I put away childish things. There was a finality about death that would not allow him to be obsequious. He recognized the look in William Littlejohn's eyes. His emotions were being supplemented by the spirits of alcohol. He had had too much to drink. He slurred as he said, "This is what happens to niggas who don't stay in their proper place." He delivered a searing lash across Emanuel's back.

"William, stop it, this instant! I mean it!" Kathryn said as she grabbed hold of the whip, preventing the next strike.

William became more infuriated than he already was and flung Kathryn to the ground before he realized what he had done.

Again, he turned his rage on Emanuel. He drew the whip back far back and again it was caught. This time, by David.

"Come on, William, leave the boy alone. Can't you see that he has had enough beatings? You gonna lynch him tomorrow, isn't that enough?"

William's rage was even more uncontrollable. "You stay out of this, little brother. I'll beat my slaves as long as I want and when I want." Again, he drew back the lash. This time David grabbed the whip and threw it to the side. He delivered a decisive blow to William's jaw, knocking him to the ground.

To say the least, William was humiliated. He tried to retaliate but was so drunk that he fell back to the ground. He eased himself to his feet with the help of Hughes and Knight, then he stood unsteadily but managed to jerk himself from the men's grasp. "All right, li'l brother, you win this time. But, there'll be another. I've had my suspicions about you all along. Too many slaves disappearing from everybody's place 'cept yours. Been hiding runaways, have you, li'l brother? Well, maybe the other plantation owners would like to hear about that. And then, maybe we'll lynch a nigga and a nigga lover all at the same time from the same tree." William ambled away toward the plantation house. There, he had more to drink.

Winnie guessed that it was about 9 p.m. She had collected her thoughts. She knew what her last resort would have to be, that is, if David and Kathryn's plan wasn't put into action soon.

She had made her bed with clean sheets—clean white sheets. The coal oil lamp was filled to capacity and the extra oil was by the chair. There was only one chair in the room and she sat in it stiffly. Teary eyed, she waited.

David and Kathryn rushed back to Echo Holler. There wasn't much time to put their escape plan into action. The plan was simple. While Kathryn was in the plantation house keeping William occupied, Tom Baldwin and his agents would subdue Hughes and Knight and release Emanuel. David would slip into the house to get Winnie. Their last stop would be to pick up the baby as they left the plantation and they would take a carriage out of the county as fast as they could, staying, hopefully, one step ahead of news of their escape. Tom Baldwin, along with one other male slave, would accompany the group, posing as a master on sojourn to Virginia.

David looked at his pocket watch. Both hands pointed straight up. It was midnight. Time to leave.

At about 1:29 a.m., William awakened from a drunken stupor. At first, he felt around as if he were in bed and Kathryn was at his side, but neither was true. He was on the sofa in the sitting room. He surmised that Gertie had covered him with the blanket that he flung to the floor as he sat upright. The room was dark. He felt alone and lonely. He thought of Kathryn—the hell with her. He thought of Winnie. There was no hesitation on his part as he walked toward the cellar room with an unopened bottle of liquor in his hand.

Winnie had not moved from the chair. She knew the moment would come, and it was here. William Littlejohn walked through the open door. A surge of excitement pervaded Winnie's body. Vengeance was so close at hand that she could smell it, and tonight she was not going to be denied. It was too late for any alternatives. She had to remain calm, but her thoughts of how much she hated this man, her own father, made it all the more difficult. William Littlejohn was a sloppy mess—unshaven, disheveled, and mostly drunk. There was a liquor bottle in one hand and a cotton ball in the other. He had a penetrating, lurid look about his face—one that she had seen when Bertram had accosted her. This time would be different. There would be screams, but not hers.

William walked closer. He put one arm around her neck. With the other, he raised the newly opened liquor bottle to her lips. Winnie took small sips. Then he gulped the liquor. He set the bottle down and lay the cotton ball aside, then he began to undress Winnie. She didn't resist. Every passing moment brought revenge closer. Once she was completely disrobed, he picked up the cotton and softly massaged her breast, stomach, and thighs. Slovenly, he took off all his clothes and reached for the liquor bottle and drank more, spilling the pungent liquid all over his body. The bottle was half empty when he pushed Winnie onto the bed and roughly lay on top of her. She did not resist. But nothing happened. William's penis was as soft as breakfast butter.

William rolled onto his back and directed Winnie to reciprocate his massage with the cotton. She did not resist, but first she reached for the liquor and generously poured it on his lips, soiling the sheets and pillowcase as well. . .

Meanwhile, Hughes heard a ruckus in back of the cabin that held Emanuel captive. He went outside to see what it was. He never knew who or what delivered the killing blow to his head.

"Hughes! Hughes! You out there? Say sumpin', boy," said Knight, frightened by the sounds from outside.

A strong arm with rock-hard muscles grabbed Knight by the neck, almost lifting him off the ground. Even though the grip eased, Knight could barely grunt. He felt sharp metal against his neck. Knight was dead before the knife completed its global swing.

Others in the group freed Emanuel. "You is free now, Piana. You is free. Go git yo' woman and baby and git."

It was too dark for him to recognize any of the faces, but

Emanuel recognized the voice of the person speaking. It was a slave girl who always danced outside the window when she heard him play. He ran toward the plantation house as fast as he could.

William was in a drunken stupor, and finally fell off to sleep. Winnie eased off the bed. She lifted the coal oil lamp and removed the globe that imprisoned the flame. The new air caused the miniature flame to jump more briskly. There was a brief, gentle breeze from the open cellar door. Sounds from the diminutive blaze grew louder when Winnie tossed the lamp onto the pillow where William lay. The moistened pillow ignited around William's head, quickly spreading onto his skin. The thirsty flame had suckled all the liquid on his face before he could deliver the first scream. But the screams did come, and they were interminably long. Gertie was nearby and rushed down the cellar stairs. Emanuel heard the screams and he, too, rushed down the cellar stairs, unnoticed by Gertie.

Winnie heard Gertie call out, "Massah William, Massah William. . . " Winnie splashed the cold oil all around the room and, inadvertently, on herself. When Gertie entered the door, Winnie threw the burning lamp at the slave's hem, then picked up the coal oil and slung it all on Gertie. The room burst into flames.

There was an explosion of hot, piercing fire that plastered onto Emanuel's face just as he tried to enter the room. The flames knocked him back on the stairs. He grabbed his face, suffocating the fire. The screams within the room faded as the relentless blaze roared. He tried to see, but there was only darkness.

"Winnie! Winnie!" Emanuel screamed as he crawled backward up the stairs to escape the suffocating smoke and heat.

From depths familiar only to the spirits, like so many times before, he silently called out to his mother. He couldn't speak now; his lips were burned shut. Emanuel also couldn't see. The fire had siphoned his vision just as rapidly as it had the alcohol on William Littlejohn's face. There were only the memories. He thought of the piano. The fire would soon reduce it to ash. He made his way to the music room, stumbling over furniture until he found the piano stool. He sat before the priceless instrument one last time and placed his fingers on the keys. The spectrum of his life flashed before him just as if he were still sighted. He began to play and as he did, he felt his mother's presence. Emanuel called out to her with his music—energetic, vibrant, incendiary tones that implored her: Sing for me, my mother, sing for me.

They had to acknowledge each other—somehow confirming each other's presence and understanding of what was about to happen.

Emanuel began to play their favorite melody. As he did so, his mother began to sing:

> *I sings to yo'*
> *'cause you makes me happy*
> *I sings to you 'cause yo' makes me sad*
> *I sings to you 'cause you makes up*
> *for all that I lost*
> *an' some that I neba had.*

The fire had engulfed the house, except for the music room. There wasn't much time. The two were in unison—separate but one with the music, just as if they had practiced every day for years. The soulful rendition that followed captivated the would-be audience, the field slaves that gathered behind Bell, almost forgetting the fiery furnace before them as they listened to her sad song:

He'll be ridin' on a smoke cloud
I want yo' ta ride dat smoke cloud
to heaben, my son,
I'll meet you dare som'day.

I want yo' to ride dat smoke cloud
to heaben, my son,
Dat is de only way.

When yo' smoke cloud lands
in heaben, my son,
Give yo' respect to de grace of God
and when he gets time to lend you an ear
Tell him dat life down here is so hard

I want yo' to ride dat smoke cloud
to heaben, my son,
I'll meet yo' dare som'day
I want yo' to ride dat smoke cloud
to heaben, ma son,
dat is de only way.

When ma smoke cloud lands
in heaben, ma son,
I'll give ma 'spects to de grace of God
den I'll turn to de business
of looking for yo'
and dat won't be so hard.

You'll be on his right or his left side, ma son,
You'll glow and gleam in his grace

I'll hug yo' and kiss yo', ma son,
Beside yo', fo'eber mo', will be ma place

So ride that smoke cloud to heaben,
ma son . . .

The fire was well onto the roof, cracking and popping loudly as it chewed up everything in its path.

In the distance, Kathryn and David could see what was happening.

Kathryn was filled with doom and remorse as she envisioned what must be happening. The relentless, glowing fire shot sparks high into the air. No matter. Above it all, Kathryn heard music—piano music. "Emanuel! Emanuel!" she screamed. A black child—a little slave boy, a gift from God with a special talent. She had unleashed his brilliant mind, trained his agile fingers. She had watched him grow from student to maestro. And yes! Yes! She could hear his playing above the noisy inferno. Emanuel was in that house.

Kathryn struck her horse hard with the reins and was off like a flash before David knew what was happening. He raced after her, but to no avail. Her horse was simply too fast. She continued to scream. "Emanuel! Emanuel! No! No!"

She fell silent, then thought, this is my last chance to pay him back. Kathryn rode faster and harder as the fiery noise pierced the silence. She rode the horse right up to the porch before it bolted, throwing Kathryn to the ground. There was only ash and rubble as she fell to her knees beside Bell, repeating, "No more! No more!"

The End

A Mayhem Tale

374

A word about Blind Tom:

During my research on this book, while shopping in a novelty shop in Charleston, S.C., I came across an article in *Harper's Weekly* dated February 10, 1866.

Blind Tom no doubt was the 1st black and blind famous pianist. The last paragraph of my description of Piana's one concert performance was excerpted from that paper's description of Blind Tom's abilities. I did this in hopes of forming a spiritual connection between the one real and the one imagined great talent.

Piana